DESTINY'S BLOOD

The Cursed Ones Book Three

DANI KRISTOFF

Copyright © 2024 by Dani Kristoff

All rights reserved.

No part of this book may be reproduced in any form or by any electronic or mechanical means, including information storage and retrieval systems, without written permission from the author, except for the use of brief quotations in a book review.

This book is written in Australian/British English which has different spelling to USA English

Print version ISBN 978-1-922360-18-2

Ebook ISBN 978-1-922360-17-5

Edited by DP+ debbie@dpplus.com.au

Cover by Cathy Walker www.cathycovers.wix.com/books

DRAMATIS PERSONAE

Sydney

Gene Cohen, werewolf alpha, Sydney City pack, and property magnate (first appeared in *The Changeling Curse*, Cursed Ones book 2)

Reeva Cohen, den mother, Sydney City pack, Gene's mother (first appeared in *The Changeling Curse*, Cursed Ones, book 2)

Elvira Denholm, elder witch of Sydney coven (first appeared in *Spiritbound*, Spellbound in Sydney, book 1)

Grace Riordon, witch in Sydney coven, necromancer (first appeared in *Spiritbound*, Spellbound in Sydney, book 1)

Rory Penderton, warlock in Sydney coven, husband to Elvira (first appeared in *Bespelled*, Spellbound in Sydney, book 2)

Lily De Vere, foundling ward of Elvira, half-witch, former police officer and now private investigator

Silvio Bentino, prominent vampire

Canberra

Rolf Bauer, werewolf alpha, Canberra pack (first appeared in *The Sorcerer's Spell*, Cursed Ones, book 1)

Abigail McGregor, werewolf alpha, Canberra pack, former journalist (first appeared in *The Changeling Curse*, Cursed Ones, book 2)

Dane Archwright, sorcerer, current leader of the Collegium (first appeared in *The Sorcerer's Spell*, Cursed Ones, book 1)

Annwyn Flaydin, sorceress, wife to Dane (first appeared in *The Sorcerer's Spell*, Cursed Ones, book 1)

Ireland

Domhnall Dockerty, the White Wolf of Donegal

Connor Dockerty, son of Domhnall

Note

Bespelled in Sydney series meets The Cursed Ones series in this book.

PROLOGUE

In a small reception room at the Stamford Hotel in the city centre, Sydney's paranormal elite gathered. As alpha of the Sydney City pack, Gene Cohen hosted, allowing him the luxury of inviting the guests. His half-brother, Rolf, and his mate, Abigail, along with a few of his beta wolves, had arrived from Canberra earlier in the day. Not Sydney pack, but a strong association given the family connection and geographical closeness.

Rolf brought along his sorcerer friend, Dane Archwright, who brought his equally sorcerous wife, Annwyn; they also hailed from Canberra. Sorcerers had little to do with witches and weres in an official capacity, but the rise of dark forces in the world not only threatened the Collegium, the sorcerer's governing body, but all paranormals. Dane and his wife had the task of fixing things at the Collegium. To fight this unknown force required all paranormals to band together, cooperate, and put aside old animosities. Keen to make friends, Dane oozed charm. Known for being stand-offish, vampires had not showed. Gene's nose appreciated their absence. Vampires stank like death and old perfume to his nostrils.

Elvira, one of the elder witches from the Sydney coven, who Gene had known for a while, arrived with her entourage. Tall and plump, she knew how to dress to make the most of her assets. He always sweated a little when they met, as he'd never get used to her just popping out of thin air as she did. Thank goodness not all witches were capable of such feats of magic. Gene stepped up to meet the new arrivals. Elvira had assisted him after his father was murdered, letting him know there was a witch on the police force. Gene would never give up searching for his father's killer or killers. A witch on the force provided an opportunity to find out more.

"Elvira, thank you for coming."

The elder witch inclined her head and smiled. "My pleasure. Handsome devil, you're making mischief with women everywhere you go. I read the social pages." She tapped his wrist. Gene blushed because it was true. He had at least two women lined up for the afterparty. She turned to the two women flanking her. One was tall, with thick dark hair and a very pretty and amused face. She was also very pregnant. "This is my daughter, Grace." Gene racked his brains. He'd heard of Grace, the talented necromancer, useful in keeping people alive when they were close to death. He shook her hand and greeted her. "And my ward, Lily De Vere."

Lily's light perfume tickled his senses pleasantly. She had high cheekbones, a straight nose and full, pink lips, currently upturned in a smile. Her olive-toned skin contrasted with her white-blonde hair, which was gathered into a ponytail. A compact, athletically built physique and intelligent pale blue-green eyes completed the package. She only came to his shoulder height, and he liked his women to be tall and willowy. Attracted to her, even though she wasn't his type, he rallied his charm. "Pleased to meet you."

She put out her hand to shake. Instead, he lifted it to his mouth to kiss her knuckles and watched her reaction. Her eyes narrowed and her smile faded. He felt judged.

Elvira coughed. "Lily is working with NSW Police and is stationed in the city."

Gene stiffened and studied her in a less amorous way, realising she was a useful resource with smarts and magic working for her. "Ah ... I'd be interested to hear anything you might know about my father's murder investigation."

Her gaze locked onto his, measuring him, he was sure. "I am sorry for your loss. While there have been no breakthroughs yet, I know there is a dedicated team working on the case."

This was not the place to discuss his father's murder, so Gene resumed his host duties and introduced Elvira to his mother, Reeva, who surprised him by greeting the witch like an old friend. He gave a little shrug. His mother had been around a long time; so too had Elvira, so it was not surprising. Dane joined the older women, and they chatted about politics, so he left them to it.

Rolf sidled up. "Thank you for organising this. Dane was keen to make alliances."

"We must work together if we are to fight what is coming."

Rolf peered at Lily. "The police lady is interesting. Abbie says she smells strange."

Gene eased a crick out of his shoulder. "I didn't notice anything odd about her scent. The perfume she is wearing is light and alluring. I've got members of my pack in the forces. She's something else, though."

"I can see that."

"I mean, she's smart. You can tell."

Gene had only discovered that Rolf existed just over a year ago, his mother's child from a previous relationship. It had been painful to learn about him, coming hard on the heels of his father's murder. Gene had hated him on sight. They had each thought the other a prick, at first. But Rolf had grown on him after a while, and he realised it was their similarities that had annoyed him. Both of them being alpha werewolves hadn't helped, but in the end, they had bonded. It had been a tumultuous time when they first met, with his brother fighting a curse that was killing people by forcing them to change into werewolves with horrendous results. The only survivor had been Abigail, who had made a full transformation to werewolf. Then she became an alpha. Rolf and Abbie's relationship was fiery and passionate, but he understood that, as co-alphas, they were a good team and governed the Canberra region pack with fairness and strength.

A few minutes later, when it appeared everyone had arrived, Gene went to the stage to thank everyone for coming and introduced their guest speaker.

Then Dane took the podium. "Thank you to Gene Cohen for organising this get together. I've come to talk to you today about a growing threat. You have all heard about the attacks on the Collegium and I know that witchkind has experienced growing dark forces that are twisting their young, causing strife. Werekind, too, have been hit with curses and attacks that threaten to expose them to humans. These threats are derived from the same dark entity, and we must unite to fight this threat to our very existence." He paused and fixed random attendees with a hard look. "Not only do they have little regard for humankind, they want to turn humans against us, tell humans about us, expose our world to ignorant eyes. I don't know the why and I don't understand the how, but I do know we must fight it. If we don't fight, we will be so reduced in numbers we will be as nothing and in the end we will cease to be."

Rumbles in the crowd greeted Dane's speech and then died down as he continued. It was sobering. Dealing with the day to day was hard enough, Gene thought. Having to fight some nefarious dark force that overshadowed everything was going to be harder.

Later, he cornered Lily as she grabbed a glass of prosecco. "About before," he began. "I didn't mean to be politically incorrect."

Lifting her glass to him, she grinned, amusement dancing in her eyes. "Politically incorrect? I'm off duty, Mr Cohen. And before you ask, I don't have any information for you. Your mother has everything the investigation team knows."

Gene frowned, annoyed to realise that she was immune to his charm. That glint in her eye had him worried. Was she judging him? "If you find out anything new, you will let me know, right?"

She gave a small smile and was about to respond when Grace joined them. "Lovely to have met you, Mr Cohen. We must be off." Before he could blink, they were gone.

Damn the woman ... witch. She could do that travelling thing, just like Elvira. But he didn't need her help, anyway. If it was the last thing he did, he would find out who killed his father and why.

CHAPTER 1

S*ix months later*

GENE PROWLED THE BACKSTREETS OF NEWTOWN USING HIS WERE senses and the map app on his phone to find the place he was looking for. He turned a corner, sniffed and then crossed the road, squeezing between parked cars. When he found it, the old semi-detached house appeared to be defying gravity—its gutters sagged, the angle of the roof was off, like a truss had broken, and its paint was peeled and curled. Rubbish lay in clumps in the front yard and the house looked abandoned. How could anyone do business in such a dilapidated place?

Taking the narrow path between the fence and the building, Gene had to slink sideways to make it through to the backyard, where he found rats foraging in a knocked-over rubbish bin. A wave of scents assaulted his nose—rot, sour milk, decay and mould. The streetlamp from the lane behind the house shot light into the space. Turning, he found what he was looking for, an ugly construction that appeared thrown together, leaning onto the back of the building proper. No signage, but that went with the type of business that operated there—backstreet moneylenders. Scum! If the poor weren't miserable enough, these leeches fed off them, bled them dry, made their life a misery. But railing against it wasn't going to help the situation, so he breathed out slowly and focused.

With a twist of his hand, he forced the doorhandle, hating the feeling of skulking around like a low-life criminal. The reason he was there was too painful to think about. He inhaled, the taste of spilled rubbish sat on the back of his tongue, along with the lingering scents of people who had been there recently. He cracked open the door to reveal a dingy office. There didn't appear to be anyone was inside.

He pushed farther in, waiting for the squeak of hinges to give him away, and breathed out slowly when the door opened silently, and he slid inside. This was a simple reception area, with six hard chairs that a charity shop wouldn't consider taking. In the corner sat a table, with ratty old magazines fanned across it. A high counter to hide the receptionist's chair. A door behind led, he imagined, to a small office. Dead tendrils of a fern hung down from the countertop, and on the desk was one pen, ready to slide off the edge. No computer to be seen. The office chair bore stains and frayed upholstery.

A noise alerted him he was not alone, as he had thought. He frowned, puzzled because his nose hadn't detected anything. Besides, it was one in the morning. Who would be working now? He crept forward, inhaling deeply. There *was* a scent, a perfume in the air. It could have been from the receptionist who worked here, yet it had familiar tones that teased his memory. The door to the inner office was slightly ajar. A thin sliver of blue-tinged light framed it. He stepped up and slid the door open slowly. At first, he saw nothing, just a blur of silvered shadow. He blinked and shook his head. No way was it a ghost. Something supernatural, though. He brought forward his were magic and the blur solidified into a human shape that was bent over the filing cabinet, rifling through documents. The person's outline grew more distinct—a lithe figure, dressed in black leather pants and jacket, with long white hair held in a ponytail. Taking a breath, he closed the door with a snap and leaned his back against it, arms crossed. "Looking for something?"

The figure froze, sighed audibly, and turned.

"You?" Annoyance gripped his gut. He may have growled at her.

The woman twitched her lips, not quite smiling and not quite frowning. "Yes. Me. Can I help you?"

He moved forward, trying to hold back the aggression surging into him. "I've told you before, Ms De Vere, to stay out of my investigation." Since she had left the police force, she had no business sticking her nose in, even if she was supposedly a private eye now.

She folded her arms, and cocked her head. "Likewise. You don't take a hint."

Taken aback by her audacity, he fumbled, not sure what to do next. He noted the pile of files she had extracted on the edge of the desk. He saw two sets of the same files. Was she magically copying them? Curiosity drew him in. "Did you find something?"

Her gaze switched from him to the files. "Something of interest to me. I—"

He thrust out his hand, palm up. "Give them to me."

She stepped between him and the files. "No can do."

Her scent teased his nostrils and her perfume curled around him, lulled him. "Stop it!"

She smiled then, a flash of straight white teeth in a luscious mouth. "Stop what?"

He could still smell the aroma of her perfume, but it no longer threatened to dull his mind and actions. "You know exactly what, witch!"

She laughed. "You say that like it's an insult. But magic is half my charm." Then she sobered. Her eyes, which appeared dark in the unlit room, narrowed. "Stay out of this investigation. You'll only get yourself into trouble, maybe killed. My client won't like that."

"Who is your client?" It irked him he didn't know who was trying to thwart him from finding his father's murderer.

"Can't say. I'd love to stay and chat, but the owners of this place are aware there are intruders. They will be here any minute now." He tensed when she stepped close, her hot breath caressing his neck. "I wish I had time for more." Her teeth nipped his neck. Before he could react, she stepped back, smiled, drew a flowery pattern in the air with her hand, and disappeared. His gaze went to where the files had been, but they had disappeared as well. A door slammed. He needed to get gone, too. Damn that witch, Lily De Vere. She could have helped him get away.

He raced back to the door. Outside, a torch shone. Damn, he'd need to shift. He undid his clothes, pushed his possessions into a little pocket knapsack and called on his wolf. He changed, grabbed his belongings in his teeth, and leaped when the door opened. A man, dark-haired and tanned, recoiled. The one behind him fell back, caught by the first one's backward motion, and yelped in pain. Gene loped from the backyard over the fence. A neighbour's dog barked. "What the fuck. Was that a dog in the office?" a man's voice asked.

"Dunno." The voice was full of pain. "Fuck. I think I broke my ankle."

In the lane, Gene shed his wolf form and hunkered down to get dressed again. Soon, he'd find the witch and have words. He'd use his connections with the Balmain coven, and Elvira was the best place to start.

CHAPTER 2

Lily sank down onto her couch with an enormous sigh. She tugged at the tie holding her hair and let it fall down her back. Her apartment was small, but it was home, and right now it felt like a safe haven.

Timing was everything, and she'd stuffed up. She should have magicked herself out of that office before the big brute Gene had tried to muscle in. Why had she stayed there reading files that had no bearing on the case? Because she was a diehard, goody-two-shoes, that's why. Half of the files she'd stolen were important because they represented people who were suffering and people who were potentially in harm's way. They were debt defaulters. People who'd borrowed in desperation from crooks, because they couldn't borrow from legal financial providers. One had borrowed money for bail for her son who was in trouble for break and enter. A note in the file ordered the bashing of the mother in punishment for defaulting on the repayment of interest. Another person had borrowed for emergency surgery for their mother overseas. There was a note for them to have their car torched as a warning. Another had borrowed to fund a trip to recover a stolen child, taken across the continent to Perth. She was behind in repayments and the child had vanished. They were planning on setting her flat alight. It angered Lily. These were all valid reasons to borrow money, just not from these crooks. What was it about human nature that made some people prey on the weak? She jumped to her feet and paced the room. Coven rules prevented her from shrinking their dicks or covering them in sores. No spells to harm the humans, even the bloody nasty bits of trash humans. That sucked!

In the fridge, she found some sparkling mineral water and poured herself a glass, tossing the empty bottle into the recycling bin. At her window, she looked out into the night, at twinkling streetlights, dim stars, and a flash of headlights. Being keyed up meant she was in no mood for sleeping.

When she'd calmed down a bit, she left her empty glass on the counter and returned to the couch, taking up the one file she thought related to the Cohen murder. The file contained information about an unexpected and anonymous repayment of twenty thousand dollars of one Ms Violet Smith's debt, which occurred the day after the murder of Cohen Senior. Smith had been scheduled to have her kneecaps broken because of the outstanding payments of interest. It said she'd been making deposits and then had refused to comply with the arrangement. The original loan had been five thousand dollars to repair her house, damaged by a fallen tree, because the woman didn't have insurance.

Notes on the file showed a Western Union transfer with no information on who had settled the debt. But who? Some kind of good Samaritan, or was it payment for a favour? It might be a dead end, but her witch's nose thought there was more to it. That kind of money didn't come easily. Also, it came in three separate payments on the same day, presumably to avoid the threshold for mandatory reporting. Whoever paid didn't want to attract official notice. Nor did they want anyone to know who they were.

Her phone rang. She eyed the number and recognised it. "Yes," she said.

"How did it go?" asked a gravelly, slightly accented voice.

"Not as much progress as I had hoped, and I was interrupted."

"Interrupted? By him, I suppose." A curse. "I told you to keep him out of it. I want him protected."

"I'm doing my best. But he's a werewolf. He can look after himself better than I can."

A groan of exasperation filtered into her ear. "Despite what you think, werewolves are mortal. If you can't keep him out of it, keep him close."

Lily sat up straighter, nearly launching out of her seat. "Keep him close? No way! That wasn't the deal!"

"I'll double your fee. I want answers and I want him safe. You understand?"

"Double?" The money would be useful. Lily groaned. "But he's such an asshole."

The voice laughed. "That he is. He'll grow on you, especially if he gets you into bed. Just don't let him walk all over you." They cut the call. Lily pulled a face. *As if! No way was she letting that womaniser near her bed.*

Lily sat back and closed her eyes. She'd done a pretty good job of staying hidden from Gene Cohen. Now she had to let him find her, or she had to find him. She knew where his office was, knew he worked from seven in the morning to seven at night, sometimes longer. He was predictable that way. His turning up at the moneylenders' place had been a surprise. Damn him.

She headed to the shower, but even under the hot water she was not able to relax completely. She thought about the double fee. The extra money could be useful. She could pay those poor people's debts. It was only a drop in the ocean, she knew, but once she'd read those files, her sense of fairness and justice took over. At least she duplicated them so the moneylenders wouldn't know which ones she had taken. She couldn't let the victims suffer and she couldn't curse the criminals ... unless she put in a case to the coven elders ... she shook her head. It would take too long. She could dob them into the police. She had contacts there among her old workmates. But if the police didn't act fast enough, then those people would get hurt and the moneylending operation would just move on. It was a big operation, but a transportable one. She needed a lot more evidence before she could convince the police to take action.

After exiting the shower, Lily looked lovingly at her bed. The hot water had finally helped her relax and allowed the excitement to dissipate so she was actually sleepy. She was about to turn out the light and climb into bed when the doorbell chimed. A quick glance at the clock told her it was two-thirty. She didn't want to disturb the other residents in her block, so she moved to the spy-hole and took a peek. When she saw who it was, her forehead hit the door. "Blast it. Couldn't you wait until morning?"

"No," came a gruff reply. His angry vibes were crawling under the gap in the door. She opened up and Gene Cohen stood there. She should be annoyed, but he was a clever werewolf and had obviously called Elvira. That was the only way to account for him being here. He looked her up and down. She was dressed in a slinky, dark blue nightie that fell to her ankles and hugged her on the way down. Over it she wore a matching wrap, with silver piping to match the bodice on the nightgown. She liked the feel of the fabric on her skin. Her feet were bare, and her hair hung down her back, with shorter bangs curled around her face. While initially angry, there was a glitter of interest in his eyes as he took his time looking her over.

Lily opened the door wider. "You may as well come in."

He walked straight through and stood in the middle of her living area, looking out of place and uncomfortable. The room seemed incredibly small with him in it. He was tall, well built, had cleanly shaved skin, a proud, curved nose and intense blue eyes. He also had a reputation. While she was now required to keep him close, she would not be another of his conquests.

"Can I get you a drink?"

His eyebrows lifted. "Sure. What have you got?"

She'd drunk the last of the sparkling water. "Tap water. Milk, but I wouldn't vouch for it being fresh."

"Water then. May I sit?"

She paused on her way to fetch a glass. "Why not?" She wasn't expecting manners. She'd expected ranting and raving. Now she was just confused, and that wasn't good. Not with Gene Cohen. She needed to keep *him* confused. More importantly, she needed to keep him safe. Second thoughts were digging their way into her brain, but the thought of those poor victims pushed them back out. She could do this job. Find a man's killer and keep his son safe. Not beyond a snooping witch's skill level.

He pulled out one of the two chairs at her small dining table. "Who hired you?"

She shook her head. "No can say."

She filled the glass and walked back to him.

"Why did they hire you?"

Lily pursed her lips as she passed him the glass. He'd obviously figured that part out, so was seeking confirmation. Since they had met six months ago, she had avoided him on more than one occasion. "To find those responsible for your father's murder."

He sat back and rubbed his chin. "It's my mother, isn't it?" He twirled the glass on the table. "The one you're working for."

"How would I know that? I'm not exactly in your pack's social order, am I? I'm hired through a service." That was partly true, but mostly a lie.

"What did you find at Ramsey's? You took files."

She chewed her lips and took the other seat. "Some of the files don't relate to the case. I have taken a personal interest in some other prospective victims of that moneylending service."

His eyebrows rose again. "And the other files?"

"One potential lead."

He shook his head. "Will you stop shitting me and tell me what I want to know?"

She sat back in her chair and frowned. "It's not so simple, Mr Cohen."

"Gene, please."

"Mr Gene," she said and inclined her head. He grimaced but kept quiet. "Potential lead means I found something that might," she lifted her hand to stop him from interrupting. "be a lead. It's a gut feeling, that's all. I'll need to do background research on it first to see if I can track that lead down, see if it comes to anything, then I'll let you know."

He nodded once. "Well, then, tell me about it in more detail."

Lily sighed. *What part of avoidance didn't he get?* "Only if you promise not to go off half-cocked, shoving your brawny arms into this mess, without my say-so."

"Don't presume to tell me what to do or how to do it. I have sources and resources, too."

She shook her head and folded her arms. "Fine, I'll keep mum, shall I?"

He leaped to his feet, fists clenched. The water sloshed out of his glass as he bumped the table. "Look you, interfering witch ... woman. I don't take kindly to you meddling in my business. I'll find who did this and then they'll pay."

She shook her head again, more emphatically. "They will be found and brought to justice and not by you."

He paused, studied her face. "So you think they're human, then? Not paranormals?"

She scratched the back of her neck, making her shortened bangs droop across her face. She hadn't decided yet. From what she could see, this incident—Cohen's murder—straddled two worlds. Nothing was clear-cut, neither motive nor suspect. She flicked her hair back and met his eyes. "Not sure yet. It still could be either or both."

"Both?" He ran a hand through his hair and let out a low whistle. "That's too horrible to think about."

"I agree."

As Gene loomed over her, she was in a quandary. Her orders were to keep him close. She wasn't sure how she could do that, unless she invited him to stay. Her couch didn't seem big enough for him, even if he was so inclined. He would no doubt leap at the chance to share her bed, but that would irk her completely, and she feared he would not enjoy it as much as he thought he would. She looked down at her nightdress. Time to change. If he went home, then she'd need to track him to where he slept. Luckily, she knew a few spells to keep her sleepiness at bay.

"You agree? Explain."

"Humans knowing about us would be bad. Any joint operation between human and paranormal is going to be terrible. One that can take out the Sydney alpha, a powerful werewolf, is a nightmare to contemplate. It threatens the very structure of all our lives."

"It would be disastrous for the darker elements of the human and paranormal world to band together. Believe me, in my line of work I come across dangerous humans in this city often. So definitely not good for humans nor good for us."

"World of trouble," she replied earnestly.

"Other world of trouble."

It was very nice that they agreed, but what was this conversation about? His eyes were hooded. She sensed a swirl of enchantment around her and grinned, understanding. "You trying to use your alpha influence on me? Make me submit? Spill the beans?"

The surge of power dissipated, leaving a light scent of wolf in the air. "Yes, of course. I want to know what you know. Not working?" He inclined his head, admitting defeat.

"No, you charmer." Lily flipped her hand. "Look, I have to go to bed. I'm sorry I can't invite you to stay."

He blanched as if she'd insulted him. Then he glanced around the room and lifted an eyebrow. Her flat wasn't flash. She knew that. He lifted a finger. "I want you in my office at seven a.m. I want a briefing on what you're doing next." He turned and was at her door in two steps.

She laughed lightly as she followed him. "I don't work for you."

He swung round, met her almost nose to nose. "You do now. I'm hiring you and I'll pay double what you're currently being paid. I don't care if you still work for them, as long as it doesn't conflict with the central mission—finding out who killed my father. Deal?"

She blinked at him. *Double? More money?* That's more people she could help. She didn't need money, per se. It was nice and everything, but magic helped with most of her immediate needs. Then she thought about working for him. It had advantages. It would give her an excuse to be close to him, which was part of the new job. "Let me think about it."

"Be quick. I haven't got all morning."

"Okay. Give me five minutes to change and pack."

His chin jerked up. "What?"

She was halfway to her bedroom. "Bugger seven a.m.," she called back. "I'm coming with you now. Until this is done, I'm sticking close."

He shook his head. "I want you on the job finding these bastards. Not getting under my feet."

She shoved clothes into an overnight bag and walked around the room stuffing odd bits of essentials in. "Seriously?" She looked over at him, looming by the door, hands on hips. He took up a lot of space and his angry vibes were back. "I own a laptop. I can do research. You don't need to worry about me. Just find me a corner of your place to park myself in."

Stepping out of view, she shucked her night clothes and re-dressed in her dark leathers, dark top and black leather jacket. She knelt on the floor to look for her boots, which she might have tossed under the bed.

He cleared his throat. "You're saying you are coming to live with me now?"

Grabbing her boots, she moved back into the living area, and pulled them on. His eyes were wide, and she sensed some visceral terror as he realised he had bitten off more than he could chew. It sent a wave of joy through her to disconcert him so.

"Yes, for the time being. And coming to work with you, too."

He laughed. "With me? Not for me, like a bodyguard?"

"No, that costs extra." His appalled expression made her grin. She might as well have some fun teasing him. "But I'm keeping my eye on you and keeping you out of my investigation."

"My investigation," he countered.

"My investigation." She hit her chest. "Ex cop, remember. You can fill me in on what you know tomorrow."

"But ..."

"I'll give you a briefing after I've had some time to pull the threads together. Okay?"

He eyed her with a wild, defeated look and then slumped. "You're going to drive me crazy, I can tell." He stepped back into the hall and let her come through the door.

"Probably. Shall we go?" She covered a huge yawn. "It's past my bedtime."

"Why does she have to be a witch?" Gene muttered as he headed down the hall.

Lily sighed. *You big brute. I don't like werewolves much either.*

The door locked behind them and she placed a magical seal and renewed her wards. She might only be gone for a few days, but it paid to be careful. If Gene had found her within an hour, then others, not as resourceful, may find her as well, just a bit behind Gene. While it annoyed her to have to hang with the big, bad werewolf for the duration, she belatedly realised that she herself might be in danger and it was timely to shift abodes for the duration. He had a network of werewolves to mind him, and they might come in useful as a deterrent.

Out on the street, she followed him to a sleek black car. The car came to life as he approached. "Is that a Tesla S?"

"Sure is." Gene got in as Lily tossed her bag in the back and crossed to the passenger side.

"Nice ride."

Gene grinned. "Don't you ride a broom or something?"

She favoured him with an innocent, wide-eyed stare. "Wouldn't you like to know?"

He blinked and slid into the driver's seat. The car moved quickly and silently. She checked the seatbelt was secure as gravity pressed against her. Gene didn't speak and for that, she was grateful. The streets blurred and her eyes closed. She really needed proper sleep. Recently, she'd overdone the magically enhanced wakefulness and would probably have a hangover for days. The night wasn't over, though, so she hoped the spell she gave herself in the car would clear her head. With the werewolf next to her, she was in dangerous territory now.

CHAPTER 3

Gene's mind was turbulent. This witch had him in a spin. She knew something, and the only way he was going to find out what, was to keep her close. He told himself that was the only reason he wanted her there. Although, her coming along with him right then was a surprise. He thought he'd have to threaten her to be there in the morning. Yet here she was, sitting in his car. Her unpredictability made his teeth ache, and her resistance to his alpha power unnerved him.

It wasn't only that something about her attracted him. He'd had women with great bodies and faces to die for before and never succumbed to their charms. They had been drawn to him, and he'd enjoyed them. He felt safe on that score.

As well as being interesting to look at and fit, she exuded something. Probably some magical allure. He didn't think she was traditionally beautiful. Not tall, willowy and buxom, but small, compact and athletic.

But she was a witch and, for him, that meant something else. Suspicion. Distrust. Fear. His pack kept their distance from the Sydney coven, only cooperating when necessary, including sharing information. Every time he met Elvira, one of their most powerful witches, his balls clenched painfully just being near her. He never knew if she was going to ravish him or vanish him. She could turn him into a toad or twist him into something else entirely. That's what he had heard. His werewolf would have something to say about that, of course.

He glanced sideways at Lily, who had her eyes closed. She lived in Balmain, in the heart of the Sydney coven, and he was taking her to his home in Bondi. Not the heart of his pack, though. Just one place in his property portfolio, inherited from his father, that he liked a lot. There was something soothing about the waves crashing against the sand—the persistent rhythm of it calmed his nerves. And the full moon rising over the ocean? Magical in all the realms of his senses. It was also very convenient to the city and his place of business.

The witch's colouring was odd. She had pale blue-green eyes. This he'd noted when they had first met. Her hair, though, was silver white and appeared natural and contrasted with her olive complexion. With her short straight nose and largish mouth, she was an odd but still attractive mix. It was as if she had been brewed from different magical potions to be unique in this world.

"Is your family in Sydney?" he asked as he took the turn that would send them down Oxford Street.

Without opening her eyes, she replied, "No. I don't have any family."

He blinked. "How can you not have family? I thought you witches were a tight-knit clan."

"The coven is pretty close, but none of them are related to me." She sighed, opened her eyes, and cast him a sideways glance. "I was a foundling. They think I'm from Ireland originally, because the ship I was on had originated from there. Clairvoyants could not confirm it. They said their research of my baby memories was inconclusive. They had the flavour of my mother and nothing more. I have yet to travel to Ireland and pick up the threads there. The consensus is that I have magical ability and that points to me being a witch or part-witch."

"Why wait? Aren't you naturally curious?"

"Sometimes I'm more curious than other times. I have yet to have the yearning, the driving need to know. I grew up happy enough here."

"Families can be full of mystery. I only recently found out I had a brother."

She turned to him. "Really? And how did that go? Did you like him?"

Gene chuckled and pulled up at a red light. "I hated him at first. I thought he was an annoying prick. But after being forced to spend time together ..." He paused, as if considering. "I learned to respect him and his abilities."

"Were you jealous?"

He scoffed and cast her a sideways look. "What do you mean?"

"Your mother. He was her son, wasn't he?"

He frowned. "Why do I feel you know my story?"

She shrugged. "I'm intuitive. It helps with the job."

He took off at the green light. "Why did you leave NSW Police?"

"You've been doing your homework. I left after three years of service. My abilities were raising suspicions. The coven asked me to quit before I inadvertently exposed them."

He nodded. "I can see why they might be concerned. Elvira is very protective of the coven."

"Yes, she is. And of me. While I'm her ward, I didn't live with her growing up. We have grown closer once I became an adult. We get along well."

He lifted his eyebrows. Useful to know that their connection was a strong one, even if not by blood. "So you became a private investigator?"

"Yes, for special cases, if you know what I mean."

"What have you got on the supernatural angle of my father's case?" He had to pry some information from her.

"He was a werewolf and alpha of the Sydney City pack. A silver bullet was used to kill him. So, yes, that's a supernatural element. Whether there is a further conspiracy originating within our world, I don't know yet. To tell you the truth, I hope not."

"You'd like it to be clear-cut murder then?"

She looked at him sideways again. He spared her a quick glance and then concentrated on driving. "I'm sorry for your loss. I truly am. Don't think me hard-hearted. I need to be clear-headed on this, not swayed by feelings or prejudice. I need to be objective and keen-eyed to see what needs to be seen. My intuition helps, but all it does is guide me. My investigative skills will be what gives us the information and evidence that we need."

He pursed his lips. "Cursed thing is, I hope he didn't die for nothing."

Again, she flicked her gaze his way. "I don't think he died for nothing. There was a reason. I just don't know what it is yet."

They were now on Bondi Road as it arched to become Campbell Parade. Stars glittered in the dark sky and the curve of the beach hove into view. "This is Bondi."

"I know. I have been here before. Great beach for swimming. You live here, I take it."

"Yes. Just up Hall Street." He drove into the garage of his knock-down-rebuild house. His father had owned the land, with a derelict building on it, but had allowed Gene the freedom to design and build the replacement dwelling. It wasn't big, but it was his favourite place.

He grabbed her bag out of the car before she could and opened the door, which hid the stairs to the upper floor. "I'll set up a desk for you at the office. For now, though, you can have the guest bedroom to sleep and work in."

After tramping up three flights of stairs, he showed her the generous-sized room, which had its own bathroom. After placing her bag there, he led her back down the stairs to the kitchen and showed her where everything was. "Help yourself and let me know if there is anything you need." He turned and walked to the large glass doors, opening the blinds to show her the balcony. The sound of traffic and people drifted in. It was a relatively quiet early morning, but still people lingered in the streets. The cafe bookshop over the road leaked conversations and music, as well as the scent of espresso coffee. He breathed in the clean sea air and let it out slowly.

Lily came up to stand beside him. "Nice. Do you often stand out here where anyone can see you?"

He repressed the urge to snap at her. "Yes, I like to be out here when I can. I'm anonymous here."

"No, you're not. You need to stop doing this. Is this where you normally live?"

"Yes, except when I visit my mother or I'm being entertained." He wanted to say getting laid to irritate her but hesitated. He blinked, wondering why he had such a motive. Was it because she was attractive, as well as exotic, and apparently not attracted to him?

"We need to move you, then. We should be okay for now, because I'm here. But later on today, we need to move you elsewhere." She flicked a glance at him. "Somewhere not so obviously associated with you or your family's business interests."

He growled. He really didn't want to have to change his ways. She was acting as if he was in danger as his father had been. "We're investigating my father's murder, not mine."

She lifted her face to his. "You hired me. So listen to me. My intuition tells me you are in as much danger as your father was. You have other properties, don't you? Let's go somewhere else and then somewhere else again. Keep moving every night. Let's keep them on their toes. I realise it is an inconvenience, but not I hope one that is life threatening."

"You have a suspicion, then? You know who they are?"

"No, I don't. But I know you're being monitored here. There's a tracking spell in your house."

"What? So it's witches after me?"

She shook her head. "No, not for certain. It's a purchased spell, so it could be anyone. Until I have it examined, I don't even know if it belongs to a sorcerer or a witch. There are differences." Frowning, she paced around the edge of the room. "Have you had the house swept for mechanical listening devices?"

"No. But I will. I wish Abbie was here. She can smell magic spells."

"Abbie?"

"My brother's alpha mate."

Lily blinked. "I think I saw her at that reception you held. A werewolf that can smell magic. Useful. You should invite her to stay with you. I can't be everywhere and with you all the time."

He narrowed his eyes. "Let me get this straight. Someone right now knows I'm home. Can they see me? Do they hear what I'm saying?"

"Yes. And they know I'm here as well."

"No sleep for me tonight, then."

Lily sighed. "You can sleep. I'll watch over you. I can use spells to keep me awake and alert for a few nights."

He stood aghast. "You're not going to stand over me and watch me while I sleep?"

She smiled slightly, her lips curving. "I don't need to do that. Outside your door will be fine."

He looked at her and wondered if he should be objecting to having her in his room. Her scent was light, like a delicate perfume: he could get used to it. The only reason he hadn't made moves on her was his distrust of witches. *And she doesn't fancy you.* Besides, there were plenty of human and weres eager to share his bed. A witch was not as desirable as a partner, so it was best not to dally in case some magical spell caught him unawares. He thought of tales of hard-ons that didn't go away, or a limp dick that wouldn't rise to the occasion. There were rumours about witches and their subtle revenge. He thought she might be the vindictive kind, so best not go there.

"Show me your bedroom."

"Sure." He reversed their steps, taking her up two flights of stairs to the top floor. On one side of the short corridor was the door to his home office. On the other side, he opened the door revealing his oversized bedroom containing a king size- bed, a comfortable chesterfield couch and a door to an ensuite bathroom. Both the office and the bedroom had full-length glass doors with access to a balcony and a view out onto the street. He loved waking up to the sunlight pouring in.

He glanced at her, expecting awe, but she was shaking her head.

"What?"

"This will not do. There are so many ways someone with malicious intent can get to you. That rooftop over there and the balcony below give access to this room, and the windows provide very little shielding."

Bristling, he bit back a retort. He looked at his room with fresh eyes, seeing the flaws she pointed out. He loved the space and the light, but now he just saw the vulnerability.

"Do you sleep in pyjamas?" she asked.

He blinked at the sudden change in topic. "Depends. What's it to you?"

"I just want to make sure you're comfortable." She walked towards him, and he backed up, hitting the edge of the bed with the back of his knees. There was a vibe coming from her, aggression, sexiness and something else rather intense. He fell back, wondering if she was going to have her way with him. He almost grinned at the thought, until she waved a hand in front of his face, heard her whisper words and next thing he knew, he was under the covers, eyes closing, sleep dragging him down. His last conscious thought was 'bloody witch spelled me'.

CHAPTER 4

Lily stood outside the bedroom door once Gene was under her spell. It was short-lasting and his own need for sleep would keep him dormant until he woke naturally. He was going to be pissed about her magicking him and she didn't care, really. She'd seen his expression when she approached him, seen the excitement and desire light his eyes. Oh yes, he was going to be pissed all right, because he found her attractive and thought she was into him. But Lily knew he was attracted to most women, so was not flattered into thinking anything special had developed between them. What had annoyed her, though, was that she detected a thread of attraction for him in herself. It would not do. This was a business arrangement, and he was a werewolf alpha and philanderer. Not a good alliance for a witch, even a strange kind of witch like her.

She lowered herself to the carpet, propped herself against his bedroom door, and tried not to pry into his dreams. As she was a tad bored with her monitoring of the house and maintaining her alert spells after a few hours, she was tempted to have a little peek. However, such an act might lead to a deepening of their connection. If he had erotic dreams about her, she might like that, but they were more likely ways in which he could harm her. He was a werewolf, and the werekind were inherently violent and unreasonable. Not that witches were perfect. Far from it. She had learned from a young age to be resilient and logical. It wasn't that she wasn't loved and nurtured. She had been. The community within the coven had been accepting. Because her origins had been unknown, and still were, she was not connected in the same way as those born into the coven.

Lily was an observer and often she would study people, their ways and habits, to try to ascertain the why of what they were doing as well as the how. It was how she developed her intuitive sense, she supposed. No one in the coven would believe that, though. It was put down to her inborn talents and unknown origins.

Outside Gene's door, she listened. It was quiet, so she snuck a look inside. He was out, breathing deeply. Not a snorer, then. She silently checked the room, the windows and any spy charms. Nothing in there. She thought about placing one of her own and changed her mind. Gene had a reputation, and she didn't think eavesdropping on his seductions would be entertaining and, while he looked to be an impressive specimen, she didn't go into perving on unsuspecting people.

She shut the door softly behind her and she went downstairs and started a check of the other rooms, plus the external doors, windows, security room and feed. Heading to the garage, she searched the car. On her haunches, checking wheel rims, she found a tracker. Not a magical one, but a state-of-the-art electronic device. The idea of smashing it came to mind. A better course would be to let Gene make that call. The garage door had a small caged spell up near the motor casing. She studied it, not quite able to make it out. It thrummed when she got close, so she backed off, wary of triggering whatever it was. This required a specialist. She made a mental note to contact the coven, as the elders would know who to send.

She patrolled through the remaining hours of the early morning, checking on Gene, the doors, the windows and for any active spells. Around five in the morning, the sound of a door opening brought her head up. She raced to the first floor entry to find two burly men in dark suits standing there. One sniffed. He was built like a bulldozer. The other, slightly shorter and leaner, hunched his shoulders, ready to attack.

"Who are you?" they asked in unison.

Lily shook her head. "I'm working for Gene. New recruit."

The one ready to bowl her over relaxed slightly. "Shouldn't you be naked, then?" The other laughed.

Lily flashed a snide smile. "Shouldn't you?"

They came further in. "We're the security detail. Gene sent a request."

Lily blinked, wondering when he'd had time for that. They were either very slow to mobilise or bad liars. "Prove it." Her stance was relaxed, theirs wasn't. They had the air of werewolf about them, so they weren't necessarily organised crime.

"I'll get my phone out." The man behind the bulldozer slowly put his hand in his jacket pocket, drew out his phone and held it out for her to see. Her eyesight was good, but not that good. But no way was she moving forward to read it.

"Put in on the floor and slide it over to me."

He nodded and bent to push the phone along the floor. She could see then what looked like an email from Gene, sent just after they'd arrived here. He requested two bodyguards from his pack to come ASAP. He said he had company.

She relaxed, given the message and their behaviour. "Okay then. Guard away."

"Where's the boss?" bulldozer asked.

"In bed."

The eyes widened. The men shared a look. "Alone?"

"Yes, and asleep, so keep the racket down."

They looked her up and down, and she didn't like it. "Stop that. I'm not one of his conquests. He hired me and I'm keeping him safe."

They both laughed. She felt suddenly tired. "Now you're here, I'm going to sleep in the guest room ... alone ... and undisturbed, if you please."

She didn't think they suspected she was a witch, and that was fine by her, as she didn't need to advertise that fact. Bulldozer took up station by the front door. The other followed her upstairs. He snuck a look in at Gene and then pulled his head back out and nodded to her.

"I'll check the security feed and take up station here."

Lilly nodded and went down to the floor below to the guest room. She set a ward to wake her if anyone came into the room and then stripped down to her bare essentials, leaving her black leather pants and jacket on the back of a chair, her black T-shirt on the seat and stripped off her bra and undies. A shower wouldn't go astray, so she stepped in. The hot water pummelled her skin, massaged her muscles and made her groan with delight. There was an array of shower gels and shampoos, so she availed herself of them and then dried off before crawling into the queen-size bed. She must have drifted off quickly and slept soundly. A yell of outrage woke her.

"What the actual fuck!" The sound of heavy feet coming down the stairs echoed outside her room. "Where is she?" The door flung open. Her ward woke her at the same time. Her hair was all over the place, from being wet when she fell asleep. She blinked through her bangs and saw a very angry, very naked Gene filling her doorway. Perhaps she should have left him clothed after all.

It was rather a marvellous view, and she was going to say so when he came up to tower over her. "How dare you spell me!"

She scratched her head, not realising at first that one breast had slipped out from under the covers. "You needed to sleep. I thought it best." She tugged the sheet up to cover her wayward breast. "Did you sleep well?"

The growl made her cringe. So, he was indeed pissed. Too bad. He looked refreshed. Alert. He clenched his fists. She saw a shadow move outside the door in the hallway and guessed it was one of his bodyguards. "Don't you ever do that to me again."

With a sigh, she lay back against her pillow. "I promise, unless you give me permission first. What time is it, anyway?"

"Get dressed. I'm heading to the office, and you're coming with me. Bernie, order coffees for pick up, will you?" He stormed out and stomped up the stairs to his room, and slammed the door. He had left her door open, so she had use magic to swing it shut to dress. His alarm must have woken him. It was five forty-five. By six-fifteen she was standing by the car, with her laptop and bag, waiting for him to come down.

When he appeared, he was dressed smartly and smelled like a spice cologne. He barely looked at her. She rolled her eyes. She didn't have time for grouches and was beginning to regret agreeing to work for him.

He didn't invite her into the car, but when the garage door went up, she snapped open the passenger seat and slid in. "I wanted to warn you of two things," she said.

He sighed. "What?", he asked, as he started to back out.

"There is an electronic tracker on this car. Rear wheel driver's side. There are no incendiary devices or tracking spells, though. There is, however, a complex and dense spell up near the garage door opener." She pointed at it as they passed out into the drive. He hit the brakes.

"Why didn't you tell me before?"

She lifted her lips in a sort of embarrassed smile. "I'd put you out for the evening before I discovered it. I've put a barrier spell around it so it's safe for now."

"Why didn't you tell Bernie and Geoff?"

She squinted at him. "Why do you think? I don't want to advertise what I am. It's complicated."

He sat back in his seat, staring at the roller door. "Do you know what it does?"

She shook her head. "I was going to organise a specialist to assess it."

"What do you think it does?"

She sat back. "The position indicates that it might prevent the garage door from opening. Or if it was something designed to explode, it might ..." she did a mental calculation. "Take you out in your bedroom."

His eyes widened. "Okay. We'll relocate to a new place. I'll decide where, later."

"Do I have your permission," she emphasised the words, "to organise someone to look at it?" She pointed to the suspicious spell lurking in the mechanics of the garage door machinery.

He gave a jerk of his head, which she took for agreement, thrust the car out into the traffic, keyed the garage door shut and used the car's amazing acceleration to avoid a collision, much to her relief.

After they had coffees in hand they were on the road into the city. Gene took a sip from his cup and said, "I'm taking you to my office. You should be able to make arrangements there."

She nodded and tried not to flinch at the way Gene was driving. Often he was too close to the car in front, always a tad faster than she liked. His driving hadn't been this intense last night so perhaps the stress was getting to him. She managed to get most of the coffee into her mouth and only had a few splashes on her black T-shirt.

At the office, he led her to a small room with a desk and a phone on it. "You can use this room. The ladies' is next to the lift. Tea and coffee in the break room over there. Don't go anywhere without consulting me first."

She lifted an eyebrow. "Anything else you require? A sacrifice to your statue at dusk, maybe?"

He just snarled and shut the door. Lily dug out her phone and dialled her client. "Hello."

"Give me an update," the voice said, more accented than usual and clogged with sleep.

"I'm with Gene. The Bondi house is compromised. Magically and electronically."

"Both? That is strange."

"Agreed. I'm going to contact the coven and get someone out there to assess a spell in the garage."

"Smart move. Will they agree? They have their own issues."

"They will. I have a friend. She's soft on Gene."

"And Gene? Is he suspicious?"

Lily coughed out a laugh. "He guessed it's you who hired me first off. I did not confirm, but you two know each other too well. He's just a bit more aggro than you so he's rattling my chain."

"I'll have you know I am way more aggro than him. I'm better at hiding it." Her sigh echoed across the connection. "He' hurting. He lost his father, and he wants to know why, just as I do."

Lily pursed her lips. "I wish I had some answers for you now. It's just so murky. The leads appear to go both ways—organised crime and paranormal involvement."

"Could the coven be involved, infiltrated? Or is it outside of that?"

"My gut says not the coven directly. It's not the leadership's style. I need more time to find out. Let me get that spell analysed first and that might give us a clue to who and then why."

"Keep me posted."

Lily ended the call and stared at her phone. She hated asking favours from the coven, because she felt the debt went too far in her direction and asking just swung the scales further. The thought that there was a conspiracy involving the coven made her gut churn and her heart ache. She dialled Elvira.

Elvira gave her a contact, who she chased down and gave him the details. Then she had to get Gene to relay the message to Bernie and Geoff and whoever took over from them to expect a visitor.

"What do you want to do about the tracker on your car?" she asked, leaning in to his office while holding the doorframe.

He lifted his gaze from his computer screen. "It's been removed already."

She nodded. "So whoever put it there knows you're on to them."

He let out a groan and rubbed his hands through his hair. He glared at her. "What choice do I have? You said to move houses. What's the point of doing that if we're being tracked?"

"Yes, I agree. We don't know who they are. They don't know that we don't know. Hopefully, they will make a mistake."

His phone rang. He picked up straight away. She left his office and returned to hers, studying the files once more and keying up information on Violet Smith. Nothing showed up in her search, so either Violet was very particular about her internet presence or her name was fake. She put in a request to a solicitor friend, who could search land titles and the electoral rolls. That would take at least a few hours. Her gut feeling, though, was that something wasn't quite right. If Violet wasn't a real name, the money could be for something else. The amount of money paid was a little low for a hit on someone. Also, why the elaborate story about a loan to fix the house? She brought up the local news pages for stories on a storm around the time. There had been a storm, but no damage reported on that street or in that suburb. She scratched her head, feeling sleepy. It made little sense. If it was a fake loan, why was it repaid? Money laundering? They were already criminals, and wouldn't they just be deceiving themselves in trying to hide it? It made no sense.

CHAPTER 5

Sitting at his desk, Gene sprawled in his chair, trying to calm down. He was so wired; he could punch something. Today's business had been dealt with, and still he mulled things over. He knew he was grinding his teeth but couldn't stop himself. What had he done bringing that witch under his wing, making her stick close to him? It stuck in his craw that she wouldn't just fess up to who she was working for and wouldn't hand over any information she'd found. He was angry. He was vulnerable. He was angry because he was vulnerable, and he couldn't blame her for that. Depending on her to find out what he could not irked him. From what she had discovered today, he was a marked man. Followed, bugged and who knew what else?

His father had been a clean operator, not a crook or involved with organised crime—not knowingly, anyhow. In the construction world there were a lot of places where crime crept in, and he had a gut feeling something like that had gotten his father killed. His father had been too honest to stand by and let others be duped.

Around three o'clock, his intercom sounded. "Yes?"

"Mr Cohen. I have a reminder here for the gala ball in Enmore tonight."

"What? When did I sign up for that, Gail?" He rubbed his face and held back a moan.

"You're a major sponsor and you agreed to hand out the prizes. I've sent the tickets to your phone." He rubbed his face again.

"It's formal too?"

"Yes, Mr Cohen. Your second tuxedo is in your office closet, just back from the cleaner."

"Thank you, Gail. I'll talk to you tomorrow." He was about to end the discussion when he remembered. "Is Ms De Vere still in the office?"

"Yes, I believe so. I haven't seen her leave."

"Thank you." He disconnected and frowned. Not seeing her leave was no guarantee that she hadn't popped off. She could magic herself away. He threw himself out of the chair and through the door and didn't bother knocking as he strode into the spare office. He had to check himself on the threshold. Glancing over his shoulder at his receptionist, he shut the door. "Where did you get the whiteboard from?"

Lily sat at the desk with a laptop open, hunched over it like she was waiting for something to jump out at her. "Oh, do come in," she said without looking up.

He came around behind her so he could see what she was working on. "What's that?" On the screen was a series of boxes with names, connected with lines and coloured patterns.

She sat back and sighed. "It's a program I'm using to map out connections. It can help me to see things more clearly."

"And the whiteboard?"

"Gail fetched it for me. Apparently, there's a storeroom in the building where they hide all the junk, so she got one of your boys to bring it up for me. I like to write my ideas down."

He studied the whiteboard, but she had written in initials or code so he couldn't make sense of it. "Have you found anything yet?"

"I have found things, but none of it is connected to anything yet." She sounded tired to his ears.

With a cough, he clenched his hands and began. "Here's the thing.

I've got a gala tonight and you're coming with me. Got any formal wear in your knapsack?"

She sat up straight. "A gala?" She turned to face him. "You can't go to a gala."

He sighed and then clenched his teeth again. "Get ready, we're going." He looked at his watch. "I'm going to shower and change, and we will leave in half an hour."

"Half an hour?" The outrage seemed to steam out of her pores. "I suppose you're headlining. Sitting duck you'll be."

He shook his head. "Well, lucky I will have my bodyguard with me."

"I'm not your bodyguard."

"You are now. Buy a dress and put it on my account."

Cussing, she packed up her laptop, then she took a photo of the whiteboard before erasing it. Within five minutes, she had her little bag packed and all her gear put away. She looked at him and squinted. "You better get ready, then. The clock is ticking."

He was expecting more opposition, maybe arguments, insults, screaming, whining (which he hated), complaining or pouting. He got none of that.

He turned on his heel and went to get ready. Gail was packing up. "See you tomorrow, Mr Cohen."

"Good night, Gail. Have a nice evening." He smiled as she left through the main door. She was a nice young woman. The daughter of one of his pack members.

In the shower, Gene scrubbed and fumed and thought and wondered. He had a lot on his mind. He hadn't even got to pack business today. Luckily, he had three seconds who managed the day-to-day concerns and only briefed him when something difficult arose. Having a witch in his life had thrown everything out of kilter.

He stood there naked as he shaved and mused further about the situation. There was no choice about keeping her close. It had been the right decision, yet he was uneasy. She got under his skin and not because she tried to piss him off. That was nothing. She was small and skinny and a strange-looking witch, but there was something alluring in that.

After he shaved, he dressed. As he fixed his tie, he thought Lily was unlike his normal preference in women. He rolled his eyes. Perhaps he should not think of her as a woman. He slid his arms into his jacket and surveyed his reflection, pleased he had scrubbed up well. He had no idea what Lily was going to wear, considering he'd given her half-an-hour's notice.

He stepped out into the front office and gasped. Lily was there, dressed in a slinky, body-hugging black dress. Strappy, silver shoes peeked out from the hem and a matching purse dangled from a chain on her shoulder. Her silver hair was curled and cascaded down her back and she had a very fine diamond-like necklace at her neck with matching earrings. Her face was tastefully made up, and she looked well-groomed and rested. He hadn't expected ... hadn't thought she would even try to dress up. "How did you ... I mean ... you look ..." He coughed to hide his confusion. She had blindsided him. "Thank you for being ready in time. Shall we?" He indicated to the lift with an arm.

Her lips lifted in a lopsided smile. "Just because I don't think it's a good idea to go to this gala, doesn't mean I won't go with you or look the part."

Once in the lift, he recovered himself enough to be grateful. "I appreciate your efforts." He glanced down at her carryall. "You had all that in there with your laptop and stuff?"

She looked up, and her grin broke into a smile. "I'm a witch. I have resources, remember?" She clicked her fingers to demonstrate. Nothing happened, but he got the picture.

"Do you have a gun strapped to your thigh?" He made to look down her leg. The dress had a long split to her thigh, and he was more than interested to see.

"Wouldn't you like to know? I have many concealed weapons."

His heart fluttered. Were they flirting? His face flushed. He had been a little familiar, and she had responded in kind. He stared at the lift door and controlled himself. Hadn't he just told himself she was not his type? She irritated him all the time. He was pretty sure she was close to hating him, too. Looks like tonight was a truce.

The lift doors opened, and they stepped out. He decided on the

Tesla again as she liked that car and, more importantly, it was a swift vehicle in a pinch.

The traffic around the venue for the gala was a nightmare. He called Reuben and Rudy, more werewolves who were assigned bodyguard duties, and in five minutes they were there. Gene stopped his car and let Reuben take the driver's seat and handed him the key card. The Telsa used his phone to operate or a designated card. "I'm out of time. Park next to the venue when you can and take the key card with you." He touched his trouser pocket, checking he had his phone. Rudy drove the car the pair had arrived in. Gene opened the passenger side. "Come on, we'll walk in from here."

Lily put her hand in his as he assisted her to get out of the car. Inhaling, he caught a whiff of her perfume and suddenly felt very conscious of her closeness, the way she moved, the feel of her hand in his. He glanced down at her and saw that her gaze was focused on the people milling around, her expression thoughtful, if not concerned. He tucked her hand into his elbow. "Just so I don't lose you in the crush."

"Just so *I* don't lose *you* in the crush," she replied, and he felt the firmness of her grip. She had such a smart mouth on her. "This is a nightmare for security. I hope you don't have to pee, because I'll have to come with you, unless your werewolf buddies are going to be inside."

"No, they aren't. I can hold my water. Besides, we won't stay for the whole shebang."

"That's a relief," she replied as they walked up the steps where a queue had formed.

"I'm going to have to introduce you as we go in. What name should I use?"

"Just call me Lily."

He inclined his head in acknowledgement. "I fear your photo may be in the society pages."

"I can live with that." She didn't look impressed, but she didn't complain further.

The queue moved swiftly and once he had presented his ticket, the VIP crew stepped in. "This way, if you please, Mr Cohen. We have you at a table near the stage."

Gene eased his shoulders as he took a seat, hoping his tuxedo jacket didn't annoy him. It was bespoke, so it rarely did. Tonight, though, he was on edge.

A flute of champagne appeared in front of him. Lily waved the one for her away. "Won't you join me? One can't hurt, can it?"

She smiled. "I could say being with you is intoxicating enough, but you would call me a liar." She lifted a hand. "I'll pass. I don't want to dull any of my senses."

Her gaze travelled around the room, and a small crease in her forehead showed her concern. "What is it?"

She flicked her gaze to his. "Just the usual. Too many people, too many avenues of attack."

He harrumphed, and then the ceremony started. Gene was called up to present three awards. Lily had her eyes on him, and he tried not to be self-conscious. What did her opinion matter, anyway? He shook hands with the winners of the art prizes and posed for photos. When that was done, he returned to his seat, acknowledging acquaintances as he made his way back.

The first course arrived after he sat down and dug in, not wanting to make eye contact or hear any comment from Lily that might worsen his mood. When he was finished, he sat back and pushed his plate away. There were no other guests at the table, which could fit six people. Of that he was glad because making small talk right now with so much going on would have been a pain.

Music started up. Couples moved to take to the floor. He flicked his gaze to Lily. She had eaten her food and was sipping a glass of water. She met his gaze.

"Shall we dance?" he asked. "Best get it out of the way now."

"It's part of your role then, to dance?" she asked, placing her glass back on the table.

"Yes. Like I said, I want to leave early, so I get all the necessaries out of the way first."

Her gaze flicked to the dance floor and back to him. "It's a slow dance."

He looked out and saw that some couples were dancing close,

others were waltzing. "If you don't know how to dance, I can manage for both of us. Just follow my lead."

She pushed out her chair and stood up. "I can dance perfectly well. Can you?"

He took her hand and twirled her onto the floor. Their eyes met. She lifted her eyebrows in challenge. He took her in his arms for a waltz and something happened. She fit against his body so perfectly he had to slow his breathing. His hand pressed against her waist, almost spanning it. He was so big compared to her—in height, in breadth, in might. He drew her closer instinctively, and she didn't resist. Her perfume teased his nostrils, and he was mesmerised. It was as if she had cast a spell on him. His cock began to respond. Oh God. He had to fight the urge, the attraction. She was a witch, and she could be manipulating him. He looked down at her as she looked up at him, and there was a strange expression on her face. He stared back at her, losing himself in the depth of her eyes as they moved as one across the floor. The song had changed, but he barely noticed. She opened her mouth to speak, but all he could see were luscious lips begging to be kissed. His head lowered and her eyes widened, her chin lifting slightly.

A shot rang out. Then another.

Gene froze, felt a sting in his neck and back and dropped to the floor. Lily's cry was loud in his ears.

CHAPTER 6

At the sound of the shots, Lily dived to the ground, dragging Gene with her and then covering his body with hers. She patted him down, looking for wounds, and couldn't find any. No blood. No ripped flesh. It made no sense. Yet he was down, unconscious and vulnerable. Not bullets then. Not magic either as far as she could sense. Chaos surrounded her. People screamed, were running in all directions. There were yells, cries and another shot—a soft phut sound and she sensed something zip past her head. She had no choice but to remove Gene as fast as she could. He was too big for her to physically drag him herself and his bodyguards were outside. She would have to use magic, but it would cost her. Removing herself wasn't hard, but taking another was next level.

Where to go? Another two shots rang out. More cries of fear. Sirens sounded in the distance. She had to move. Her mind raced. The car. She could take them to the car. Where had he told the boys to park it? Next door in the car park. She hoped they had done that.

Making the gesture that helped focussed her magic, she disappeared them from the dance floor to arrive next to his car. Jumping up, she checked their surroundings. People were running out of the hall and people were running in. A police car skidded to a halt at the base of the steps. She needed to move. They didn't need any legal entanglements or questions, either. She rolled off Gene and frisked him. In his trouser pocket, she found his phone. The car door opened as if by magic. He was too heavy for her to move by mortal means. After opening the doors, she magicked him into the passenger seat, did up his seatbelt and climbed in the driver's side. She keyed up a number, put her phone on the charging plate in the centre console and then backed out in a wide screeching arc. She checked herself, as this car was more powerful than she was used to. Luckily, there was no one behind her and only a few cars were trying to leave. More sirens blared as the cops responded to the incident.

Reeva answered, "What?"

"There's been an incident. I'm coming to you." She angled out of the driveway onto the street.

"Gene?"

She looked sideways at Gene's inert form. His breathing was shallow, but at least he was breathing, which was a relief. "I can't see any blood. He's out cold, though."

"Where are you now?" Reeva asked, her accent noticeable with the stress.

"Enmore. In the car. We'll be there in half an hour." She pulled to a stop at the lights, trying not to gape at the emergency response vehicles and tapping the steering wheel while she waited for the lights to change.

"Forget the car. No time. Just come here."

"But ..."

"Just bring him now," Reeva ordered.

"Okay. Give me a minute."

She couldn't deny she could transport them both, but it would drain her for a day or two, maybe more. It was a risk, as her magic would be more depleted than it had ever been. What if they needed her magic before then? She glanced at Gene. What if he needed help right now? She had no choice but to do what his mother asked of her.

She turned into another car park and pulled the car into a free spot. Bringing his phone, she climbed out, went to the passenger side, undid his seatbelt, adjusted the seat to as far back as it could go, and climbed onto Gene, straddling his inert form. After taking a few breaths to prepare herself, she pictured Reeva's lounge room, and she made the sign, putting all her strength into it and transported them.

Gene fell backwards when they materialised, luckily not too far and his head was cushioned by a thickly carpeted rug in the middle of the floor. Lily rolled off him and dizzily tried to get back up. Reeva was there immediately, calling his name and slapping his cheeks. With professional efficiency, she patted him down, and started pulling off his coat and undoing the buttons of his shirt. Lily crawled over, trying to fight off the post-magic tiredness. She hadn't jumped that far before with such a huge burden. Her heart hammered and her head thumped. She thought she was going to faint.

"Is he okay?" she asked weakly, running her hands over to Gene's naked chest. His skin was cool and pale. She helped lift his shoulder so Reeva could tug his coat sleeve off. Once they had his top half uncovered, they looked more closely.

Reeva didn't look up from her survey of her son's body. "He's not bleeding, as you say, but he isn't waking up." She glanced up, meeting Lily's gaze, with an assessing look. "A hex?"

"Not that I can tell ..." Lily sank to the floor, her face pressed against the lush carpet. Her magic stores were depleted. Too many nights not sleeping properly and now this. "Wait a minute."

She lifted her head and delved into Gene's aura, shaking her head to clear the memories and focus. "There were shots fired and he fell down," she explained breathily. "I thought he'd been hit." She narrowed her gaze. "I can't sense magic on him. It must be something else." She bent down closer and inspected his skin and looked at his shirt, which Reeva had peeled him out of. She saw a small pinprick of blood on the collar and then another along the seam. As she brushed her fingers against it, a small item fell out from the folds of the fabric. "Look!" she said to Reeva.

It was a small dart. She put her face close to Gene's neck and saw the puncture wound. She checked further and found two more pin pricks. "He was shot multiple times, but not with a bullet." Puzzled, she shared a look with Reeva. "Drugged?"

Reeva glared and nodded. Reaching for her phone, she added, "I'll get the doctor here. I've got some Narcan in the fridge, so if it is an opioid overdose, we can reverse it."

Lily stumbled over to the fridge and found the vial. It was inside a plastic container and clearly labelled. She brought it over to Reeva who injected Gene. Lily looked to Reeva, eyebrows raised in query. "Why do you keep Narcan in the house?"

Reeva flicked up her gaze and shrugged. "Some of the younger ones play with drugs. If I'm in time, I can help when things go wrong. Because they are weres, they take too much to get a high and even they can die from an overdose."

"That sounds practical, if you ask me. A problem many communities face, too."

They waited, not speaking, both staring down at the inert body on the carpet.

A few minutes later and Gene showed signs of improvement as he came around, moaning softly. "Good," Reeva said as she made little touches on Gene's arm and cheek.

"Why would they drug him?" Lily asked. "I mean, they could have just killed him outright."

Reeva's gaze was intense on Gene's face as he let out a sigh. "It's easy and accessible. They could be testing him, too, see if the drugs will kill him. If they found a drug that could do that, the whole pack would be vulnerable."

"But there were shots fired. It must be humans then." Lily pushed her hair out of her eyes and looked down at her dress. How it survived without being ripped and crushed she didn't know. It had felt so good wearing it. "They don't want him dead then. Not yet."

Reeva snorted. "I find that hard to believe. They could've killed him if you hadn't been there and got him to me in time. He's a touch arrogant at times, and has rubbed some people, human and paranormal, the wrong way." She frowned, though. "But yes, they didn't succeed. They will try harder next time, and you will be in their sights, too."

Lily shifted position, not getting up yet. "Maybe they're sending a message: *We know who you are, and we can get to you. Back off or we'll get you*. He had a tracking device removed from his car this morning. I told him that would alert them."

Reeva's head shot up. "Like his father. You know, there was an attempt on my husband before the fatal attack. We thought nothing of it, at first. Now, though ..." she sighed slowly. "We might think again."

Lily climbed to her feet and swayed. The room spun as she righted herself. Reeva stood also and steadied her with a hand on her shoulder. She had really overdone the magic this time. She couldn't remember being so drained. Reeva studied her. "There's nothing you can do now. You should go rest and I'll stay with him and help him to bed when he's more mobile." Just then, Gene moved a leg and flexed his foot. His complexion was grey and his lips pale. "You look worse than he does."

"But Gene ..." She gazed down at him. His handsome features were unaffected, proud nose, strong brow, full lips. She blinked in alarm. Why was she thinking like that? He was whole, was what she meant. Unbloodied by bullets. She had not failed completely, and she had brought him here to where he would be safe.

Grabbing Lily by the arm, with the phone pressed to her ear, Reeva half-dragged her to the door. "I'll take care of him," Reeva said. "Go to sleep, little one. I've made up the guest room. You look dead on your feet."

Lily was too exhausted to even check her words. "I don't remember ever feeling like this before."

Reeva spoke into the phone. "We need you now. Gene is down. Drug or poison we don't know yet. I've dosed him with Narcan and he's coming around." She nodded. "Great, thank you. See you soon."

Swaying with dizziness, Lily used the wall to feel her way along the corridor. Reeva walked along behind her, a hand reaching out now and then to guide her or prevent a stumble. The edges of Lily's vision blurred, and she aimed for the doorway, hoping the dark rectangle didn't move before she got there. Arms came around her waist as Reeva guided her to the bed. "Rest now," Reeva said softly as she eased her back to lie against the pillow and lifted her legs up on the bed. "I'll look after everything. Let me help you out of that dress." Lily rolled so that her zip could be lowered and could do little to assist Reeva in stripping it off, as her arms didn't obey her commands. Reeva faded from view and Lily sank into a dark, dreamless sleep.

※

LILY DIDN'T KNOW HOW LONG SHE HAD BEEN ASLEEP WHEN HER very full bladder woke her. It was still dark, and she couldn't be bothered checking the time. She stumbled to the ensuite toilet, made herself comfortable, and then flopped back on the bed. Sleep enveloped her straight away. The dreams began then—strange, powerful dreams with erotic elements growing in intensity. She fought against them, mumbled arguments with vague figures who refused to accept her side of the story, until her exhaustion meant she could no longer stop the images unfolding.

In the dream, Gene kissed her, his mouth hot, demanding, dredging desire from deep inside. He held her, body pressed against his like it was made for that purpose. It shocked her. The way she responded, the way the need for him was like needing air. She knew it was a dream, but also detected a truth component, a predictive element that rocked her to the core. The sane part of her mind screamed: *You don't even like the arrogant son of a bitch and would not fuck him. Ever!*

The dream images broke apart, reforming to become more heated, more intimate. Gene's hot mouth was on her clit, thrumming away with strong flicks of his tongue. She was close to orgasm. It's a dream. A dream, she told herself, but she could not break free. As the orgasm hit, it exploded through her body, her mind. The consummation of desire it foretold was frightening. But still she did not wake up. The dream continued, shifting to where he was riding her, his muscled arms cradling her gently as he moved inside her. *No. No. No!* She tried to break free of the visions. Her cries of delight were traitors. She didn't want this. Had no desire to be another of Gene Cohen's trophies. Yet, there was something deeper at work, a connection, a bond. Opening her dream eyes, she looked into his and the light there overwhelmed her—powerful magic, energy and essence. His voice was soft, caressed her as he spoke. Then he growled and nibbled at her ear, and it was as if he touched her soul because a connection locked in, snapped into place, and—

The door to her room slammed against the wall. Lily bolted upright in bed, panting hard. The dream's claws released as she did so. Lily shoved her hair out of her face, trying to get her bearings.

"Get out of my head," Gene bellowed. He was naked, impressively naked, with his cock upright and engorged. He might be an arrogant so and so, but he didn't hurt the eyes. What was he on about, though? Surely they hadn't shared that dream? *No, not possible.* The very thought scared her.

Her breathing was not quite under control. "What time is it?" she asked, as if he hadn't just burst into her room naked and aroused. She needed time to think, to sort through the confusion, her own arousal.

Having him there in the flesh was disturbing. He had been the object of her erotic dream just moments ago and having him naked while she felt so worked up was a dangerous combination. The taste of him was still on her tongue and the memory of his heat on her skin and the light in his eyes lingered. The connection felt so real.

"I told you to get out of my head," he repeated, outraged, stepping further in.

"Get out of my room then," she replied tersely.

Lily swung her legs off the bed. She had only her underwear on. "I'm not in your head, and I have no idea what you are talking about." It came out grumpily. Her head ached something fierce.

He folded his arms. She tried not to look at him, but he was very hard to ignore. His skin was evenly tanned, a nice olive. Probably a trait inherited from his mother. His physique was muscly without being too obviously worked over. He was tall, well over six feet. Well-endowed in the cock department. She could see what women found interesting and alluring. She was not going to dwell on his erection.

"I don't believe you. I can sense your arousal from here."

"Fuck off!" she growled at him, rubbing at her aching head.

"Huh? You have a nerve to speak to me like that, like you weren't casting erotic dreams to me just now. Dreams of you and me fucking!"

Lily glanced up at him and knew she was blushing. "I didn't cast anything to you. Last thing I remember was saving your skin."

He shook his head once. "No, I experienced it. You were there right with me. You know what I'm talking about. Admit it."

She stood up, put her hand on the wall to steady herself. She was still weak as piss. "I didn't cast anything to you. My magic is depleted, so I can't use magic at all right now. I don't know when I will be able to. It got used up transporting us here."

"I don't believe you."

Aiming for the bathroom, she flapped a hand at him as she moved past. "Fine. Believe what you want."

The room shifted around her as her stomach sank to the floor. She didn't know she had fainted until she woke up again in Gene's arms. She thought it was a growl that woke her. His gaze penetrated, searched for all her secrets. He righted her, so she was standing on her own two feet, but still supported, with a hand on her back and an arm on her waist. Her defences were non-existent and she could barely think. She should have shut her eyes, fought her way out of his embrace, but didn't.

Her heart beat erratically trying to climb out of her chest and she blinked, once, twice, and then he growled again, before his hot mouth, the one she had dreamed about, found hers. The hand on her back moved until it was behind her head, strong but gentle, holding her as his tongue sought hers. His other arm went to her lower back and pressed her to him, melding their bodies together, just like in the dream. The kiss went on and on and something quite extraordinary happened—she kissed him back, really kissed him, until her breasts were heavy with want and her clitoris throbbed as if his tongue was there stroking her to climax. It was just a kiss, and yet it was more. A fulfilment of premonition, a fusion of desire, a—

"No!" a voice shouted, a voice that barely penetrated. Lily was deep, engrossed in the moment and Gene didn't stop, didn't let up, just drew her in until she was ready to come just from the feel of his body, his hot cock pressed against her and the erotic way they kissed. It shouldn't have been happening, but Lily was only vaguely aware of her past dislike, her vow not to be one of his casual lays.

"No, Gene. Stop!" Reeva's voice penetrated, and a wave of were magic, coercion, rocked them. Were magic could override emotions or drive them. Reeva had been den mother, a powerful werewolf in her own right, and she shoved that coercion between them as if she was splitting a log with an axe.

Gene's mouth disengaged, his breath hot and moist against her face. He let out a fierce growl, one that woke her as if from a daze. Her body throbbed with pent-up desire, reawakening the titillation from the dream—the dream Gene had come to her to complain about, and accuse her of making. She was in a weakened state and dared not move from Gene's embrace as he was currently propping her up. "Not now, Mother. Can't you see I'm occupied?"

Reeva stepped closer, her elegant nightgown and matching robe swirling around her ankles. She made sure Gene could see her. "No. Let her go. She is not for you."

Her words were like ice water. Lily took them in, felt them to her core. She was not good enough. She was not accepted. She tried to fight this gut reaction, tried not to experience it as rejection, but it was always her default position. Ever an outsider. The Sydney coven brought her up, and they treated her well, but she was not one of them. She was too different in looks and abilities to fit in well. She could use magic, and even though she was thought to be part-witch, she was something else, something different, something foreign.

Like a switch had flipped, Gene edged Lily out of his embrace and eased her gently back on the bed. She sat there, pushing her unruly hair out of her face, and panting away the lust that had accumulated in her blood. Her brain began to work again, shuffling through her emotions, her desire, trying to sort them into neat little piles where they wouldn't hurt, wouldn't control her. She was so tired she could melt and meld with the mattress.

Reeva was right. She couldn't get involved sexually and romantically with Gene, as she was supposed to be protecting him. She nodded. Nothing to do with rejection, she told herself, even though in her gut that is what she expected, what she experienced.

Gene turned to Reeva, not concerned that he was stark naked. Bloody werewolves—nakedness was second nature to them. Part of the need to transform and shed their skin she supposed. "Mother, it's none of your business."

Reeva straightened her spine, seeming to tower even though she did not. "It's my business and my house. You will not do this," she said emphatically, swiping her hand down. "You cannot have this woman, and I forbid her to have you. She works for me, and she can't do her job if she's fucking you, because you will throw her away when you are done, and she'll be no use to me or to you then."

Lily glanced up and nodded. What had she been thinking? She didn't even like him and she definitely hadn't wanted to fuck him until he walked into her room or into her dreams. "I'm sorry, Reeva."

The woman sent her a hard, flinty stare, mouth in a thin line. She seemed so unyielding that Lily felt the depth of her words again. Real and not imagined, she thought. *You're not good enough for my son. You can't have him. I won't let you have him. You are not one of us.*

Gene spared Lily a glance and grunted. "Mother ..."

"Get dressed now, Gene. And then we will talk. All of us."

Reeva stood with arms folded by the open door, waiting expectantly to be obeyed. Gene growled again, not the sexy come-hither growl that curled around her innards, but a sharp one of outrage and protest as he stomped from the room. Lily stared at the floor, the aftertaste of desire as good as a hangover. What was she thinking getting entangled like that, and what had caused that dream, that ethereal connection? She shook her head and cast a quick glance at Reeva.

Reeva made eye contact and nodded. "Get ready. We will wait for you. We need to talk. There will be food. You need food if you are to recover your abilities. And you need rest, but I can't see you getting any right now with him like that." Reeva turned to the doorway and then paused. "You know I speak truth," Reeva said quietly, and Lily felt the words like a tattoo on her skin. *Don't touch, don't even think of touching.*

"I know," Lily said on a sigh and pushed to her feet, stumbling to the bathroom. She needed to wash Gene's scent from her body. His glorious scent. She scowled at herself in the mirror. *You are only saying that because you can't have him. You didn't want a bar of him before. Now he's off limits, so you want him.* Her scowl softened. She shook her head as she flicked on the shower. Werewolves!

CHAPTER 7

Lily stayed in the shower longer than necessary. Thank goodness Reeva had instantaneous hot water that never ran out. The hot needle spray helped her regain some alertness, and she needed help to rid herself of the arousal that would not leave her alone. With desire coming off her in waves, it was safer to see to her own needs before meeting Gene again. Werewolves had ways of detecting such things, apparently. He had sensed her arousal, and that was damn annoying. She still had no idea why they had inexplicably shared a dream or simultaneously dreamed about each other in an intensely erotic way. Was it because she had no magic left at the moment, that her defences were down and his were magic took over? Possibly, but she had no definitive answer. It wasn't likely that Reeva was using her were powers, given the effort she took to break them up. Was it something from Lily's own heritage then, something from her unknown past? She had never been this depleted, this weak ever before. Luckily, she had fetched up with Reeva, who was prepared to protect her. It might have been terrible if she had been powerless out there in the world.

After dressing, she took time to do her hair, plaiting it slowly, pausing and then redoing it. It was deliberate stalling, because she was trying to mount a mental defence, a wall to keep her thoughts protected and appear level-headed and in control. Not the weak, magicless puppet she had become. There was no point in trying to do magic at all, with her reserves so depleted. Her stomach burned with hunger, so she decided it was time to face them. She needed to eat.

Just as she was about to leave the room, her phone rang. It was her contact at the police. "Michael?"

"I found that information on Violet Smith you asked for."

"And?"

"She was found dead in the alley behind her house. She'd been dead a few days, and it took a while to identify her. Here's the thing. Her name wasn't Violet Smith, it was Violet Tremblay."

Lily's heart sank at hearing the woman was dead. The moneylenders had gotten to her already. "How did she die?"

"Apparently she had been exsanguinated."

Lily's eyebrows rose as her mind began working furiously. Vampires? "Wounds?"

"She was a registered blood donor." He laughed.

"What?" Was he making a joke? He couldn't possibly know about vampires.

Michael coughed. "Well, someone or something had hacked her up pretty bad." He chuckled. "Neck wounds mostly."

"Right," she said coolly. "Thanks for the help. Any family come forward for the burial?"

"No. No living relatives, as far as we can tell. No one that will own to it."

"Okay, thanks."

"Let's catch up for a drink sometime," he said.

"Sure. Talk to you soon."

Lily ended the call. It was the link she'd been looking for and, although it was tenuous, it was better than nothing.

Reeva greeted her as if nothing had happened and even Gene appeared to have forgotten their interlude as he was startlingly neutral when he wished her good morning. Breakfast was a huge meat platter in the centre of the table. A bowl of scrambled eggs stood nearest her plate and there was chopped tomato, avocado, with fresh basil and little chunks of bocconcini. Lily sat down with a thump. She had never felt so empty in her life. Reeva spooned egg onto her plate, while Gene dumped some medium rare steak next to it. Toast with melted butter appeared on her side plate and Lily reached for the fresh salad and spooned it onto her plate as well. She knew the salad was for her, because werewolves could live off meat alone. She gave a slight nod to Reeva and started eating. They all ate, although Gene by far outstripped them all in appetite.

Fresh coffee followed the food, and Lily was no longer shaking and ready to faint. More alert, yet deeply bone weary, she was able to converse even though the place where her magic dwelt was empty and cold and she had to accept she needed time to recuperate.

"I'm glad you're not dead," she said to Gene.

He flicked up his eyes from his plate. "I am too."

"How are you feeling?"

"Like shit," he replied.

"I know that feeling."

Reeva coughed. Gene's eyes went sideways to her and then back to Lily. "Thank you for protecting me and bringing me back here."

She acknowledged his thanks and tilted her head. "Why drugs? Why not bullets?" Lily asked. They could have killed Gene at the gala if they wanted.

Gene shrugged. "It depends who is behind it. I think it was a warning from someone who doesn't know who, I mean what, I really am."

"That's bullshit. Warning? If not for your werewolf metabolism, that overdose would have been fatal." She turned to Reeva. "I am right, yes?"

"Those drugs would have killed a normal human fast," Reeva added. The den mother lifted a shoulder and scraped some bones off her plate into a waste bowl, obviously for that purpose. "I am not a hundred per cent clear what they drugged him with. The Narcan helped, and Dr Umwale was able to bring you out of it. He said there was something in there to repress your heart and another unidentified substance. Most likely a combination of Heroin, Ketamine and Fentanyl."

Lily's gaze assessed Gene across the table. "Did the doctor take some blood to check?"

"Yes. But that analysis will take a few days. He will text me the results."

Lily furrowed her brow, wondering if some supernatural element had been injected. In her state, she couldn't tell. Even if she hadn't had that rather vigorous encounter with him earlier, she could see he was recovered with seemingly no side effects. His skin looked good, his eyes were alert and, even dressed in track pants and a sweater, he looked raring to go.

"You work from here today," Reeva said to Gene.

"No, I can't," Gene said, upping his coffee mug to finish it. "I have meetings."

"Then postpone them or have them here."

"No."

Lily blinked. He was angry with his mother, and that wasn't fair. She hadn't done anything. Had only helped him.

"You can have online meetings," Lily suggested.

"No." His scent kicked up, and she breathed deep, unable to stop herself. It was heady, mind-cloying, and her clit began to throb again. *I can't do this.* She wanted to shout at him to stop it. If he used his were magic on her, she'd be lost.

"Lily isn't recovered yet. You could work here today to give her more time." Reeva used a reasonable tone instead of a demanding one.

Gene met Lily's eyes. She got no hint as to what he was thinking or feeling. "One day, then. That's all."

"I can make a few calls. Check on that spell in your garage. And I need to do some analysis."

Gene grew suddenly more alert. "You have news?"

"A possible link."

"Tell me."

She shrugged. "It's nothing conclusive. One of the moneylender clients I pulled a file for was found dead."

Gene studied her face. "And?"

"I used an old police contact to get more information. The name she gave the moneylenders wasn't her name. Not Smith but Tremblay.

Tremblay was a registered feeder. She was found exsanguinated in an alley."

Gene's fist slammed down on the table, making Lily jump. "Vampires!"

Lily lifted her hand to get his attention. "It's a connection, nothing more, so don't jump the gun. It could be coincidence. Vampires have quite a few feeders in Sydney. People like donating their blood and their bodies, hoping to obtain eternal life. It's a counterculture thing, mostly going under the radar, but it's a risky business and accidents happen."

"They are advertising themselves?" Gene said.

"Low key ... unofficially. I checked it out after my police contact made a joke about Violet being a blood donor. I found news stories and advertisements in underground BDSM newsletters and online groups. Also, some were written as articles, advising on how to find a vampire, how to submit to them to be accepted, and so on. They're semi-serious in tone, but obviously accurate if you know the truth."

Gene's mouth screwed up. But it appeared Reeva kicked him under the table, and his expression was suddenly neutral but interested. "Werewolves don't like vampires much," he said in a grumbling tone.

Reeva laughed. "Werewolves don't like anyone much, even other werewolves."

Gene laughed too, then, and Lily joined in.

"Right. Lily, you go back to bed and rest. When you feel like it, research on your laptop. Your main aim is to recover your strength and your magic." Reeva stood and began to clear away dishes. To Gene she said, "Use your father's den for an office. I'll stay out of your way."

Gene pushed to his feet. "Thank you, Mother." To Lily he said, "Get better quickly. My mother and I clash if we are caged together too long."

Lily turned away and rolled her eyes. Why had she agreed to work with them? She must be crazy. Werewolves were so different to witches. Lifting herself out of her chair, she stumbled back to the guest room and was asleep in about a minute.

CHAPTER 8

A shout woke Lily from the sleep of the dead, the next morning. Sitting upright, heart pounding, she listened for the sound again. Was it danger? Was it Gene and his mother talking? They tended to be loud.

A laugh echoed up the hall, and she let out a long, slow breath. Not danger, then. Just werewolves. There were other sounds as well. Maybe visitors. Lily flopped back against the pillow. Her body ached, and she still felt weak, but there was an improvement. Some magic had returned to take up residence. Not much though.

Her stomach growled. Hungry again. She sniffed under her arms and pulled a face. Cursed with an unusual body odour, she showered at least twice a day. Wearing a borrowed nightie from Reeva, she threw off the covers.

Shuffling to the bathroom, she rested her head on the cool tiled wall, flicked on the tap, and adjusted the temperature. Hot water enlivened her skin and while she rinsed shampoo from her hair, she thought maybe, just maybe, she had the resilience to face the werewolves. Tedious bunch. At least there had been no erotic dreams about Gene this time. Not that she recalled, at least.

Her handbag and her carryall had been delivered to her room. Her slinky evening gown was a bundle in the corner. She stumbled over, flicked it and placed it on a hanger in the wardrobe. She unzipped her bag and dug out her work clothes. A quick spell cleaned off her pants, top, and jacket. The underwear too. She wished she had packed more choices, as the ones she was wearing were the lacy ones from the gala. The gala. Recriminations flooded in. She had to do better, but directing Gene was like trying to stop a bull charging by waving a buttercup. It was difficult in a place full of people to set wards, but not impossible. She hadn't even tried. Had she been enjoying looking sexy and let herself be taken up by the moment? Shaking her head, she swallowed the denial. A bit of a buzz, maybe. The way Gene looked at her added to the thrill. It wasn't often she thought of herself like that, and the way Gene had practically drooled made her feel attractive. *Right. Time to put that bullshit in the tucker box for later. If you don't get your act together, you'll be burying Mr Charming, and his mother will gnaw on your bones.*

"HERE SHE IS NOW," REEVA SAID AS LILY WALKED INTO THE LOUNGE room, pausing on the threshold. The large room seemed full. And there was a musk smell lurking there. Werewolves. There were two other people in the room besides Gene and Reeva. The stunning redhead, who pierced her with a knowing gaze, was the sister-in-law, Abbie, and the man was Gene's brother, Rolf. She hadn't been introduced but had seen them at the paranormal get-together. They were hard to forget, being a stunning-looking couple and werewolves too.

Gene slapped the other werewolf on the back. "This is my brother, Rolf. I mentioned him."

Lily smiled. Rolf was an eyeful. Pretty where Gene was rugged. Built, with these mesmerising citrine-coloured eyes. The woman stepped between them, cutting off her view. Lily blinked because she thought she heard a growl.

"And this is Abbie, his mate and co-alpha."

"Nice to meet you," she said, meeting their gazes and not quite smiling. Abbie was a beautiful woman, and Lily had learned she was a survivor of a spell that turned her into a werewolf. With her alpha tendencies and very, very demanding libido, general report said Rolf had had no choice but to marry her, make her co-alpha and fuck her crazy every chance they got. She also had a reporter's analytical brain. Lily tried to imagine how the curse had changed the woman's life so completely. On the surface, Abbie seemed comfortable with herself.

Gene pulled out a chair. He grinned and said in a welcoming tone. "Come sit and eat."

"She smells funny," Abbie said, tracking Lily with her gaze as she moved towards Gene. "Magic and something else."

Rolling her eyes, Lily sat and turned to face the table. *How rude was that?* "I did shower just now," she supplied, her comment not seeming to land.

Abbie moved to close in on her, but Rolf put out his hand and shook his head. Some silent communication passed between them and Abbie nodded.

Gene took a seat opposite her and Reeva brought out another large platter of food. Without further ado, Rolf and Abbie sat and everyone reached for a morsel or two. A bowl of green beans and a smaller one of chopped tomato sat by her elbow. "Thank you for the food, Reeva." Lily scooped a lot of the plant food onto her plate and added some chicken drumsticks. Already the mound of meat piled on the platter had been substantially reduced.

After she spoke, the others mumbled and growled between mouthfuls of food. "It's nice to see some manners around here," Reeva said and smiled at the gathering.

Lily could see the love and fondness she had for her sons. Abbie, too, she thought. While Abbie was very beautiful, there was a ferocity to her that Lily could detect.

After dropping a large bone onto his plate and wiping his mouth with a napkin, Gene stood. "Anyone for coffee?" Each put in their order and soon the aroma of freshly ground coffee beans wafted over to her. She inhaled deeply, feeling so much better. Gene placed a cup in front of her and glanced up at him. "Thank you."

She was nose deep in it when Gene said, "Rolf and Abbie are here to help."

Lily lowered her cup and looked up. "Help who?"

"You ... us."

"Help how?"

Rolf lifted his chin. "Abbie can smell magic. We both have good noses, so we can track."

"I can track magic." She wasn't about to argue that she had a sense of smell that would match a wolf. It was just that two extra werewolves to deal with would complicate things. Take more time. Create more barriers.

Reeva met her gaze. "They can help protect Gene."

Gene erupted. "They aren't needed for that, Mother. I can take care of myself."

Lily nodded. "I see what you mean."

Rolf put down his coffee cup noisily and shifted his attention to Lily. "Gene said you found a vampire connection. We know they have made incursions into the fringes of society. That works against us and for us."

"How?" Lily asked.

Rolf tilted his head. "Their enclaves are easy to find."

"And against us?"

Rolf sat back, his gaze intent. "They have human and paranormal allies. If they notice us sniffing around, it could rebound."

Lily had had little to do with vampires. They stayed away from witches and witches stayed away from them. It was true that there was an underground culture in which they featured. Mainstream news might mention them in passing, like a modern myth or dodgy conspiracy theory. Similar to drug lords, they lurked on the fringes, doing damage along the way. When she was a cop, she had encountered one or two of their victims. Obviously, she'd been out of touch since she'd left the force, because they had grown bolder since she resigned. Now, Michael's comment made sense. The police, hence the government, knew about vampires. They weren't putting up billboards and featuring on talk shows, but they were there and knowledge of them was spreading. How had this happened without the rest of the paranormals knowing? Her gut churned, and it wasn't because she'd eaten too much. "Tell me about what happened at the Collegium. Apart from Dane's speech, I heard of upheaval, but not much else."

Rolf cleared his throat and gave her a lengthy run-down.

Lily reiterated the key bits of information. "So Dane's father, who was part of the Triumvirate, was killed?" Her gaze slid to Gene. "And then your father was murdered?"

Gene nodded. "You think they're connected?"

Lily gave a firm nod. "It's an angle worth exploring. There's usually no such thing as a coincidence."

Abbie narrowed her gaze. "I had not previously connected them myself. I know the vampires are angry that the sorcerers have the power and aren't good at sharing. I thought it was because they were disorganised, you know? No hierarchy, just sort of clannish. They aren't well liked among other paranormals either, and they smell so bad." She waved a hand in front of her face, as if waving away a stench. "But maybe they're more organised than we thought."

Lily bit her lip. Abbie had also described how werewolf packs organised themselves.

"Their plots might go deeper than we ever expected," Rolf said. "Now, that's not something I want to think about."

Gene grunted. "I'd like to clear them out. They threaten all of us with their overt practices. Since our discussion, I requested some research on them and just received a report. They have a media liaison and a whole consulting firm managing their public face. They pass themselves off as if they are poor people with an inherited medical condition."

Eyes widening, Lily digested this. "While I was in the force, they had only just crept up to the fringes of society. Like a little pocket of concern. The media wasn't picking up on their stories much then, but they must have sympathisers in government and in the force to grow in influence so quickly."

Rolf screwed up his mouth. "I'll have to talk to Dane about it. Weres are on the outer too, but we don't mind as much. We like doing our own thing as long as people don't get hurt. Damned if we're going to start managing our public profile. But the enmity between vampires and weres is of long standing. The most recent attacks have come from within the Collegium. The curse that affected Dane and then Abbie were traced to Rafael and whoever else was manipulating him.

"Rafael?"

"He was a top sorcerer at the triumvirate who was supposed to be on our side. The side of right. That's why Dane is so busy and so concerned about the dark forces at work. They are slippery and we still don't know who or why. Only that they were trying to expose werewolves and other paranormals to normal humans."

Abbie spoke up. "It's not only that, but we have allies among some high-powered sorcerers, and I suppose that can cause jealousy. We aren't officially connected but known to be wielding influence. Perhaps the vamps don't like that." She shrugged. "Who knows!"

Lily didn't like hearing this one bit. Things were mostly sunshine and roses in the Balmain coven. Sure, they had dramas and dark warlocks causing havoc, but in Sydney, with the sun and the harbour, well, those problems didn't stick. The coven was more concerned about maintaining its population through having children, keeping humans safe, and having fun with magic.

With this upswell in paranormal political intrigue, there could be a spillover. She made a mental note to put Elvira on alert. "Witches are affiliated with the Collegium, but run their own show, abide by their own rules." Lily shifted in her seat. "They won't like this disharmony. There's enough going on with dark forces spreading worldwide to keep them worried. Dane's speech caused waves. It made the elders realise that this dark movement isn't only affecting witches, it's affecting all paranormals like some kind of rot. It also made them see it wasn't something that began with us, either."

Gene opened his mouth to speak, but Reeva got in before him. "There will come a time when we paranormals will have to fight for what is right and for survival, too, if we don't address this now."

With a nod to Reeva, Lily faced Rolf and Abbie. "I take it, then, that you want to take out the vampire enclaves. The ones we know about?" Lily said, meeting their gazes in turn.

"Yes, that is a good place to start," Gene said.

Lily shook her head.

"What?" Gene blurted.

"That will take a lot of resources and likely advertise that we are on to them. They could retaliate and I don't think we are ready for that."

Reeva nodded. "It could lead to an all-out war. We have the wolves, but we aren't prepared for battle. Think of the repercussions if we move too soon, before we are ready. I agree with Lily. We must tread carefully."

Gene stood up suddenly, sending his chair flying. He banged his chest. "They killed my father!" he yelled.

Reeva blinked. "Eugene was my husband, too. Sit down, Gene. Someone, some faction, is responsible for his death. It may be vampires, it may not. We need proof before we act."

Lily had been holding her breath. She knew Gene to be a hothead, but that sudden outpouring of rage and grief affected her. She was wary of Gene's volatility, but also sad for him.

Even as she kept her head down, she knew he was looking at her, willing her to agree with him.

Abbie raised a hand to get their attention. "We need some intelligence first. Like how many vampires there are, how many enclaves and where? Who is their leader, the seconds, the full vampires, their progeny, their keepers, their blood donors? All of it. We need to know who they fraternise with, who they control in the human world."

Lily agreed. "Yes, some research will help. We can work out who to target."

Gene growled, and the hairs on her arms lifted in response. Rolf growled back. "Don't be unreasonable, brother. They talk sense."

Gene banged his fist on the table, making the cutlery jump. "I want action. I want who did this to suffer. I want to rip their throats out."

Lily blinked and tried not to look at any of their faces. "Lily!" Reeva exclaimed. "You keep him safe. Stay with him."

With a large swallow of saliva, she gaped. She wanted to say: *Are you out of your mind? He's a loaded shotgun, an unexploded bomb.* All she managed was. "Yes. I can do that."

Reeva reached out and patted Rolf's hand. "Son, can you start some snooping? I know you have a nose that can detect vampires."

He nodded. "Absolutely. I will start straight away."

Reeva turned to Abbie. "You were a reporter once. Can you do some investigating? Lily is good, but she's not up to snuff right now. Can you help her?"

Abbie nodded like a salute. "Can do."

"Right then. Get going all of you. Back here by sundown. I want no altercations with the vampires. Understand? Gene, you go to work as normal. Take Lily with you. Keep it in your pants."

Gene looked ropeable. "Mind your own damn business, Mother. I put my cock wherever I want." He grinned, then caught Lily's expression, gave a small wince. "Where it's wanted, I mean."

Reeva rolled her eyes. "Let him find someone to bang before his head blows off in frustration. Just not you. I want you focused on keeping him safe. And make sure he's back here before sunset."

Lily stood up. Gene glared at his mother a bit longer before he tossed his napkin on the table and stood. The brothers shoulder bumped, and Abbie kissed Gene on the cheek. "See you later."

CHAPTER 9

Lily had to run to keep up with Gene. "But I thought Reeva said we should work from her place."

"That was yesterday. Today I have other ideas."

He took long strides down the corridor and into the car park. She leaped into the car as soon as it unlocked and buckled up quickly as he tore out of the parking spot and headed for the exit. She held on to the overhead handle to keep herself from bouncing around. He turned his head briefly, giving her a withering look.

Wincing, she asked, "Where are you working today?"

"Back at the office." His response was sharp and angry. She could tell he clenched his jaw as his cheek muscles bunched and flexed. "Just being normal, as my mother instructed."

There was nothing normal about Gene Cohen. After meeting Rolf, she realised there was nothing normal about either of Reeva's sons. Upon reflection, she hadn't had too much to do with weres, not this up close and personal. Occasional interactions when on the beat. As a paranormal herself, with witch training, she could sense what they really were. They were less able to detect her, though, or so she had thought. Breathing out, Lily ventured. "You know she's right, don't you? You should keep a low profile."

A growl was all the answer she received.

Once they reached the office, she chased after him as he strode towards the elevator. "Gene, wait."

He swung around so quickly she nearly barrelled into him. "What?"

"Do you mind if I put up a few wards in the building? Just monitoring ones so I know who is coming and going?"

"Magic surveillance?"

"Yes."

"Then you're restored?" His eyebrows lifted in query.

"Some ... wards take little power. Not like transporting someone else over distance."

His expression softened and his voice lowered, becoming warmer, gentler, as its tones washed over her. "I'm glad to hear that you're feeling better. I was worried." A ghost of a smile played around his mouth as he held her gaze. "I don't think I have thanked you for getting me out of there, getting me to safety. My mother explained it to me once I was recovered. She said you acted quickly and bravely and that you had been in the line of fire."

Lily blushed and swallowed the lump in her throat. Gene could turn on the charm, say the right things and she was in danger of liking him. "Just doing my job."

"Nevertheless," he said, putting his hand on his heart. "I owe you. I thank you."

Lily shifted her gaze to the floor. A wave of power rolled over her. Not a compulsion, but some alpha thing Gene had going. "It's fine."

In the lift, he angled his body towards her, snagging her attention. "About accusing you of getting in my head ... with that dream ... Mother explained it couldn't have been you."

Lily relaxed. "That was good of her. Did she have a theory?"

Gene lowered his gaze, his cheeks pinkening. "Not exactly," he began, and then coughed. "She thought it was something to do with my alpha powers affecting you."

"I see," she replied and looked down to avoid his gaze. "It must have been the close proximity." Not being were herself, she shouldn't have been affected the way she had been. That dream had been so intense, her arousal so marked. She got the sense that he was undressing her in his mind, that he remembered that erotic dream where she screamed out her orgasm as he sucked on her. Her own face radiated heat and the mere memory had the pulse throbbing between her thighs. Right then, she didn't know how she was going to last the day. Maybe she should take things into her own hands, so to speak. A touch would likely set her off, give her some relief. Hopefully, Gene would get laid, as well, and his overpowering werewolfiness would dissipate.

Ah, but then she'd have to go with him while he did the thing. *Goddess, life could be a bitch.* She rolled her eyes. Reeva was a cow for doing this to her.

Once he was ensconced in his office, his were bodyguards in place, Lily made an assessment of the floor space, the entrances and even the foyer, to determine what kind of watch ward she needed. She placed several in strategic places. The one in the men's room was a bit of a risk, because she was sure she wasn't going to like the conversations or the sounds from there. But it seemed to her a likely place where secrets might be uttered. She did the same in the ladies' room.

After she made a call to Elvira to alert her to possible vampire shenanigans and the threat of all-out war, she needed a big, strong coffee. Elvira had a lot to say, and Lily's ears were still ringing as she made her coffee. Elvira's daughter, Grace, was a necromancer and Elvira said she'd talk to her about whether that talent would be any good in rooting out vampires and their conspiracies. However, Grace had two young children, one a baby, and may not be able to be spared.

As she was leaning against the counter in the kitchen, sipping her coffee, Gene surprised her when he walked in. He seemed calmer. She gave him a nod of acknowledgement. Had he dealt with his arousal issues already? She hadn't picked up anything. Then again, she had been busy setting the wards and making calls.

"Any news?" she asked.

"Rolf called. He's found two enclaves on sense of smell alone. He's marking them on a map."

Lily smiled. "Progress then."

"Yes. Unfortunately, it's been too long since my father's murder to track vampires at the scene of the crime."

"Oh, right. No one noticed their scent at the time?"

Gene shook his head. "We were at the hospital, Mother and me. The cops were all over the scene. Then, there was a week of storms, which washed away a lot of olfactory evidence."

"Those storms that ate a chunk of the coastline?"

"Yes, they did, but they happen with regularity these days so hard to track which one this far along so security camera footage was not much use."

Lily finished her coffee and placed her cup in the dishwasher.

Gene spoke. "I need to go out for a meeting."

"Oh? Where? With whom?"

Gene rolled his eyes. "You sound like my mother."

Lily shrugged. "Well, I am working for her ... and you."

"Restaurant meeting. I hope you like fish, because we are off to Watsons Bay."

Mentally recreating a map of the place, she nodded. It was as good a place as any for a meeting and a bit isolated, so easy to manage access.

"Do I need to dress?"

Gene looked her slowly up and down. "I think you'll do nicely. Black leather is sexy on you."

Lily sagged. "Black leather is sexy on anybody. Do you mind not sexually harassing me while I work? I'll tell your mother."

Gene laughed. "Point taken."

He headed for the lift, and she bolted after him. The tension from the morning had eased somewhat. He had been bursting with anger and sexual tension then and now he was mellow. No wonder the coven kept their distance from werewolves. Unpredictable creatures. Sex mad creatures too. Witches liked sex, were not prudish, so it wasn't a clash of appetites that was a concern, nor was it an incompatibility thing when weres were in human form. Because they desired to keep the witch line pure, the elders encouraged witches to mate with other witches or humans in a pinch because there was a warlock shortage in the coven. Given they were so different in temperament and race, witches and weres didn't tend to fraternise. Sex was not outlawed between them, but not encouraged. Lily had not heard of a witch/were joining or offspring before, so it was probably not possible for couples from the different groups to breed. Mentally, she slapped herself. *Stop thinking about sex with werewolves. Goddess, damn your eyes.*

The drive up to Watsons Bay was nice enough. Gene drove less maniacally than previously, which suited her. "Any pick-ups on your watch wards?"

Lily grimaced. "Nothing concerning you, but I had to warn the receptionist in the Flight Bureau shopfront downstairs that the security guard has been stalking her."

"What? Building security?"

"Yes. He was watching the feed when he was on the bog." She screwed up her face just thinking about what she'd heard.

"Ah ... was he um ..." Gene made the wank sign, and she nodded. "What a creep."

Was he just saying that or did he really think perving was a bad thing.? He was a highly sexed man—okay, werewolf—so weren't women all just like prey to him?

He looked at her sideways. "I don't need you to tell me what you're thinking."

"You don't?" she acted surprised, because acting appalled would give it away.

"I like sex. But the women I'm with want to be with me and they know the terms that it's on."

"Oh ..." Dammit. He could read her mind.

"I have never stalked a woman, ever. Never perved on them when they didn't know I was. I can't say I haven't sexually harassed anyone, because you called me on it this morning—for which I apologise. However, I don't usually engage in that way with my staff. My receptionist is the daughter of one of our betas and newly married."

His arrogance had been so much a part of their interaction that she wasn't expecting an apology or even an admission of wrong doing. "Thank you." She didn't know what else to say. While she hadn't sexually harassed him, she had enjoyed looking. Now that his mother had banned them from consummating their attraction, it was rather hard going. Nothing like forbidden fruit to grow desire.

"My mother ... can be a bit relentless and controlling."

"Ah ..." Having him know what she was thinking was quite disturbing. He had to be guessing, though, surely?

"She meant no insult to you."

Lily lifted her eyes and met his gaze. "She didn't?"

He smiled. "No. I detected that you might have construed her words that way. She has never interfered in my sexlife, ever. She has nagged me to take a mate, produce grandchildren and the like. Just normal mother stuff.

"It's just that's she's worried about me. She obviously thinks very highly of your skills and wants you focused on the job. She doesn't want me bonking your brains out and distracting you."

That comment created images she had to suppress. "Oh, right." She cleared her throat and looked out the window. "That makes sense."

They pulled into a car park and exited the car. A light breeze delivered scents of salt and sand. As they approached the restaurant, kitchen smells of hot fat, cooked chips and fish batter became stronger. The view of the harbour was amazing as they waited for the maitre d'.

Gene inhaled, his eyes assessing. "They're here."

"Who?" She dragged her gaze from the see and the bustling tables that fronted the beach.

"The men who were involved in a project with my father when he died. We're here to settle our negotiations. They tried to take it over, but I've put them straight on that score. They were backers, not owners. Dad had the legalities sealed up pretty tight. Even then, they fought. I suspect you might find that one of them associates with vampires."

"I see," she said as she followed him inside. "I don't have your nose, you know."

"You have other skills just as useful."

Four men looked their way when they walked in. Gene was twice the size of the youngest man, who wore a grey suit and red tie, with dark hair spiky on top. He had to be near forty. Two of the men were grey-haired, in their sixties, black suited with blue ties and pale eyes. One was rather tubby and the other leaner, with heavy floppy jowls like he had lost weight recently. The fourth man was swarthy, around fifty years old. He wore a white coat, open shirt revealing dark chest hair. His black hair was slicked back and when he smiled, his teeth flashed white. He stood to greet them. "Cohen," he said. "Good, you could make it." His eyes shifted to Lily. "And who is this charming woman?"

Gene shook the man's hand. "This is Lily, Ruiz." He gave no other introduction, leaving her status ambiguous. He must have had his reasons. The man studied her as Gene introduced her to Mr Owens, Mr Costas and Mr Capillo.

Gene sat close to her, pouring her some water while he caught up on pleasantries. Ruiz appeared to be the lawyer. "About the settlement," Mr Costas began.

"It will be paid by bank cheque when you sign the papers and, no, I will not increase the amount."

Mr Costas deflated somewhat. "Let's eat," suggested Mr Capillo. "They have fresh lobster today."

Gene waved to alert the server, and the rest of them hurriedly studied the menu.

"I haven't had lobster before," she said to Gene. "What's it like?"

"Do you like prawns?"

She nodded. "Well, similar to that, only richer, and there's more of it. Choose it if you like."

Real French champagne arrived, which the server poured out for them. "A toast," Mr Ruiz said. "To business, good food and beautiful women." He met her eyes and lifted his glass.

Her face heated a little, and then she shook herself. She was not beautiful, so wondered what the spin was, what angle was this sleazebag lawyer playing.

Gene, though, took him at his word. "Indeed. To beautiful women."

He nudged her with his shoulder, and when she met his gaze, he winked. She didn't know how to take that, so took a sip. It was excellent wine, a little dry for her taste, but it slid down easily.

They placed their orders, and then Mr Ruiz presented the documents for signing. Gene looked at them without touching. Obviously, he wasn't about to trust that the documents reflected what had been agreed.

He slid his arm around her, and she froze. He leaned in, pretending to nuzzle her neck. "Can you tell if anyone is hiding something?"

She sank into him as if they were lovers. With her hands under the table, she did a quick spell. Pretending to enjoy his nuzzling, she replied. "All of them."

He kissed her cheek, just a little peck that twanged her arousal tendons. "Thanks, beautiful."

Lily did her best to not roll her eyes.

"I'll get my solicitor to go over these. Provided all is well, I can sign tomorrow."

Ruiz rested his hands on the table. He opened them out. "I assure you everything is as we agreed."

Gene smiled, hiding his teeth. "I'm sure they are, but if you don't mind, I'll have my expert check them."

Ruiz's smile didn't change, but something inside him did. He was quick to hide it, but Lily noticed, and she was convinced that Gene had as well.

The food arrived, which diverted everyone's attention. A great platter with a cut up lobster, all red, with long legs fanning out along the edge graced the centre of the table. In amongst the cut lobster were jumbo king prawns. A dish with lobster mornay also landed next to it with sides of greens, both fresh and cooked. A nice side of roast Kipfler potatoes wafting of rosemary and garlic arrived as well. Gene placed a serving of each dish on her plate before serving himself. "I think you'll find this is the best seafood restaurant around. It's family run and has been in operation since the late 19th Century. Lily tasted her first piece of lobster and enjoyed it. The tender white flesh tasted very rich and fresh.

Ruiz appeared distracted as he ate. Lily's eyes were drawn to the contract that now sat by Gene's elbow. The more she stared, the weirder things became. It had a friggin' spell on it. Lily tried to interpret it, knowing that the intent had to be malicious. Under the table, she grabbed Gene's knee and squeezed. He grew still.

"Can't get enough of me, babe?" he asked drolly.

He nuzzled her neck again. "Maybe we should take this outside for a moment," she responded, arching her back as if he was turning her on.

Gene broke away, turned to the table and said in a cool voice. "I won't be a moment. Just a little business to attend to."

He grabbed Lily's hand and dragged her out the door. With his back to their audience, he swung her around and enveloped her in his big bear arms and kissed her soundly. With his reputation with women, his actions wouldn't raise an eyebrow. They would have been clearly visible through the glass doors. She tried to break off the kiss because she needed to speak with him urgently, but he was intent on putting on a show. Her mind went into a spin when he drove his tongue into her mouth, teasing her own. *For Goddess's sake*, she thought, and gave him as good as she got, mashing his mouth like there was no tomorrow. In response he changed his grip and pressed her to him. Despite their clothing, she could feel his heartbeat as it crashed around in his chest and his body heat washed over her. Her heart wasn't behaving itself, either. "Tell me," he said breathlessly.

Pleased she had affected him as much as he had her, she grinned and then grew serious. "The contract has a spell on it. I'm not sure what it's meant to do, but it can't be good. If you sign it, there might be a magical compulsion that you consent to. Or if you take it away, it might blow up. We need high-level technical assistance."

"Elvira?"

She nodded, pecked him on the lips spontaneously, not sure why she did so. The aftermath of their passionate embrace, perhaps.

His eyes widened, and he leaned closer, giving her a solid kiss. "Good work. Call Elvira and get her here while I stall. I think we need another bottle of champers and some elaborate dessert."

"I'll take myself off to the ladies' room. Maybe mess up my hair or something, so I have an excuse to set it to rights."

It was in a braid, so she snapped her fingers to loosen the tie. He grabbed her to him again, smashed his mouth against hers while putting his fingers into her hair, and massaged her scalp. It wasn't easy to focus. Gene kissed like an expert and the first one had set her off and this one threatened to tip her over the edge. Nothing but being tossed into the ocean was going to cool her down quickly. A large wave made a splash on the pier, caused by the wash of a motor cruiser heading out of the heads. That was a reminder that she was on the job. He eased her back, looked her up and down, and grinned like a loon. "You look impressively ravished, if I say so myself."

Gene walked confidently back into the restaurant, stopping to adjust his trousers. Either that was an act, or he had been aroused as well. Lily headed to the ladies' room. She found Elvira's number in her favourites and pressed call as she studied her reflection in the mirror. Her skin was flushed. Her dishevelled white hair stood on end as if she had just got out of bed after a mad night of passion. This she spelled back into place just as the phone answered. "Elvira? How soon can you get here? I need your expert opinion."

"I've got a life, you know. Where are you? Is this more of this vampire business?"

Lily filled her in. "I see. Well, some space has just opened up in my calendar. Who am I going to be? Your mother?"

"That'll work."

"I was joking," Elvira said. "Can't I be an acquaintance accidentally bumping into you?"

"No. I know you were joking, but I think mother will work best. Be the outraged mother-in-law type. I need you to get a close look at the document that's sitting on the table next to Gene."

Luckily Elvira was a traveller, one of the best in the coven, so she would be here soon. Lily sat back down next to Gene. "That lobster is divine. It's nearly as tasty as you are." She leaned in close, putting her hand on his thigh. "Is there more bubbly?" she purred these words out.

Gene signalled, and the server came over and took the order for more champagne. The businessmen and their lawyer looked at each other and she could tell they had grown wary, despite the playacting. Gene had a reputation with women, but there was something they weren't buying. That was weird, because Gene had done a good job of arousing her and from where she sat, Gene was always horny.

Gene lifted his full glass. "To great deals and many more."

They smiled and lifted their glasses. Only Ruiz had a cagey look in his eye. His gaze flicked to Lily and back to Gene.

"Lily De Vere! Is this the man you've been seeing behind my back?" A loud, irritating voice washed over the table.

Everyone jerked, even Lily. "Mother!" Dressed elegantly in a yellow pants suit with a floral scarf in autumn tones draped around her neck, Elvira approached. With her tall frame and regal bearing, Lily expected a royal wave.

"Don't you 'mother' me." She drew in close, right into Gene's face. "I bet you're only after one thing. You lech, corrupting my pure, innocent daughter!"

Ruiz stood up. "Look here, you can't just burst into this private meeting."

Gene used both hands to gesture in a downward direction. "Sit, sit, you'll only make it worse."

Gene leaned away from Elvira, looking entirely freaked out by her verbal attack. "Mrs De Vere," he began. "So lovely to meet you. Can I get you a drink?"

"A drink? No, I don't want a drink." She poked Gene in the chest. "I want a marriage proposal, right now."

Lily's heart thumped painfully. Where did that 'marriage proposal' idea come from? Lily saw Elvira squint at the contract.

Gene threw up his hands in surrender. "A marriage proposal? I haven't even bedded your daughter yet."

"Yet! You cheeky bastard. My family doesn't believe in sex before marriage. What do you say to that?"

Gene blustered, fumbling for a response. "I will think about it."

Elvira poked him with a finger to the chest. "You stole her out of my house, right out the window like some beast in the night."

"I did?" He nodded. "I did." Gene grinned in spite of himself. "A beast? Them's fighting words, Mrs De Vere."

Elvira reached down and grabbed the contract. Ruiz yelled and thrust out a hand to stop her. Rolling it up, she aimed it at Gene's head, but Ruiz touched her and then she hit him with it instead. Ruiz screamed in fright, threw up his hands and tipped his seat over before leaping up and bolting out of the restaurant.

"Interesting," Elvira said, dropping the contract back onto the table. She eyed the other men, squinting at them like insects. She was very good. Lily was glad the elder witch was on her side.

Gene tilted his head to regard the three other men. They had their mouths open, then when they saw the look on Gene's face, their hands went up. "We had no idea," Capillo said.

"No idea about what?" Gene asked.

"Er, that he was so flaky?" shrugged Capillo.

Gene shifted his gaze to the other two. Owens shook his head. "I have no idea what just happened."

Lily saw genuine confusion in his expression and aura.

Mr Costas shook his head and shrugged. He obviously knew something, but perhaps not what the actual issue was. Gene glared at them all. The older men grew restless, their faces mottled with red. Lily hoped they didn't burst a blood vessel. The younger man stuck a finger in his tie to loosen it.

"You should leave," Gene said with a jerk of his chin. "I'll cover the meal. My solicitor will be in touch about going forward from here."

The men stood as one, chairs scraping. They gathered up their briefcases and umbrellas. Lily detected disappointment in Owens, suspicion and wariness in the older men. Mr Costas seemed like he had something to hide. They wandered out the door as a group, then once outside the door, each went their separate ways. Elvira slid into Ruiz's vacant seat just as a platter with an enormous bombe Alaska was lowered onto the table.

Gene told the server that the others had to leave but not to worry as they could manage dessert. Then he turned his smile on Elvira. "I hope you'll join us," Gene said. "There is plenty to go around."

Her eyes lit up at the flames on the meringue, which died quickly as the rum dispersed. "I think I will. I'm sure my husband won't mind if I'm a tad longer than I said I'd be. A woman has to get her priorities straight."

Elvira cut off a huge section of the dessert and levered it onto a plate while keeping it in one piece. Without further ado, she picked up a spoon.

Lily rested her chin on one hand, watching Elvira. The witch noticed her regard, stopped eating, wiped her mouth and said, "You were right. It was a compulsion spell with a nasty spike." She flicked her thumb over her shoulder. "That's why your friend ran off when I hit him with the contract."

"Did you hook him with it?" Lily asked.

She grinned, took another spoonful of meringue and lifted it, pausing dramatically. "He might find a compulsion to do something embarrassing in about an hour. Hopefully, when he is far from here."

Gene scooped a portion of the bombe Alaska onto a plate and settled it in front of Lily and then did the same for himself. "Thank you kindly, Elvira. As he ran off, I detected some vampire taint as well."

Elvira pulled a face. No love lost there between the coven and the Sydney vampires.

"Let me know how I can return the favour," Gene continued. "If you need any construction work done for the coven, I'll give you a good price." He then refilled their glasses with champagne and lifted his in a salute to the witch.

They had made inroads to the dessert already when they started up the conversation again.

"Did you know him? Ruiz? Was it his spell?" Gene asked as he picked up his spoon and played with the melting ice cream.

"No, I don't know the man, but I might know the conjurer of the spells." Elvira dug her spoon in again.

"Spells?" Lily asked. "Do you mean there was more than one and they were pre-purchased from a vendor?"

Elvira nodded as she scraped the plate clean. She eyed the remaining dessert, and her eyes danced as Gene cut another enormous slice for her. She picked up her spoon, dug it in, and then bit into the mouthful. Her eyes rolled up. "So good." Then meeting Lily's eye. "Same signature as the one in the garage."

Lily had requested someone from the coven study the spell she had found that first night at Gene's. She hadn't realised that Elvira had been the one to do the inspecting. "Rogue?"

Elvira nodded and then took another spoonful. "Yes. Difficult to track down, but I know her work. She's been in trouble with us before." Elvira lifted her hand in a chopping motion and then wiggled it. "She's been flirting with the dark ones for a while. She always has been borderline."

"Her?" Gene asked.

"Yes."

"Name?" he asked.

Elvira cut into another section with her spoon. "That's coven business."

"Not when it's aimed at me and mine."

"True. That puts another light on it. I will have to consult with the other elders before divulging. I'll get back to you. She may have gone underground and, if so, we might need your particular skills to sniff her out."

Gene agreed. "That I'm happy to do, or I will send someone even more skilled than me." He took a sip of champagne. "By the way, that was a brilliant performance. Very convincing."

"Nearly had you proposing, did I?" She flashed Lily a grin, which made Lily concerned and embarrassed. "I'm not losing my touch, then. I have been known to facilitate some matches now and then."

Lily's stomach churned. Surely, she wasn't suggesting that Lily marry Gene? That made no sense, even in jest. Witches did not marry werewolves. She frowned at the thought. Did the older witch know something about Lily and her parentage? Now was not the time to get into it, but when she had some spare time, she was going to see Elvira and ask some pointed questions.

Elvira picked up a napkin, wiped her mouth, belched quietly. She stood up, picked up a champagne glass, and emptied it. Placing it back on the table, she grinned. "That's quality. Thank you." Her gaze shifted until she spotted what she was after. "I need to use the ladies. See you when I see you, Lily." To Gene she said, "I'll let you know by tomorrow."

CHAPTER 10

Back at Reeva's house, they gathered in the dining room, each taking a seat. The smell of roast meat lingered in the air. Reeva was cooking for them. These werewolves always seemed to be eating. Lily would have to watch her weight, as she didn't eat as often or as much as she had been while working for Gene and his mother. Just thinking about how much dessert she'd eaten at lunch made her head spin. Her stomach was so full, she could just slide into a corner and power nap.

Abbie sat forward, her red hair luxurious as if she had just showered and blow-dried her hair. Rolf's hair was damped, as if he had also just showered. Lily narrowed her eyes. Obviously, they had sex and then cleaned up afterwards. If Reeva noticed, she didn't let on. Anyway, she suspected that was perfectly normal behaviour for wolves. A certain amount of resentment grew in her chest. They got to indulge, and she didn't. That sucked. Gene had been close to her all day. He was in her nostrils, his scent on her skin, his breathing detectable from where she sat. After their shared erotic dream, her sensitivity to him had grown. His presence was like a huge weight in her mind. If he was doing it deliberately, she would throttle him.

Reeva handed out drinks and sat down. "What did you find?" she directed this question at Rolf and Abbie.

Rolf took a sip of his drink. Whisky by the looks of it. Lily sniffed hers. Mineral water. *Why thanks, Reeva.* She rolled her eyes and tasted it. Definitely plain mineral water. This was getting tedious. No sex, no booze. What next?

Abbie unfolded a map and laid it on the table in front of them. Rolf leaned forward. "We found twenty enclaves today alone. Just large houses with compounds. Some looked like former brothels. I think there are more, though. Much more than you would expect."

Reeva screwed up her mouth. "That many. In Australia? But this is the arse end of the world to most paranormals. Why so many?"

Rolf shook his head. "It has me baffled as well. We might have to alert other packs to check out the other cities. Just in case this is peculiar to Sydney."

"From what we could determine," Abbie explained. "There are about twenty to forty people in each location. From the scents alone, most were blood servants, bound but not vampires. Each location had about four to five vampires of various strengths, so they could be progeny with one or two older vamps."

"Were there any witches among them?" Lily asked.

Abbie blinked. "Not that I noticed. What do witches smell like?"

Lily shrugged. "Like me I guess."

Abbie shook her head. "You smell like magic, sure, but there's something else to you I don't understand yet."

"What?" Lily asked.

Reeva waved her hand dismissively. "Don't get off track. What happened to you two today?"

Gene recounted the meeting, and the hexed contract. "Ruiz had vampire taint on his clothes. Maybe he's sleeping with one of them. There were no signs of bites."

"You think these men are behind the killing of my husband?" Reeva aimed her question at Lily.

"They were hiding something. I don't know what, though."

"A tail on Ruiz then," Gene said, picking up the phone and issuing the order.

"And the witch Elvira?" Reeva asked.

"Useful and she will get back to us about the rogue witch selling spells."

Reeva stood. "Let's eat. We're going to need our strength. While I'm bringing in the food, Gene, ring a few of the alphas around here and ask them to get the word out to other states. I want to know how many vampires are in the country."

"Why are they multiplying so quickly?" Abbie asked. "They don't breed, and it takes time to make progeny otherwise."

"Yes," Rolf responded. "And they usually cap their numbers, to keep their population low. They would soon run out of food if there were too many of them."

"But could they be increasing their numbers for an attack, for war?" Lily asked.

Gene placed his hand on her shoulder and squeezed. "That's the scary part of the scenario. I hope not. A coup maybe against the Collegium."

"I've spoken to Dane. He's trying to find out what the Collegium knows and what they can do if our worst fears are realised." Rolf said and put his arm around Abbie, letting her snuggle into him.

Gene made a few calls, nodding as he signed off each one. "They're on it. Word is spreading, and we should know more in a day or two."

Reeva brought platters of meat and placed bowls of vegetables near Lily. They ate and chatted, although Lily grew tired before she had finished her first helping. Gene nudged her with his shoulder. "Go to bed. You look beat."

Reeva nodded. "You're still recovering. With Rolf here, Gene is safe. Let your guard down and go relax."

Lily pushed her bowl away. "That was great. I'm sorry I didn't do justice to your food. I think I will go nap now. Wake me if you need anything."

"I'll knock on your door in the morning," Gene said.

"Thank you."

After a shower, she regarded the guest bed. With a sigh, Lily folded her naked body into the sheets, her head a swirl of information and her body abrim with unsated lust.

Abbie and Rolf's cosy snuggling just fuelled the desire she already experienced by being near Gene. They had an earnest, potent attraction and sex drive that leaked into the very air. She turned over and put her head under the pillow, trying to block it out. She needed to bleed off some of this arousal, as she felt like a walking time bomb. Yet, she knew if she did, they would all know. They would smell her desire and detect the vibrations of her orgasm. *Bastards!* Why did she ever agree to work for these werewolves?

She closed her eyes and tried to sleep. As soon as she did, she relived that kiss with Gene, except in the dream they were naked and his hands did more than mess up her hair. His large hands cupped her butt cheeks and pressed her against his erection. *Oh Goddess! I'm going to come.* He moved her slowly up and down so her labia and clit were rubbing against his hard cock. Her breath grew short and fast. Her breasts tingled, and her nipples hardened. He bent over her, catching a nipple in his mouth, and suckled. Her orgasm hit, rocking her body like she was having a seizure. She awoke panting, her clitoris throbbing as the orgasm waned. She didn't even need to touch herself, she thought, as she drifted off to sleep. Bloody werewolves.

Gene lifted his forehead from Lily's door and stepped away. He couldn't really explain why his alpha powers interacted with her, but he had experienced her erotic dream just now. Adjusting himself, he went to take a shower and deal with his erection as best he could. Before he could go to bed, he had business to attend.

"Gene?" his mother said, stepping into the hall.

"Yes, mother."

"Leave her alone."

He turned around. "I am leaving her alone. I'm leaving her very much alone."

Reeva huffed. "As if." She turned away, shaking her head. He remembered that gesture from when he was a kid. *Oh, Gene, what have you done now?* That sort of thing.

He took a shower, took care of his arousal and ventured out into the living area to speak to his mother.

Gene shook his head when their eyes met. "This isn't easy, you know. There's something there, something powerful connecting us."

Reeva rested her butt on the back of the couch. "Forget it. When this is over and she goes back to her life, you'll get over her."

Gene nodded, superficially accepting her words. He thought of Lily and her alluring scent. Magic and spice and something else. Abbie said there was something strange about it. He didn't think she'd be easy to forget. And when they found the culprits and when his life was no longer in danger, he was going to have Lily De Vere in every way he could. If she agreed, of course. Although he was certain he could sway her, given she found it as hard to resist him as he did her. Never mind what his mother said.

In his office, he checked his emails and voicemail. Reports started to come in by phone, text and email as he sat at his desk. The Brisbane alpha, Troy Menzies, reported five enclaves around Brisbane and a large one on the Gold Coast. Reuben Dingo from Darwin said there was one up in the distant north. By the time all the reports had come in, Gene knew there were at least one hundred and fifty enclaves all around the major cities of Australia. That had to be just some of them because, surely, they all wouldn't be just in the cities. He sent some emails to the rural packs and told them to investigate on the down low. Where had all these bloodthirsty bastards come from? How did they accumulate without him or other werewolves knowing? He wasn't averse to blood himself. He did like his steak rare after all, but those nasty, walking corpses creeped him out. There was too much bad blood there. Too much history of abuse. Were blood was potent and vamps could get pretty intense when they had too much of it. Like drug addicts, they wanted more and more. Hundreds of years ago some vampire enclaves went too far, draining weres and using them as slave labour or sex slaves. Once free of the vampire yoke, weres kept their distance. If socially necessary, each tolerated the other and that was it.

It was very late when he was done, and he found his mother still in the lounge room, sitting on the lounge with her feet up. He kissed her on the cheek, his former annoyance dispersed. "Good night, Mother. See you in the morning." He slouched out of the room to hit the sack.

In his bedroom, he was tugging on a T-shirt when there was a knock at the door. "Yes," he said.

Rolf entered.

"Come in," he said with a grin. "Can't sleep, bro?"

Dressed in boxers, Rolf took a seat on the easy chair, shifting some of Gene's clothing to the arm so he could sit without crushing them. Once settled, he looked Gene full in the eye. "I confess I'm keyed up this evening. Abbie and I tried to clear our heads, but even fucking our brains out isn't helping. She, at least, has gone to sleep."

Gene sat on the bed and crossed his legs. "Rub it in, why don't you?" All this talk of fucking brought a certain white-haired witch to mind. "So, anything bothering you in particular?"

"Two things. I've heard from Dane. He doesn't know for sure, but he suspects the European and English vampires have recently migrated to Australia."

"Why, for heavens' sake? I thought it was a penance to be sent here."

Rolf nodded. "That is what I thought was the current and past thinking, yes. It is also a good place to hide."

"Why didn't we notice?" Gene asked.

"Apparently, they have done it slowly and in small batches over time, to avoid being noticed."

Gene was not impressed. "We've noticed now. And any advice or solutions?"

"He's going to call a meeting with the leaders of the vampire nation, such as they are. We don't truly understand how they govern themselves. A few liaise with the Collegium. He hopes to do that by tomorrow, next day at the latest, if he can organise it. Then he'll let us know."

"And his opinion?"

"Given the upheaval in the Collegium and the ruling triumvirate, he thinks it's a power play, possibly a schism. With Australia set to break away from the rest and go their own way."

"And taking all other paranormals here with them?"

Rolf lifted a shoulder. "Probably. He can't rule out that they are behind the business with murdering Dane's father and yours, along with the other deaths and curses."

"What a bloody mess. They fuck it all up and we get caught in the wash."

"You think Dane's right?"

Gene rubbed his short-cropped hair. "I can see the logic in his analysis. That doesn't mean I like it. This could get ugly. My parents came to Australia because it was a paradise. Open spaces, no war, plenty of opportunity and freedom. Now all of this is at risk."

"I can't see werewolves and witches going along with it, though. Either siding with the vamps or cutting off ties with the Collegium."

"Hence the spectre of war. A war I'm not ready for and definitely don't want. The only way I see to stop an escalation is to find proof. We need to link the vamps to the attacks. That might head them off at the pass. I'll speak to Elvira tomorrow. She might have more information on the witch selling the spells. I'll let her know about the vampire build-up and the issues with the Collegium as well."

"And what about the vampires that are already here? Flaunting their existence, draining the human population while pretending to offer eternal life?"

Gene rubbed his chin with a thumb and forefinger. "Mmm. The only way I see to fix that is to make them really want to go back to where they came from."

"Difficult, particularly if we can't find proof they have ulterior motives."

Gene nodded slowly as he considered what might be in store for them, for Australia. This paradise could be ruined way too easily. Besides his own interests, he hated the thought for anyone else. What they had wasn't perfect by a long shot, but being governed by vampires? No way he'd let that happen. He'd die before they got in cooee of that happening.

Rolf stood up and stretched his arms out to the side, muscles bunching. "I might call it a night."

"Wait. You said there were two things. What is the other?"

Rolf sat back down and met Gene's gaze. "It's the witch, Lily."

"What about her?" Gene was suddenly tense.

"She is not what she seems. Abbie's concerned."

Gene drew back and blinked rapidly as he tried to process what Rolf had said. Abbie had a great nose, could smell magic. "What does that even mean?"

Rolf shrugged. "It's nothing personal. I like her. But Abbie can't work her out. Something about Lily's scent has got her back up, got her mind in a twirl. Reeva says she was a foundling, brought up by the coven."

Gene sighed and let himself relax. Lily might be a puzzle, but she wasn't a threat. "Yes, I know that much. They brought her up, as she has magic. Apparently, they don't know who her parents are, where she came from, or whether she is really a witch. From what I know of Lily, she's an outsider and when slighted—like Reeva did by banning her from my bed—she takes it personally. Does Abbie know something more?"

Rolf lifted a shoulder and frowned. "Not exactly. It's something about her scent. Abbie can't pin it down. You know she was once a journalist. She wants to look into Lily's story, find out more. If that's all right with you?"

"With me? Shouldn't you be asking Lily? It's her life."

Rolf nodded as he walked to the door. "As long as you are okay with it, I'll run it past Lily." He paused, holding the door open. "What if it's not good news?"

Gene shrugged. "I don't understand. What do you suspect? She looks human, has witch powers. How much worse can it get? Unless you think she's a vampire witch! Because that would be quite a nasty combination. But from what I know of her, she has a good heart, cares about people, helps them even if they don't know about it. The money she's earning from me and Reeva she's giving to victims of loan sharks. She's not doing it for herself. And the coven give her a good report. No evil tendencies ever. Elvira keeps an eye on her out of love, I expect. Elvira isn't a bad sort."

"I can't say," Rolf said with a shrug. "Just that something doesn't add up, and that could cause ripples, have ramifications, for you and her."

"Me?"

"Yes, you."

"I have nothing to do with it." Gene threw out his hands to the side, all innocent-like.

"Really?" Rolf grinned. "I can tell you are hot for her. Maybe even something deeper."

Gene laughed it off. "I'm hot for any woman I see, particularly if she's beautiful and willing. Besides, Mother has warned me off. No touchie."

Rolf frowned. "Really? That's strange. I wonder if she knows something. I'll ask. See you in the morning."

It took a long time for Gene to get to sleep. Only this time, it wasn't arousal that kept him awake; he'd dealt with that in the shower. No, it was conspiracies and lies and convoluted paths that led him everywhere except to the truth.

Lily was ready and waiting for him when he exited his room in the morning. Reeva held out a sandwich for him and a coffee mug. Lily had the same in her hands. "Thanks, Ma!"

Reeva pouted. "Don't call me Ma like that. You're not too big for me to box your ears."

Gene burst out laughing and hugged her. "Reeva, you made my day."

Still chortling, he got into the car. Lily gave him the side eye until he explained. "I don't mind strong women. The thought of Reeva wrestling me is hilarious. We haven't rumbled since I was a teen. She's a ferocious wolf, you know. I'm just big and muscly. Apparently, only a mother would love me in wolf form."

Lily bit her lip. "I haven't had the pleasure."

"Believe me. Me in wolf form out of the moon cycle would be pretty intense indeed. I'm mean when I'm pissed."

Lily laughed. "Well, I'll make sure I don't make you mad then."

Gene sobered. He had felt so relaxed with Lily just then that he'd talked about werewolf things in a way he wouldn't normally do. He'd ask her to forget it, but that would just bring it into focus—the difference between them. She a witch with no experience of werewolf ways, what the change was like, and how he had to adapt his life to fit into the human world. Some wolves mated with humans, but it was hard work on both sides. She was more than human. Wait, what? *Stop even thinking that*, he told himself. He bit into his sandwich and kept one hand on the wheel. Lily took small bites of hers with sips of coffee in between. The sun came up on a grey, watery day. Buildings and sky blended in the wan light. Traffic lights glowed brighter than normal, no longer washed out by bright sunlight. He liked this time of day. There was less traffic and usually he could think through a few things, even make a few calls.

When they arrived at his office, he had a big meeting first up. Lily took herself off to survey the building or whatever she did when he was occupied. This meeting was with his engineers and architects for a new development up near Newcastle. He had just received feedback on their planning proposal. With good roads and train connections, Newcastle was opening up to the Sydney market, which meant profits could be made. Although changes suggested by the council needed to be discussed, costed and also alternatives considered, they needed to decide if they would set the project back and delays cost money. However, the bottom line was still looking good.

It was two in the afternoon before the meeting wrapped. All that haggling and arguing drained him. He was hungry as well and thought he might step out for lunch. "Where's Lily?" he asked his receptionist, Gail.

"I haven't seen her for a while." She gave a little shrug. "I'm sorry I didn't take much notice."

Gene dug out his phone and called Lily's number. There was no answer. It was about that time that he had a very bad feeling.

"Gail, can you check the surveillance cameras from here?" he asked.

She shook her head. "Downstairs security can bring up the images if you like. Why, what's wrong?"

"Lily is missing."

"But ... how do you know?"

He was already on the phone and heading to the lift. "Feeling," he said as the door closed.

Security had the footage ready to roll for him by the time he arrived. Gene leaned over as they called up the images, his hand on the back of the chair. They checked cameras covering the front, the rear, the car park and the corridors. Nothing. "What about the loading dock?"

The security guard was about to argue, and then shrugged. Keying in the camera, he started the recording. Lily was in the footage, appearing to be looking for something. She crouched down, peered into dark corners, and then stepped slowly around. The shutter doors opened. She jerked around and stepped back as an arm went around her throat. A man had appeared from the dark corner and reached out to grab her. Before she could do anything, he injected her in the neck, and she went limp. Gene's breath hitched and his heart beat hard. Did they kill her? He heard a cracking sound and realised his hand had broken the chair he was leaning on.

A nondescript white van backed in. Two men dressed in black ran up to Lily and the three of them carried her and swung her into the back. They jumped in the van and sped away. The whole thing took less than three minutes.

One guard, a woman, reached for the phone. "I'll call the police."

Gene straightened. "Do it. See if you can identify the van. I didn't see a registration number. I'm going down there."

"But, sir, you can't do anything?"

Gene rolled his shoulders. "Oh yes, I can."

It was a bit of a trek to the loading dock. He stalked it, inhaling deeply, searching for scents. He dug out his phone and called Rolf. "She's been kidnapped. I'm going after her."

Rolf said, "What, Lily? Are you sure?"

"All on the security feed. I have a trail and I need to pursue it while it's fresh."

"Okay. What do you want me to do?"

"Come after me with backup and a set of clothes. I've no time to plan or carry my gear in my mouth."

"Will do. I'll let Reeva know. Good luck, bro."

Gene backtracked out of the view of the cameras. He found a changing room and shucked his gear. He summoned his wolf, and by God, it was angry. His growl was loud in his ears. It was about a week to full moon, too, so he had to hold the wolf in check. It was eager for freedom. A dash out of the open door and he was hot on Lily's trail. She had an unusual scent, and in this case it helped a lot.

CHAPTER 11

A strange vibration in one of her wards had drawn Lily to the loading dock. So strange was it, that she couldn't tell what had caused it, so she'd had to check it out in person, as there was nothing in the security feed. Outside on the dock, the sun peered through clouds that were dispersing in the light breeze. *A few showers left in those clouds*, she thought, as she bent to check one of the wards. Nothing wrong with it. Peeved, she went to inspect the other one. That one looked like someone had tampered with it, though not successfully. That must have been the sensation she had detected earlier.

It didn't look like it had been a witch or other magical being that had been trying to break the ward as she would've been able to tell. No, the person who interfered with the ward carried a talisman or magical ward of their own that had clashed with it. Whether it was intended, she didn't know. Lost in thought, she studied the space where her ward sat.

A motor groaned. An alarm beeped as the shutter door started to roll up. She backed up to get out of the way of whatever was coming through. It was then she detected a movement, too late. An arm encircled her neck, pressing hard on her throat. Intentional, she thought. In a split second, a needle stabbed into her neck.

A moment of fear. *Too late to fight!* Her heart thumped, throat burning for air. Her legs folded and wham! The void took her.

Sometime later she awoke facedown on a smelly old mattress in a dark room. *I'm not dead!* Her head thumped and her vision was blurred. Disoriented, she struggled onto all fours and then vomited up her breakfast. Whatever that drug had been, it was playing havoc with her body. What the fuck had they stuck into her? *Why? Fucking why?* After emptying the contents of her stomach on the rubbish-strewn floor, she flopped back down onto the putrid mattress. Her innards were empty and regretted the loss of the breakfast sandwich.

She lay there trying to sort out her brain and then tackle her situation. "Why the fuck did they grab me?" she asked in the darkness. She closed her eyes, calmed her mind. To trap Gene, of course. *Nah! He's too smart for that. And why would he care if someone snatched me? I'm just the hired help. No, he's going to come after me. It's a slight against his honour, his pride. He'll come just to prove the point that no one touches what is his. And he wants to know what is going on and who is behind all of this. Worst of all, he's a bloody hothead. Fuck, fuck, fuckity fuck!*

Holding her head, she groaned aloud. She was meant to be protecting him, not becoming bait so they could capture him. The thought that Reeva might step in and keep him away flitted across her mind. Except Reeva wasn't at the office and Gene wouldn't tell her, because he wanted to enforce boundaries. *Dammit! Bloody alphas and den mothers! Who needs these politics anyway?*

At least in the coven, she was on the periphery. Left to her own devices most of the time and able to join in when she wanted. That suited her. The werewolves were way too involved with each other in comparison.

Another wave of nausea hit, and she puked thin bile onto the floor. Her stomach contents really didn't make the stink in the room any better. With a sigh, she lay back, hoping her brain would start working properly, but it kept returning to Gene and what he might do. Hopefully, he wouldn't notice her absence. Then, if he looked for her, he might think she'd absconded for the day. At least he'd be safe if that was the case. She moaned. *Goddess! What if this wasn't about luring him here, but leaving him exposed and open to attack?* Without her there to protect him, he'd be vulnerable. Removing her cleared a path to him. Her head thumped, and she winced. Why did even thinking hurt, and every scenario that came to mind was more dire than the previous one?

Covering her eyes, she breathed deep, waiting for the pain to recede. There were cameras in the dock, but it had all happened so fast, and that part of the building was not the normal pedestrian access. No one was going to notice. Would they even think of looking there in the first place?

The drug had done something to her, set her back. She had recovered some of her magic, but now it had been punched back down where even she couldn't find it. There wasn't enough to chant a spell to clear her body of the drug. From the time she had transported Gene to his mother's apartment after the attack, her magic had not fully restored. Now it was as if it was non-existent. *Damn and blast.*

Groggily, she tried to get to her feet. The room spun and she faltered, dropping to her knees and resting her head against the wall. After a few breaths, she felt ready and pushed to her feet again, took a few steps and then went to her knees again and crawled over instead. It was hard to see in the dimness. Her fingers detected the edges of the door and found the handle. Not surprisingly it was locked. Further investigation revealed it had a high-grade doorhandle with a lock and a bolt mechanism. She groaned as another wave of dizziness hit, sprawling her on her back, head thumping with the exertion.

The building was quiet, so those who had taken her either weren't close by or were asleep. She couldn't tell what time of day it was, and she wasn't good with scents, not in the way werewolves were. As they had drugged her at the outset, she had no idea who had taken her, how long she had been out or where she was now.

If Gene was smart, he'd wash his hands of her and get a new bodyguard. Although she had an inkling that Gene wasn't that smart or completely uninterested in her. With cynicism, she surmised she was an unconquered mountain he was desperate to climb. She grimaced at the idea. What a stupid metaphor. He might forget about that aspect, as he had plenty of beautiful women to choose from. That was a better idea. That thought soothed her. Then her kidnappers would have to let her go after a few days, when he was unconcerned about what had happened to her. That, strangely, was a comforting thought. *Gene, please go bed another woman and forget I exist.*

As the dizziness calmed, a sense of optimism made her try to touch her magic again. Nothing. What kind of drug had they slammed into her? It should be banned. She needed to tell Elvira …

The quiet, the toll on her body and her stamina, had her eyes closing. She'd open them and then close them again, completely unable to measure how long she had her eyes shut. Sleep took her. This she knew because she had drooled and snorted as she woke. Disoriented, and with no idea of how long she'd been out, she knew the drug still affected her. Futilely, she tried to summon her magic. Nothing. She punched the mattress because she couldn't cast a spell, couldn't escape. That irked her more than anything. Helplessness was not something she was used to or planned for.

There was no water or food in the dark room with her. After another nap, the effect of the drug diminished, and she was restored enough to farther scout around her surroundings, hoping to learn something that would help her escape, or at least keep her alive. A horrible realisation hit. It wasn't a given that they'd let her go if Gene didn't come for her. That was wishful thinking. If they wanted to erase any link to them, they'd kill her. That upped the stakes. She had to fight for her life. An hour or so passed while her strength improved, and she felt marginally better. However, her head ached something fierce.

A key in the lock sent her heart ticking. Before she could stand, light arrowed in, temporarily blinding her. She scrambled backwards on the mattress, her hands shielding her eyes.

"Here is water and food," said the voice, a blurred figure of a man. She tried to inhale to get the scent of him, but the fetid, rotting mattress overwhelmed her senses.

The door shut, and the lock engaged before she had even climbed halfway to her feet. Necessity drove her to inspect the tray. She needed to eat to keep up her strength. Lifting the tin picnic mug, she sniffed. The water smelled untainted, so she drank it all down. Feeling around on the tray, her fingers made contact with a sandwich. The bread was hard and curled at the edges. She lifted it, inhaling the aroma of cheese. She stuck her finger between the bread and cheese, and it appeared it was only a slice, nothing fancy like butter or pickles. Continued feelings of nausea meant she could only nibble the bread. Too late did she realise they might have drugged the water. She couldn't taste anything, but the thought undermined her confidence. To survive, she had to recover quickly and ingesting more drugs would thwart that.

Time passed and her strength came back slowly. No drugs in her food or water, then. Thank Goddess for small mercies. She needed more time. Just because they hadn't drugged one meal, didn't mean they wouldn't drug or poison the next one. What if they came back to drug her again before she was strong enough to fight them? Her chances of escape or survival diminished. An exploration of the room revealed no weaknesses to exploit. The tips of her fingers detected exposed brick walls broken by panelling, which hid the masonry behind. No windows or panels hiding crawl spaces or fake walls. It smelt of mould and old socks. It was a locked door and whatever waited beyond it. There was no noise, no voices or echoes of footsteps. Either they had left, or the building was well-insulated with a reinforced floor. It was dead quiet.

Her phone was gone and so was her watch. She had no idea how long she had been gone and no idea if it was night or day. She thumped the wall in frustration. What a waste of time! She had been so focused on protecting Gene that she completely missed that she could be a target and used as bait. It was a hard realisation that she was vulnerable.

Suddenly, the air changed. Her senses went on alert. On the floor above, a loud growl and a thump reverberated. No screams or anything. She waited, listening so hard she forgot to breathe. The crash of broken glass bled into the room. There was definitely something going on up there. She dared not hope that it was a rescue. Lily crawled back over to the door and studied the lock. If only she could wield a small amount of magic, she could get out. In here she was a sitting duck.

A scream gave her a jolt, and another. Now she could hear footsteps running, boots hammering across the floors. A gurgled, garbled cry sounded too close.

Panting, she closed her eyes and concentrated, a little force here and a push there. A scream split the air on the other side of the door. It was human, and she jumped back, wondering what the fuck was going on. Who was killing who? Was there another faction? Was it Gene?

A low, repetitive thumping followed, and she didn't like the images it made in her mind. She was focused on the lock again when something smacked against the door she was trying to open. It sounded like the impact of a body.

Frowning, she tried again to concentrate on the lock. Did the door open out or in? Would a body block her exit, or would she just have to climb over it? It looked like it opened inwards so she would need to step back and then possibly scramble over a body or two.

Get your emotional shield on, woman. She'd seen bodies when she worked as a cop and thus knew how to prepare. Adrenaline-filled situations like this were risky. Heightened senses and emotion could cause someone to make a wrong decision.

Bending to focus on the lock, she pulled a tiny thread of her meagre magic and focused it until she was panting with the effort. The lock clicked, and the bolt slid. With a tug, it swung open, and she stepped back. A large furry shape leaped into the air, sailing above her head. Instinctively, she ducked and fell back as her cry of surprise echoed off the walls. In a smooth move, she pivoted and climbed to her feet as she studied the creature. A werewolf. Her heaving chest forced the air in and out of her lungs. While she knew Gene, Rolf, Abbie and Reeva were werewolves, she'd never seen them in wolf form. As a police officer and a private investigator, she hadn't come across any in wolf form either. Even though her heart raced, she knew she was safe with this wolf.

It was an enormous wolf. Totally fascinated, she studied it, and it kept its eyes on her, lips pulled back over teeth.

It had blue eyes, she realised. Familiar blue eyes. "Gene?"

A growl was her answer. So surprised was she that immediately she went into panic mode. "What are you thinking? Get out!"

She waved her arms, an instinctive move to shoo the creature away. The growl grew louder, a short yip of defiance.

"No, no, no! You can't be here. Get out! It's a trap."

The wolf just tilted its head as if she was crazy.

Shaking her head, she crawled out of the room and up the stairs outside it, hoping Gene followed. It wasn't very dignified, but the drugs had left her woozy. She made it to the top of the stairs into a kitchen and was considering how the bench might allow her to climb to her feet, when five black-clothed figures came rushing through a doorway across from her. One had a gun, another a machete. "Fuck!"

"Kill her," the lead one said, making eye contact. His eyes were weird and dead-looking and the whites were the colour of red wine.

Not fully recovered, Lily hesitated, in a quandary about what to do next. The thought of backtracking to the basement prison seemed like a good idea. The click of claws on the stairs alerted her to Gene approaching. She had momentarily forgotten about him in her surprise.

Both of the armed men in black leaped at her. She rolled into a ball as the big wolf sailed over her head and barrelled into the man who had ordered her death. Her two attackers split apart to avoid the beast. Gene's wolf jaws connected to the leader's throat. There was a short struggle. Dark blood spouted, and the man gurgled as he fell to his knees.

The two who had broken away raised their weapons. Gene leaped on one. Lily sat up, studying the attackers. One had a gun, and she knew, just knew, it had silver in it. Surging to her feet, she stepped forward, captured his wrist and twisted. The gun was now pointing at her assailant. Sweat dribbled down her spine. She was still weak, and her magic came with difficulty. Holding her compulsion steady, she used her grip and magic to force the nozzle of the weapon to his gut. He struggled and tried to let the gun go. "Pull the trigger, you bastard."

The gun went off, and the man slumped. She wasn't normally murderous. However, it was her job to protect Gene, and this lot had already tried to kill him. There was a step behind her, but she turned too late. A woman she hadn't noticed before reached for her with red-taloned fingers, aiming for her eyes. Blocking with both her forearms, she thwarted the woman's aim. Lily grabbed the other woman's extended arms, dropped and performed a controlled backward roll, bracing the woman's hips with her feet to flip her over. The woman flew through the air, hitting her head on a cupboard and smacking into the legs of one of the remaining attackers, bringing him down. The woman was out cold, but the man in dark clothes disentangled his feet and picked up the machete he'd dropped. He was coming for her. The other attacker was throwing kitchen equipment at Gene's head.

Gene growled and pawed the ground, the utensils only irritating him. The smell of blood filled the air. There were two attackers left. Gene pounced and the kitchen utensil guy screamed as he fell under the heavy load of fur and muscle. His blood-filled cry gave Lily the shivers.

The machete-wielding guy hesitated, eyes wide as he gazed upon the remains of his fallen comrades. Gene growled low and he tensed to leap. Lily readied a spell to snatch the bladed weapon. The guy dropped the machete and ran out the door.

Gene, poised to leap, stopped when Lily cried out. "No!"

Shaky, she tried not to sway or fall over. The drugs had lasting after-effects. A car screeched to a halt outside. Booted feet tramped up the stairs and the front door shook in its frame as they pounded and rammed it. Another howl filled the air as a werewolf just as big and beautiful as Gene burst through one of the windows at the front of the house. Glass shards fanned out, but none managed to cut the beast. The wolf with yellow eyes yelped at Gene. Gene's wolf shook its body. In response, the new arrival howled low and disappointed. It had to be Rolf. There was nobody left to fight.

Lily, near to collapse, held it together as the wolf who had come to her rescue changed form. It looked painful as fur peeled away and muscles and skin reformed. The crack of bones and the cry of pain as the jaw reabsorbed and the familiar face of Gene reassembled. When the change was complete, he stood before her, very impressively naked, built superbly everywhere, and she didn't mind the view at all. His concerned expression did something to her.

She clenched her jaw and balled her fists. *I was meant to protect him.* She wanted to explain, to upbraid him for putting himself in danger. Instead, the room spun, her vision grew dark, and her stomach roiled. As she fainted dead away, Gene took her into his arms. "I've got you," he said quietly into her ear.

Lily came to in the back of a van. Two large guys were in the front seat. She and Gene were alone in the back seat. Rolf wasn't there. Gene was no longer naked. *Damn, why did I have to be weak at that crucial moment?* He was very impressive underneath his clothes and that wolf skin. Her head rested on Gene's shoulder and her butt rested on his lap, with her legs draping to one side. Heat radiated from his body, and she snuggled into it like a cat. It was weird to be held that way and, also, disconcerting to realise how small she was compared to him.

"You should put me down," she said, realising it looked bad to be cradled like a baby, even if she liked it.

"We'll be at the new safe house soon," Gene said in a soothing voice.

She lifted her head to meet his gaze. "New safe house?"

"It's closer. New and hopefully well shielded. You need time to recover. I need time to plan. I can work remotely and keep the business running."

Lily swallowed, feeling guilty but also weak, which was something that she wasn't used to and didn't like. She also didn't like being this close to Gene because the closeness was distracting. He smelled nice, a spicy scent that drew her in. "I'll be all right." She met his blue gaze and saw only compassion in his. That wasn't what she was expecting. Anger, annoyance, even boredom, maybe. But compassion?

He squeezed her shoulders gently, reassuringly. "Nevertheless, Elvira is sending someone to check you over. Apparently, a regular doctor with witch connections has moved to Sydney. A Dr Wentz."

"Oh!" she laid her head against his chest and closed her eyes. "Right."

His voice rumbled under her ear, reverberating in his chest. "Rolf and Abbie will meet us there. They have to make sure they aren't followed. They may be furry when they arrive." She lifted her head and met his gaze. "You okay with that?"

"Sure." Her cheeks grew pink. He was going to think she was crazy. "I'm fine with furballs." She was trying to be nonchalant and failed.

A crease grew between his brows and his mouth formed an 'oh'. "You are? Not seen too many wolves up close, I imagine."

Her face snuggled in to his chest. He was comfortable to lie against. "No, not at all. Not up close, at least. The theory is there, and I saw worse beasts when I was a cop." She gasped and lifted her head to meet his gaze. "I didn't mean that how it sounded. Honest."

Gene's eyes narrowed. "We are not for everybody."

She touched his cheek, felt the rough bristles of his beard's growth. "I wasn't afraid of you or repulsed, if that's what you think. You and Rolf are very impressive in wolf form. I'm a paranormal. I get it."

His gaze was intent. "Do you?" He shook his head. "I find that hard to believe. Are you going to request I find another bodyguard?"

Shame flooded in. "Only because I didn't do my job properly. Stupidly, I got myself abducted and drew you into danger. That wasn't well done of me. I'll understand if you want to replace me."

Gene threw his head back and laughed. "Replace you? No, not yet."

They turned a corner, and she clung to Gene to keep her place on his lap. The van dropped onto a ramp, down into a car park and then swerved into a parking spot with a screech of tyres on concrete. The men in front climbed out and slid open the side door of the van. "We're here," the larger one said.

Lily rolled her eyes. That was stating the obvious, but she guessed they were more brawn than brain. "I own this apartment building," Gene explained as he placed her on the ground. "I have were families living here and two apartments joined up that are mine. The apartments around that are empty, so we have a buffer."

"Won't Reeva be expecting us?"

Gene put an arm around her shoulders and guided her as they followed behind his two men. She liked the feel of him close to her, and that also weirded her out. Those drugs must have been powerful if they made her drop her defences so low. She'd gone from wary to accepting.

"Reeva knows, and she's concerned for you. She didn't expect them to attack you."

"Me neither," she replied. "A serious oversight on my part. Again, I'm sorry."

He scoffed. "I should have guessed myself. I won't have you taking the blame for a lack of foresight. We were all caught off guard."

They travelled in the lift, heading to the fifth floor, while Lily digested Gene's words. Either he was trying to soothe her wounded feelings for some obscure reason, or he was telling the truth, and no one had foreseen this abduction. What had they been doing to cause the opposition to act this way? They had put Abbie and Rolf on the case, that's what. Had their snooping caught the wrong attention? That pointed strongly to vampires, but that could be a frame up job. It was hard to think. Lily wiped a hand across her eyes.

The lift opened on the fifth floor. Apparently, that was the top floor. High enough not to be an easy target and not too high that a wolf couldn't leap to safety. "I need to scan for spells."

Gene shook his head. "Not until you have medical clearance and a shower. You stink."

Her face grew hot with embarrassment. "But you've been holding me close." She wished he hadn't held her or treated her so tenderly.

Gene sniffed his clothes. "I stink now as well. I'll shower and change my clothes." He cocked his head and grinned. "I was worried for you, so I didn't notice the stink until now."

Lily sank down into herself, instinctively trying to make herself smaller. "But I smelled bad."

Lily remembered the fetid mattress she'd been tossed unconscious on.

"It's fine. It will wash off in no time." Gene kept his hand on her elbow as he guided her through a large bedroom to a bathroom. "Rolf and Abbie are bringing some clothes and personal items for you from Reeva's." He ducked out of the room and came back with clothing and shoes. "In the meantime, use this robe and these slippers." He shrugged. "The slippers might be too big, and I guess so will the robe, but as much as I hate to say this, it is better than you being naked." He shot her a grin, and she blushed from head to toe. That look seemed like he had already undressed her with his imagination.

"Thank you," she said. "I'll manage from here."

He shut the door, but not completely. "Just in case you need help," he called from the other room. Lily hated feeling weak as a kitten and tried to ignore the fact that the door was ajar and that Gene could hear her every movement. He was right. In her current state, it made no sense to shut the door, lock it and then have her fall on her face or her butt. *Naked on my butt. Geez, stop!*

First things first, she needed to get clean, rest and then get her head together. Now was not the time to get distracted by Gene, the image of the naked Gene, the remembrance of being on Gene's lap, his warmth and the tender way he held her and talked to her. No, that was for another woman, one who wasn't a half-witch and off limits.

It was a struggle to get out of her clothes. Her trousers needed peeling off and to her embarrassment she saw that there were vomit splashes on her top. Her jacket was long gone. She tossed her trousers and top into the laundry basket, but wondered if they should just go in the bin. If she had magic to spare, she could've fixed them with a spell.

There were thick lavender-coloured towels rolled up and slotted into shelves on the wall. She pulled out a bath mat and then inspected the array of toiletries to take into the cubicle with her. Shampoo, conditioner and some body wash. She continued searching and then found what she really wanted: some body scrub. Her skin needed to be rubbed clean. The water was hot and plentiful. Afterwards, marginally improved, she was tired, and a bit dazed. She slid her arms into Gene's bathrobe and his slippers dwarfed her feet.

Feeling clean was a boon to her soul. She stood there, staring at the door, as she worked up the courage to face him. He saved her the trouble by pushing open the door and looking at her. "Good. You managed all right then?"

"Yes, thank you."

He led her over to the bed. "You can rest here. I've got to have a shower myself."

Lily looked to the bed and to him. "You're okay for me to sleep now?"

"I insist upon it. I'll leave the door open so I can check on you after I've had a shower."

Lily pulled back the covers. This tiredness that dragged against her bones and muscles was unnatural. "Okay, but I want to know how you found me. How did you even know I was gone?"

Lily snuggled into the bed but kept her gaze on Gene.

He lifted his shoulders and threw out his hands to the side. "I noticed. Okay? I looked, and I looked until I saw you in the security feed. Then I picked up your trail." He tapped his nose. "I had backup."

"But you shouldn't have come after me."

Gene's expression closed down, his eyebrows lowered. "They took you because of me. Of course, I wasn't going to let them keep you. What kind of man or wolf would I be if I allowed that?" He smacked his chest. "I am the alpha of the Sydney City pack."

Lily let out a sigh. There was little point in talking sense to him.

"Besides, I had backup. Rolf wasn't far behind me. Between us, we could sort just about anything."

Lily nuzzled the pillow and closed her eyes. She felt like shit. Hopefully, the rest would help. If not, then the doctor. A strange coincidence that they used drugs on Gene and then on her. She wondered if her contact on the force would know anything about that. A drug that targeted paranormals. One that wiped a witch's power. One that could fell a powerful werewolf. It was too scary to contemplate, but they needed to.

For the moment, feeling safe and clean, the sound of running water and Gene's humming in the shower soothed her off to sleep. A few hours later, by the growing darkness outside, a knock on the door woke her.

The door swung open, and a man stood there. He was blond, clean-shaven with regular features and a cleft in his chin. He had intelligent green eyes and a medium build and was about five-ten. He wore jeans and a plain pale blue T-shirt, and was carrying a black backpack. There was some ripple there against her senses. Not strong, but he had some magic in him. "Hi. I'm Dr Wentz."

"Hi," she replied, trying to lift herself higher up the pillow. He was casual looking for a doctor.

"Let me help you," he said and came over to ease her further up the bed and fluff her pillows.

Once she settled comfortably, he asked if he could check her over.

"Sure," she replied in a weak voice.

He lifted her wrist and took her pulse and then checked her eyes and her reflexes. Then he threw in a few questions about the drug and its effect on her. While listening, he frowned and nodded. "Without a blood test, I can't be sure what they gave you. It could be a mixture of street drugs and prescription."

"Okay. Can you do a blood draw?" she asked.

He rummaged around in his backpack. "Yes, I have the necessary equipment."

She held out her arm, and he dug the needle in. "Sorry for the pinch there."

He held the vial of blood between thumb and forefinger, up-ended it and then wrote her details on the label. "It will take a few days before I have the results. I suspect whatever they gave you would have killed a human, but with your paranormal physiology, you have come through. I can give you a shot of something. Not something you get from the chemist, just something I know works for witches. A bit of an energy boost."

"I'm part-witch."

His eyes lit up. "Me, too. My mother was human. You have a heavy aura, so I think even as a part-witch you are strong. What is the other part, may I ask?"

She shook her head. "I don't know what else I am. Not part-human, as far as the elders could tell."

His smile faded. "I'm sorry if that's a sensitive topic. I've only been down in Sydney for a few months and I'm still finding my way around coven politics."

Something about the doctor's name caused memories to surface. "You're the doctor who looked after Declan when he crashed his bike."

"Yes. A few years ago, now, but that was me. I was in Newcastle then."

"Yes, Grace and Elvira talked about you a lot at the time. They were quite excited by your move to Sydney."

"I see I'm a legend." His smile didn't quite reach his eyes.

She screwed up her face as she tried to drag the memory forward. "I recall Grace said you were married with kids."

His smile faded and his expression grew sad. "I was. My wife and kids went missing just over two years ago and I've been looking for them ever since."

Lily closed her eyes. "I'm so sorry to hear that." There was more to the story, she was sure, but being so tired, she couldn't really pursue it right now. She would file it away for another time, when she could actually offer some help.

"Ready for your shot?" he asked.

She nodded, and he rummaged around in his backpack. Items clicked together and then he drew out a vial and a syringe.

Again, Lily put out her arm and Dr Wentz slid in the injection. She could feel the contents of the needle speed through her body. It was like a warm wave of happiness. Her breathing deepened, her heart fluttered, and her mind cleared as if a window opened and sunshine rushed in.

"Oh my. That feels good." She turned her head to study him. "You could become very popular with that concoction." She sat back and revelled in the pleasurable sensation filling her up. "Wow!"

He packed away his things, wiping his hands on a sanitary wipe and then tossing it in the bin. "Give it an hour to work through your system. It will chase out the bad stuff and fill you with light."

Lily enjoyed the sensation as the warmth and light spread. "Thank you, doctor," she said, dreamily.

The doctor regarded her for a moment, a thoughtful expression causing creases on his forehead, then with a nod, he said, "Call me Lyle. I'm sure I'll be seeing you around. You're a private investigator, right?"

Her eyes narrowed. "Yes, ex police."

His expression relaxed. "You might be able to help me in the future."

"I'd be happy to," she replied, but felt as if she was intoxicated, which didn't happen often. She waved her hand a bit floppily. "Okay, Lyle, that's great. Thank Elvira for me. Much appreciated." She didn't think she was making much sense as the words spilled out of her.

He paused as he opened the door and looked back at her. "There's a werewolf guy here who wants to see you. Should I tell him to go away?"

Lily met his gaze. "If it's Gene Cohen, then let him come. Any other werewolves can bite me."

Lyle laughed. "I'll pass on the message."

CHAPTER 12

Lily jerked awake. She must have drifted off after the doctor left. The shot had been more hefty than expected. Someone was in the room with her. Her eyes snapped open and her heart pounded. Gene sat on an office chair by the desk in the corner of the room.

"Oh, thank God!" she said. "For a minute I thought ... well ... never mind." She patted the bed, inviting him to sit on the edge. If he thought that was odd, he didn't give her a sign. He moved to sit next to her and picked up her hand, studying her fingers one by one. After a minute or two, he lifted his head and met her gaze. He stroked her knuckles with a small, circular motion that was soothing but also distracting. This was a different side to him, one she had not experienced. Her own mood was also difficult to interpret. She was grateful he'd come for her, saved her, and also very glad he had not been hurt.

"The doctor gave me a good report," he said, not quite smiling with his mouth but it showed in his eyes. "He said to let you rest, and I did. I'm sorry if I woke you. I had only come in to check on you." His neck flushed. If he was just checking on her, why had he been sitting in a chair? "How are you feeling now?" He glanced at his watch. "It's been three hours since you flaked after the doctor left. You must be hungry by now."

Dazed and strangely mellow, she found it hard to focus on things—the kidnapping, the deaths and what she was feeling for Gene at that moment. "I'm not too hungry," she replied, and then her stomach rumbled, making her a liar.

He chuckled. "There's food if you want it." Gene appeared relaxed, but also intense, as he studied her face. His movements were constrained, as if he didn't want to disturb the air in the room.

She brushed her fingers against his hand. "Are you all right? Has something happened? You seem subdued ... or less angry, maybe."

His eyebrows drew together. "Nothing else has happened since your kidnap and rescue. A few hours' reprieve is not much to ask, is it?"

"I guess not." She nodded slowly and smiled. "How much time do we have until the next thing happens?"

His gaze narrowed further. "Hopefully longer than we expect. Are you feeling all right yourself? You seem a bit ... well ... out of focus."

She lowered her eyelids. "A bit strange, to be honest. I'm hoping it will pass. Soon."

"Right, then." He stood up. "I'm going to bring you something to eat. There's soup and there's a steak sandwich, if the boys haven't eaten them all by now."

"Oh, the sandwich. I lost the last one from breakfast."

He drew his head back, not understanding. She mimicked puking, and he nodded with understanding. "I'll be right back."

Lily wished he didn't have to leave the room but was too fudged in the head to call him back. She could eat later. For some obscure reason, she wanted him there with her, where she could see him ... where she could protect him. She laughed way too over the top. *Protect him how? Mash the intruders with your pillow?*

In less than five minutes, he returned with a tray. He narrowed his eyes. "Were you laughing just now?"

Avoiding eye contact, she screwed up her face as she tried to think clearly. "Yes, I was. That's odd, isn't it?" She lifted her head to meet his gaze.

"It is. Another call to Dr Wentz, I think." He frowned and placed the tray over her legs. "I wasn't sure what you would drink, so there's water, milk and a soft drink."

The aroma of the sandwich immediately snagged her attention. "That smells so good." She picked up a half of the sandwich, which had been sliced diagonally. Besides the hot steak, which was so soft and medium rare, there was lettuce, tomato, avocado and some tasty sauce. Before she knew it, the sandwich was gone, and then she drank the milk, chasing it with the water. She was so absorbed in eating, she had forgotten Gene was still standing there. She flicked her gaze his way and blushed. She had smashed the food as if there was no tomorrow, like she had no inhibitions.

His wide-eyed expression was half surprise and half admiration. "You'll get indigestion eating that fast," Gene said with a hint of a smile. "You were hungrier than you thought."

She covered her mouth and belched. "Sorry. Yes. Definitely hungrier than I thought."

He put the soft drink on the side table and then took the tray from the room. She took a sip of the soft drink, hoping to rinse her mouth. Gene came back again. "How do you feel now? Nauseated?"

She grinned. "I feel good, but still a bit tired. You look tired. You should sleep, too."

His grin stayed in place. "I'm quite refreshed. We wolves can go for a few days without sleep."

"Are you sure?" She patted the bed. "Want to join me?"

The tanned skin on Gene's face paled, his expression stilled. "Are you inviting me to sleep with you?"

Lily considered this. "No, I'm letting you know if you need a nap, there's room in here."

"Thank you for the invitation. Are you sure you're feeling all right? I think I need to call the doctor."

"Fine." She yawned hugely, smiled at him before closing her eyes and drifting off to sleep.

He must have left the room, because she heard the door click. A while later she woke again, and he was still sitting there. "What are you doing?"

He blinked. "I'm processing this new mood of yours. I'm afraid my head is spinning. The doctor said that the shot he gave you should not have affected you this way."

"What way?"

A V-shaped crease grew between his eyebrows. "You do know inviting me to nap with you is the same as inviting me to fuck?"

"No, it isn't." She sat up and poked him in the chest with a finger. "Your mother said we can't fuck, so there." Lily lay back down. His voice was doing things to her, and it was fascinating. Her skin tingled and her mind mellowed as if she was a cat ready to purr. Her sex throbbed and her mouth yearned to taste his.

Gene chuckled. "You think my mother's prohibition on sex with 'the help' would stop me if I really wanted you?"

"Well, if that's all I am to you, 'the help', then I rescind my invitation, and you can bugger off and find someone else to annoy."

"I'm annoying you? But you asked me to sit on the bed."

"You called me 'the help'!" Her voice rose with this delivery and she blinked. *Did I just yell at Gene?*

Under the covers, she pulled her arms out of the robe and tossed it out of the bed. His eyebrow arched and there was a trace of a smile. Then he grew serious, picked up her hand and studied it while he rubbed his thumb in small circles across her palm. "That was wrong of me. You're a colleague who's being paid by my mother and by me."

There was a touch of irony in his voice that she found funny. She repressed a smile. "Damn straight."

Her thinking was a bit disordered. Was she punch-drunk? She hoped Lyle hadn't dosed her with a love potion. Nah! The doc seemed wary of Gene and the other werewolves, so she didn't think he'd leave her to their mercy. But what about side effects? Was her kind of paranormal reacting differently to other witches? "What did Dr Wentz say?"

"He said that as your other half is unknown, but not human either, then you might need to take it easy until the drug he gave you flushes out of your system."

Lily blinked. "How long will that be?" She had no time to laze about waiting for his potion to get out of her system. But Gene just looked delectable right now and his voice was doing things to her. If he talked dirty, would she come? She shook her head. That's just crazy thinking.

"Maybe twenty-four hours ..."

She frowned, tried to feel concerned, only that didn't stick around. "Oh, well," she shrugged. "I just wanted a platonic snuggle up. Your skin is so warm."

Gene frowned, rubbed his chin and then shook his head. "You want me to snuggle with you while you nap?" he asked, as if clarifying a clause in a legal document. "Nothing else?"

Lily considered this. "Yes, that sounds right to me. Snuggless fuck ... I mean fuckless snuggle."

Gene laughed out loud then. "You're aware that you're naked under the bedcovers?"

Lily glanced down and then wiggled against the sheets. "Oh, I am too." She almost laughed. Definitely weird behaviour.

"I've got a few things to do and maybe you need time to consider things." He looked her up and down. "We need to meet with the others and discuss the situation, when you can think straight. I'll going to tell them to hold off, given your current state."

Gene left the room and Lily shifted over to give him some room, in case he joined her after all. She had thought he'd jump at the chance to get close to her. Had she misjudged him? Maybe it was the 'no fuck' condition. They could have fun, though. Gene didn't return straight away, so she drifted off to sleep.

<hr />

GENE RESTED HIS BACK AGAINST THE DOOR TO LILY'S ROOM, TILTING his head back to stare at the ceiling. That had been the hardest thing to do. Walk away from that oh so very tempting invitation. He couldn't get the sight of her bare shoulders out of his mind. Along with the way her eyes sparkled and the way she licked her lips, it turned him on. Just the thought of holding her close, skin-on-skin, sent his mind reeling. It was a war of desire against what was right. Despite wanting to fuck her senseless, he couldn't. She wasn't herself. When she was in her right mind, they could fuck if that's what she wanted. Doing it now would make him an asshole and a sexual predator, and he was neither of those things.

A knock at the front door and Rolf's scent in the air told him he had visitors. He could have hugged Rolf for giving him a valid excuse not to go snuggle with Lily, but that didn't mean he didn't think about her lying there naked and needy.

"We brought her things. How is she?" Abbie asked. "Her phone and wallet were recovered from the house where they held her."

They walked into the lounge room and relaxed onto the couches. "Not quite herself. The doctor dosed her with something, and it's had some interesting side effects."

Abbie nodded, lowering her eyelids. "Oh, that explains it. You smell like you're ... well ... on heat ... but as you're a male, you can't be."

"Abbie," Rolf chided. "He's just horny as all hell. Nothing on heat about it. Besides, it is his usual state when there is an attractive and unattached woman around."

Abbie's lips twitched as she met Gene's gaze. "Interesting. You want her, even though she's a bit off."

"Watch it, Abbie. There's nothing 'off' about Lily. Over and over, she's proved herself. Just being a half-witch is normal enough. Maybe it's the other half that has your sense of smell in a twitch. She could be half pixie. She looks it, with that colouring. Or elfkind, even, but without the ears or faery wings. Who knows? Just don't judge her. You don't know her like I do."

Abbie's eyes widened, and she flopped back into her chair. "My, you have it bad."

Gene growled low in his throat. Before he could respond, Rolf intervened.

"She's just needling you. Her nose distracts her sometimes and we like Lily even if she's a puzzle."

Abigail smiled and tilted her head. "Yeah, sorry. No offense intended. I'd like to see you bedded and wedded."

Gene's hackles rose. He was not about to get shackled with a mate and kids. His life was just fine, even if his mother nagged him for grandkids. Letting out his breath slowly, his anger bled off, along with his anxiety for Lily and all that was going on.

"What else can you tell me?"

"That lawyer, Ruiz, is dead. Suspected suicide, but we think someone knocked him off for failing to snag you with that spell in the contract."

Gene lifted his shoulders. He didn't care about Ruiz. "Elvira sent me a message. They have captured the spell caster. She won't be selling any more spells and charms, but apparently, she can't remember who she sold them to. A memory wipe."

Rolf frowned. "Who is capable of that? Another witch, a sorcerer?"

"A vamp, maybe," Gene suggested. "I've heard they can mesmerise. That's how they can attack unwilling victims. Although these days they have so many willing donors looking for eternal life that they don't need to use it. But they have that power all the same."

Abbie nodded. "Right, I didn't know that, but that could stuff up the witch's memory. You would have thought they'd be resistant."

Rolf grunted. "Different magics, I'm guessing."

They continued talking for a couple of hours.

※

WHEN LILY NEXT ROSE THROUGH THE LAYERS OF SLEEP, SHE FELT A large, hot body pressed against her. Gene was spooning her. His hand came around her waist and then drifted to her breast. *Oh, I'm naked.* His touch sent shivers across her skin and her clit stood to attention. He caressed the handful of breast, easing the flesh forward to her nipple. She couldn't stop herself from groaning. Desperate for him to suckle her nipples, suckle her nipples until she cried out, she pressed herself back against him, feeling his heat, feeling his erection burn into the skin of her butt. Was she out of her mind to invite him to nap with her? He shifted, moving his lips to her neck, just under her ear. Waves of desire leaped across her skin, and she moved her head to give him better access. He bit softly into her flesh, and she groaned louder. His hand left her breast to slide along her ribs, down to her hips.

"No," she said. He couldn't touch her there. She'd come in two seconds, and she wanted more. She turned in his arms, placing her nipple close to his face. He caressed her breast again and then his lips lowered, capturing her nipple. Her back arched as she called out her delight. He increased the suction, and she could feel the tug on her sex, the growing warmth in her belly, the heat on her clit as her breaths came fast and hard. This was crazy. He couldn't make her come by sucking her nipple, could he?

There must be something else at play. The potion the doctor had given her. *Oh, my Goddess! I want to fuck him so bad.* The more she moaned, the more diligent Gene became. He leaned on his elbow and caressed her other breast and then took that nipple into his mouth. Hard pressure that was akin to pain and pleasure combined. Her hips bucked, and she was so close to coming. Gene urged her to face him. He gathered her into his arms, pressing her close so that his erection was between her legs. Then he moved his hips, holding her there as he mock fucked her. The feel of his hot flesh sliding over hers was too much. She grabbed his head and mashed her mouth to his while they moved together.

"Can I put my mouth on you?" he whispered when she released the kiss.

"I'll come too quickly," she whispered. "I'm so close already."

He growled. "Is that a yes?"

"Yes, if you want."

He slid down her body, and she opened her legs. "Oh, my God, you're so beautiful," Gene whispered. His tongue dove in and she cried out, so close to coming. He took her clit into his mouth, and she could feel the rush of her climax approaching and then he paused, licked her elsewhere. Her heart thudded. *Don't tease me, you bastard, just do it.* Again he dove in, and she arched her back. His tongue was hot and hard as he brought her close yet again.

"Dammit! Stop playing with me."

He chuckled and dove in again, taking her clit and licking hard. Her orgasm was earth-shatteringly strong. She might have screamed. Her moans filled her ears and then she passed out.

"Lily?" A hand was shaking her. "Lily, wake up. The meeting is ready to start."

Her eyes snapped open. She was no longer feeing dazed, but she was disoriented. A fully dressed Gene stood there. Looking him up and down, she tried to parse what had happened. Had she dreamed that encounter? The other erotic dream they'd shared had been so real and hot. This seemed different, even more real. She was naked, like she remembered, but surely Gene hadn't just let her go to sleep after she had come like that? She hadn't even bothered to try to pleasure him. She had no recollection of reciprocating, of taking him into her mouth. Damn and blast, she couldn't remember.

"Oh?"

"Rolf and Abbie turned up after I left you. Sorry, I didn't get to take up your invitation."

Her face felt like a beacon. She had dreamed that? No way, but ... "I'll get ready."

"Your things are here." He pointed to her bag. "See you outside."

Gene shut the door. She launched into the bathroom, hit the shower. While she washed herself, she felt her breasts, remembering his caresses, the tightness of her nipples as he sucked on her, the way she pressed her body against his, delivering herself to him in a way she never had with anyone before. She let out a breath. Remembering the heat of his skin, his lips on her neck. The way they were attuned, the way she had felt safe enough to surrender. It had to be a dream. Her fingers brushed her nipples and there was no tenderness there. "Oh God, I dreamed that whole thing. What is going on with me?" He was her boss. She was supposed to protect him. She rolled her eyes. *And you invited him into your bed.* Had Rolf and Abbie come as he said? It had felt so real, but so had the other dream.

"You have totally lost your shit!" she said. She exited the shower, grabbed a towel and vigorously rubbed herself dry.

She inspected the pile of clothes and nodded. They were exactly what she wanted to wear. As there were people waiting, she dressed quickly, putting on her spare leather pants, dark roll-neck sweater and boots. Her hair was damp, so she wove it into a single plait down her back.

Her reflection showed her normal face. Her brain clicked into gear. She was no longer dazed and ready to jump Gene's bones. However, she was now really conscious of being attracted to him. The intimate dreams had to have an explanation and she would find out, eventually.

As she headed to the door, she realised she had been in a vulnerable state, and he had not, despite her urging, taken advantage of it. Mr Gene Cohen, alpha of the Sydney City Pack, was a gentleman. Who knew?

CHAPTER 13

When Lily opened the door and joined them in the apartment's living room, Gene tensed, assessing how she moved her body, aware that she was more herself.

"Hi," she said, as she looked around the room. Abbie was seated, with Rolf sitting on the arm of her chair.

Gene tapped the arm of the chair next to him. "Sit here. There's coffee."

Lily didn't meet his eyes but took the seat and then leaned over to the coffee table to pour herself a cup. She added cream and one sugar, stirred it and sat back, the cup nestled between her breasts. Her breasts? Why did she do that? It only made him want to touch them, kiss them. A flash of something teased his brain. Him sucking on her nipples. He inhaled sharply and flicked a sideways glance at Lily, hoping she didn't notice his gasp. He hadn't been asleep so it couldn't have been his dream. Was that an echo of something she dreamt or just the image of what he wanted to do to her?

Abbie had been studying Lily, but her eyes shifted to him, and her nostrils flared. Damn, she can taste the attraction. He needed to dial it right back.

"I've been able to track the owner of the house you were held in,

Lily," she said. "It was rented by a company that was owned by another company, whose owners are nominees for other people."

Lily frowned. "Are you saying you don't know?"

Abbie shook her head. "I've done some searches. It's a long trail, but it's definitely a vampire. One Silvio Bentino, formerly of Cagliari in Sardinia, an island belonging to Italy. He's been here five years, so not part of the new wave of migration."

Gene hit the arm of his chair. "I knew those bastards were involved."

Abbie shook her head. "It's not certain. Rolf spoke to Bentino."

This surprised Gene, and he turned to Rolf. "You did? But you never said."

Rolf met his gaze, then twitched his head slightly to encompass Lily. "Lily was resting, and we had agreed to wait until she could join us," he said neutrally. "Besides, he called me and invited me to meet with him."

"What?" Gene sat forward, feeling his blood rise.

Rolf shrugged. "I don't know how he got my phone number. We have been seeking vampire enclaves, so maybe he heard about that. There are phone trackers."

Gene blinked. Lily put her coffee on the table. "You *met* Silvio Bentino? The head honcho?" she asked. Even Gene had never met him, though he knew him by reputation. It looked like Lily did, too. He was rumoured to be in his prime, handsome, a suave dresser, affluent and owner of a few nightclubs in Kings Cross, Bondi and Parramatta.

Rolf grinned and gave a nonchalant shrug. "He thinks he's God's gift, but I don't find him a great specimen myself. While he is clean and wears nice cologne, there's no disguising the musty, dead smell he exudes." Rolf tapped his nose.

"It obviously went well," Gene observed. "You're still you."

Rolf grinned. "Not tempted." He rubbed leaned closer to Abbie and rubbed her back. "What he said was interesting."

"Well, what did he say?" Lily put her cup down and was nearly out of her seat.

"He said, and I quote: 'It is not me. It is not any of my minions. I cannot vouch for the new immigrants. But my contacts tell me they were not involved. You need to look elsewhere before you try to fix the blame on me ... on us.'"

"Do you believe him?" Gene asked.

Rolf snorted. "As much as I can believe one of their kind."

"Abbie?" Gene asked.

"I'm divided. It could be an attempt to frame Bentino or implicate the vampires. More importantly, it doesn't shed light on why there are so many vampires moving from Europe and the Americas to here. They know something is going on. Whether it is related, I can't be sure." She shrugged. "Sorry."

Rolf brushed his goatee with a finger and thumb. "He did own, though, that one of his progeny has broken faith with him. Her, he could not vouch for."

Abbie nodded. "It could be a lover's tiff or something more. I'll look into who his progeny may be and see what I can find."

Lily bit her lip. "Witches have been having issues with a dark cult. It originated in Europe, but we have had signs here." She cast a glance at Gene. "The spell on that document. That would never have happened before this dark cult came along."

"Elvira told me they have captured the rogue witch."

"She did? Excellent." Lily let out a long sigh and he could see the tension ease out of her posture. He guessed that the rogue witch had worried her as much as it had him.

Gene narrowed his gaze. "In the past, Elvira and the other elders have not spoken of this cult. It wasn't until I called that meeting and Dane spoke that they spilled the beans."

Lily nodded, licking her lips before speaking. "I'm not surprised. They're ashamed. They definitely don't want it talked about."

"I should talk to Elvira again."

Lily shook her head. "I'll ask her to brief you. The elders didn't think it was big enough or dangerous enough to cause problems on this scale." She met Gene's gaze. "Besides a few rogue spells."

Gene rubbed his hair, making it spike. "Are you sure you can be objective?" he asked her.

Her skin flushed, and she lowered her gaze. He pondered that. She was back to being herself, but there was something else going on. "I think the power struggles at the Collegium are at the centre of this," she said. "Maybe they are linked."

Abbie narrowed her gaze. "You smell different," she said to Lily.

Lily jerked up straight in her chair. "I've just had a shower, used different toiletries."

Abbie glided to her feet and moved closer.

"Abbie?" Gene said.

Abbie shook her head. She circled Lily as she sat in the chair. Abbie's lips twitched. "I can smell Gene on you ..." Lily's flush grew deeper, and she wouldn't meet his gaze.

"I'm sitting next to her," Gene interjected, annoyed by Abbie's repeated acts of sniffing around Lily as if she was some stray who played in muck.

Abbie nodded. "And there's something else—the magic is part of it, and still something I can't quite name."

Lily rolled her eyes. "You've previously established that I smell strange. I'm half witch and half something else. It doesn't mean you can't trust me. I'm still me."

Rolf perked up as Abbie took her seat, running her hand along his thigh as she did so. "Didn't Reeva say no fucking?" she asked.

Lily rolled her eyes. "We did not fuck."

Gene tilted his head. "I agree, we did not fuck. We didn't even canoodle."

Lily glanced sideways at him and then refilled her cup. There was a look of surprise on her face. Had she thought he'd taken advantage? He'd have to sort this out.

"Canoodle?" Rolf said. "That's an interesting term."

Gene stood. "Just don't mention it to Mother or she'll ban me from that, too."

Abbie scoffed. "My God, Reeva will smell it a mile off. There is some very strong sexual attraction between you two."

"Damn," Lily said, putting her cup down. "Perhaps I should stay away from Reeva for a bit."

Abbie shook her head. "No choice in that, I'm afraid. Reeva has asked us to join her." She checked her watch. "In about an hour."

DESTINY'S BLOOD

"Bugger!" Gene said. "Can't she wait? We have nothing solid to tell her."

Abbie studied him, eyes narrowing. "She said it was urgent."

"Well, we need something a bit more concrete to tell her. Whoever they are, they killed my father. They tried to kill me. They kidnapped Lily to either hurt her or to draw me out."

"I think it was to draw you out," Lily said. "Besides drugging me, keeping me locked up and feeding me crap food, they didn't ask me anything, didn't talk to me at all."

He rubbed his chin. "They tried to get me through my business dealings, the same project that my father was working on when he died."

"That seems like a human underworld type of crime, though," Lily observed. "Have we checked which paranormals are linked with your father's human business associates?"

"Yes," Abbie said. "It was the first thing we did."

"Besides the rogue witch's spells, no other connection," Lily added.

Gene leaned towards Lily. "What about your lead? The one your friend on the force told you about?"

"He told me Violet Smith, the name of the woman I had found in one of the files was dead. Her real name was Tremblay and she was exsanguinated and that sort of ties with vampires."

"Not necessarily," Abbie said. "We would need to see the body."

Lily sat back and made a helpless gesture with her hands. "But she's dead and buried or cremated. At least I think she would be by now."

"But there would be photos, autopsy results. Can you get your hands on them?"

"I can but try." Lily left the room to make some calls.

Gene poured himself more coffee. "Did mother say why she wanted us there?"

Rolf shook his head. "She was rather mysterious about it."

Abbie stared at the floor as if she was a million miles away.

"About Lily," Gene began.

Both Rolf and Abbie locked gazes with him. "She wasn't herself yesterday. Something the doctor gave her. We didn't, you know … She asked me to cuddle her."

Rolf laughed. "Cuddle her with your whole body?"

Abbie's lips lifted in a knowing smile.

"Look, it didn't happen. You arrived and I've been with you ..."

"But you wanted to, right?" Rolf asked.

Gene shook himself, nearly up-ending his cup. "Of course I'm interested! Just not when she's not properly consenting. Besides, she's not for me. Mother is right to warn me off. She's a witch, and weres don't mix with them, not in a serious way."

Rolf narrowed his gaze. "Yet you're in danger, brother. I can tell."

Gene wanted to thump Rolf. He wasn't talking about the threat to his life, but his heart. What did he know? Sure, they were half-brothers, but only recently known to each other. They hadn't grown up together and on first meeting they had disliked each other intensely. Only shared experience had allowed them to appreciate each other. "I'm not in that kind of danger. I'm the alpha of the Sydney City pack, and I know my responsibilities."

Rolf nodded but seemed unconvinced. Gene really wanted to wipe that smug expression off his face.

Lily came back in. "I've arranged to get copies of the autopsy report and the death scene photos."

"When?" Gene asked.

"We made dinner arrangements. My former colleague and I will meet in about four hours."

Gene shook his head. "You're not going on your own."

Lily gave him a 'what did you just say? look'. "Pardon?"

"You have a prior engagement with Reeva."

"No, I don't. I called her, and she's postponed tonight's meeting. Some hiccup with her surprise."

Rolf looked at his phone and nodded. "Yeah, there's a message. I didn't feel it ping."

"Well, you're not going to meet this former colleague without me," Gene said, folding his arms and looming over her.

Lily narrowed her gaze, looked from Rolf to Gene and back again. "I thought you'd be safe enough with Rolf and Abbie while I popped out."

"He is," Abbie said with a smirk.

"That's not what I'm talking about. I'm fine ..." He wanted to say he was fine without her, but that could be interpreted wrongly. She still had a job to do, and it had nothing to do with him wanting to taste her nipples and feel the weight of her breasts in his hands. Lily was back to herself: sharp, decided and very irritating.

"Where are you meeting this character?" he demanded.

Lily folded her arms, lifted her chin. "Some Turkish place in Enmore."

Gene considered. "Where in Enmore?"

"It's for your own good that you don't come with me. I'll text the details once I'm there. Now, before I leave, I'll need to sweep for magical and electronic surprises. If you won't be needing me for an hour or so, I'll start in this apartment and work my way back to the exterior of the building." She drew out her phone and waved it at him. "Full charge, so call me if anything happens."

She left, but they could hear her as she went in and out of every room, opening and closing doors. She came back in briefly, ignored them, and then left again.

The front door opened. Gene turned to Rolf. "You have to get me to that meeting. I don't trust this contact. He will not give that evidence over for nothing."

"Are you afraid that what this contact wants is what you want?"

Gene pivoted. "Yes! No! But consider this: He's giving over evidence from police files. That means he's probably bent. Even if she's ex police and a private investigator, that's not Kosher. She'd be better off hacking into their systems than getting it from him." He touched the side of his nose with his index finger. "There's more to it."

"You think she's blind to it?"

Gene shook his head. "I honestly don't know."

Gene made several pressing business calls while Lily did her scan of the premises. She came back just as he hung up from the last call. "It's clean." She nodded and jerked her head to the window. "It's a good set-up. Well done."

Gene wanted to growl. Was she trying to flatter him? Or did she think he was so stupid as to let his guard drop after the Bondi episode? "Good to know. About tonight ..."

She turned on him. "Look, whatever happened last night after the doctor's medicine, it was nothing. Don't sweat it."

Gene blinked. "What are you talking about?"

She walked up to him, and he didn't back away. She poked his chest. "You know exactly what I'm talking about."

He met her gaze. "You mean you asking me to snuggle you?"

She grew still. "Yes, um ... it was ... um."

"It was a really touching invitation. But by the time Rolf and Abbie arrived, you were asleep."

She frowned and blinked. "I fell asleep? When?"

"Just after you asked me. I had to leave the room and when I came back, you were curled into a ball and fast asleep. I left the room and spent the next few hours with Rolf and Abbie."

"So we didn't do more than talk? Are you sure?"

Gene threw out his hands wide. "More? No, Lily. I'm sure I didn't take advantage of you, if that is what you are asking. I'm not into non-consensual sex. Why? Don't you remember?"

"No. Yes. I remember things." She ran a hand over her head in a nervous gesture and didn't look him in the eye.

"Did you dream about me ... Us?" Gene asked.

She coughed, turned bright red, and walked away.

He guessed that answered his question. He wished he'd been able to share that dream. A grin spread over his face. She'd had an erotic dream about him. Now he was curious about what she had experienced.

※

LILY TOOK ANOTHER SHOWER AND USED THE SHOWER HEAD TO TEASE her throbbing clit to a climax. *Bastard! Bugger! Goddess!* She remembered clearly her naked flesh against his, her offering to snuggle. The nipple sucking had seemed so real, but he'd said it hadn't happened. She could ask Rolf and Abbie, but she believed Gene. That experience had been her dream, her imagination, yet it had been so real. Her footing with him was a bit off now. The line between real and imagined had grown quite thin. In her dream, he had made her come with his tongue. It was weird that it had felt so real when she had imagined it.

If the root of her dreams was her mind and heart processing the everyday, then she was bound up in Gene, a werewolf, who was totally unacceptable as a partner. Casual sex maybe, but could she be casual with him? He evoked something much stronger—a need, a deep-seated bond and a cellular-level desire that she could not understand. She had the hots for him, even though at first that was the farthest thing from her mind. What had changed? The potion the doctor had given her was gone from her system. Yet, she still wanted to march up to Gene Cohen and push him to the floor and mount him. She wanted to mash her mouth to his, take off his clothes, and fuck him senseless. That was no drug. *Goddess, I'm in trouble. I'm also out of my mind.*

But Reeva had said Lily wasn't the one for him. She wasn't good enough for him. Half-breed that she was, and the wrong breed to boot. There was no point in pursuing this attraction. She had to admit that, like other women before her, she wanted what Gene had to give—no promises, no commitment. Just fuck me hard and be damned. It was not a good realisation. She was no better than his other floozies. Now, she was a potential conquest as well.

Gene had shown restraint, too. He could have taken advantage of her, but he hadn't. She had invited him to join her in bed while she was naked. She had invited him to cuddle her. No wonder she had dreamed about him. After her invitation, her state of mind, and him holding her hand.

Even now, as she dried off from her shower, her breasts tingled and throbbed in memory. She had to fight not getting aroused again. She re-dressed in her black leather gear.

"I'm going to walk to the main road," she explained to Gene and the others. "I'll call a ride from there so as to not lead anyone here."

Rolf nodded. Gene stood solid as stone, and his expression was not inviting.

"I'll send you a text when I've made contact, and I'll try to get away as soon as he hands over the evidence."

Rolf and Abbie nodded, but Gene's glare felt like a knot in her back. She paused and looked over her shoulder at him, sent him a reassuring smile, and left.

Traffic was only mildly heavy, and her ride arrived within seven minutes. As they drove, she tried to focus on the meeting. She needed a clear head. After she alighted the car, she walked to a Turkish restaurant just down from the Enmore Theatre. Michael Sloane was waiting for her. In street clothes, which was a relief; it would have been awkward if he was in uniform.

"Hi," she said, taking a seat. "Thanks for agreeing to meet."

He wore grey trousers and a brown-striped shirt. He was tall and thin with acne scars on both cheeks. He'd been friendly on the force, but nothing more. Michael had a half-drunk bottle of beer in front of him. He stood, kissed her cheek, and sat back down. He picked up the menu and waved it. "You okay for the banquet?"

Lily hadn't come for the food, so shrugged. "Sure. I'm so hungry I could eat a horse."

The waiter took their order, and the restaurant filled up. "Why are you interested in this particular case, Lil?" he asked.

Lily picked up her glass of water and took a sip. "Something about it tingles my spidey senses."

He chuckled. "And?"

"It's linked to an investigation I'm doing into illegal moneylending and extortion. She was one of the victims." His eyes widened and she saw the question there.

"Can't really call her a client now, can I?"

He shook his head. "You should leave it to us professionals. It's a police matter."

She put her glass down carefully. A platter of bread and dips arrived. "I am a professional as well, you know. I agree the murder of this woman is definitely police business, but the rest is open for discussion."

"So why ask to see the autopsy details?"

"Just curiosity about how she died. It might give me some leads."

"I told you whoever did it exsanguinated her." He sat back in his chair. "I shouldn't have told you that."

"Yes, you told me, and I want to know how she was exsanguinated."

He shook his head. "You want to know by who."

Lily smiled. "Or what?"

They stared at each other until Michael dipped bread into the hummus. He ordered another beer. Lily started eating as well, trying the carrot dip first. The dips were tangy, and she used small pieces of bread to scoop them up so she could save some room for the main meal.

"Are you glad you left the force?" Michael asked.

Lily lowered her shoulders and stared into the middle distance as she thought her answer through. "That's a hard question. I loved the work and the people, too, except for a few arseholes. But I would never climb the promotion ladder. Well, not for at least ten years."

"Why leave? Why go private eye?"

"I liked the work, so that's why I'm working for myself. As for leaving, that's harder to explain. If I had to sum it up in one word, I'd say freedom. Freedom to do it my way."

The main courses arrived: kebabs, grilled lamb cutlets, chicken skewers, salad, rice and zucchini balls. The meeting with Michael aggravated her mixed feelings. She had enjoyed being a cop, but the danger of being outed as something 'other' had grown daily and she'd had to curb her use of magic to get answers. Using magic brushed up against the strict rule of law. You couldn't really testify in court that you followed a perp's trail using magic.

Michael shook his head, cut some meat and put it in his mouth and chewed.

"You're not thinking of leaving the force, are you?" she asked.

He swallowed and paused. "I might be. Things are a little off, you know?"

Lily's brain fired up. "What things?"

Michael leaned across the table and put his hand on hers. Lily froze. This was a very odd play for him. They had never been close and definitely never in the flirtation stakes. "It's different without you there," he said, softly.

Lily couldn't suppress her laughter. "I'm sure it is. No one to tease. No one to look sideways at when something odd happens." She drew her hand away, and he frowned.

"I never teased you, Lily. You were the best to hang with. Non-judgemental. Thorough. You got results. We get results now, I suppose, but it isn't easy and, well, to be honest, some commands from upstairs are just plain weird."

Lily extended her witch senses, just in case her old workmate had been hexed or something. He seemed all clear. He was behaving within his normal parameters. She had never been attracted to him in that way. He was nice enough looking, chatty on the job but not a hand-holding, miss you, wish you were here type of person.

She breathed out slowly. "What commands?"

"Not commands, actually. Just, you know, strange decisions like no overtime, for example."

Lily exhaled and let her tension release. That old gripe. Government tightwads who don't want to spend money on crime fighting nor on crime prevention.

"And not resourcing certain inquiries, like into your friend there. There was an autopsy done." He patted an envelope in his pocket. "But it was late and if there was a lead there, it had gone cold. I'm only giving you this because I think that's wrong and that you might crack it."

He took out the yellow envelope and passed it under the table. She took it and slid it under her butt. She frowned, though, as she picked through the salad looking for slices of tomato. "What types of inquiries aren't they resourcing, exactly?"

"Any homicide that is not straightforward. If it's a gang stabbing, all good. If it's a drive-by shooting of known bikie members, we get in there and tidy up. It's the odd bits. A body on the beach, no signs of a struggle, no clear cause of death. More people disappearing and then turning up dead later. Either in pieces or thoroughly drained." He poked the table with two fingers. "They're the ones we aren't to go near. Not enough resources, they say."

Lily swallowed the last bit of tomato and contemplated the remaining lamb cutlet. She offered it to Michael. He took it while she mopped up the last of the hummus with a bit of bread. "That's certainly unusual. Have you thought that maybe there's some secret ops going on? They keep those on the down low. Surely the press will stoke the fire under the bosses if there is too much stuff not being investigated."

He shook his head, biting the meat off the bone of the cutlet. "Press is strangely silent."

Lily's brow furrowed. "That is concerning." She looked at her watch. "I've got to head off soon. You take care."

"Don't go yet," Michael said and reached for her hand again.

She was about to get up but stayed put, her gaze on his hand. "Michael, I don't think you ..."

"Get your hands off her," a familiar voice said.

Michael snatched his hand back, jerked his head up, and gaped.

"Oh. Michael, please meet my current client. He doesn't like it when I'm late." She said the last with emphasis. What was he doing here? Had he followed her? He better have brought Rolf and Abbie or she was going to have words with him. She narrowed her gaze as she thought of a nice little hex she could lay on him. Something that made him itch and burn in all the wrong places.

"The fuck!" Michael said, pushing his chair back. He looked between them, then he leaned in close, even as the other diners were angling to see what was happening, and hissed. "You're working for one of them?"

Lily met Gene's eyes and then turned back to the policeman. "One of them?" she asked.

Michael had gone pale. His mouth worked, and she swore she had never seen him this lost for words. His voice was quiet when he spoke. "Supernaturals."

Gene laughed lightly, and Lily gave Michael a quizzical look. "I'm fairly sure the police exams screen for belief in the paranormal, ghosts and the like. Have you been taking any mind-enhancing or -altering substances lately?"

He had had four beers while she was there. Every nerve was on fire. If he knew about paranormals, even though he called them supernaturals and recognised Gene as one, then they had a serious problem.

"No," he said, seeming desperate for her to believe him. "I saw the file!" His eyes pleaded with her. "That's Gene Cohen, right? His name is on a list of people who are non-human."

"Oh?" Lily laughed, as if this accusation was a fine joke. "How shocking."

A look of uncertainty crossed his face as he processed her comment. "I saw his name." His gaze flicked up to Gene, looming behind her, and he swallowed. He looked ready to bolt.

Gene said nothing, but she bet he was listening with both ears burning. "Who made this list, and where did you read it?"

Michael shook his head. "I don't know. Don't remember."

"It must be a joke of some kind. You see, I've seen quite a bit of Mr Cohen, and he has all of his human bits."

Michael blushed. Her comment betrayed an intimate knowledge of Gene's body. Lily let her tension slide. At least it threw cold water over Michael's attempt to create something between them.

"I see," he replied. He frowned and shook his head. "I've said enough."

There was nothing for it. Lily had to hex him to get it out. Now that Dr Wentz had treated her, her magic was nearly back to normal. With her hands under the table, she cast the spell, twining around his head.

"Would you like to come back to my place for a drink?" she asked in a soft, purring voice.

A growl behind her chair threatened to break her concentration. She shook her head. "Not now, Gene," she said out of the side of her mouth, keeping her gaze meshed with Michael's.

He must have understood, because he remained quiet as Michael looked longingly into her eyes. "Yes. I thought you'd never ask. I'll get the bill."

He signalled the waiter. While she was taking her jacket off the back of her chair, she slid Gene the envelope. "Where can we take him?" she whispered.

Gene slid the envelope into his shirt to nestle against his skin. "I have a place nearby that's currently empty."

"Of course you do," she said and shook her head. After Michael paid the bill, she looped her arm through her former colleague's and led him outside.

"Where are we going?" Michael asked as he tried to nuzzle her neck. She pushed his head away.

"To my place, where we can be private."

Michael gazed at her, longing dripping from his gaze. "I want to be private with you in your privates."

Lily rolled her eyes. "I'm sure you do." She touched Gene on the arm. "You don't mind driving, do you, Mr Cohen?"

"I want to kiss you," Michael said and wrapped his arms around her.

Lily smiled. "Of course you do." She neatly folded his arms so he couldn't grab her and dodged his lips.

Gene had parked curbside. How he had managed that she didn't know, given the traffic and limited parking. He helped her get Michael into the back of the car and she jumped in with her former colleague. She felt guilty about the hex, but they had to know about that list.

Gene sped off, keeping her in view in the rear-view mirror. He took a series of side streets to Newtown. Gene pulled up in front of a small terrace. It was lucky for them he was a property magnate. Although she had to wonder why so many were vacant, how he made money from them, but had no time for questions. They climbed out of the car and walked up to the porch. There was a key safe and Gene keyed in the code, retrieved the keys and let them in.

"Nice," Michael said and tried to snuggle his face into her neck. She guided him down the hall into a sitting room. It was tastefully furnished in a bed-and-breakfast style. Not quite sterile, but not quite lived in.

"Come and sit on the couch next to me," she said, and Michael followed along.

She stroked her fingers through Michael's hair. "Now, Michael dearest. Tell me about that lovely list with the supernaturals on it."

Michael's gaze went over her shoulder, where Gene glowered.

She turned her head, met his gaze. "Gene, could you make a cup of tea or something?"

Gene grumped and left the room. "Who had the list?" she asked in a caressing voice, weaving her compulsion spell into it.

"The police commissioner."

"Oh ... and who gave it to him?"

"I don't know. He said it was from a reliable source. He said there were creatures among us, feeding off us, and that we had to be careful because ... because ..."

"Because?" she prompted.

Michael frowned. "I don't know. I don't remember."

Lily tried a few different lines of questioning and frowned at what she suspected. A pot of tea arrived on the table in front of her. She brushed her fingers over Michael's eyes. He lowered his eyelids and went to sleep.

"Your friend is a bit of a whinger," Gene said as he poured her a cup of tea.

She took the cup and shook her head. "You're not wrong."

"So, what did you find out?"

"Not much. I'm sorry to say this, but someone has already hexed him and wiped his mind. I'm not sure why he could tell us about the list. They must have missed an association that allowed him to keep part of the memory. He definitely recognised you, though, so that's something. The downside of being in the social pages, I suppose. Never took Michael for a reader of popular press."

"Is there actually a list?" he asked.

Lily thought it through. "Look, I think there must be. I don't know who compiled it, or why. There is definitely something weird going on with the police and the press. Before you came and introduced yourself ...not," She peered at him. "Why did you, by the way?" Gene took a sip of tea and lifted his eyebrows. "Oh, never mind. Before you interrupted things, he told me that there are weird things going on. Murders not being investigated. The press staying quiet about it."

Gene blinked. "You mean like interference, some infiltration? By who?"

"I don't know!" she took another sip of the hot tea. "If it's crooks, then why target supernaturals? If it's supernaturals, why the list?"

"We need to see the list, to work it out. I don't think that whoever's behind this would put themselves or their kind on this list."

"I agree. It's almost like they are preparing for something. A coup, maybe. Or a rebellion."

Gene sat down. "Before I came after you, I had a quick chat with Rolf and Abbie and what strikes me is what they said was going on at the Collegium seems to mirror what is happening here. A disruptive force pushing us all to a particular pointy end."

"And your father? Is there anything in his background that makes you think he was part of it or that he knew something?"

Gene shook his head. "I've been through everything. I can't find anything underhand that he did or said or was part of."

"What about pack politics?"

Gene met her gaze, a sort of stunned expression on his face. "I can't see how. No one challenged me when I took over as alpha. He was the most powerful alpha in Australia, with a vast network of allied packs."

"It can't be a dead end. We need to think this through another way. Your father was the defacto leader of werewolves in Australia. Dane's father was high up in the Collegium and was murdered. Then Dane himself was targeted too, so Rolf said. A curse that turned him into a werewolf every full moon, taking his mind a bit at a time so it would have left him as a mindless being, something to be put out of its misery." She tapped her knee. "It's a bit of a tangle. Plots and counterplots and that's why we can't see clearly. We have to see where the connections are. Maybe we stumbled on something big without meaning to."

Michael let out a snore.

"What are we going to do with your friend?"

"We can drop him home. I don't know if he drove, but he's too drunk to drive in any case. But first, let's look at what he brought us."

Gene drew out the envelope and spread the contents on the table. There were photos and a report. The report confirmed exsanguination. There were several bites on her body: ankles, vagina, neck, wrists, elbows. Some were obviously older than others, indicating she was a long-term donor for a vampire. The report didn't say that, of course. It suggested possible bed bug infection or rodent bites to explain the wounds.

She picked up the photos of the fatal wound and studied it. It was larger. Jagged flesh made an uneven groove. No DNA sample taken. She wondered at that. She passed the photo to Gene, and he frowned. "It could be a werewolf's bite, but it's too restrained and no one in my pack would kill an old woman, feeder or no."

"Why would a vampire do it if she was a dedicated feeder? That makes little sense, unless there's some rivalry between the vampires. We might have to talk to Bentino again."

Gene nodded. "And this woman," he tapped the photo, "was linked to that moneylending place?"

"Yes. They could have killed her to make it look like it was a werewolf. But to do that, they would have to work with or be paranormals. There was no hint of that at their office. Did you notice any stray scents?"

He shook his head. "I feel like I've spent a lot of effort for very little gain. As much as I love having you around, the disruption to my life is starting to grate. And how does all this fit into the attack on me?"

"That is the question, isn't it?"

CHAPTER 14

After dropping Michael home they headed back to the apartment complex. On the way they continued to argue about the importance of the connections, without much success in determining who was doing what to whom. Just as they were arriving, Lily noticed a big grey dog. On second look, she realised it was a wolf prowling around in the flickering lights of car park. "Did you see that?"

"See what?" replied Gene as he navigated the parking lot.

There was another wolf bounding along towards the exit. "There's something wrong. Your pack has changed into wolves."

His alarmed expression faced her for a split second before he shot his gaze out into the wider surroundings. "What the actual ..." he said, when he saw the wolves himself. "That's Percy and his wife, Cynthia." Gene swerved into an empty parking space and stopped the car. He was about to get out when Lily shouted. "Stop!"

Gene paused and turned to look at her over his shoulder. "What now?"

"I have to check that it's safe first," Lily said. "Something caused this and you might be in danger."

"Fuck that! This is my pack." Gene grumbled as he climbed out of the car and slammed the door. She didn't quite get what he said, but she understood the tone. *Ungrateful bastard*, she thought at him as she swung open her door and slid out. She sent her witch senses as far as she could, detecting nothing out of the ordinary, except there were at least fifteen wolves prowling the perimeter. There was a disturbance in the air, like the aftermath of magic, but not actual magic.

"Anything?" he asked her as she ran up behind him.

"No major threat that I can detect from here without actually looking." Her tone was not friendly. "My wards have not pinged."

"I am the alpha of this pack. I can't hide behind you when there's a threat like this. I'm their leader and I'm responsible for them. Something happened."

Gene whistled and two wolves ran up to him. Soon after, another five wolves trotted up, their claws scraping on the concrete and their pink tongues lolling. Gene shook his head. Lily wasn't sure if he could communicate with his pack mates without changing himself. However, after about five minutes of silence, Gene turned to her. "It appears we have a visitor waiting for us in my apartment."

"A visitor?" Lily thought this visitor must be very scary for the pack to change into wolves without a full moon's power to assist. At least it was night-time, and few people would notice. She did wonder how the vampire had entered without her wards alerting her. "Who exactly?"

Gene shrugged and let out a long sigh. "A vampire. Silvio Bentino, if I'm not mistaken."

Lily jerked to attention and reached out with her magic to see if she could detect the visitor. She shook her head. "He doesn't register with my senses or my wards. To be honest, I haven't come up against vampires in person before." She tried again, arrowing her senses in the direction of the apartment. There was a space where nothing seemed to exist. "How did he get in? I thought vampires had to be invited?"

Gene pursed his lips and flicked an annoyed glance her way. "They do. Somehow, this one didn't need one or someone invited him in. What worries me is how Rolf and Abbie stand in all this."

Lily jogged to keep up with Gene's long stride. She couldn't imagine that either Rolf or Abbie invited the vampire across the threshold, and that only added to her concern. Gene was in a hurry and heading straight into danger. He wasn't about to be deflected by anything she could do, unless she hogtied him with magical ropes, which she wasn't sure would work given his own were magic and strength. However, she made a note in the back of her mind to learn how, because dealing with werewolves was fraught with issues that required restraints. If she was going to continue in the private eye business, she could definitely see them being useful.

"Can't you let me go first?" she asked.

Looking over his shoulder as they entered the lift, Gene grimaced at her. It certainly wasn't a smile. "No. As interesting a development as this is, I'm facing it. You can back me up, if you like. We werewolves have a long history with vampires and it's not an exaggeration to say we don't like them, and we definitely don't trust them."

Lily considered this. He had the experience, and he *was* on home territory.

"Besides," he added when the lift door pinged. "The timing is right for your first time."

"What do you mean?" she asked, a twist to her lips because she knew she wasn't going to like the answer.

The doors swished open. "For me to protect you."

Lily flashed him a fake smile and thought *smart-arse*. Just because she hadn't met a vampire didn't mean she didn't know how to protect herself, or that she was frightened or, worse, useless in a fight.

The vampire had not walked into the apartment down these halls or through the main entry points, which is why the wards hadn't alerted her. While she was wary, she could detect no danger and had no reason to not let Gene lead the way. Besides, she had lost the argument with Gene already about who went first. His pack, his apartment building and he was her boss. In his current mood, she bet she'd lose again if she tried to physically take the lead. The thought of being bodily moved out of the way was rather disconcerting. She was a lot smaller than Gene and hexing him because he tried something like that wouldn't go down well, either. She grit her teeth.

A couple more wolves lurked in the corridor, clearly unsettled by the visit of one of the undead—or the undying, depending on your point of view. "What about Abbie and Rolf? Surely if they were there, they would have objected to this vampire visiting? I don't understand."

"Neither do I. They must have left. We're about to find out."

The door to the apartment was ajar and Gene pressed his right shoulder against it, opening it further and then stepped through. Lily was close behind him, all of her senses on alert. Leaning casually on the breakfast bar was a lean, suave-looking man in a black designer suit, crisp white shirt, complete with a red tie, and expensive-looking loafers. Bentino was beyond handsome, Lily decided. There was something in the package he presented, a coiling allure that swirled through the air like an invisible hydra. She shook her head, realising it was affecting her. That was a powerful bit of magic; not witch magic, vampire magic. She stood beside Gene and studied their intruder. He had dark eyes, an aquiline nose and full, red lips. His dark hair curled around his forehead and ears, and he was clean-shaven. She estimated him to be around five foot ten, a few inches taller than herself and a good half foot shorter than Gene.

As they entered, he stood up straight, inclined his head a fraction, and smiled slightly. "Gene Cohen, I presume." He didn't move forward to shake hands. He inclined his head again to her. "And you must be the enchantress bodyguard. You are not what I expected."

Lily wanted to ask what he was expecting. However, she resisted the urge to rise to the bait and folded her arms across her chest, refusing to be charmed because charming is what Bentino was trying to be. With his good looks and vampire allure, he was probably used to getting whatever he wanted. His voice, though, was pure liquid honey. She savoured it, let it wash over her skin, her mind and it excited her, made her pulse leap, her sex pay attention. Oh, yes, those tones would lure anyone to sleep with him, let him bite their necks or other places. Quickly, she erected a ward against it. The unsuspecting wouldn't stand a chance against the caress of that voice.

He didn't introduce himself, which was rather strange. Was he that famous?

Tension coiled around Gene. She didn't know whether he was going to unwind or lash out. "Where are my brother and his wife?"

Bentino stepped forward and gave a Gallic shrug. "I have no idea.

They were not here when I came in. My arrival caused quite a stir amongst your people, and I apologise for that. But as night had fallen, I thought it opportune to pay you a visit and tell you in person I had nothing to do with the attack on you, the kidnap of your bodyguard, or the death of your father."

It was possible Gene tensed even further. "How did you get in here without an invitation?"

Bentino waved a hand nonchalantly and then shrugged. "The Mayor of Sydney gave me the keys to the city around three years ago. She may not have realised what I was and what it meant. Within the boundaries of the city, I have no impediment to enter any building."

Gene inhaled sharply. Bentino raised a hand. "Do not be alarmed. I rarely take advantage of it. However, in this instance, as the politics and rivalries are fraught, I found it necessary. As you yourself have experienced, a direct approach is sometimes best."

"You seem well informed. You obviously have something else to say, besides *I didn't do it*."

Bentino nodded slowly, as if gathering his thoughts. "You are correct. I have made enquiries with my support team, if I can call it that, and of my progeny, of which there are only three. One of them, sadly, did not answer my enquiries sufficiently. Further investigation on my part led me to believe that they are involved in what is going on. That they have interfered with the administration of this city more than they ought and, perhaps, provided information imprudently."

"You know about the list," Gene said, with certainty.

Lily gasped and gave Gene a sideways glance. How had he guessed that? With a frown, she wondered whether someone had followed Michael and listened in on their conversation. She had been alert for magical or paranormal presences spying on them, but had overlooked the obvious: normal human eavesdropping. She was very disappointed in herself.

"Belatedly, I have become aware of attempts to out the paranormal among us. While it suits me to have the myth surrounding vampires circulating so we can attract blood donors, I do not agree with outing everybody, particularly without their consent."

"You will give me the name and details of this progeny," Gene said, not relaxing at all.

Bentino lost a smidgen of his charm, his mouth drawing tighter, his nostrils flaring. "It does not sit well with me to give you that information. I have a sense of loyalty to her, and I care for her, despite the fact she has rejected me and struck out on her own." He shook his head slightly and bit his lip.

Lily glimpsed his elongated incisors, and the sight gave her a chill. It brought the threat of vampires and what they represented to the fore. Even though she was a paranormal, she didn't trust vampires and how they treated humans, how they targeted their weaknesses and promised them eternal life. Humans didn't understand, not until it was too late. There was so much exploitation and so few that actually achieved what they wanted.

Gene relaxed his shoulders, dropping them down. "We have the means to rumble a few of your nests. The immigrants might not like that either. I gather they are annoying you?"

Bentino's eyes flashed. "Even though I do not agree with this mass migration, you cannot stir things up. There are other ways to deal with the influx of immigrant vampires. I do not need your help there."

Lily grinned. "You've lost your place in the hierarchy, haven't you?"

The influx of so many new vampires would have upset the status quo and disturbed the lifestyle he had enjoyed since he arrived some five years before. Keys to the city and all that. Exposure could cause that to be taken away. Now, he probably had to compete for food, with all the new vampires relocating from Europe and the Americas.

Bentino gave a slight shrug, resumed his casual position, once again leaning his elbow against the breakfast bar. "Given your situation and the amount of angst your surveillance of our premises has created, I will give you her name and address. I'm not even concerned if you tell her where you got it. She has been a thorn in my side and has not adhered to our agreement."

He tossed a piece of paper onto the breakfast bar.

Gene relaxed slightly. "Your word is not enough. Evidence is what I need. Besides, I'm not here to do your bidding and help you round up your progeny and make them obey you. I want information and justice, or whatever you want to call it."

Bentino nodded slowly, as if he expected nothing less. "Very well. I will deliver what evidence I have to you." He sniffed. "I will do my best to wrangle my progeny. She has, however, been very slippery of late, and keeping bad company. If rumours are to be believed."

"I appreciate your cooperation."

"Wait, what rumours?" Lily asked.

Bentino drew himself up as if there was a string attached to his spine that had suddenly grown taut. "Rumours that her lover is the police commissioner."

Wow! That will certainly make things awkward. If Bentino's information was good, it was fraught with trouble. If Gene attacked this vampire progeny directly, then he risked outing his werewolf pack and other paranormals. It had the potential to be disastrous. She wondered if Bentino was concerned enough to help other paranormals stay under the radar.

Obviously, Gene was thinking along the same lines as he whistled and nodded his head slowly. "What else do you know? Screwing the police chief is not a bad thing in itself. Just risky."

"Bianca has stuck her claws into the criminal gangs. I'm not sure which one, because it could be more than one. Before her elevation to vampire, she was a criminal lawyer. She has many contacts among Sydney's underbelly."

"Oh, fuck!" Gene blurted.

Lily rolled her eyes. How much had this progeny vampire told the underworld thugs? Too much, she feared. The ramifications were far-reaching.

Gene glared at the vampire, while Lily felt a stirring of sympathy. The creature didn't have to come and give them a heads-up. Unless, of course, their surveillance of the vampire hives was causing him difficulties. Maybe there was something else that he didn't want others to know, possibly related to the cause of the mass migration of vampires to the Australian continent.

As if there had been a silent signal, Gene stepped out of the way and with a grand gesture, pointed to the door. Lily also shifted out of the way to allow the vampire to exit. This he did with a lithe step, appearing to glide along the floor. Without a backward glance, he entered the hallway. Wolves waited and trotted after the vampire. Lily raced out to see Bentino depart. He was at the window, standing in the silhouette of the streetlight, and in the next breath, he was gone. "Impressive," Lily said to herself.

Now that the vampire had departed, the wolves transformed back into their human shape. She backed into the apartment, trying to ignore the bone crunching, moaning cries of those transforming. It seemed excruciating. And their nakedness was only slightly disconcerting. Werewolves! Was she getting used to their ways?

Gene slammed the door after she came inside and dug out his mobile phone. "Rolf! Thank God you're okay." Rolf spoke, but Lily couldn't understand what was being said. Gene said into the phone, "We're on our way." He pressed the off button and swung around to face Lily. "If you're ready, we need to head to Reeva's, but first I have to restore order here. Apparently, Bentino arrived not five minutes after Rolf and Abbie left. Nerves are fraught, I'm afraid, as vampires are not usually welcome in pack territory."

Lily nodded and rolled her eyes. "He's impressive, that's for sure. His exit right now had a certain style."

"Funny. Planning on working for him now?"

"I was just making an observation, not changing my loyalties."

Gene frowned, and she thought she heard a growl. "It won't take me long."

She jerked her thumb over her shoulder. "All good. If you give me a few minutes, I'll freshen up and then I'll be ready to leave."

Gene watched her enter the hall on her way to the bathroom, and then she heard the front door slam.

By the time she had showered and changed her clothes, Gene had composed himself and had apparently dealt with all the nerves that needed soothing. There was barely any trace of his previous tension and irritation. He had showered and changed his clothes as well. He was wearing blue jeans, a pale blue-and-white-striped shirt, and a sweater. On his feet were a pair of black Nikes. Looking relaxed, he greeted her entry with a firm nod.

"Let's go then," he said and opened the door. He wasn't waiting, so she scrambled after him. She had a feeling she had upset him but waved that away. Surely, he wasn't jealous of Bentino. The vampire was attractive on a surface level only. There was no fire—nothing to lure her down that road. Gene was way more attractive. She had a bunch of erotic dreams to testify to that. Having his compound breached by a vampire was bound to upset his mood for the foreseeable future. Now they were on the way to his mother's house and more angst, if she wasn't mistaken. Something was obviously up, because Rolf and Abbie had left to go there without waiting for them. They also needed to confer urgently regarding the information they received from Bentino and Michael.

They had been driving for about ten minutes when she asked. "Did you bring the name and address of his wayward progeny?" She had only just recollected that the slip of paper had been on the breakfast bar, and she hadn't retrieved it.

Gene threw a glance in her direction, his blue gaze intense. "Of course, I brought it." He turned back to face the road.

"That's good, then." She wasn't going to admit she'd forgotten all about it.

"You were attracted to him," Gene said quietly.

She sat still. "He's a vampire. He puts out lures, so one thinks he is attractive. His voice was very seductive, though. Is that what you want to hear?"

Gene pursed his lips and nodded. The light from a traffic signals shone red on his face, giving him a slight demonic appearance. "You're truthful then. A witch and a vampire are not a good mix."

She stared out at the street. There had been a rain shower and puddles of water glistened in the streetlights and the road was a glossy black. The light changed and Gene accelerated.

"Are you speaking hypothetically? Or categorically? Vampires can't usually breed, so having a witch lover is not so bad. But if a witch becomes a vampire, that is the wrong mix, I agree."

He flicked his gaze her way. "Unstoppable I would say."

She nodded and cocked her head. "Yes, particularly if that person had evil intentions. Why are we talking about this?"

"I sensed you were tempted."

"Tempted to what? I liked the sound of his voice even after I screened his allure casting."

"You can do that?" he asked, obviously surprised.

"Yes, I can screen out the allure magic he casts. But his voice is genuinely sexy."

Gene smacked the steering wheel. "You will not drool about a vampire in my car."

Lily turned her body so that she was facing him. "You're going to kick me out of your car because I said his voice was sexy? That's a bit of overkill."

"I never said I'd kick you out. Just don't drool."

"I shouldn't drool over you, then?" Why had she said that?

"What?"

She turned her body to face the front again. "Nothing."

"No, you said something about drooling over me. You think I'm ... I'm ..."

"Sexy ... or attractive?"

He squinted out the rear-view mirror. "Seriously? I thought you were immune to my charms?"

"I can be, but that doesn't mean I don't notice."

"You aren't still suffering from Dr Wentz's potion, are you?"

"No. What is it with men? You can come on to a woman, say all kinds of stuff. You look hot tonight and so on. Then if a woman says you're sexy or attractive, it's like she's committed a mortal sin."

"That is very unfair."

"It is, just not in the way you think."

"For the record, I think you're attractive, and I would really like to explore that further, but things are rather complicated at the moment." He took a turn at an intersection. "I mean, I've had some pretty erotic dreams that involve you."

Lily's face heated. "I didn't send them to you. And you know I've had them too, featuring you."

"So it's not you casting a spell or something? Sometimes I wonder. Witches are new to me."

Lily rolled her eyes. "No. That would be unprofessional, for starters. And if you recall, I used up all my magic rescuing you. Just when I got some magic back, I was kidnapped and drugged, which depleted almost all my magic again. Then Dr Wentz gave me something to boost my energy. That's when ... I ... er ..."

Was she really going to tell him about that?

"What?" he asked.

It looked like she was. "After I asked you to snuggle with me. By the way, that was very gentlemanly of you not to take advantage."

"Yes, I suppose it was. I don't take advantage of drunk women and you gave all the signs that you weren't yourself."

"My inhibitions were lifted for a time," she agreed. "I had a very enjoyable dream that you were in bed with me."

"A dream?"

"A very realistic dream. One where I couldn't tell if I had been dreaming or if it had been real when I woke up."

"Tell me," he said, lowering his voice to coaxing level, or was that his bedroom voice?

Lily swallowed. They were drawing closer to Reeva's, so she was going to run out of time. "Your skin was very hot, and I wanted to rub myself against you."

"Did you?" he asked quietly.

"Yes, Goddess, yes. You spooned me and snuggled up close and it drove me out of my mind." She cast him a glance. He didn't appear to be breathing. "I woke up in the dream and you were holding my breasts and then kneading them."

His eyebrows rose. She kept going. "The way you touched me in the dream drove me out of my mind. I wanted you to take my nipples into your mouth and suck hard and you did. Desire in my dream was off the charts."

"Heavens, did we fuck in this dream?" His comment broke the spell.

"Not exactly."

He drove into the parking lot and into his designated spot. "We need to discuss this dream of yours further."

"It was just a dream," she replied. "I don't know why I told you."

"Yes, you do. You think I was involved somehow, influencing your mind, directing your dreams. I can't deny I want to do those things, but I didn't consciously project those thoughts to you."

"Then Reeva's alpha magic theory might be correct. Somehow, you could be affecting me?"

He growled. "Yes. Maybe. The bottom line is you want to know if dream matches reality and after what you told me, I do too."

Her mouth fell open. "But ... but ..." She climbed out of the car and followed him to the lift.

He faced her, resting his back on the marble-lined lift wall. His face showed no emotion. "There is something at play here, Lily. The erotic dreams, the tantalising attraction and Reeva's constraint."

"Reeva? She's right, though. I'm working for her, and we shouldn't be mixing business with pleasure."

"And?" he prompted.

"She said I was not for you."

He crossed his arms. "Something my mother has never ever said to me. If I presented you to her as a mate, maybe she could veto that. But that is not on the cards. You took her comment personally, didn't you?"

"Yes. I've always been on the outer in the coven. Never quite good enough. I guess I must believe it down deep, because her comment did gouge me a bit."

"I'm glad you told me about the dream. When you were asleep, I was awake. I didn't get to share it like that first time. Something strange is going on here, and I figure my mother knows what that is."

"What on earth could it be? It's not something I've heard about before."

The lift opened on Reeva's floor.

CHAPTER 15

"Finally!" Reeva said as they stepped through the front door. "What kept you?"

Gene kissed her cheek, nodded to Rolf and Abbie and stepped further into the room for Lily to step through. "We had a visitor. To cut a long story short, a vampire, one we have been discussing recently, Silvio Bentino." Rolf and Abbie gaped, obviously appalled.

"That vampire came to your apartment?" Abbie asked. "Without invitation?"

Her gaze flicked between Lily and him. "Yes. He caused a bit of an uproar," Gene said, heading to the drinks trolley. "Apparently our revered mayor gave him the keys to the city so he can go wherever he pleases. It wouldn't surprise me if he waited until you two left before dropping in."

"What was so important that he turned up?" Rolf asked, coming forward to accept a finger of whisky from Gene.

"I think your surveillance has rattled his cage and with the kidnap of Lily, he was pre-empting a retaliatory attack." Gene lifted his glass and downed it in one gulp. He poured another and enquired if anyone else wanted one. No one did.

"Did it?" Rolf replied, eyes narrowing. Abbie leaned into him, and he put his arm around his wife's shoulders. He sipped his drink and waited for Gene to answer.

"With some information Lily has received, and what Bentino told us, we have a name and a web of connections that may lead us to who killed Papa."

Reeva put a hand to her chest. "Truly! That is progress." She beamed at them. "That was worth the delay." She hugged him and then Lily.

Gene still didn't know why Reeva had summoned them or why she had hugged Lily. He would never figure women out. His mother was on top of the list as a difficult to decipher specimen. The dining table had the best china on it and champagne chilled in a cooler. Reeva was dressed up to the nines. Gene narrowed his gaze. "What's going on? What's the occasion?"

His mother smiled. "We have special guests arriving." Her gaze left his and settled on Lily. "Are you feeling well now, Lily?"

Lily glanced between him and Reeva. "Yes. Much better thank you. Is there something wrong?"

Gene sighed and tried not to roll his eyes. Even Lily had trouble working out what was going on with his mother.

"No, but if you would like to change into something more elegant, we have time."

"Me?" She looked down at her body. Gene loved the black leather pants and jacket she wore and the black polo top. She appeared so badass looking and such a tantalising feast for his eyes. Her telling him some of her dream had been hard to listen to without taking action on his desires. She thought he was hot, and he definitely reciprocated. However, there was more to it as well, he could tell. Something that he couldn't quite put his finger on. He wondered what might have been if he had accepted her invitation to snuggle. It wouldn't have been fuckless, of that he was sure.

"She looks fine as she is," Gene ventured.

His mother swiped him across the shoulder. "What do you know? Go on, Lily. There are some clothes in your room. A gift from me for all your hard work. I think it would be good if you dressed up for this occasion."

"You're the boss." Lily shrugged and took herself off. Reeva was not one to argue with.

Once Lily left the room, he rounded on his mother. "What are you doing? Why does Lily have to dress up when we don't?"

She stepped up to him, her index finger aimed at his chest. "Because in this, you don't matter," Reeva said and turned away and threw out her hands. "Another drink anyone? I have bubbles."

Mystified, but knowing it was useless to cajole his mother, he sauntered over for a refill. He'd take his time with this drink as he needed his head clear. Not that booze affected him overmuch. After she had handed out drinks, his mother excused herself and went down the hall, presumably to assist Lily.

A thought struck him out of the blue, that his mother was matchmaking Lily with someone else. He wouldn't put it past her, first forbidding him to bed Lily, then rolling out some competition. His heart lurched at the thought. No way would he stand by and let someone else take his place. Surely, his mother didn't want Lily out of the way that badly. It had been more than a 'she's working for me to protect you, so keep your hands off' kind of warning. He stood there, baffled, trying to work it out. Rolf joined him, bumping his shoulder companionably. "Do you know what is going on?"

"No." He replied testily. His brother's eyes widened, and he shook his head. "I wish I did. More whisky?"

"Yes, I'll try that new single malt."

Gene opened the bottle. "Good choice. Very peaty and very smooth."

Abbie joined them. "Me, too. Two fingers, neat, no ice." In a whisper, she leaned in to say, "I want to know what's going on. Reeva has been cagey and jumpy ever since we got here. All I know is she's expecting a visitor or visitors. Important ones, given the preparations."

Gene poured the drinks and angled his head to the fully set table. "The best china is out. I've seen it twice in my life."

Rolf snickered, and Gene chuckled. "Should you check on Lily?" he asked Abbie.

Abbie twisted her head so that her neck clicked. "No, I'm not getting between those two. I have no idea why Lily agreed to change clothes without an argument. I thought Lily knew her own mind."

Rolf clinked glasses with Abbie. "Smart thinking is my bet. She assumes Reeva knows what she's doing and will not stand in her way, even if it's odd and inconvenient."

Gene shook his head. "You two are no help. Obviously, the visitor has something to do with Lily, but I don't know in what way."

"A long-lost husband?" Abbie ventured, stabbing Gene with a sharp look.

Gene glowered at her. "Lily wouldn't forget to mention something important like that. She's straight as an arrow."

Rolf sighed. "You two, enough. Let's talk about something important. What about the vampire's information? We should plan our next—"

Rolf stopped talking abruptly. Abbie's eyes widened. Gene turned as Lily walked into the room. The dress she wore was long, black and glistening with embedded crystals. It clung to her form all the way down to her knees, then flared out like a fish's tail. The bodice clung to her breasts, displaying them like they were on a platter. On her feet were strappy shoes that matched the fabric of the dress. Somehow, Reeva had persuaded Lily to take her hair out of a plait and then curled it around her shoulders and back so that it now flowed with her movement. A light touch of make-up made her skin glow, and her lips were dark red and glossy.

"Breathe," Abbie whispered into his ear, a snicker in her voice.

Gene's cock immediately took notice of the vision of Lily before him. He inhaled deeply, as instructed, and tried not to gawk. His mother had just upped the ante, and he didn't know why. Was she trying to turn him into a slavering mess, drooling after a half-witch? The desire to howl at the moon possessed him. As he couldn't change right then, he had to endure chills and heated stabs of pain in all his muscles as desire fought constraint.

He found it hard to drag his gaze away from Lily and nothing else in the room registered. Rolf leaned in and whispered in his ear. "Pick up your jaw, brother. The visitors have arrived."

Gene's alpha powers surged to life. Someone powerful was closing in. Another wolf. "Thank you for coming," Reeva said at the open door.

The man, a powerful werewolf if Gene was correct, was tall and had an impressive mane of white hair. He was broad-chested and well-muscled, his arms bulging and his legs thick and strong looking. A very impressive wolf. He and his companion wore black wool coats that went past their knees. He couldn't see what they were wearing underneath.

"This is Gene Cohen, my son," she said. "Gene, this is the White Wolf of Donegal."

Gene shook himself and met the other alpha's gaze. The fuck! The White Wolf of Donegal? His battle in the north of Ireland was legendary and his training camps for weres a place alpha's fought to send their best and most trusted. This hulking, white-maned werewolf was akin to royalty.

Gene wanted to find a quiet corner somewhere and huddle just to get his head around these two astounding things. Lily dressed to kill and a werewolf king in the space of three minutes. Too bad he didn't have that luxury. He stuck out his hand instead.

"Name is Domhnall Dockerty," the man said as he took Gene's hand and squeezed it hard. His Irish accent was strong and lyrical. He turned to the side. The second man entered, leaner and younger than Domhnall, with a similar white mane of hair. "This is my son, Connor."

"Pleased to meet you, sir," the younger man replied as he shook Gene's hand. He appeared to be around twenty-one years old, if Gene was to guess. *The moon take me. The bloody prince is here as well.*

Dazed, Gene stood stock-still as his mother introduced Rolf and Abbie. Either this visit had to do with whatever was going on in Europe with the paranormals, or it was to do with Lily and, as he couldn't join the dots, he remained perplexed. His heart didn't particularly like that state of mind, if the rapid thumps against his ribs were any indicator. With a roar in his ears, his gaze sought Lily. She stood transfixed, gaping at the big white-maned wolf. Gene's pulse leaped. Something momentous was happening. It was more than the wolf king's power that washed over him, easing his anxiety and desire to change. Gene blinked at that. Domhnall could hold him in place, and he had never met a wolf who could do that. His gaze slid to Rolf, and he suspected he could hold his brother as well. This was a mighty wolf who could stop two alphas from shifting into wolf form. *Moon save me*, he thought.

"And this is Lily De Vere," his mother said in a soft but triumphant voice, as if presenting a prize.

Domhnall just stood there, quiet, not even breathing. "Lily?" he said breathily, with a trace of uncertainty and repressed emotion.

Lily narrowed her gaze. Gene noted her complexion paled. There was a wetness in the corner of her eyes, and she clenched and unclenched her fists at her sides. He had never seen her so rocked emotionally. "Am ... Am I meant to know you?" she asked in a voice that shook.

Reeva came up and put her arm around her. "Not really. I don't think you have met."

Lily looked ready to faint. "But ..."

Gene sprang into action and went to her, taking his mother's place in supporting her. "Come and sit down, Lily. I think there's a story here."

Reeva's eyes sparkled, and Gene knew that look. "Indeed," Reeva said.

Energies, magical and mythical, swirled in the room. Lily was trying to assess the situation, he was sure. Gene had to keep his power reined in to not conflict with the visiting alpha werewolf. The other could hold him in place, but that did not mean he could prevent energy tides and subliminal conflict leaking out. Gene was very uncomfortable, as he was not master of this situation. His mother, though, was calm and enjoying every moment.

At Reeva's direction, they pulled out some dining chairs so they could all sit in the lounge room with their guests. Lily sat in the dining chair he pulled out and he drew another to sit next to her. He took one of her hands and squeezed it gently. She didn't look at him, but neither did she take back her hand. Reeva drew out chairs for her guests, too.

"I've come a long way to meet ye," Domhnall said, taking a seat opposite.

"Meet me?" Lily replied, her eyes widening. She cast a sidelong look at Gene, and he shrugged as he knew as much as she did.

"Yes, you see Reeva told me a story of a small child, with magical abilities, who had been found on a boat from Ireland about twenty-five years ago. She told me that girl had been brought up by witches but was only a half-witch herself. The coven that cared for her didn't know what the other half was and maybe they didn't keep looking for her family to find out. This girl had a distinctive look, particularly the white mane of hair." He gestured with both hands at his own white mane.

Lily squeezed Gene's hand hard. "White hair?" Her voice was faint, as if speaking up had suddenly become impossible.

"I had a relationship with a young witch, years before I became alpha of the Donegal pack. My father was a harsh man, and he didn't approve of my liaison with Aoife."

Gene kept his gaze on Lily, watched her chest rise and fall. He really needed to speak to his mother about springing this on them, on Lily. He worried she was going to break apart, shatter in front of them all. He returned the pressure of Lily's hand in his.

"Aoife disappeared and I couldn't find her anywhere. I didn't know at the time that my father had a hand in it. Nor did I know she was carrying my child. Our child. It never occurred to me, you see, that a werewolf could make a child with a witch."

"It's not possible," Lily said in a choked voice. Her distressed, distracted gaze latched on to Gene. "Is it?"

Gene shook his head, shrugged. It had to be possible.

The White Wolf of Donegal nodded sagely. "It's not meant to be possible. But something went right in our union. Some alignment of magic."

Lily looked between the white wolves, and he saw the fear in her eyes. "Anyway, Reeva told me about you, and I did some digging at my end. I'm certain you are that child, Lily."

"No, it can't be." Lily had tears in her eyes. "I'm not part werewolf. I can't be."

"But you are part something," Reeva said.

Lily faced his mother. "Yes, but the coven theorised I was part pixie or something. I don't have werewolf in me. I don't have any werewolf inclinations. The moon doesn't change me. I have a terrible sense of smell. You must be mistaken."

Reeva shook her head. "There are signs."

The white wolf started speaking again. "I found your mother, Lily," Domhnall said quietly. "She told me about your birth, about how she took care of you for a couple of years until one day you were taken."

"My mother?" Lily replied, her voice choked with tears. "She's alive?"

"Yes," he replied quietly. Gene was surprised how gently this large werewolf spoke, how still he held himself. "She's alive. She couldn't come here, though. Not right now. But she told me enough. I also found the wolf who took you and hid you on that ship. He was meant to kill you but couldn't do it. He couldn't do what my bastard of a father wanted of him."

"Reeva sent me a photo of you from when they found you. You were wearing the same clothes."

Rolf blurted. "She's half werewolf!"

Abbie grinned. "I told you she smelt funny."

Gene jumped at his brother's interjection and Abbie's comment. He remembered her making it and hadn't taken it seriously. He thought Abbie was just being snarky. Lily always showered, twice to three times a day if she could. The witches must have been able to smell the wolf on her and taught her to wash it off. He had never smelt anything, just the spice that was Lily.

Lily seemed to sink into herself. There was a lot to digest. It also explained a few things. The way her magic coiled around him and the fierce attraction between them. They had shared dreams, so real, so erotic. Not something he had experienced before, such things were the stuff of romantic fantasy, but her being half-were could account for it. He narrowed his eyes. Even then it would have to be a strong connection, like that between mates. He shivered at the thought.

Lily sat unmoving, though tears spilled down her cheeks. He squeezed her hand again, and she squeezed back, not taking her eyes off the White Wolf of Donegal.

"I'm Irish?" she said and laughed, a laugh that had a hysterical edge.

The white wolf smiled, light shining in his eyes. Gene thought he wanted to grab Lily to him and hold her tight, but as a father who had no history with his child, he could not unless invited. Gene bit his bottom lip, his heart twisting in sympathy with the large wolf. He tried to think of what it would feel like if it was him in this position and just froze. His gaze slid to Rolf and he remembered all the emotion he had felt finding he had a brother—the denial, the anger, and then the acceptance. This moment must be a hundred times worse for Lily.

"Mother, bring Lily a stiff drink. She needs it," Gene said.

That comment broke the mood. Domhnall barked out a laugh near to raise the ceiling. His son just gazed at Lily as if he'd met a goddess.

"You're my sister," he said in a quiet voice. "That's amazing."

Lily shifted her gaze to her younger brother. "And I have a brother. Who knew?"

Reeva shoved a small snifter of brandy into Lily's hand. Lily upended the drink and gasped. Looking from face to face, Lily sniffed and then burst into tears. The snifter dropped into her lap as she covered her face with her hands. Gene picked it up and handed it to his mother. Their gazes locked and there was something strange in his mother's eyes. He tried to assess it but couldn't. He would have to find out later when they had some time and privacy. Right now, Lily needed him, and he needed to focus on her, on her needs.

❧

THROUGH THE TEARS, LILY STRUGGLED WITH A SURGE IN EMOTIONS and the disarray of her mind. She was speechless, the most speechless she had ever been in her life. This was not the moment she expected such revelations, either. She clung to Gene's hand; he seemed to be such a rock, a solid, unwavering presence. She could barely look his way, so she leaned her head on his shoulder and blubbered like a baby. His warmth enveloped her, and he held her close to him, whispering comforting words.

After the storm passed, she pulled away and wiped her eyes with the backs of her hands. Reeva passed her a box of tissues. She took a bunch of them, blew her nose. "Sorry," she said to Gene. There was a big, wet patch on his sweater. Gene gave her a slight smile, concern evident in his expression. "This is big news, Lily. You're entitled to feel everything."

She nodded and fought a new onslaught of tears. This revelation warred with everything she had thought about her heritage, the position she had forged in her mind a cross between curiosity and not caring to know. She had accepted that she may never know. Never, ever, had she thought her heritage involved a werewolf. She had every right to be sceptical and bewildered and upset.

Reeva had cleaved her with this revelation, with this meeting. As far as she knew, Reeva meant nothing evil by it. If anything, she sensed the other woman's delight, as if she had won the lottery. Even more so, if she had wanted a spectacular father, she had certainly delivered. A brother too.

The timing of this meeting was not good. There were so many things going on, and now she had to take time to understand her heritage. That was most inconvenient. Of all the things she imagined herself to be, it was not half-werewolf and half-witch. She had no particular affiliation with the moon, other than standard witch rituals. It did not call to her in any weird way. She was going to argue against what she had been told again when her father brought out a file from inside his coat.

Her heart stopped when he brought out the photos. The one of her mother snared her attention, hooked into her heart. She picked it up. Small and dark-haired, with a pixie look on her face so much like her own. She ran her finger down the picture and just then, a memory surfaced. That face laughing and calling to her. But her name wasn't Lily, it was Shauna. Her mother had called her Shauna. It was like a large bell had tolled in her insides. Her hands shook, tears fell. "Mama!" she said, as if from the past. She looked up at her father. "That's my mother."

Nodding, he let out a long sigh. "Yes," her father said. He picked up another photo of her mother and him when they were younger. She could see how much Connor looked like his father at that age. Then there was a photo of her as a child. She couldn't have been more than three and wearing the same pinafore and blouse that she had arrived in on the ship. The same outfit she'd been wearing the day she had been kidnapped, apparently.

The news pressed into her. Belief warred with disbelief. She studied her father and her brother, assessing, trying to press them into herself. "I'm your daughter?"

Domhnall nodded, tears leaking down his olive-skinned cheeks. Her colouring was very similar to his. She was part of him. But a werewolf? That was beyond anything she had ever imagined. It wasn't that she was against werewolves or had a prejudice against them. She had fancied Gene, after all. It was something she had never considered and was thus an alien concept.

She needed time to process this news. Never had she allowed herself to dwell on her origins or even imagine what they might be. She had accepted what the coven had said. It was Reeva who pushed beyond that to find the truth. Why?

She lifted her head and locked gazes with Reeva. "How did you put it together?"

The older woman nodded. "Instinct at first. There was something about you, something I had to know." She shrugged and wiped at a tear on her cheek. "It's big news, important news, and once Domhnall here found out about you, it was impossible to stop him from coming to meet you. Even if the timing wasn't perfect." Her gaze shifted to her, Gene and then to Rolf. "I know how family secrets can tie one up, deny a person knowledge of who they are and where they come from. I was complicit in that once. Not again."

Gene sat back and gave her some room. Her father leaned in and picked up her hand that lay in her lap. His hands were big, calloused and warm. It was their first ever contact, skin on skin. Power tingled over her fingers. She could feel his alpha strength. It registered in her bones, her skin, and her mind. A gasp escaped her.

Narrowing her eyes, she stared into her father's eyes, a hazel green, like meadows under storm clouds. Something stirred inside. Like a cat darting out of a closed cupboard door. It meshed with her magic self. Her heart lurched and her skin sweated. "Goddess, what was that?"

Her father smiled. "Meet your wolf, Lily."

Lily stilled, feeling this sensation that swirled in her gut, in her chest, and in her mind. It was familiar, and she'd always thought it was her magic, but now she could see it was separate. She was not a werewolf, as far as she could tell. She couldn't transform or anything like that. It was the spirit of the wolf inside her, part of her. It had always been part of her.

"My mother's name for me was Shauna," she said, as if from far away.

He nodded and sniffed. "I know. You have been Lily for so long, it's fine for you to keep it that way. No shame in that."

A little laugh escaped her. He had come here and turned her life upside down. It would take time for her to process everything. It would take time to get to know him and Connor. And she did want to get to know him. It wasn't his fault that she had been kidnapped. That her mother had kept her existence secret. That the coven didn't trace back her passage on the ship she'd been found on. She always knew she was different, separate. Now she felt a part of something, even though it was not what she had expected.

He inclined his head, eyes glowing with kindness. "You could be known as the White Wolf-Witch of Donegal."

Her eyes widened in surprise. Then a laugh burst out of her. "I would if I wanted to be pretentious." She wiped tears from her eyes and blew her nose. They were all watching her, and she couldn't meet their gaze. "And if I had ever been to Donegal."

Her father laughed aloud and drew out a handkerchief to wipe his own eyes. She figured her father was quite aware that his title, White Wolf of Donegal, was rather pretentious sounding.

"Aye, well we can remedy the not been to Donegal, but the pretentious part comes in useful now and then."

It warmed her heart to know that he owned it. After blubbering all over Gene, she couldn't face him. She could feel his heat, feel his watchful wolf's presence, and it was scary because the wolf in her was entirely too aware of him. It lusted after him. That realisation hit home, and it explained so much. Her wolf must have a thing for confident and arrogant beings because Gene had irritated her at first and, now, he was a comfort. Elvira was really going to crack when she heard this latest development about Lily's life. She imagined Elvira saying; 'You want to bed a werewolf and now your father is one. Only in Sydney could I hear such a tale'.

"Let's eat!" Reeva announced, and that broke the mood.

Lily was running on empty and all the emotion, the crying and stress, had taken all her energy. She had to refuel before she melted into a puddle of flesh. Reeva asked them to put their chairs back around the dining table. Gene stayed by her, ready to steady her. Her father loomed as well. He was tall and broad and although he was an older man, the echoes of what he must have been lingered there. No wonder her mother fell for him, werewolf or not. Lily had a sudden desire to meet her mother.

Emotion levels dropped as the practical part of eating came to the fore such as the taking of places at the table. "Time enough for more conversation later," Gene said.

"Yes. We must refuel." Reeva went into the kitchen and, a few minutes later, brought out the first large platter. As Lily had seen these platters before, she was doubly surprised when Reeva brought out another one equally full.

"Come on. Take a seat. Eat!" Reeva's summons was a call to action. They moved towards the seats. Rolf homed in on a platter of meat, with Abbie close behind. They just piled meat onto their plates. Connor appeared to be in competition. He had a plate, he forked food onto it and sat down, picked up a piece of meat, saw something else, put it down and grabbed the new thing and then repeated that action. Her father stood and waited, and she realised he would not join in until she took a place at the table. Gene hovered by her side, and she didn't know what to say to him or how to look at him.

"Lily? Are you all right?"

Lily pulled at her lip, mostly to stop herself from shouting at him in front of everyone that no, she wasn't all right. This had rocked her, rocked her sense of self. It changed everything. It changed her relationship with him.

He put his arm around her shoulders and hugged her to him. "Don't," she said. "Don't ask me. I'm not ready."

Gene lifted his arm away. "I get it. I'm here if you need me. We all are." He talked with Rolf and Abbie, nodding to Domhnall and Connor and offering them food.

Reeva came over. "Come along and eat something. It will get easier."

"Easy for you to say," Lily said without heat.

Reeva chuckled as she dumped a huge serve of meat onto her plate. Her stomach churned. How could she eat and make small talk with these strangers that were the first close family she had ever met? But what else was she going to do? Run to her room and cry into her pillow? Run to Elvira and complain that the coven got it wrong? *Poor me. I'm a werewolf!* That made her smile. No way would she do that. She didn't know what she was going to say to Elvira and the rest of the coven. It was fine to make light of it. The reality, though, would be something else. Ripples, she thought. Ripples in the coven and in the werewolf world here in Sydney.

Reeva leaned into her, drawing close. "Darling, Lily. Don't you understand? You're special. Always have been and always will be." Reeva picked up a plate. "You're also one of us, and we look after our own."

Lily blanched. That couldn't be right. Didn't Reeva say she wasn't good enough for Gene? No, she hadn't said that. She'd said Lily was 'not for him', and she had interpreted it that way.

Her gaze shifted sideways to Gene as he was talking to Connor and eating. They seemed to get on well. She swallowed. Of Gene, she was more aware than before. If anything, the attraction was stronger. Reeva might say she was special, but she was still neither one thing nor another. She still didn't fit in, didn't fit anyone's norm. *But at least I know what I am. Who I am hasn't changed. I'm Lily De Vere and I have a job to do.*

The storm of emotions made her feel exhausted. She ate. She didn't recall what food passed her lips. Nor did she recollect what she said to anyone. Her father sat close to her, and she was aware of him on so many levels. However, he gave her some distance. He didn't try to talk to her, he was just there, smiling whenever she made eye contact. His werewolf magic comforted her, and she drew it in instinctively. He was trying not to crowd, to overwhelm her, even though his very presence did that. It was going to take time to get used to him, what he was, and she wished herself forward to a day when their relationship was one of familiarity and comradeship. She trembled with the knowledge that there was going to be a long-term relationship, and she wanted that relationship to happen. Her life would change.

Too soon, the party broke up and that cocooning warmth of her father's were vibe dissipated. "May we talk again?" he asked her, putting out his hand.

She put her hand in his and met his gaze. "Yes, I'd like that." His hand dwarfed hers and he squeezed it gently before releasing it.

Connor nodded to her, a wicked smile on his face. "See you again, sis."

Lily lifted her lips, trying to smile, only feeling awkward instead. "See you."

It was inane, really, that response. As the door shut on them, she realised there was so much she didn't know, that she didn't ask. It was all about her and the revelations of her birth, her kidnapping. But Domhnall had obviously married, taken a mate who wasn't her mother. Connor was her brother, but was there more? A sister? Cousins? It was Ireland, of course, she'd have cousins.

Mechanically, Lily walked over to the table and started to clear the plates. In a dream, she scraped the leftovers, rinsed the dishes and stuffed them in the dishwasher. Abbie, Rolf and Reeva were there, too, but she didn't notice their interaction, just their presence on the periphery of her awareness. When everything was all tidied up, she turned, and they were gone. The overhead lights were off, only a table lamp was on. She was alone. All except for him.

Gene stood there, just looking at her. She met his gaze and sank into it. She didn't know how long she stood there, just staring until his arms swept around her, drawing her close.

"Oh Lily, I'm so sorry this has happened to you. Without warning. Without a hint. I swear to you I didn't know."

Lily rested her cheek on his chest as he spoke these words over her head, his breath brushing against her hair. "I ... er ..."

She wished she had a witty comeback. Being floored had derailed her ability.

"How are you handling things?" Gene asked in a soft voice. His heat surrounded her, penetrated her, and she relaxed into him.

"Badly?" she said, rubbing her cheek against his chest. "I don't know what to think or feel."

"Understandable. It must be pretty confusing."

"Yes," she said. "And also no, in some ways."

"Does it make sense to you, though, what Domhnall told you?"

"Yes," she said, rubbing her face into his sweater, hearing his heartbeat. "I remembered my mother. Just for a moment, a scene that sprang at me when I saw the photo. A buried memory."

"Oh, my God."

"Yes, like an arrow to the heart. Take this you. Truth."

Gene exhaled slowly and hugged her tighter. "What a turn up. And my mother knew."

"She said she suspected at first. She can't have known when she hired me."

"Why did she warn me off?" Gene shook his head. "She said you were not for me. I didn't like hearing that."

Lily nodded. "I didn't either. Possibly because I didn't like what it meant."

By then, they were pressed tightly together. Nothing much was left to her imagination. His erection made its presence felt.

She leaned back, meeting his eyes, and said, "Perhaps it has something to do with werewolf rituals and politics."

Gene's eyes rested on the creamy flesh of the top of her breasts, arrayed in the bodice of her dress. The dress she had argued with Reeva over. She had loved and hated it, but had worn it because Reeva had begged her to. No one had begged her to do anything before. It had made no sense at the time. She liked how she looked, liked how

Gene looked at her in it. Liked the hot coals of desire that had flared to life in his eyes when she had walked into the room.

That desire was now rampant in his gaze. Excitement curled in her gut. The wolf prowled inside her, aware of Gene, wanting him. Her breath caught at this realisation. The wolf was her, too. She wanted him.

His head lowered, and she lifted her mouth to meet his. His heat spilled into her mouth, his tongue stoking her desire. She opened to him and then she detected it. His wolf meeting hers. He broke the kiss and aimed for her neck, nuzzling under her ears, sending bolts of weakness into her legs and small shocks into her brain.

He growled, a deep resonance that had her body undulating as passion flooded into her veins. As if his voice called to all her cells and demanded that they pay attention to him. Her breaths sped up as his lips trailed kisses down to the top of her left breast and then along the right. Pools of heat made her nipples contract, and she had this hankering for him to put her nipples into his mouth. Suck until she screamed out, until her clit throbbed so hard, she'd come.

She couldn't be that bold in person. She could not demand. This was crazy. What was she doing? What were they doing? Gene worked a breast free, and his hot mouth latched on. Her knees buckled, but his other hand had her by a butt cheek. The noise she made was inarticulate but joyous. Her breast felt heavy as he firmly stroked it, making the nipple peak, the suction taking her to the very edge of desire and pain. She wanted him to stop, and she wanted him to never stop. Her back bent, giving him greater access. "Gene!"

Her mind was turning white with need. Coherent thought fled. Gene made his way to the other breast, flicking her breast free and capturing that nipple with his tongue, sucking it. Lily's brain was short-circuiting. There was only his hot mouth and her teased nipple, creating havoc in her body. She was wet and ready and, Goddess, how could he keep doing that, making it thrill and hurt and drown her in want?

His hand slid up her thigh. She was about to fly apart. A moan escaped her. She said his name. His lips returned to hers, hungry, determined as his fingers slid into her panties. Goddess, she was hot and wet and so close to coming. He touched her, and she bucked. So tender, so close. His fingers moved urgently over her clit, once, twice. His mouth once again on her breasts, slipping from one nipple to the other. Incoherent sounds escaped her throat, groans and cries. Frenzied with lust, she broke apart, her ecstasy spilling out, her legs buckling.

Gene held her, whispered into her ears, as the quakes settled. "Oh, Lily. Beautiful Lily. How hot and spicy you are."

She clung to him, shuddering as the climax washed through her. He pecked her on the lips, his blue gaze studying her. "Are you all right?"

Edging away, she met his gaze. She was confused and not confused, bold and not bold. It was definitely weird. "Yes." She moved her tousled hair out of her face. "I ... er ... it's been a mind-blowing evening all round. That was ... er ..."

"Fucking wonderful," Gene said with a smile. "A promise of more to come."

She held his gaze, seeing more than a promise there. Weakness claimed her limbs. He ducked down, put his arm under her knees and lifted her. "You, my dear one, are in dire need of bed. Tomorrow is going to be another big day and you need your beauty sleep."

Bemused, she tried to shift her breasts back into her dress and gave up trying when he kicked open the door to her room. He laid her on the bed and stood up. "Will you be all right?"

"Yes. Thank you." Her head lay on the pillow and her eyes closed. He pressed his lips to her forehead, and then she heard the door click closed. Opening her eyes, she saw he had turned out the light. She struggled up, took off her shoes, and unzipped the dress and wiggled out of it, and then lifted the bedcovers and slid in.

Things had definitely changed on so many levels. She had family, she knew what she was, and she knew she wanted to fuck Gene's brains out the first chance she got. Bugger Reeva's veto. Her wolf definitely called to Gene's. He didn't need a voice of liquid honey to get into her pants, he just had to growl, and she'd be wet and ready. Her body still rode the orgasm he gave her It was great to understand finally what was going on between them.. She giggled to herself. Animal attraction.

Whether there was a future for them, she didn't know. However, she had a whole new future to explore. She hadn't thought of going to Ireland before. Now there was someone there she wanted to meet. Her mother lived. Her mother had wanted her. Her father would have wanted her, if he had known about her. He wanted her now. She slipped into sleep, troubled by dreams and scenarios that she rode like a rollercoaster. Until everything went quiet and deep sleep claimed her.

CHAPTER 16

Lily woke early the next morning, pushing a tangle of hair out of her eyes, feeling hungover and tired. Events from the previous evening piled in, filling her up with dismay and excitement. She wasn't keen to get out of bed. With Rolf and Abbie there, she didn't have to hurry to guard Gene. They were ample. She had met her father and her brother. It still blew her away.

With everything that was going on, she had not been prepared for such a revelation. How long had Reeva been organising this visit? Of course, they could have flown as soon as they found out about her, but she remembered there was a scent of the sea on them but maybe that's because they lived near the Donegal coast. She wondered why her mother had not come to see her too. Something prevented it. Lily had no way of knowing or even guessing that, so put it on the backburner. She needed to rally to deal with what was in front of her. Time enough to see her mother. It was important to get used to these changes to her life, so she could try to gain some equilibrium. A sense of balance was necessary to access her powers, to function at her best. At the moment, she was not at her peak potential.

The recollection of her interlude with Gene flooded back in. Goddess, that was hot. Gene was very hot. She wanted him. No more erotic dreaming, she wanted to actually fuck him until he begged for mercy. Her father had released her wolf, and her wolf wanted Gene, like light attracted moths. It hurt to think that Reeva would oppose them getting together. She admired and respected Reeva, as a person, as a den mother, and many more things besides. She reminded her of Elvira, which had symmetry to it. Mentor mother types on both sides of her heritage.

"Fuck me, I'm a wolf and a witch."

Saying it aloud created a permanence about it. Like acknowledgement was halfway to acceptance.

She thought about whether knowing about her heritage earlier would have helped her navigate her relationship with Gene and shook her head. "No idea." She couldn't think straight. Her phone pinged. It was Reeva.

Are you awake? I'm meeting Domhnall and Connor for a harbour cruise. Are you up for that?

She typed a response. *Yes. Okay. Who's coming?*

Me and you. Gene, Rolf and Abbie are off to follow a trail of the renegade vampire.

Lily lowered the phone and stared at the ceiling. The choice conflicted her. She wanted to go with the others to find who was behind the attacks, and she wanted the opportunity to get to know her father and brother. This was a unique time. The first time doesn't come twice.

Reeva sent another message that included the time they were leaving. Lily climbed out of bed, squinting from a headache. A shower would restore her. She glanced at her phone, thinking to call Elvira, and thought better of it. She needed to get this day over first, get to the end, and then assess everything all over again.

Hot needles of water massaged her aching body. Who knew emotional surprises could make one feel so tired and sore? Her breasts tingled, and that sensation brought back the feel of Gene's mouth on her, the heavy draw on her breasts at the suction that caused so much delight. He had made her come with just the briefest touch on her clit. What a powerful climax! She wanted more of that, but it wasn't going to happen today. She could have used the secondary shower nozzle to take the edge off, but where was the fun in that? Better to be ready for her next encounter with Gene Cohen. She would have her wits about her then, and he would be the one begging for mercy.

There was so much going on, and the introduction to her father and brother had certainly sent her into a spin. Time enough to sort through all this and what it meant. What could she wear for a day on a boat? She rummaged through her bag. Shorts, a singlet top and an overshirt. Flip-flops were all she had besides her boots and the strappy things that Reeva had given her yesterday. There was definitely something going on with Reeva and, despite being a private eye, she didn't know what. She was going to find out, but it felt like she had to wait for the end of the movie to discover the truth. The den mother had no ill intent, she knew, so it didn't bother her that much.

An hour later, she was standing on the wharf with Reeva at a yacht club near the northern beaches. Reeva was dressed elegantly in a wafting silk pantsuit with a sailor-type theme. It looked simple, but she bet it cost a fortune. On Reeva's feet were classy leather pumps. It was a private wharf and a motor yacht bobbed off the side. It had three levels and looked very schmick. "Not mine," Domhnall said as he held out his hand to assist her on board. He was also attired in a naval theme: navy cargo pants, white polo shirt, with a captain's hat askew on his head. "It's a loan from a friend. It's got two cabins, a nice lounging area called the galley, and goes very fast. As the swell isn't too bad, we should have smooth sailing."

"Do you know your way around the harbour?" she asked, stepping onto the boat. Connor assisted Reeva.

Domhnall smiled, and his chest expanded as he laughed. "Oh, I'm not driving this thing. Pete there is. He's one of Gene's pack." He winked at her. "We can talk freely about anything, and you can tell me about this beautiful city of yours. It has to be the most picturesque harbour I've ever seen. So blue too, the sky and all. And so warm."

Lily narrowed her gaze. Was he kidding? "Don't you have blue skies in Ireland?"

He smiled broadly and lifted his head as if taking in the wide expanse above him. "To be honest, not often. Not like this." He said this with an accent that she had to listen to carefully to understand him.

Connor came over. Like her, he was dressed plainly. Cut off jean shorts, black T-shirt with a Black Sabbath logo, and loafers with no socks. He had a wide-brimmed hat on. Very sensible. He had fine blond hairs on his legs, she noticed. He was lean, but well-muscled. "You might get sunburnt once every ten years," her brother said. "You're more likely to get windburn or your skin scoured by wind and rain." He shrugged. "The only difference between the seasons is in winter your bollocks get frozen off."

She laughed and tried to imagine the weather. Sydney rarely got cold in winter. Not that kind of cold.

"You need a hat," Reeva said, making a face. She ducked inside the main cabin and came back with a straw hat, wide-brimmed with a pink band and dried flowers attached. Given how sunny it was going to be, Lily didn't argue, but accepted it with thanks. She didn't put it on straight away, but if she was going to be outside she definitely would. Being sore and beetroot coloured was not part of her plan. A healing spell would sort that, but why tempt fate?

Her father guided her into the main cabin and showed her to a seat. "Ireland is very green, you understand. That's because it rains a lot. We have some marvellous countryside, though. Mountains and cliffs and rugged coast land—"

"And peat bogs," interrupted Connor.

"Get away with you," Domhnall said. "It's a beautiful land, an ancient land, full of ghosts and faerie and songs. Great food, too, and some good booze."

Pete, the pilot, greeted her. Connor and Pete went to cast off the mooring lines. Reeva stayed on the back deck, looking out at the view as they pulled away from the dock. Lily was alone with her father. It didn't feel contrived, just a natural occurrence as people arranged themselves.

"Why didn't my mother come?" she asked, studying him to see if she could read him.

He sighed. "Your mother is in a spot of bother and can't quite get here."

Lily sat up straight as her mind raced through the possibilities. If she was sick, he would've said. "She's in prison?"

"Aw no, not exactly prison. Her coven has her under an interdict. She's not allowed to go anywhere."

Lily blinked. She hadn't heard of the Sydney coven putting anyone under interdict, but there was that guy that ran off before they could. A bad seed, apparently. He would certainly be locked up if he came back.

"Is she all right? Did she do something wrong?"

He shook his head. "I don't want to lie to you. She's okay, if unhappy. The coven thinks she did something against their law, associated with the wrong people. She's not a bad person, truly."

Lily sighed. "So I will have to go there to see her."

"Aye, well yes. For the moment, yes." He poured her a drink of mineral water. "If you want something stronger, just let me know. We have all kinds. I think Reeva has ordered a big lunch, too."

He patted his belly, which had kind of a spread but not much of one compared to the bulk of him. "Water is fine." Her gaze slid to Reeva again. "Reeva has been very kind and thoughtful."

He also looked over to the den mother, who appeared absorbed in looking about her, at the waves, the shore and the passing boats. She waved at one. "Indeed. No one has ever sent me such wonderful news. I'm very glad to be meeting with you. Thank you for agreeing to it."

Lily wiggled her head as she took this in. She hadn't really had a choice about meeting him and, it being a surprise and all, she'd had no time to think about or prepare a refusal. Luckily, she liked what she had found and knew deep inside that she belonged with this man and her brother. They were a part of her and, until she met them, she didn't know how much she needed to know about them. "I'm happy to be here, too. May I ask, do I have other siblings besides Connor? Are you married? Where do you live?"

Domhnall nodded after each question, not quite able to answer given they were delivered so rapid fire. "You do, another from your mother. Fiadh is fifteen and as dark as you are fair. She's taken after your mother. Her father I don't know about and, as it's not really my business, I never asked. As for me, I've been married twice. My first wife, Niamh, died in an accident. That's Connor's mother. I have another wife now, name of Bessie and we have a wee girl called Marigold, hair as red as a sunset after a storm. She's turning six years old soon. She's a bit of hard work for an old man like me."

Lily laughed. She wasn't that sensitive to his werewolf power. She could detect this older man's status, but his physical presence was quite strong, and he looked robust and barely old enough to be her father. He didn't look a day over forty. "That's lovely."

"They want to meet you, when you're ready. We live in Donegal, on the coast, in a small village. You won't know it and you probably can't pronounce it either, but if you can get yourself to Donegal airport, I'll collect you and then you can see for yourself."

"I'd like that." She sipped her drink, her mind agreeably engaged thinking about that trip, that land, that place, and those people. People who belonged to her. It was weird.

"How long have you and Gene Cohen been friendly like?" He studied her and she noticed.

"I don't know what you mean, actually. Reeva hired me to investigate the murder of her husband, his father. Then he hired me."

He gave a quick flick of his head. "You seem a bit more friendly than that."

Her cheeks flushed, and she broke his gaze to look out the window. After a shrug, she glanced back at him. "Why do you ask?"

"I can smell him on you. That's why I was curious." He narrowed his eyes. "I wanted to know if your heart was here."

"My heart?" she asked, surprised.

"If you're free, you can come back with us. Meet your family, your mother, get to know your people."

"What makes you think I'm not free?" She frowned. While she liked the idea of visiting them at some stage, going back with them now was a bit too soon. A bit immediate. What about the investigation? What about Gene? Her gaze flicked to Reeva and then back again. If Reeva had heard, she gave no inkling. She wouldn't put it past the den mother to have very acute hearing.

His gaze slid to Reeva, who was still outside, pretending to enjoy the view. She understood the look, but didn't understand his meaning.

"Reeva? But ..." Lily frowned. "You've got it wrong. She told Gene I wasn't for him and forbade him from touching me."

"But he has touched you, aye?"

She wasn't used to being quizzed on her life, her sexlife or any other part of her life. She was half annoyed and half ... she didn't know ... touched, maybe?

She let out a sigh, cast a quick look in Reeva's direction, and then whispered. "A little."

Domhnall half shut his eyelids and then opened them and his mouth. "A little? I've not heard of that before. What do you mean a little?"

A groan escaped her and her fists were tight as they rested on her thighs. "It means we haven't ... consummated our relationship ... and I'm not saying we have a relationship. There's an attraction there. Meeting you explained everything. I have an inner wolf." She tapped her chest. "My inner wolf has the hots for Gene."

Her father nodded. "I've never heard of being a werewolf, or part werewolf in your case, as explaining everything. It usually makes things complicated."

Lily lowered her chin and regarded her father. "What do you mean?"

"Well, what do you think about him, otherwise, without the inner wolf being involved?"

A sigh escaped her. "Oh, well, at first, I thought he was a dick. Then I thought he was just a ladies' man who wanted to bed every attractive woman he sees with no sense of commitment or emotional engagement. Now that I know him better, I'm not so sure. I haven't figured him out. He's also a bit of a pain in the arse. Argumentative. Stubborn. You get me?"

"You find him attractive?"

Lily's mouth fell open. "Frustratingly, yes. I have succumbed to his charms, I think. He can certainly kiss." She coughed and blushed. Why did she tell him that? "But I know it would be nothing more than a quick liaison."

Her father blinked slowly, twice. "And that's the definition of a little bit."

Reeva came into the galley at that moment. "A little bit of what?"

"A joke, Reeva," Domhnall said before Lily could blurt out the truth. He climbed out of the lounge he was sprawled in. "We should sit where we can see the view. Have you had your fill already?"

"Oh, no. I came in to encourage you to come outside."

Lily sat for a moment to reel in her emotions. Why was he asking about Gene? Did he think Gene would prevent her from visiting Ireland? Why would Gene give a rat's arse about what she did? She put on her hat and smeared sunscreen on her exposed skin. It was 50+ so it had better work.

They went onto the deck, and Reeva did a good job of pointing out the highlights. She pointed to a house at a place called Coasters Retreat. "That's my little holiday place. I haven't been for a while, which is such a pity. You can only access it via water and my runabout needs a new motor. I will have to make time, though. My neighbours will think I'm dead." Later, they passed Scotland Island. Reeva pointed to a small cottage. "That's Gene's place there. He built in himself when he was a young man. He was very pleased with himself. It's a one-person place. Not flash like some of the other properties."

Lily studied the building, little more than a boatshed, and tried to imagine a young Gene there, building it, being alone and enjoying the solitude. There was a lot of bush on the island, so a young werewolf would have plenty of space to roam. She shook her head. Why was she thinking about him? Was he safe? Had they found the rogue vampire progeny? Her phone was quiet. No message even. She couldn't bring her device out and sour this trip and her time with her father. Reeva wouldn't be happy. As Gene's mother appeared unconcerned about her son's safety, so should she.

Around lunchtime, they pulled into another wharf where a caterer waited for them. After they transferred the food over, Reeva set out the meal. "This is terrific, Mrs C," remarked Connor as he shoved a king prawn into his mouth. "Tastes as good as scampi!"

Her father had taken a liking to a seafood-mac-n-cheese dish and some delicious meatballs. Lily had taken some fennel salad and smoked fish on a delicate roll. Reeva smiled as if them loving the food was the best thing ever. She knew Reeva was way more than just a thoughtful hostess. She was shrewd, manipulative, and calculating. A lot of what she did was accomplished through meeting people, putting them together, pulling them apart. She was Gene's mother, after all, and he must have learned his methods from her.

After lunch, they lounged around on the benches in the galley, nursing their full stomachs. Lily had relaxed enough to lean against her father as they made room on the other lounge for Reeva. Connor was trying his hand at fishing on the little platform at the back of the boat. Being young, his stomach had the capacity to expand around the meal.

"Tell me more about your childhood. Why was your father so harsh?" she closed her eyes and listened to Domhnall talk. She loved the lilt and tilt of his voice, even though the tale was quite sad. Times had been tough for them all. No work. Hard to find food and keep a roof over their heads. Fishermen drowning. Then the whole fishing industry closing down once they joined the European union. "Things are better now. Mostly."

She listened to him breathe, inhaled the scent of him and just felt at home. It wasn't the same as knowing him her whole life, but it was a beginning. After a bit of activity, Pete tied the boat to a buoy. It rocked gently while Connor and Pete fished off the back of the boat. Lily snuggled next to her father, closed her eyes and dozed off.

Sometime later, a yell from Connor had them surging awake. Lily sat up, rubbed her eyes and shared a look with her father. "The lad's caught something," Domhnall said, as he surged out of his seat and scrambled toward the stern.

She followed. On the platform at the back of the boat Connor struggled to land a large fish. "That's massive," she exclaimed, seeing the silver fins beneath the water.

"Don't lose it, lad."

Concentrating on the fish at the end of his line, straining to draw it in, he snarled over his shoulder. "I'm trying not to, Da, but he's a fighter."

Domhnall patted him on the back and refrained from any more talk. It took a few more minutes and Connor finally brought it on board. "My, that's a beauty. What is it?" his father asked as he looked on.

Pete came over to look, whistling as Connor held it in front of him with both hands. "That's a very fat kingfish, mate. What did you use for bait?"

Domhnall bumped shoulders with his son. "Don't tell 'em."

Connor shrugged and laughed. "The squid you gave me." He shook his head at his father. "Da, he gave me the kit and the bait. It wouldn't be fair now, would it, to keep mum?"

Domhnall tossed his head back and laughed. "I suppose now you've had your fun, we should get back."

Reeva stood with hands on hips, regarding them all. "Yes, I wonder how the others got on today. Are you feeling well now, Lily?"

Lily looked over, surprised by the enquiry. "I feel fine. Thank you for arranging all of this. The food was amazing."

"You've got my son to thank for that. His boat, his pilot, his money."

Lily stilled. "I didn't know that. I didn't expect ... You have both done so much for me. Finding my family ..."

Reeva slid her gaze to Domhnall, and he nodded. That meant something, but Lily didn't know what. Inside the galley, Lily packed up the leftovers and the caterers' dishes, ready to be delivered back to the wharf. She pulled out her phone. No messages from Gene. She didn't know if that was a good thing or a bad thing. Not quite able to work it out, she chewed the inside of her cheek. As for what Reeva was up to, she wasn't even going to try to understand.

CHAPTER 17

The engine whined as Rolf shifted gears in his beat-up Golf, the car he and Abbie had driven up from Canberra in. They were headed to the address Bentino had supplied. The major road had two lanes, with parked cars along both sides. During peak hour no parking was allowed. Cars sped along the street and trucks rattled along, barely keeping within the lane markings. It took two turns of the block before they spotted a car leaving and hastened to lay claim to the parking spot. It hadn't been easy to park within view of the building and it was a fluke that they had.

Bianca Maroni's block of flats contained four apartments in a two-storey building, a rather nondescript construction built around the 1920s in dark brown brick with cream-coloured, curved mouldings under the front gables. There was limited parking and two garage doors at the front. He did not let appearances deceive him. While the aged façade was there, it could be completely modern and full of protection on the inside.

On either side were two taller 1970s apartment blocks in sand-coloured brick with generous balconies to the front and side. Not many people appeared to be about on this weekday. Gene looked up and noted that the sky was bright and clear.

A young man with an impressive hipster beard, black jeans and an open-throated white shirt walked down the driveway. He looked up and down the street, then headed away from them. Given the entire building belonged to Maroni, the man had to be one of her attendants. He didn't have the hollow look of a long-term blood donor, but that didn't mean he wasn't compromised, either through sex or blood or both.

"Wouldn't you rather be on the harbour?" Abbie asked him. "Rolf and I could've handled this. It's pretty straightforward."

He lifted an eyebrow. "If you must know, I would. I was not invited." That smarted a little. His mother had been adamant that he not be present and to let Lily enjoy some alone time with her newly found father. He was still processing that whole encounter and what it meant. Reeva played a deep game, but how any of it impacted him and his pack he did not know. An alliance? Ireland was a long way away and he could see no immediate benefit. As for how it affected his relationship with Lily ... He shook his head. What relationship? All it did at this stage was help him understand that physical attraction he had for her and maybe kindle the emotional connection between them into something more. He didn't quite understand the ramifications.

Rolf snorted. "I'm so glad my mother did not bring me up. I'd be completely henpecked."

Abbie thumped him on the shoulder. Rolf winced and then grinned at him, pointing his hand palm up at his wife. "You see what I have to put up with?"

Gene rolled his eyes at their antics. "I'm not henpecked. I respect my mother and her abilities. We clash a lot, but l love her, and I know she would never knowingly harm me." He knew Rolf and Abbie shared decision-making in their pack, and they had a healthy, if not vigorous, relationship.

Gene studied the building. "I don't believe this situation is as straightforward as it looks."

"What makes you say that? You think Bentino was lying?" Abbie asked.

"Not telling the whole truth, is more like it. You can't trust a vampire as far as you can throw him."

Abbie, new to werewolf politics and history, returned a blank stare. Rolf leaned over. "Long history between werewolves and vampires. It is rumoured we were their servants once, and they liked our blood because it gave them additional power."

Abbie sighed. "I had heard some things. I thought they liked werewolves because they like to fuck and their blood is delicious. But I should read up on it and check the facts. Anything in the library at home?"

"Hey, look." Gene pointed with his chin out the car window.

They were there to gather evidence of Maroni's involvement with the police commissioner and a dark sedan with government plates had just rolled up. The driver stayed inside and a man in a dark blue suit alighted. He was a familiar figure. However, they had to be sure. Had to have irrefutable proof. Rolf started the camera rolling. The man was facing away from them, heading into the building. It wouldn't be enough.

"I need to get closer." Gene slid out of the car. Changing shape in broad daylight was risky so he darted through the traffic in human form to get nearer. When there was a break in the traffic, the driver eased away from the curb. He'd be back, thought Gene.

It was the wrong time of the day to be visiting a vampire. She was progeny, so he doubted she had the longevity and stamina to be awake and functional in daylight. There must be some other business going down. What that could be, he had no idea and, frankly, didn't care. He just needed a better look at the man and to grab a good face shot. Better yet, a sniff. The olfactory evidence wouldn't stand up in a human court as part of testimony, though it would add conviction to his statements to his community. It would be evidence enough for weres and other paranormals.

Gene ducked down behind two very smelly rubbish bins as his quarry turned his way before disappearing inside. It was the police commissioner. He waved at the stench with his hand as he hunkered down behind the bins. He hoped Rolf got a shot of that as he had no chance to get a photo without being seen himself. Gene stayed put, figuring it wouldn't take long before the commissioner came out again. Only the human attendant would be awake now.

"Anything I can help you with?" a voice said behind him, just as something cold and hard poked him in the back. The hard thing felt like the barrel of a handgun. A big handgun. Why hadn't he smelled the man? Ah, the stench of household waste would have swamped his nose, and he had been distracted by seeing the police commissioner's face. It was something a stupid, inexperienced cub would do. He dared not turn his head towards Rolf. His accomplices would be watching, he was sure.

"Not really," Gene replied. He didn't know who it was but guessed the hipster beard guy who left before. It didn't really matter as he'd been sprung. If he didn't get shot, he thought it likely he would find out what was going on.

"Care to come inside, Mr Cohen? My mistress said you'd be dropping by."

Gene kept his eyes forward. Never trust a vampire. Bentino had warned his progeny, obviously. Werewolves knew not to trust vampires. Had known it for thousands of years and Bentino was cut from the same cloth as all the other vampires. Or his progeny had a very good spy network. It didn't matter. "I wouldn't care to disturb your mistress in her slumber."

"What makes you think she's asleep?"

Surprised, Gene tried to turn. "No," his assailant said, poking him between the shoulder blades. "Don't turn around. Take out your phone and text your friends to stay put."

He'd seen enough to know it was the hipster beard guy. Slowly, he dug out his phone, keyed in the text, showed the screen to his assailant, and sent it to Rolf. He surreptitiously sent his gaze out and spotted the small cameras that obviously covered both sides of the street and a fair way down both sides. Much more high tech than it seemed. He should've checked.

The gun jabbed in between his shoulder blades again. "Right, let's move, shall we? We have a visitor who needs proof of your true identity."

Gene shook his head, lips pulled tight. He didn't know whether to be more angry with Bentino or himself for being trussed up and delivered to the police. He didn't have to imagine what the proof was going to be.

Walking in front of the building, they turned into the entryway in full view of Rolf and Abbie. How arrogant were these vampire hangers-on to act with such impunity? They took the stairs up to the top floor. Gene was sure he could have taken the gun and toppled the guy prodding him. Tempting as that might be, he needed to crack this thing open, and what better way than to be escorted in? He was not that desperate yet.

The door opened at their approach. He looked up and saw another camera. Bianca Marconi didn't take chances. This place was wired for all contingencies. He wouldn't be surprised if they had escape tunnels, panic rooms and the like. They stepped inside the door onto a lush grey carpet. Pale grey walls and interesting artwork decorated the hall. Encouraged to keep moving, he walked past a large, modern kitchen in shades of grey and a bathroom, all black, including the throne.

The police commissioner, Ramsay Court, paced on the carpet in a large living room. It was dark, as the curtains had been closed against the daylight. A lamp cast yellow light into the room. Cloaked in shadow, one other person sat in an easy chair in the corner. To his surprise, it was a woman who, by all appearances, answered the description of Bianca, the progeny. His werewolf senses confirmed she inhabited a blank space, which is what a vampire felt like to him, and the musty smell of dead thing also lingered in the air.

"Why is he here?" Ramsay demanded. "You didn't tell me one of them would be here. I can't be seen fraternising. I've got a reputation to maintain."

Keeping to the shadows, the woman spoke. "This is Gene Cohen. I believe you know each other."

Ramsay stood up straight, neck rigid as he stared at Gene. "In passing, only." His wary expression was tinged with disdain, curling his lips as if he'd tasted something rotten.

Gene flashed a grin. "You didn't say that when I donated a large sum to the policemen's charity ball. *Old friend*, I think you said. *Good mate.*"

The atmosphere in the room was tense. Ramsay was nervous, on edge. The progeny was awake. Not moving, but clearly able to command attention, and that put Gene's nerves on edge too. Hipster beard guy kept his eyes on Gene, his gun out. Gene inhaled, and he was pretty sure besides fear coming from the young man, he smelt silver. Silver bullets in the gun, then.

A rustle of movement from the shadows. "Enough of this bullshit. Ramsay, my love, you wanted proof. Here it is."

Her pale hand made a flourish as she indicated Gene. "The alpha werewolf of the Sydney City pack. Right under your nose for years. I bet you've even shared a beer at the pub."

Gene did his best to remain calm as he tried to assess the scenarios which might unfold. He didn't like any of them, but some had options that could ease things over.

He didn't have to make eye contact with the commissioner to see he was staring at him, or detect that his blood pressure had shot through the roof. "And what of you, Bianca Maroni? Your master, Silvio Bentino, is a vampire with keys to the city, would you believe."

Ramsay made a gasping sound and switched his gaze to Bianca.

"Gene Cohen would say anything at this moment to cloud your judgement, Ramsay. I know Silvio, he's a friend and a business associate. Nothing more."

"We know there's a small group of degenerates calling themselves vampires," Ramsay said. "Common knowledge."

Hipster guy lifted his gun, aimed it at Gene's chest.

Ramsay turned around. "What are you doing?"

"Change for me, Gene," Bianca said in a seductive voice. "I need leverage right now and showing your true form fits the bill."

Gene flashed a grin and held out his hands in a helpless gesture. "If you want to prove to him there are paranormals, why don't you change for him?"

"What does he mean?" Ramsay asked. The police commissioner remained on edge, and there was a spectre of suspicion surrounding him. He was not comfortable at all. Gene wasn't either, but that always happened when someone pointed a gun with silver bullets at him.

"Forget it. He's trying to deflect. I'm as human as you are, Ramsay. You know this." She glided out of the shadows, took two steps to reach the police commissioner, draping herself along his torso. She looked amazingly alive. Flawless, smooth, olive-toned skin. Dark red lips framed a generous mouth, and her dark hair swam around her shoulders in luxurious waves. Her figure was taut, breasts high, hips slender in the short tight dress. He narrowed his gaze, wondering how she could look this good and be this awake, if she was only progeny. Had Bentino lied about how progressed Bianca was? He wished Lily was there, because she'd be able to sense if there was magic at play.

"Jem," she said in a soft voice. "Safety off, if you please."

Hipster guy clicked the safety.

Ramsay nuzzled her neck. "Now darling, I don't think ..."

"Shush, my love." Her fingertips brushed his lips. Caught by her mesmerising gaze, the commissioner stilled. "Watch." She turned the commissioner's head so that they both faced Gene.

Her expression changed as she glared at him. Underneath the congenial surface rippled rage and spite. Losing all patience, she commanded him. "Change for me, Gene. Now."

The compulsion in her words slid off him easily. He was an alpha werewolf with magic of his own. The gun never wavered. Gene inhaled, readying himself to gather his wolf. If the hipster guy was too slow to shoot, he'd attack. Which target to choose gave him pause.

A crash of glass breaking snagged their attention. Rolf, in wolf form, plunged through the window, taking the curtains down with him. Sunlight blazed in through the windows, strong afternoon sun. Hipster guy cried out, changing the direction of his aim.

Gene leaped, pushed the police commissioner to the floor, and knocked the gun out of Jem's hand. A scream filled the space where the commissioner had been standing. Gene's attention centred on Bianca as she cringed in the light from the bare window. Her hair smoked, the ends catching alight like kindling. Then her skin bubbled, small blisters at first, on her face, then larger on her hands and then her legs. Her screeching mouth malformed, fangs protruding. "No!" she warbled, her tongue no longer able to form words.

The smell hit him hard. He gagged and fell to one knee. Dead body stench, charred flesh, fire and something else. The fetid internal organs glowing within the peeled back skin.

"Out, Rolf!" Gene ordered, and his brother bounded out the window again. There was a balcony out there and Gene stumbled over and saw how Rolf had gained entry, using the adjacent buildings' balconies.

Hipster guy was on the floor, shaking his head as if he'd been knocked out. Gene assisted the commissioner to his feet and eased him into a chair. Dazed and shocked, Ramsay looked around him, mouth opening and shutting. Bianca was a whimpering, smoking, writhing form, spilling bodily fluids onto the carpet. "That, sir, is the creature you were dealing with. Sunlight isn't kind."

Ramsay recoiled. "Bianca?"

The clothes were recognisable. It was what was in them that was not. "She's a vampire progeny." He took pity on her and went to pick up the fallen curtains and placed them over her body. She was still alive, but not for long, he thought. "It means that eventually she would be a fully-fledged vampire. Her sire is Silvio Bentino. He made her. She was once the human you knew.

"Perhaps we should leave now and let her people tend to her," Gene suggested. Ramsay nodded and stood up from the chair.

"Yes. I'll send for my driver. Best be quick." He took out his phone, sent a text. Recovering quickly, the commissioner shook himself as Bianca's influence faded. He narrowed his eyes, glanced around the room.

Still on the floor, Jem was already on the phone, calling for specialist help, but not having much luck from what he could hear.

"Try Silvio, young man," Gene said as he made his way to the hall. "He can help more than anyone else can. He created her and they have a blood tie."

Ramsay allowed Gene to take him downstairs, where he shakily waited for his ride. "What was that thing that came through the window?"

Gene shook his head and lifted a shoulder. "A rival vampire gang, I expect. No one likes another gang to get close to authority, to have the power to influence the police or the government. It's important they stand apart."

"I didn't know," Ramsay said. He shook his head. "I cannot trust my judgement."

Not wanting to let the commissioner off the hook, Gene replied. "You can never be too careful. And you were set up."

His ride pulled up. Ramsay stuck out his hand, and Gene took it with a firm grip. Ramsay stared into his eyes and Gene detected the doubt there, the questioning. Gene returned the look, unfazed. It was all he could manage at that moment.

Rattled, Ramsay, darted into his car and after a brief delay, the vehicle wove into the traffic and sped away.

Relief washed over him. He had averted part of a disaster—the exposure of himself and his kind. The commissioner still had the list of paranormals. To deal with that, he'd need Lily, maybe with some help from the coven.

Gene sauntered back across the road. "Well done, Rolf. Your timing was impeccable. I thought I'd have to get the coven in there to wipe his memories if I was forced to change."

He explained the scenario playing out when Rolf had broken in. "What were you thinking anyway?" he asked his brother.

"Surprise. Enough time for you to act. That the curtains came down and let in the daylight was accidental."

"How did you know I was in danger?" Gene asked, buckling up his seatbelt.

Rolf snorted out a laugh. "You butt called me and I could hear what was going on, the danger you were in."

Abbie sat forward. "They could have shot you once you changed. Did you think of that? Showed the police commissioner how to kill us."

Gene whistled. He hadn't thought of that scenario. "I admit I did not think that far ahead. There were a few ways things could have gone. Luckily, I have you on speed dial, brother."

Rolf nodded and fingered his goatee. "Lucky, he didn't think to take your phone."

"Is she dead?" Abbie asked.

"Maybe," Gene said. "She looked a goner to me, but knowing Bentino he will bring her back. We made no friends there. Bentino might owe me a favour, now his progeny will soon be back under his control."

"The police commissioner?" Rolf asked.

"Hopefully reconsidering where he sticks his ... loyalties."

Rolf and Abbie laughed. "Let's go eat something."

Gene nodded, mentioned a good place, a favourite grill of his. Then he closed his eyes and hoped Lily was enjoying the nice sunny day on the water.

CHAPTER 18

That evening, they gathered back at Reeva's place. Lily showered and put on a dress of her own choice. As it was a warm evening, sweltering even, she didn't mind. At least it was one of her own—a string topped, cotton sundress in pale blue. The whole 'meet your dad, you're half werewolf' thing still had her head in a shambles. Her heart was filled with a confetti of loss, love and kinship and she didn't know how she could put it together again. A strong wind would blow her away. Of that, she was certain.

When she joined Connor and her father in the lounge room, her brother handed her a drink. "I really like Sydney," he said. "I wish I could stay longer."

Lily frowned. "Why can't you?"

Connor's gaze slid to his father, and he shrugged. "Da needs me. I couldn't let him down."

Domhnall shook his head. "Son, if you want to stay, and I can get Gene to keep an eye on you and allow you visiting rights in his pack, then I can spare you. As long as there's a timeframe on that. I don't want you leaving our home for good."

Connor's eyes lit up. "Really? I'll ask first chance I get." He grinned at Lily, and she sensed something there, something not stated. Her gaze slid to her father as well. Her witch sense could not penetrate the wall surrounding them. They were, on a certain level, enigmas.

When Reeva entered the room, her father lowered his voice and said to Connor. "Mind your manners, now."

As her brother seemed well-mannered, she wondered at the warning. He was enthusiastic, and she wondered if that meant he could get out of hand. How she wished the ground didn't keep shifting under her.

"Will your son be joining us again this evening, den mother?" Domhnall asked Reeva as she refreshed the drinks tray, bringing out a fresh bottle of whisky from a cupboard underneath.

"Yes, both my sons will be joining us, along with Abbie. Drink?"

"Yes, please." Domhnall nodded sagely. "Ah, Abbie, now there is an interesting she-wolf." He tapped the side of his nose. "I heard she has hidden talents. She can smell magic, right?"

Reeva passed Domhnall a whisky. "Yes, she can, and it was very useful. A curse transformed her into a wolf. It killed the other victims. Only she had some latency that helped her survive the change."

"I didn't know that," Domhnall said.

"My son, Rolf, helped her too, of course. He's a powerful alpha, with connections to the Collegium." Reeva returned to the drinks tray and poured herself a whisky. "Combined, my sons are a force to be reckoned with."

Domhnall was nodding as he listened. "That accords with what I've heard. We could use someone like her at home. We have some small problems of a magical nature."

Lily's ears pricked up. So that was the way of it. They need magical help and Lily had witch powers and could detect magic, too. They hadn't asked her if she was interested. The topic of the conversation definitely informed her of their needs. She had to worry if it was a plot to get her to Ireland or if they were manipulating her. This was all happening too fast.

Lily wanted to get to know her family, that went without saying, but she also wanted to do things on her own terms. She closed her eyes and breathed slowly, trying to work out the were magic that swirled in the room. Reeva's power was steady, strong, and determined. Connor was akin to a camp fire, strips of bright flaring flame. Her father? Her eyes snapped open. If Connor was a small fire, her father was a compressed bonfire. He was holding his power in, disguising the strength of it. Her gaze slid to Reeva. Something coiled in Reeva, too. It must be some werewolf code or something. Her father was a visitor, and he couldn't go around flaunting his alpha powers, his great werewolfness.

Lily swallowed. "What kind of problems are you having?" Through her coven connections, she had heard there had been unrest in Europe and wasn't quite sure if it had reached Ireland.

"Dark witches," Domhnall said without preamble. "Dark deeds."

Lily caught his look and shivered. People like her were causing problems. Not quite like her, though. Dark witches. Lily was a light witch. She helped people. It was what meant most to her. That is what had started this whole mission. Wanting to help the victims of the moneylenders, by giving them the fee Reeva was paying her. Now the path seemed less certain. She'd found out about her herself and was shaken.

The door opened and in walked Gene. Without thinking, her gaze was on him, and her breath caught. Dressed in a suit this time, he looked incredible, wide shouldered, firmly muscled. Next came Rolf, who had also dressed in designer finery. Her gaze slid back to Gene and when their eyes met, there was a flash of something, a spark of fire that shot into her. She gulped and looked away, shaken. What was that?

Abbie came in, looking drop dead gorgeous with her red hair curled and hanging down her back. A figure-hugging, violet-coloured dress clung to her hips, emphasising her breasts. Her smile was rich and genuinely warm.

Lily caught her breath, calmed down and latched onto something mundane such as what was for dinner. Reasoning with herself, she thought about how much was going on, how disturbed her life was then. That flash of something between her and Gene was because she knew him, he was familiar when everything else was disturbed right now. That had to be it. He was a calm centre in this maelstrom of emotion and change.

Abbie's gaze met Lily's and then travelled down her dress, which was pretty and summery, but not really dressy. "Aren't we going out tonight?" Abbie asked, looking around the room. "I thought we were. Didn't you have a restaurant booked, Reeva?"

Reeva surged forward, bringing her hands together and smiling. "Oh my, you look radiant, the three of you. Unfortunately, there's been a change of plans. We aren't going to the restaurant after all."

Abbie shared a look with Rolf. Of the two, she looked genuinely disappointed, as she had taken pains to dress.

"My fault," Domhnall said, putting his glass of whisky on a table and coming over to shake their hands. "I don't want to advertise my presence here, you see. And these intimate surroundings make it easier to get to know you all. I hope you don't mind."

Gene shrugged out of his jacket with a grin and hung it on the back of a chair over by the dining table. "Perfectly understandable. We don't have to mind our table manners here."

His gaze found Lily's, and he smiled and came towards her. He guided her to the couch, and they sat down. "How was your day?" he asked, in a soft voice that curled around her innards. She was used to him ordering people about and being very direct. This solicitous manner affected her, put her off kilter. She wondered whether it was him who had changed or herself, because the emotional turmoil could be affecting her perceptions.

"Great. Thank you." She smiled at him and then her smile wavered at the way he looked at her. There was a glow in his eyes that tantalised something in her. She looked away, suddenly afraid of what that meant. Her father soon snagged her attention when talking with Rolf and Abbie. He lifted his drink to make a point.

The day had been amazing. It had been intimate and had allowed her to just be with her brother and father. Her gaze locked onto Gene's. "I understand the boat is yours. It was a truly brilliant way to spend the day and show off Sydney."

He reached over and clasped her hands that were sitting in her lap. "That's the best news. It was mother's idea."

"How did your day go?" she asked, narrowing her eyes. If she pierced through her own turmoil, she could detect a sense of excitement running under Gene's skin. Intuitively, she knew something important had happened. He was also easy with her, like his barriers had come down and this was the real Gene. A shiver of excitement went through her. What if her barriers had come down, too? Her whole life she'd hidden her true self, so people couldn't see the hurt, the fear, the fault in her that had let her be abandoned by her parents. Had finding her father and the reasons for her kidnapping just flicked that armour away like it was gossamer wings?

There was way too much going on in her life right then to resist the tide of change that was curling over her like a huge wave. Their eyes met and there was that spark again. Her heart hammered. Once was an anomaly, twice was a problem.

"Our day went very well." He patted her hands and removed his. "You'll hear about it at dinner."

The way he smiled snagged her attention. Lily's face heated. Reeva's voice broke in between them. "Drink, son?" she asked, standing in front of him. Her eyes darted between them, and Lily studied her hands, the hands that still had Gene's heat on them. What was happening to her?

"A beer would be great, Mother. I can get it myself." He slid off the couch, leaving cold air in the place of his warmth. "Can I get anyone else anything?"

As Gene went to the kitchen, he filled the various orders that were called across the room. Whisky for his brother, a Campari neat for Abbie, a dark ale for Domhnall and a pale ale for Connor. Lily needed to keep her head. "Just mineral water for me, please."

She got to her feet and joined the others, who stood around in a circle. Domhnall made room for her, and she stood by his side. Lily tried again, now that they were all gathered, to see with her witch sense. Rolf was a bright ball of light. Different from her father and brother. Abbie was a rose gold ember, glowing but held in check. Lastly, her gaze settled on Gene, and she let her witch sense open. Her breath hitched; her eyes widened. Gene was fire, dense with red highlights. He was contained, though. Except for Rolf, all of them were. She wondered at that and knew she'd have to ask Gene later about whether it was some were protocol. Closing her eyes, she let go of her witch sense and opened them again to see them as anyone would. The surface layers, their clothes, their eyes. Only Gene's seemed to ignite when they met hers. It was unnerving and mesmerising. She had to keep a grip on herself, unless she gave everyone, especially Reeva, cause for concern.

As they stood around with their drinks, Rolf filled them in on what happened. "This bearded guy went in one direction and then popped up behind Gene from the other direction, sticking a gun in his back. A gun with silver bullets. Gave us a turn, I can tell you."

Abbie grinned, and it was a feral expression. "The hard part was staying put, waiting for it to play out."

Lily gasped when she realised how close Gene had come to getting shot with a silver bullet. "I should have been there."

Gene spread his arms and turned around. "It wasn't that bad. I wanted inside, and that got me in."

Lily frowned. "So you caught the police commissioner inside with the vampire, Bianca?" She turned to Rolf and Abbie. "Please tell me you have evidence?"

Abbie nodded. "We do. Already backed up to about fifty devices."

"The most amazing thing," Gene began, "was Rolf leaping through the curtained windows, bringing glass shards and full daylight in his wake. It wasn't pretty for Bianca. The commissioner got a bit of a surprise."

Reeva jerked her chin. "That swine should've got more than a surprise." She lifted her hand like a claw and swiped.

"To be honest," Gene said. "I don't think he really understood what he was involved in."

"I'd like to see these photos," Lily said in clipped tones, not willing to let it lie. Bianca was a link, but was she the end of the line?

Rolf nodded. "We're having prints delivered in the morning."

Lily swallowed a retort. "That will have to do."

"No harm done," Gene said, smiling enough to melt an iceberg.

He lifted both his arms out to the sides in an expansive gesture. She got a good look at him and that suit really enhanced his build. She glanced away, concerned by this sudden, uncontrollable awareness of him. The attraction had been there: he was charming and good-looking and rich. All things in his favour. He was also a womaniser and that had irked her. Now that didn't seem to bother her as much as it once had. She wanted to jump him and make him beg. Had meeting her father and brother cracked open her vulnerability? Or was it this wolf spirit thing she acknowledged that lived within her? Whatever it was, she could sense this tie between them like a hook on a fishing line. However, she didn't know if she was the bait or the fish.

"Still, you shouldn't have taken risks without me being there."

Gene rolled his eyes. "You do know I have existed in this life before you came along?"

It wasn't meant unkindly. Lily felt it though, and Domhnall shot him an annoyed glance. Gene sighed. "I'm sorry. I didn't mean for that to sound so dismissive. Forgive me."

Lily flashed him an insincere smile. That comment gutted her. It was true. He had survived. These last weeks, looking after him, protecting him from someone who meant him ill, had been important to her. Both Reeva and Gene had trusted her. Gene couldn't see magic spells. Sure, he could hire another witch, but not one with her skills, her experience in the police force, her tenacity to strive to find the truth. Her gaze flicked to her father. Reeva's revealing of her heritage could have been better timed. Like after they had found the culprit and Gene was safe. Well, as safe as an alpha of a werewolf pack in Sydney could be in a society that would end him if it knew of his existence.

As the plan had originally been to go out, Reeva had ordered in a very swank meal from that same restaurant. However, she seconded Abbie, Rolf, and herself to meet the delivery van and carry the trays and other items. Rolf did a lot of the carrying as he felt it was faster than loading up a trolley and wheeling it in.

The restaurant had sent staff to serve the food. Reeva headed them off. "We can manage from here," she said.

A tall young man in a dark suit and white tie stood stock-still and wide-eyed. "But we were to return with the serving dishes and lay out the plates according to the chef's orders."

Reeva smiled. She pulled out a wad of cash. "We can manage from here. I see the chef has sent photos of how the dishes are to be displayed." She separated the notes and pushed them into the three waiting staff's hands. "If you would thank the chef for letting me have the meals, that would be great. I can either return the dishes in the morning or he can send someone. Tell him to send me a text message with what he prefers."

The young man looked at his workmates and shrugged. "We'll leave you to it, then. Thank you for your generosity."

Lily had a quick look at the denominations and she thought Reeva had paid them a week's salary each.

Taking the platters that Reeva had put to the side to pay the staff, she led the way back inside. Lily considered the exchange. Her father hadn't been joking that he didn't want his presence widely known. Normally, she thought Reeva would have kept the waiting staff.

The kitchen bench was full of platters and so too was every other bit of flat surface. Reeva did a quick check of the dining table and called them in.

Lily had snuck back to finish her drink and as they walked into the dining room, her father took her hand and squeezed. She glanced up at him, a smile on her face but puzzlement in her eyes. He leaned down. "Don't mind Gene. He's all male ego."

Lily's smile faltered. Was she that transparent? Gene's comment had wounded her, but she thought she had hid her reaction well. However, she was surprised by Domhnall's insight into her mood and his concern for her feelings. "I know. He's such a dick sometimes."

"Are you two whispering about me?" Gene asked, coming up behind her. "Anything juicy?"

Lily shook her head and went to where Reeva directed her to sit. Her gaze met Gene's, and he frowned and then smiled. If she didn't know better, she would have thought he was sorry for upsetting her.

After their sexy interlude the night before, Lily felt off centre. One minute thinking they had removed a barrier between them and the next erected it again by a thoughtless comment. Was it thoughtless, though? Had he meant to put her off? Perhaps he now regretted getting close to her, regretted getting intimate with her. She wondered how he could be so insensitive. She'd nearly depleted herself to save his life. How soon did he forget that? Unfortunately, her thoughts about Gene spiralled down, recalling his comments about her being the hired help. If that's what he really thought, then her feelings didn't matter. Her efforts were bought and paid for, and she was fair game. He'd dallied with her last night, and she had let down her barriers.

Her father tried to engage her in conversation, and she did her best. Fighting her own sense of inadequacy and interpretation of Gene's actions and words, she had to own that her mind and her heart were very much in disarray.

The meal was high-end Turkish cuisine. They tasted every carefully crafted morsel. Lily tried not to look at Gene, tried not to think about him. Every time her gaze strayed to him at the table, Reeva was watching her, and she hastily looked away. Reeva had banned him from being with her and now, as she studied the older woman, the den mother that she was, she was confused. Reeva had been nothing but kind. She had brought Lily's father to Australia to meet her, encouraged and oversaw their meeting.

Her father was a great talker and soon she was caught up in him, listening to the lilt of his voice, the rise and fall as he told them stories. He had them all in stitches, telling tales about his home and some of the characters in his pack. Her brother smiled and laughed along with him. It made Lily want to visit to meet these people. All of a sudden, Lily was sick of it all. It dawned on her what was going on. She was being manipulated, not only by her father, but by Reeva. Her emotions were all twisted up, with Gene stirred into the mix. Attraction and distraction and rejection. Her mind was in a spin.

"Would you excuse me for a minute?" Lily said, wiping her mouth with the napkin and tossing it on the table. "I need some fresh air."

Her father gaped at her. Reeva frowned. Abbie watched her with wary eyes. Rolf sat still. Gene she didn't know because she could not look at him.

Instead of going onto the balcony, she went out the front door. She kept walking out to the Finger Wharf. Soon she found herself in the sculpture garden confronted by a Chinese water dragon. How apt, she thought. Mythical creatures, and she was one. More than one, a mixture of two. The urge to rant and cry and pummel the statue nearly overwhelmed her. It was passing pedestrians that kept her under control. There was no point in drawing attention to herself.

A cool breeze wafted from the harbour, riffling through her hair. She hated being so confused, so at sea. She breathed out a big sigh. Her hair wafted into her face, so she grabbed it and tried to plait it, gathering the bits that escaped from her fingers as she tried to lock them down. "You should leave it. You look fine as you are."

Gene.

She turned, anger climbing up her neck and jumping out of her mouth. "What are you doing here?"

"I followed you outside." With a smile on his face, he threw his arms out to the side in a gesture of stating the obvious.

"Leave me alone."

His pleasant expression grew serious. "No, I won't."

He stepped closer to her, close enough to slap, and her hand burned to do just that.

"Aren't you listening? I said leave me alone, you ... you prick!"

Gene sighed. "I deserve that. I am a prick, but you knew that from the start. Haven't you said I was a dick ever since you met me? Sometimes you're transparent and your thoughts appear on your face, whether or not you speak them."

"I ... er ... that's no excuse to be a jerk to me." Emotion clogged her voice. She hated how she couldn't hide what she was feeling, the betrayal, the flipping off of everything she'd done. Their intimate interlude was less than twenty-four hours ago. And Reeva and her father were angling to send to her Ireland.

"Lily ... Lily," he said softly, in a coaxing way that brought out goosebumps on her flesh. "Forgive me. It was a stupid thing to say. I didn't want the others to know my true thoughts."

Lily stepped back. "No, you're right. You've managed without me your whole life. What have I done that's special?"

He stepped closer, so that his breath brushed against her shoulders. "You have done plenty. You know it."

He reached out and ran a forefinger down her cheek. Her eyes arrowed to his, her hand raised to brush it off, but what she saw in his eyes stopped her. Raw need. Hurt. Desire. "Gene?"

"Lily, I can't compete with all that's going on in your life right now. I'm afraid of how I feel. That I'll lose you to him. That I have no right to even ask you to stay. You spent the day on the water, but it is me who is all at sea."

All the hurt his words had caused slid away. "I don't know how I feel either. It's like I'm at a crossroads, with no idea of which way to go. I feel pushed and shoved and angry."

He lifted his hand to calm her wafting hair. He leaned forward, and she met him halfway, foreheads touching. They breathed each other in. "You're half werewolf."

"I know. It's weird."

"It's very sexy."

Lily laughed. "Does everything boil down to sex with you?"

"Yes."

Lily chuckled. "Figures."

"I can't promise you a commitment. I can't promise you what will happen tomorrow. I can promise you a very good time if you come with me now." He glanced around. "I have a small bedsit in this complex where we could go and," he shrugged, "fuck our brains out."

Lily laughed out loud then. "Maybe we could think clearer then? Without all this pent-up lust?"

"My thought exactly." He drew her to him, lips hot and eager for hers. When they broke for breath, he whispered. "Just don't tell my mother."

"Or my father. He said he smelt you on me."

Gene slung his arm around her shoulder, squeezing companionably. "Now don't go putting the fear of the White Wolf of Donegal into me. It might affect my performance."

She laughed as he angled them around.

"Oh, there it is." Gene pointed and then angled them toward a building.

They stopped twice more to kiss in the starlight, leaving the sculptures behind and thoughts of those who probably wondered where they had gone but could guess what they were up to.

It took Gene three goes to remember the code to his little bedsit. If it was anyone else, she would have thought it was nerves. But not

Gene. Surely not him. Always so confident, so sure of his sexual allure and prowess. The door swung open, and Gene flicked on the light. Lily looked around and laughed. His bedsit was bigger than her flat. All dark brown, maroons and black. It was very masculine and slick. There was a massive bathroom, with a sunken bath, next to an enormous bedroom, with a huge custom-made bed taking up most of the space. She thought the closet might hide a kitchen, but didn't care to look. She was too aware of Gene right then, of the energy sparking between them, the feel of her skin and the longing to rub herself against him, naked and ready.

Gene shut the door. "Reeva doesn't know about this place. Unless she changes into wolf form and follows our scent trail, she won't find us." He tilted his head, eyeing her in a way that made her insides melt. "That goes for the rest of them. They won't find us. We have the night. Tomorrow I have no control over."

For the first time since she had met Gene, she felt like prey and liked it. "Just the night? Right, then."

She wasn't going to put tickets on herself and imagine that he was going to change his ways for her. She had vowed not to be one of his conquests and had been annoyed with herself once the attraction grew and she no longer cared about being a conquest. Then she turned that idea around. Gene was going to be her conquest and the wolf inside was hungry for that. The witch in her knew that sex and orgasms were healthy and good for the soul. Fuck emotional ties. She had lived her life without them, the deep ones, the family ties. Why should she be missing them now? Gene was hers for the feasting and tasting. She could walk away afterwards, just as easily as he could. In a practical sense, maybe slaking this lust would leave her clear-headed and emotionally calm.

They met in the doorway—there not being enough room to meet anywhere else given the size of the bed, like a sodding trampoline. The odd thought made her smile, which made kissing awkward. Gene leaned away. "What is it? You finally have me where you want me."

Her smile turned into a chuckle. "Not quite." She was smaller than him, but that didn't prevent her from putting her foot behind his leg and pushing him back first onto the bed. He left out a *whoomph* of surprise, eyes glittering with desire.

"Tricky," he said. "Are you going to take your clothes off, or shall I undress you?"

Lily paused, assessing him. "That is so fucking clichéd. I expected better of you."

"My mind reading is a bit rusty and I—"

She leaped on him before he could finish the sentence. She'd kicked off her shoes and now straddled him. His eyes smouldered and his lips were tight. She leaned down and kissed him, and he let her. No attempt at grabbing her, holding her head in place, nothing. That seriously turned her on because it went against everything she had thought about him. She leaned into him, taking his mouth and exploring it with her tongue, dragging every bit of want out of him, until he was left panting when she removed her mouth from his.

The heat of his skin leached into her legs and, recalling the dream where his skin was so hot, she just wanted to spread her body against his. Rushing this encounter was out of the question, but something unhinged within her. All she wanted was his mouth on her breasts, her stomach, her thighs, her clit. She wanted him everywhere. Lifting the hem of her dress, she drew it over her head. His eyes widened, and his pulse quickened. Staring at his throat, she saw it, sensed it. That had not happened before. She undid her bra and tossed it to the side and crawled up his body. Her breasts brushed gently on his cheeks, his chin, and he growled in a way that made her breath hitch, her clit throb. "Give them to me," he said. She edged her left nipple near his mouth, and he latched on, raising his head to get a purchase and sucking her. The suction hurt at first, just like it had in the dream. She arched her back, surrendering to the delight of his hot mouth on her.

"Touch me," she said. He didn't grab for her as if unleashed. A breath, another, before his hand came up and cupped her breast, kneading it while his mouth and tongue teased her nipple. Constraint unpeeled itself from her mind. A cry left her lips, leaving her exhilarated and lust-filled. In a quick move, Gene moved to the other breast, and the abandoned one throbbed and burned as if he was still there, suckling and teasing. Her hips rocked up and down on Gene and she could feel his erection, long and strong. That thing inside her, the thing she thought of as the wolf, was demanding more. She rubbed herself along Gene's length, groaning then crying out as he swapped back to the other breast, panting and moaning in an out-of-control way.

Oh Goddess! This is better than any dream.

She'd never been so hot, so ready to fuck in her life.

"Fuck me," Gene said, laying back, panting. "Help me get these clothes off."

Lily undid his trousers and tore them down while Gene pulled his sweater off and unbuttoned his shirt. "Your panties, too."

Lily stood and dropped them, stepping out of them, kicking them to the side. He caught her as she pounced, flipping her onto her back. "I'm not done with you yet."

Lily squirmed as he kissed down her centre line, keeping one hand busy teasing her breasts, his hot mouth parted her and tasted. Her body rocked, a tantalising, pre-climatic shudder. He spread her legs wider and dug in with his tongue. It was like a lightning strike, a spark to flame, oblivion. A crackle of energy, a scream as the climax hit. When her mind calmed, she thought he'd ride her then, take and give her a goddamn ride. But he didn't. He explored her, licked her and sucked on her clit until she was trying to push him away, crying real tears as another orgasm left her a shuddering mess.

"My turn," she said.

"Not yet," he replied and flipped her again. His powerful hands pressed against her thighs, moving upward. He took her butt cheeks in his hands and kneaded them. She groaned as he released the tension there. His cock rested on the skin of her lower back, leaving a searing sensation, as he massaged her shoulders and even her scalp. It was weird. She wasn't wanting to jump him and fuck him senseless, but nor was she cold and warming down. It was like a pot on a simmer. He moved his leg, so he was no longer straddling her. She was up and on him in a flash. He was on his knees so she eased him back, running her hands over his torso, down his arms, her eyes on his delightful cock, so ready, so so ready.

Two could play at this game and she wanted to have him crying out like he had her. She ran her hands down his front, following the contours of his muscles, across his chest, and she nipped lightly at his nipples. His breath hitched. She kissed his mouth, and this time he put his hands on her head while he tried to outdo her. When she leaned back, her breath caught. The wolf was in his eyes.

She'd never fucked a werewolf before, but suspected that if she could see his inner wolf, then he was close to the edge of his control. Slowly, she worked her way down his body, and then focused on his erection. Witches had sex lessons in the Sydney coven, something she was glad of. No awkward moments there. When she took him down deep, Gene yelled and bucked as she worked him. Listening to his breathing, she knew the moment he was close and eased off, kissing the tip before sitting back on her heels.

"Oh," he managed, his chest rising and falling in rapid succession. "Can we fuck now?"

Lily lifted her head and met his eyes. "If you have anything left."

Gene moved so quickly, she didn't have time to flinch. Leaping up, he pulled her off the bed and settled her on her feet, her hands on the wall and stood behind her. One of his arms was just under her breasts, his lips were sucking at the juncture of her neck and his other hand was spreading her. He bent his knees, drawing her hips back as he angled inside of her, a slow glide that filled her up as he pressed her down. Gene was a big powerful guy, but she didn't realise he was that strong. She used the wall as support, as he moved her up and along his cock. "Goddess!" it was the strangest position. He was gentle and slow, and she wanted hard and fast.

"More," she said.

He moved their bodies again. Her on her knees on the bed, him behind. This time when he entered her, she cried out with the excitement of it. Now, as he rode her, she just let her mind go. Fuck, she loved the way he moved, his strength, his considerate lovemaking. She came so fast, but Gene wasn't done. He pushed her and flipped her.

"More," he said, echoing her words. She opened for him, and he cradled her hips in his hands. The wolf inside her was singing and exhilarating in sex as he drove his cock inside her. She loved the feel of him inside and the strength of him as he held her. For a moment she lost herself, until he tensed and then roared as he came hard. She clung to him until he stopped shuddering. They kissed and he snuggled close to her, his body half on her and half on the bed. "That was amazing," she said.

He lifted his head and smiled. "It was. You're amazing. Beautiful. Luscious."

He nuzzled her neck and then dozed off for a minute or two before they settled themselves more comfortably on the bed. As they lay together, staring into each other's eyes. What Lily saw fascinated and humbled her. Fire, yellow flames in his blue eyes. He touched her cheek, running his forefinger down to her chin. He kissed her lightly on the lips. "Your eyes are glowing," he said softly.

Lily blinked. "Mine? But there's a flame in yours."

His forehead crinkled. "What?"

"I thought it was the wolf in you coming to the fore."

He froze, then his eyes widened before he sat up suddenly. "What the fuck?"

Lily sat up too. "What is it? What's wrong?"

"Nothing." He flung off the sheet and shifted his feet to the floor. "I've got to go. You stay here if you want."

Lily stilled. "You're leaving? But we have hours yet."

He glanced at her over his shoulder. "You don't understand." He sprang from the bed, grabbing for his clothes.

Lily crawled along the bed, watching as he found his trousers and shoved his legs into them. "Damn right I don't understand. Tell me!"

He grabbed his shirt. Lily's heart fluttered at his expression. It was goddamn panic. "Gene?"

He found his shoes, a pair of loafers, and shoved his feet inside them. He paused at the door, leaned his head on it. "I'm sorry. But we can't do this again."

Then, before she could say his name or frame a reply, he was gone.

Lily threw herself back onto the bed and stared at the ceiling. "What the fuck was that all about?" She'd had some bad dates in her time, pitiful fucks that went totally down blah lane. This had not been one of those. It had been fucking marvellous. And now it was never to be repeated? What a fucking bastard! To show her the ultimate, fire up her soul and then say sorry, no can do no more. She rolled into a ball. A sob came. Tears and sometime later sleep. The dreams, though, were taunting and haunting. Gene's glowing eyes and his cock inside her.

Light entering the room woke her. To get back to Reeva's, she'd have to do the walk of shame. Momentarily, she thought about transporting into the guest room, but those wolves would know she'd used magic. She wondered if Gene was there. Sitting up suddenly, she thought, what if he wasn't? What if he was so freaked out by screwing her, he'd gone off on his own, made himself vulnerable? It would be all her fault if anything happened to him. After a quick shower, she dressed and left the bedsit. She bolted through the sculpture garden and made her way back to Reeva's. She pressed the buzzer and when there was a click, she said, "It's me."

No response from the grill, but the door buzzed, and she pushed through into the foyer. Reeva met her. Before the woman could speak, Lily blurted. "Is he here? Is he okay?"

Reeva stepped back, surprise evident. "He left for work very early."

Lily sagged with relief. "Thank the Goddess. I worried he might have done something stupid."

Reeva narrowed her gaze. "He has five werewolf bodyguards, and Rolf went with him. Are you hungry?"

Lily blinked. "Yes, I am." She followed Reeva.

Food decorated the kitchen bench. Lily filled her bowl with fresh berries, thick yogurt, and a serving of granola. This she finished quickly while standing and chased it with fresh orange juice. Reeva handed her a coffee as she went to join Abbie at the table, where the she-wolf was laying out photos.

"Oh, are they the photos from yesterday?"

"Yes, just delivered."

There were shots of a building, Gene crouching behind some rubbish bins, photos of a bearded guy walking away, photos of him holding a gun to Gene's back. A photo of the bearded guy side on and the next a photo showing three-quarters of his face. Lily stopped breathing as she picked it up.

"This guy looks familiar ..."

CHAPTER 19

A hot buttered croissant landed in front of Lily. "Oh. Thank you." She hadn't expected to be waited on.

"We need to talk," Reeva said in tones that brooked no argument.

Lily, distracted by the photos in front of her, glanced at Reeva. "Sure. I'm listening."

Lily kept thinking of the photo, her fingers itching to pick it up. Reeva stood feet apart and arms crossed, a fierce look in her eye. "Please, eat, drink your coffee and listen."

Reeva was giving off den mother who will be obeyed vibes, and Lily braced herself and looked sideways at Abbie, who quickly slid off her chair and headed out of the room. *Coward*, Lily thought at her retreating back. *Leave me alone to deal with this, why don't you?*

Cornered, Lily relaxed back into her chair and gave the older woman her attention. When no words came out of Reeva's mouth, she eyed the croissant. Nervously, she picked at the tip of it and broke off a piece and slid it into her mouth. She chased that morsel with a sip of coffee. On the move, Reeva began pacing back and forth, the period between turns getting shorter: five, four, three, two, one.

Gene's mother pounced. "I told you two to not ... Fuck it. Tell me what happened?"

Lily picked up the croissant and took a bite, chewing slowly, and swallowed. Angry and hurt, she wasn't sure how to respond. She liked Reeva, respected her. "It was just a fuck. Why do you care?"

The sound of frustration that came out of the den mother's mouth frightened her. "He is my son! He is not just a fuck. Get me?"

Lily blinked. Was there something so inherently wrong with her, a fuck was going to cause an earthquake, a crisis in Gene's identity? Her face heated and her heart rate quickened, and she held tight to her anger and hurt. That thing in her mind swelled and paced. She hadn't gotten over the way Gene had acted, the way he had run away, and she was also still trying to work out what that all meant and what that fire in his eyes and the apparent glow in hers meant. "He's a dick. That's what he is."

Reeva's eyes widened, and her mouth opened.

Lily took her speechlessness as an invitation. "A womanising arse wad, who fucks and runs. He's got as much emotional depth as a puddle." All the betrayal and hurt she felt spilled out. It surprised her she could give voice to it all.

Shutting her mouth, Reeva nodded, letting the air slide out of her nose. "Yes, that is a pretty accurate assessment ... generally. But you didn't see him this morning. He was freaked out, scared out of his senses." She leaned forward and slapped the table. "What happened?"

Lily rolled her eyes. "We had sex. I thought I mentioned that part."

"I know. I could smell you on him when he came back. What happened?"

Screwing up her face, Lily wrestled with what Gene's mother was asking her. Blow by blow description? No fucking way. Lily shrugged, picked up the photo again, and put it down without thinking. "The only weird thing that happened was I saw flames in Gene's eyes. Like I was seeing his wolf, or that's what I thought. He said my eyes glowed, too. Then in the next breath he ran out of there so fast ..."

Pulling out a dining chair, Reeva sat down, the air rushing out of her. "Oh ..."

Concerned, she turned to face the woman. "What's wrong? I know you said he wasn't for me ... or was it I wasn't for him ... After a while, I couldn't resist the attraction, particularly when I found out what I was."

"Half werewolf ... half witch ..." Reeva said this dreamily.

"Yes, is that not right?" Lily asked. "Are you saying it isn't true?"

Reeva's tear-filled eyes met her own. "It shouldn't be true. You shouldn't exist. A hybrid between our kinds is not meant to be."

A bad feeling filled her up. Fear of rejection. Fear of being different. "But I exist."

"Yes, you do. And now my son has ..."

"What?"

Reeva stood up. "I need to talk to Domhnall. We shall talk later."

"Wait! What's the White Wolf of Donegal got to do with it?" Lily asked a tad sarcastically. She wasn't used to her business being discussed high and low.

A look of pure anger came over Reeva's face. "He started it."

Reeva seized her handbag and a floral scarf and departed.

What is wrong with these Cohens? They're here one minute and gone the next. Lily sat, staring at the door Reeva had bolted out of and tried to make sense of their conversation. Having sex with Gene was being treated like some existential threat. She shook her head. Today was really turning out to be weird. With one last cranky thought at Reeva—along the lines of how dare the den mother make her feel like a naughty child?—Lily studied the photo again. That thread of recollection kept picking at her brain. She turned it over and saw that someone had written the name Jem. Jem. Jem. That name rang a bell.

Taking the photo to the guest room, she had a quick shower, then put on her black leather pants, a black T-shirt and her black jacket. As she sat on the edge of the bed, pulling on her boots, her eyes slid to the photo sitting on the bedspread.

Jeremiah Ludic. The name rushed out of her subconscious. Son of Pavel Ludic. Underworld figure with links to the construction industry. Suspected of burning down heritage sites to force their sale and rebuild. This was the link. Jem Ludic was the link to Bianca. The human criminal connection to the paranormal world. It was entirely possible it was Pavel Ludic who ordered the killing of Gene's father.

Using a spell, she materialised the duplicate of the files she'd taken from the moneylenders. She grabbed Violet's file again and reread it. There had been no repayments of the debt noted. However, the file said she was making deposits. If it wasn't money, then what was it? Blood? She looked through the other files and found similar notations. How did it work then? The criminals recruited blood donors for the vampires. As long as they gave blood to the vampires, they didn't need to service the loan. But the bastards still kept the original debt on file. Had Bianca paid the debt when Violet had been killed? Had the woman refused to continue giving blood? It sort of made sense, particularly when vampires were a secret kept from humans. To prove it she would need to match the repayment from Bianca's account but the more she studied the files, the more certain she became. That was the link.

She pulled her bedroom door open. "Reeva! Reeva?"

Nothing. Recollecting that she'd left, Lily gathered up her things and found Abbie in her room. "I need you," Lily said. She raised the picture. "I know who this is and his possible connection to Gene's father's murder."

Abbie's eyes lifted to the photo Lily held. "How do you know him?" An icy feeling followed this question, the weight of a werewolf's suspicion.

"Police work. I assisted in an investigation of his father, Pavel Ludic."

That heavy feeling lifted, and Abbie's gaze shifted from the photo to Lily's face. "And?"

"The team could see the connections too, but needed evidence to press charges. We found a witness who was offered protection and immunity from prosecution in exchange for testimony."

"What happened?" Abbie asked, eyes focused and interested.

"Someone broke in and killed the key witness in the safe house and we couldn't bring Ludic to trial. End of story."

Abbie shook her head, ran her fingers through her long hair, rearranging her waves so that they framed her face. "What do you want to do with this information? Why don't you just call Gene?"

"I'd rather do this in person. I need to confirm this before saying more. There could be danger. Gene has seen Jem, and his father may find out about it before we're ready. Can you come?" Lily asked.

Abbie grabbed a jacket and a shoulder bag and stood. "Yes, sure thing. What's the plan?"

Lily frowned. "Oh, yes. A plan. I, er ... Gene needed proof before he could act. I have the connection here." She waved the photo. "We need to talk to Pavel Ludic and his son."

"No." Abbie said, snatching the photo from her fingers. "We take this to Gene. It's his father, his revenge. He makes the call." She pushed past Lily and walked into the hallway. "Besides, I won't be popular taking you into danger."

Lily stilled and blinked. "Danger? I'm his bodyguard. Or was. I'm meant to be in danger protecting him."

Abbie sighed loudly. "Right then." The she-wolf took off down the hall. Lily followed and worried at her lips. Was she ready to see Gene again after what happened last night and, worse, the way he had run from her in a panic this morning?

Reeva, too, had acted like she had signed a pact with the devil and seduced her son. What was so horrible about them fucking each other? It was just sex. She closed her eyes. It was necessary to be a professional. She had to put all of that behind her, pretend it never happened, and not react to being in Gene's presence again. It was over. It was a one-night stand. The one thing she hadn't wanted to be for Gene. He had promised nothing, no commitment, and she'd gone along with open eyes. There was no heart in this. She had lust for Gene, not love. And he was just addicted to sex, sex with a series of women, who all understood the score. No commitment.

Now, she had the clues she needed, the potential proof, her time protecting Gene was at an end. She didn't have to see him again. It ended today. Part of her exulted in the thought of having her life back, a payday, no more dancing to Gene's tune. The other part of her mind, the part connected to her heart, wailed and sobbed and mourned. Why? They had consummated their passion. Gene had never been secret about wanting to get between the sheets. She had despised his womanising and knowingly become one of his conquests. Something had changed. She thought it was lust, but it wasn't only that. She cared about him, dammit, and now her feelings were unrequited. Could it be love? She recalled the glow in his eyes and yes, there was a deeper connection there. There was love. How it snuck up on her, she didn't know. Now, it was up to her to ride off into the sunset with no regrets, just memories that would hopefully fade in time.

She was free to do whatever she wanted. Go to Ireland and spend time with her father and meet his pack. See her mother. There was nothing in her way. Elvira could find someone to mind her flat while she was away. There would be enough money for flights, as well as helping those she had identified as needing funds to get out of their loan issues when her money arrived in her bank account. She was free.

"Right. I'll call him," Lily suggested.

"No need." Abbie put her phone to her ear, and Lily swallowed her disappointment. She wouldn't hear his voice, hear the joy when he heard she had the proof he needed. "Rolf? Lily has ID'd the connection." She listened. "Pavel Ludic, father of the bearded guy who had Gene at gunpoint."

Abbie listened some more. "Okay, we'll cab over. See you soon." She clicked off the phone. "If you're ready, we'll go now. Gene's in another safe house. We'll call a cab."

Lily inclined her head. "I'm ready if you are."

Abbie patted her shoulder bag and shoved her phone into it. "Let's go."

***

Gene seethed, threw his phone across the room just as Rolf walked in.

"What the fuck has got into you?" Rolf asked, retrieving the phone and tossing it in the air before catching it again. "You got laid. I can tell. Was it that bad?"

Gene shook himself. "No, it wasn't bad," he ground out. "It was fucking great."

"Then why are you all pissy and messed up?"

"You wouldn't understand." Gene avoided eye contact.

Rolf snorted. "I wouldn't understand? You're so wrong about that. You met your mate, didn't you?"

Gene bashed his fist on the desktop. "She saw my wolf. I didn't realise until I saw hers burning in her gaze. They connected. Fuck me. I don't want this."

Rolf rested his butt on the edge of the desk and slid the phone across to Gene. "You're scared shitless."

"I am not. I just don't want the mate-and-kids deal."

"You're getting ahead of yourself."

"What?"

"There's no saying she'll have you, Gene. You've been a jerk and now you're a prick as well. Tell me you didn't run out on her the moment you realised your wolves wanted each other."

"I can't, because I did. Never had the fear of God put into me so quickly before. I ran, and I ran and it was terrifying."

Rolf nodded and pulled on his goatee. "And because she's never been around her werewolf kin, she has no idea about this, has she?"

Gene met his gaze and gulped. "No. I just said we couldn't do that ever again."

Rolf snorted and shook his head. "You fucked her senseless. Your wolves met, and you ran away without explaining yourself."

Gene looked down and stared at the desk. Nothing was on it besides his phone and Rolf's denim-clad butt. "Yes. I did." He glanced up at Rolf. "Is there a problem?"

Rolf slid off the desk and sighed. "Depends. She may never speak to you again and if you want her—which I think you do, deep down—then that's a problem. How are you going to explain your chicken-shit reaction?"

"Hey, watch your mouth."

"It's true though, isn't it? You were scared. You're still scared."

"I'm snared, bro. That's scary."

"It doesn't have to be. At first, I had a hard time with Abbie, but I wouldn't change what we have for a second. Finding my mate made me stronger, a better alpha, a better wolf. Improved my life all round. And more, I'm happy in ways I never dreamed of."

"Oh?"

"Yes. We had a battle of wills, but she wouldn't give in. Abbie fought for her place by my side, as my equal. When you meet your mate, there's no barrier between you. She sees all of you—the strengths, the weaknesses—and she still loves you. As for kids, who knows if that will happen for us. We don't get to decide if we can have them or not. Fertility is a fickle bitch. Abbie's road to being a werewolf was not straightforward and it's not like we're abstaining from sex, but there's been no pregnancy."

Gene nodded, his heart thumping like crazy. It was more than just meeting his mate. He realised he loved Lily beyond anything. He didn't even know when it had happened or how, but he understood the why. She saw him, saw through him, and accepted him. She didn't take shit from him, either. She was a straight-talking, true-hearted person, who fought for the weak, had no avarice, and wanted to be accepted by those she cared about. And he had rejected her.

"Oh, fuck me," he put his head in his hands. "I had to ruin everything. I hurt her bad, Rolf. She's never belonged, always felt like an outsider, and I shoved her away when our true selves met."

Rolf sighed and lifted his eyes to the ceiling. "Damn."

Gene sat back and ran his hand through his hair. "I need to sort out this business."

Rolf stood up. "Yes we do. Despite your flit, Lily is obviously still on your side. Abbie called and said she had identified the human criminal connection to Bianca and then Bentino."

"Really? Who?"

"That bearded guy, Jem." Rolf jerked his chin. "He's Pavel Ludic's son."

"Oh that piece of shite. I've been trying to keep him out of my way. My father too, avoided him."

"Lily is pretty certain that's the connection. I guess you would need to talk to her to find out the details. Abbie said she's pretty convinced."

"Then let's make a plan," Gene said.

CHAPTER 20

Using an app, Abbie summoned a ride. Traffic noise assailed them, as they were near the main expressway off ramp for the Harbour Bridge traffic. A steady thrum of tyres on bitumen, horns added to the melody. The neighbourhood was an old shipping terminal that used to be an eyesore but was now renovated. It was also smack bang in the middle of traffic chaos.

They had just reached the main street when their ride pulled over. They opened the door and climbed in. Lily thought it lucky that it had arrived so quickly, given how difficult it was to navigate the traffic around Finger Wharf. Maybe the driver had dropped someone off in the complex just as they had requested it.

Once in the backseat, Abbie stared out the window, looking bored. They were soon in the tunnel with the Eastern Distributor taking them south and east. Lily checked out the cab driver encased in one of those transparent plastic shields that became popular during the pandemic and against a spate of violent attacks on taxi drivers. The driver had dark hair and olive skin and a beard. Nothing remarkable in that, as the multicultural soup that was Sydney's population provided many cab drivers.

Lily looked out the window at the passing cars and after about fifteen minutes, she became concerned. "Where are we going?" she asked Abbie.

"To meet up with the others."

Lily raised an eyebrow. "I know that. Which direction?"

Abbie sat back and looked out the window. "North. That's what I put in the app."

They weren't heading north. They were heading past the airport turnoff. Abbie was not a Sydney local so maybe she didn't notice.

A shot of panic sped up her spine. Her breath caught. "Abbie," she whispered. "We aren't going north."

Abbie frowned and leaned forward to bang on the taxi driver's partition. "Hey, you're going the wrong way."

The driver ignored them. Abbie started punching in a text and frowned. Then she gaped at the phone, lifted it up and around and shook it. "No signal."

Lily had to think fast. Her phone also had no bars and only showed SOS. There must be a signal jammer in the car. She tried to open the window, no luck. After trying the handle, she found it was locked. She and Abbie shared a look. This had to be a kidnap attempt. Her heartbeat ramped up. She needed to think clearly. Checking her surroundings, she could see that they were going to pass by Botany Bay very soon. It had a narrow stretch of parkland along the bay. "Abbie, come closer to me."

Abbie undid her seatbelt, slid closer. "What? The doors are locked."

"I know. Hold on."

Abbie embraced her, like a koala clinging to a eucalypt tree. Lily called her magic, noting that while she could transport them a short distance, she was likely to deplete her magic reserves again. Focusing on a passing park, she shifted them there. Their ride continued along the busy road at first, oblivious to them leaving. Given the traffic conditions, the driver would have trouble turning back when he realised they were gone.

They splayed onto the grass, rolling at the speed of their arrival, which was equal to the speed of the car they had escaped from. Abbie was up and on all fours in an instant, shaking her head and growling. "You could have warned me."

Winded, it took Lily a few breaths before she could speak. "Sorry about the rough landing. That driver is going to find it hard to get back, but it will. Probably with help. We need to get out of here."

Abbie pulled out her phone and pressed dial.

With her magic weakened, Lily found her physical strength depleted as well. Abbie pulled her to her feet with one hand. "You okay?"

Lily nodded vigorously. "Just ... I can't do that again."

Abbie acknowledged the point and gave her a quick once-over. Into the phone, she said tersely. "Pick up!"

Voicemail must have kicked in. Shaking her head and looking pissed, Abbie spoke into the phone. "Rolf, the cab was a fake. We were kidnapped, but we escaped and are currently near ... at ... um ..."

She lifted her eyebrows at Lily, a question in her eyes. Lily nodded, checked their surroundings. "Kyeemagh Beach, just off General Holmes Drive."

Abbie repeated that detail into the phone. "We won't be here for long. Not safe. Will call again soon. Be watchful."

Although transporting Abbie and herself a short distance did not bottom out Lily's power as much as transporting Gene across the city that time, her reserves had taken a hit. She might have enough left for one short solo shift. "We need to move. He's coming back. We should split up."

"Fuck," Abbie said, sounding appalled. "I can't leave you. Gene will have my guts for garters."

Lily gasped. "You can leave me. Gene doesn't give a shit about me. I was just an easy lay."

Abbie pursed her lips. "That's not what I ..."

"It's the damn truth." Lily realised Abbie's predicament. "Use your wolf and get the hell out. I'll manage by myself. I'll be fine. Let's split up and go in opposite directions. I'll head south, you head back to Reeva's."

Abbie squinted at her as if assessing if there was a lie. "Are you sure? I don't know ..."

"Yes, I'm sure. Go on, hurry before it's too late." When Abbie just glared at her, she added. "Don't be an idiot bimbo. Get to safety."

Abbie's nostrils flared, and her eyes flashed with rage. "Right then. You'll pay for that insult, bitch." Peeling off her jacket, she shoved it at Lily and added, "Just be there to get your just desserts." Abbie quickly stripped off her clothes and shoved them in a small bag she had taken from her handbag. She shoved her phone in there too. After checking no one was around and partially obscured from view by Lily, Abbie transformed.

Lily winced at the sound of breaking bone and tearing skin. Abbie the wolf picked up the bag with her belongings in her mouth and loped away towards the main road, leaving her shoulder bag behind. Lily scooped up the shoulder bag, put it across her shoulder, and hooked the jacket to it. Abbie was rather fond of the brown leather bomber jacket, and it might soothe relations a bit if Lily returned it.

After squinting into the distance, she could see their ride was heading back. It was like a blip in her mind. Who was on to them? The underworld thugs, the vampires ... someone else?

Lily ran along the green belt, away from where the driver would have easy access by pulling into one of the car parks that were interspersed along the edges of the various connected reserves. In a pinch, the cabbie could pull over on the side of the road, but the resulting traffic chaos would be phenomenal and would attract attention. She didn't even know if it was a real cab driver or a real cab. It was probably stolen.

She sped up, hoping to put distance between her and the road. The main problem was this was a narrow stretch of park skirting a beach and the road hugged it all the way down, for kilometres. There wasn't any kind of cover to hide in or disguise her trail. She didn't fancy swimming in the bay and there weren't many leisure boats to hide in either.

While she may have enough magic left to transport, she needed a few minutes to recalibrate and think strategically. Anger surged and coiled inside, and she recognised her inner wolf, the one that couldn't transform, couldn't ever be a wolf. As the frustration built inside, it was there, making its presence felt and making it hard to ignore. It was weird feeling these emotions. She recognised the anger, detected the inner wolf's strength, only couldn't connect to it in a tangible way.

Running deeper into the park, as far away from the road as she could get, she just hoped that whoever was pursuing them didn't have werewolves of their own to track her down. She didn't know how far she could keep to the green space along the water, and she didn't know how far she could transport. Across the road, maybe. A lot of traffic. A lot of streets with a lot of buildings to hide in. There was a train station not too far away. Maybe an hour on foot, she guessed.

Her phone vibrated in her back pocket. She reached for it and drew it out. Gene.

"Yes?" she said, panting into the phone. She looked over her shoulder and the ride was trailing her, keeping her in sight.

"Where are you?" Gene asked.

She told him. He couldn't help her, as he was too far away. "I'm sending help."

"Don't!" she yelled.

He'd hung up. There wasn't much point, as things were happening too fast for that help to arrive. She kept running, holding Abbie's shoulder bag to her side. She hoped the other woman appreciated her efforts because the damn thing was annoying to carry.

Her phone buzzed again. She held it up, and the number was withheld. Normally, she wouldn't answer, but she pressed the accept button. "Hello?"

A gravelly voice sounded in her ear. "Give yourself up, Lily De Vere. We're waiting for you."

Lily stumbled and looked about her. Ahead were about five men, evenly spaced. They were big blokes with folded arms, exuding impatience. Tats covered their bare forearms, some had tattoos on their necks as well. They were not, as far as she could tell, Gene's werewolves. She slowed down, bent over to catch her breath, phone still pressed to her ear. "Give yourself up peacefully and you won't get hurt. Put up a fight and we put a bullet in you."

"Will it be silver?" she asked breathlessly. The caller clicked off, and she nodded and gripped her phone, hoisted Abbie's shoulder bag up. A few more breaths and she stood straight, looking at each of the brawny men, her face impassive. They waited for her next move. She called her power.

Even though she couldn't get far, she transported. It had to be enough. A large wooden column hid her as she appeared in the lobby of the Novotel across the road. It was the best she could do in the circumstances. She turned, leaned her back against the column and watched people walk past. The concierge glanced her way, squinting as if he was wondering how she got there. Her legs were weak, and her power had definitely bottomed out. She tilted her head and looked up as she put the phone to her ear. She called Gene.

He picked up on the first ring. She told him where she was and why.

"Fuck! You need to get out of there. Can you trust another cab? Get them to take you to Milsons Point."

Lily thought she had little choice. Her magic was gone. She was exhausted from running. The best she could do was recoup her sagging strength during a cab ride. She ran out to the concierge desk as a cab pulled in. It was a female driver, around sixty years old and about as unthreatening as she could imagine. She had to chance it.

She slid into the back seat, and the bellboy shut the door. "You up for a trip to Luna Park?" she asked the driver.

"Sure," the cabbie replied. The woman met her gaze in the rearview mirror. The driver was plump and had wispy grey hair and very few wrinkles. She flicked on the meter, checked the side mirror and entered traffic.

"Any particular way you want to go?" the cabbie asked.

Lily was leaning over so her pursuers couldn't see her, pretending to be looking into Abbie's shoulder bag. Luckily, the jacket was still attached. No wonder the damn thing was heavy. "I don't want anyone to follow us, so go in a roundabout, but fast way."

She sent Gene a text with an estimated time of arrival. The cabbie was good. Once heading up Bay Street and away from the beach, she sat up and checked. No sign of the burly blokes who were ready to grab her. The cabbie took a side road and then another. She drove like something from a New York crime thriller and Lily had to hold on to the door. Looking behind, there was no sign of pursuit. She hoped Abbie had gotten away.

Half an hour into the ride, a text came in from Abbie. She was back at Reeva's. *I have your bag and jacket*, Lily texted back. Abbie sent a happy face emoji.

After that episode with Bianca, they must have tracked Gene back to his mother's place. He was a well-known figure and Reeva's apartment was secure, but not a secret. She thought of their little interlude in his unknown bedsit and wondered how close they had come to being attacked then. The noose had tightened, but Gene and Rolf were gone, and it had snared her and Abbie. The only reason she could think of for their abduction would be as leverage to get Gene to surrender. She wondered what the kidnappers' next move would be now they had failed.

The journey continued, and she could tell the cabbie was making a roundabout but gradual way north. She sighed when she saw a familiar landmark and relaxed. She wasn't about to trust a stranger, but this woman had shown herself to be apart from the conspiracy to grab her. Finally, as they neared Milsons Point train station, she asked the cab driver to stop. "Here is fine. I'll walk."

She paid the fare, added a generous tip, and wished the woman well. She continued down the hill to the base of the Sydney Harbour Bridge. The gaping, laughing mouth of Luna Park was to the right. The harbour water lapped against the sides of the road and a ferry pier and another private pier. People queued to enter the amusement park. She scanned the crowd and then she saw Rolf standing there waiting for her by the private pier. The relief was almost overwhelming. She raced over, put her hands on his briefly, and squeezed. "Thank God. I heard Abbie is all right."

He nodded once and stepped to the side. There was a boat there. "Yeah, she's good. Climb in."

It was a small runabout. A thin man with short hair and a beard shadow, wearing jeans and a grubby, once-white T-shirt was driving. The motor churned the water noisily, waiting to speed away. Lily didn't waste time arguing and climbed in, holding the hand of the stranger to steady herself, and sat where he instructed. Rolf grabbed the mooring lines and slid in behind her. The outboard motor revved, and they were off. They hugged the shore and then pulled up at another wharf about twenty minutes later. They were close to coven territory, down harbour from Balmain. As far as she could tell, they'd overshot Balmain East wharf, headed down Parramatta River, turned back, and then used a few larger boats to hide behind before stopping there.

"You'll be safe here," Rolf said.

She handed off Abbie's jacket and shoulder bag. "Can you give these to Abbie?"

With a nod, he helped her out of the boat and then turned away to climb back in.

"Wait ..." The photo was in Abbie's bag. But the outboard motor revved, and Rolf and the boat were off in a wash of foam.

CHAPTER 21

Lily fumed as she watched the boat grow distant and wondered what she was to do next. "That bastard!"

"Over here," called a familiar voice.

Turning around, she jolted in surprise. "Elvira?" Incredulous, she overcame her shock and then ran a few steps to where the witch stood hidden by a bush. "What's going on?"

Elvira flashed her a smile. "I wish I knew. Your boyfriend called me and asked me to keep you safe."

"He's not my boyfriend."

Elvira gave a 'whatever' shrug. She leaned closer and peered at Lily with a pinched mouth and narrowed eyes. "What have you been doing to yourself? You need a tonic ASAP. You've depleted your magic. Are you feeling tired?"

"Yes, very."

"Come along then." She grabbed Lily's hand and magicked them away.

They materialised in Elvira's lounge room. "Hello," Elvira's daughter Grace said, coming in from the kitchen, wiping her hands on a tea towel. "I haven't seen you in a while, Lily."

Grace had flour on her dress, her nose and her hands. "Mother said we were having a visitor." Her dark eyebrows drew together. "Can you tell me what's going on?"

Lily sighed and screwed up her face. "Not exactly. Trouble for sure."

"Obviously," Elvira said. "Now, where is that tonic I brewed up last week?" Elvira walked out of the room.

Grace flashed her a grin. "You know Mother. Must have your magical engines running at peak performance. I have to get back to the bread I'm baking. Do you know how long you're here for?"

Lily lifted her left shoulder and shook her head. "No idea." She tried to keep her anger and disappointment under control. She was meant to be safeguarding Gene, and now he'd shoved her here in a safe place. He really didn't want to see her again. She tried to bury the hurt and just couldn't.

Grace nodded absently. "Okay, if I don't see you before you leave, keep well."

Lily flopped onto the couch and closed her eyes. Elvira walking in jolted her awake. She hadn't realised she'd been sleeping. "Here, drink this," Elvira said. "It will help."

Lily sat up straight and took the big, long glass into her hands. The potion smelt like grass and something floral. It tasted like pond slime. She pulled a face and shifted the glass away from her mouth.

"Drink it all up," Elvira said. "Then we need to talk about your magic."

As this was an interesting topic, she held her nose and drank down all the potion. Elvira relieved her of the glass and took it back to the kitchen. Lily's stomach gurgled and complained. She burped and covered her mouth.

Elvira came back in with a plate of what looked like sugar biscuits. "Try these. As you know, Grace is a wizard in the kitchen."

Lily snaffled one and munched. She swallowed, immediately feeling light-hearted. "You were going to tell me something about my magic?"

"You keep depleting. That's not normal."

Lily took another bite of biscuit as she considered this. "I did overextend myself trying to save Gene, transporting him and myself over a long distance. Then, I got my power back slowly, but then I was drugged and hit over the head, and I was weak again."

She lifted a finger. "I meant to tell you about that. There's a drug that kills magic."

Elvira narrowed her gaze. "Right. We will deal with that soon. Tell me what else happened."

Lily blew some air through her lips. "Dr Wentz gave me an injection, and that didn't agree with me. It lowered my inhibitions, but it did restore my magic. Just now, I did a short transport with one other person and then solo across the road. I'm back at the ragged edge of power vacuum again."

Elvira nodded and stroked her chin. "I heard through the grapevine that you have found out about your other half."

Lily's eyes narrowed. "By grapevine you mean, Reeva?"

Elvira shook her head. "Gene."

"Oh! Same thing, I suppose."

"This explains a lot, but also raises more mystery than before."

She could feel the potion spreading throughout her body. It was as if she'd been plugged in to recharge like her phone.

Elvira paced in front of her, paused and met her gaze. "Your magic isn't like a normal witch. That explains why those drugs affected you that way. The connections to your magical self are not straightforward. You will recover in time, but you don't have the capacity to refill your reserves. Not quickly, at any rate."

Lily's mouth dropped open. "I didn't know. Why am I finding this out now?"

Elvira lifted a questioning eyebrow. Lily understood. She'd never used so much magic over a short space of time before. While in the police force, she'd hardly tapped into her power at all.

Elvira crossed one arm under her breast and the other she bent so she could tap her chin with a forefinger as if she was thinking great thoughts. She dropped her arms and sat down opposite. "I think the issue is that there is something else inside of you, Lily. It has magic, too, but a different kind. Sort of like oil and water. If you can combine them well enough, you will have a single source of power. At present, they are disconnected."

Lily sat back. "Really?"

"It's not like a half-witch and a human. Humans don't have magic, so there's nothing to block the magic for a half-witch. It's just weaker, diluted in half-breeds."

Lily thought this made sense. Werewolves and vampires and pixies and ghouls all had their own kind of magic. "What are you saying?"

"I'm saying at the moment you aren't functioning like a normal witch. You can't go expending your powers and expect them to come back in full."

"Okay, I understand that part. Will it always be that way?"

Elvira sat back in the chair, her eyes on the ceiling. "Mmm. I don't want to give you false hope. It could stay that way. Or ..."

"Or what?"

"Eventually, you will find a way to merge the two sources of power."

Lily's eyes widened. She meant merging the wolf and the witch. It was a scary possibility. A werewitch. A shudder ran through her at the implications. She was a hybrid that wasn't meant to be. "Can you help me with that?" Lily asked.

Elvira shook her head. "No. We can help you restore your witch magic when it's depleted, but we can't help you merge your two heritages. It's not been done before."

Lily frowned. It was up to her to work it out? Figured! At least Elvira had explained the problem. "Then I'll be like this forever."

Elvira narrowed her gaze. "Can you detect this other source within you?"

Lily's face heated. She had, but only recently had she been able to identify it. "Yes, I think. I can. I think it's the werewolf part of me. It's kind of coiled inside my mind and today when I was being chased, it was angry and frustrated."

"You haven't felt the urge to transform?"

Lily sat back and blinked. "No, never. I don't notice the moon's phases at all, except to look at the calendar for certain coven rituals. It's not like a living thing, it's more like power and energy that hasn't got an outlet."

Elvira continued to muse quietly. Eventually she said, "I see."

That was rather enigmatic, but before Lily could question further, Elvira spoke again.

"Now, about Gene."

Lily grew alert. "What about him?" She leaned over to snaffle another sugar cookie. They made her feel good. Grace's food always did that. She put spells in her cooking to fill people with love.

"He's asked me to keep you here."

Lily nearly choked on the cookie. "How long?"

"Indefinitely."

She swallowed the mouthful. "What? What does that even mean?" Her first childish thought was that Gene was done with her. She'd been bedded and was now to be forgotten. Forever! That was hurt speaking. If Gene was keeping her away, it was because of some misguided sense of protecting her. If that was true, then he cared for her more than just as an employee or a simple lay. Or, given his ego, he had a false sense that he could handle this on his own. Either way, she refused to stay put. She folded her arms across her chest and locked gazes with the older witch.

Elvira let out a long sigh. "I can't keep you longer than you want to stay. There are laws about that, human and witch." She examined her fingernails and then lowered her hand. "Besides, Gene's in danger."

Uncrossing her arms, Lily sat forward, heart once again beating time like a drum. "What, more danger than normal? And right now?"

Elvira waved her right hand in the air, in a nonchalant gesture with loose fingers. "I feel it in the air. A betrayal close to him is sending ripples out along the ether."

"No." It couldn't be Rolf, and it couldn't be Abbie or Reeva. Her father or Connor? She paused and considered. No. What would be the motive? Someone in his pack? That was unlikely, not with alpha powers.

"Can you take me to him? Just drop me there and leave?" If this betrayal was happening now, then she needed to get there quickly.

Elvira glared at her. "Of course I can. But he wouldn't like it. Not one bit. He can be aggravating when he's angry." She held up her hands and wiggled her fingers. "Such negative emotion is not good for one."

Lily locked gazes with the elder witch. "Please?"

Elvira lowered her hands and placed them on her lap, demurely. The witch's lips twitched as the smile took over. "Since when do I listen to a werewolf? Even if he is sexy and rich. I do what I think is best."

"So you'll do it?" Lily asked.

"Indeed, I will."

It took a while to sort through the preparations. Lily had to take another dose of Elvira's remedy and then Grace made her eat fresh bread and butter. This food made her eyes roll up in her head. It was the taste and Grace's magic. A baby's cry echoed down the hall. "Ah, that's my little Bethsheba waking up from her afternoon nap." Grace nipped away to deal with her baby.

Elvira explained. "Grace is visiting and letting me spend time with my grandchildren. It's for a week and I miss her already and she doesn't leave for another four days."

Elvira snuck a slice of bread and tapped her generous midriff. "No point in denying myself. No matter what I do, I just get plumper." Elvira changed her dress and had added some make-up. "I've got to pop out first before we leave. Okay? Just relax and I'll be back in a minute or two."

Of course, Lily could not relax. Negative thoughts intruded. Gene didn't want or need her. She was just sticking her nose in where he didn't want it. Elvira detected betrayal in the air. Well, maybe that was Lily interfering right now, as going against his orders could be taken as a betrayal. A recollection of the fire in his eyes and how that melded with something within her came to mind. "Oh, Gene. Stay safe."

Elvira popped back with another person. "Do you remember Martha?"

Lily did and bowed her head. Martha had been a mover and shaker in the council governing the coven. She was still an elder but was less active in the leadership these days. "Martha is going to remote monitor our situation and also keep Grace company. Let's hope we don't need Grace's services."

With a frown, Lily switched her gaze between the two. "You mean a life-or-death situation?"

"Yes, perhaps. However, we have a warrior troop now, and Martha has them on standby."

"You mean the witches and warlocks Declan trained?"

"Yes, dear. I remember you trained with him, too, before you joined the police force."

"That's great. I hope they won't be required."

Elvira gave a slight nod. "Come on. Come, stand with me."

Lily joined the older witch. The translocation twisted Lily's gut. Elvira was so powerful it was like being picked up and thrown head first across the universe. It didn't help that her gut was full of potion.

She blinked back the late afternoon sun. Trees rustled and there was green everywhere. It must be a park. "They're over there in that clump of trees. Call me if you need me." Next breath, Elvira was gone.

Lily tracked to the clump of trees in a wide arc, reaching out with her witch sense to see where they were, who was there. It was patchy. Only glimpses of blank spaces reached her and that meant a vampire or vampires. Bianca had been dealt with, but maybe Bentino had lied and it wasn't just one rogue vampire. There was no choice but to draw closer and hope she went undetected.

Crawling on all fours in the undergrowth left her feeling grimy. As well as trash, other less savoury leavings of both humans and animals littered the ground. She'd picked a place where things urinated. Screwing up her nose, she listened and looked.

Gene, Rolf and a few other weres were on one side of a clearing, close to cover, which was good and sensible. At the opposite end of the clearing only Bentino stood in view, the oldest and the strongest, in the half-light. Other vampires lurked in the shadows.

Lily checked the sky. The sun had dropped low and with the trees in this park, night was falling fast as the shadows crept forward. Did Gene know about the other vampires? Lily snuck out her phone and texted Rolf. *I'm here. There are vampires further back. About six.*

Rolf didn't check his phone. Gene could probably smell them. Both he and Rolf complained that vampires stank. At a time like this, he'd need his phone on silent, so she'd forgive him for ignoring her message.

Bentino called out. "Surrender, werewolf. I gave you what you wanted."

Gene responded. "It's not good enough, Bentino. I know Bianca isn't responsible for all of it as she was still a fledgling vamp when my father was killed."

Lily nodded in agreement. That made sense, his father was killed over a year ago.

"How do you know that? She was always very talented, advanced for a progeny." Bentino modulated his voice to sound reasonable, and it still carried. Another vampire glam feature, she guessed.

"We have our own sources. Now, you tell me who ordered the hit on my father and on me."

Bentino folded his arms and took another step forward as the shadows of night crept along the grass. "You can't undo what is done, so don't try. The humans are working with us. You can't stop that."

"I can get revenge, satisfaction. Justice," Gene enunciated clearly. "And they're after me, so that's self-preservation and protecting my own. Someone tried to kidnap Lily De Vere this afternoon."

"That hot little witch?" Bentino smiled. "I wouldn't mind having her on my team and in my bed. What a nice little hybrid she would make when I make her one of us. Witch, were and vampire."

Lily sucked in a breath. How had he known about that? She'd only just found out herself. From the look on Gene's face, he was just as surprised. Someone had leaked that information. It was a small circle who knew.

"That's some fantasy you have going there, Bentino."

"Not fantasy. I got it from a reliable source."

Gene folded his arms. "Look, Bentino. I didn't even know Lily existed when my father was killed. She is nothing to do with that. You're just obfuscating."

"Yes, I know that. Interesting development, don't you think? Such potential. Give her up and the rest will go away." He indicated the vampires creeping along the line of shadow behind him, advancing with the fall of the night.

Anger seethed. How dare they discuss her like she was some commodity? She wasn't up for being traded or negotiated. The thought of succumbing to Bentino and becoming a vampire turned her stomach.

"She's not part of the negotiations. And the Collegium will hear about your actions."

Bentino let out a belly laugh. "The Collegium has no power over us.

We pander to them, and they swallow our lies. We will not be tamed. I am master here in Australia. You will surrender the witch. Remove your claws from her."

Her gaze centred on Gene, waiting to see if he would give her up to find out who killed his father. Damn, she hadn't been able to tell Gene about the photo herself. She wanted to be the one to give him answers and see the result of her efforts. She scanned the surroundings, wondering if Jem was nearby. That was the link. He didn't need to trade.

There were a number of humans behind the vampires. There was no way of discerning if Jem was among them. She sent her gaze to Gene's side, and she sensed her father's presence there, although not her brother's. That was odd. Surely Connor would stand with his father.

Crawling backwards out from her vantage point, she made her way stealthily to Gene's side of the confrontation, moving through the shadowy werewolf figures. There were three times as many werewolves gathered as vampires.

Her father noticed her first. "What are you doing here?" he whispered as he yanked her by the arm to his side.

"Protecting Gene, and this ..." she said, flinging her hand out to the deliberations, "is a joke. There are vampires hiding in the shadows and at least ten humans."

He gripped her arm, and she struggled. "Stay here and stay quiet," he hissed in her ear.

She nodded, and he relaxed his grip. Fuming that he had manhandled her, she wanted to lash out. It was that wolf thing inside her again.

She tugged on her father's sleeve, and he leaned down to listen to her whisper. "I need to talk to Gene. I have some information he needs."

Domhnall shook his white mane. "No. You stay here."

Bugger this, Lily thought. After a moment's hesitation, she darted towards Gene. Rolf must have heard her approach because he turned, crouching, ready to counterattack, and hesitated, a frown marring his handsome face. He remained tense at her approach.

"It's more than just Pavel Ludic's son. There are vampires in the shadows and human reinforcements."

Rolf nodded. "Abbie told us. You were meant to stay away."

She ignored him and stepped forward. "Gene!" Lily called in a low voice. She was standing behind him, using him to shield her from view.

She knew Gene heard her because he froze. He didn't look around at her, but she knew he could hear her in the way his body tensed, the way it seemed he was listening hard.

Creeping a little closer behind him, she pitched her voice so he could hear. "My theory is that the vampires have been using the moneylenders to extort blood from humans."

Gene tapped his finger on his jeans. He'd heard and understood.

Rolf stepped up, stood in front of her, pushing her behind him. In surrender, she lifted her hands and backed away. Soon a bunch of huge guys, Gene's weres, stood between her and the fight. Domhnall came up behind her. "You are reckless. Don't you ever do as you're told?"

She turned and peered at him over her shoulder. "Not really. One reason I left the police force. Rules used to get in the way." That wasn't a complete lie. She needed bravado at that moment. She was more worried about what Gene was going to do to her, now that she'd become some kind of hot were property. The vampires wanted her. She felt like promising bacteria in a Petri dish, ripe for exploitation. No way would she agree to become a vampire. Surely they couldn't make her without her consent. That thought had her worrying her bottom lip.

"How long have you had an alliance with Pavel Ludic and his illegal money lending scheme, Bentino?"

The vampire didn't respond. Rolf hissed out a warning and large werewolves crowded around her. Lily ducked so she could see through the legs of the brutes hiding her from view. The vampires had slid from the shadows. At night, they would be in their power. Luckily, werewolves—and witches, for that matter—weren't allergic to sunlight and could work just as well at night.

A gunshot rang out. Gene ducked, and Lily checked to see if anyone had been hit. Her father fell to the ground like a tree lopped by an axe.

"Dad?" she cried and kneeled beside him. "Gene, Domhnall's down!"

The moon rose then. Not quite full, but there was something in it, some power that tickled across her skin in a way she'd never known before.

"Hang on, Dad." She gripped his hand. "Help is coming."

The wound was hard to see in the growing darkness. It was a pool of black spreading across his middle.

"Dig it out. It burns," her father said through clenched teeth.

Silver bullet. She didn't have any tools with her, not even a key. She hesitated. Not being a healer herself stymied her. Although she had some talent, moving things was not her forte.

"Elvira?" she said and thought with urgency. "We might need Grace." She didn't know if the witch could hear her. Lily put her hand over her father's wound. Slick blood seeped through her fingers. She closed her eyes as growls filled the surrounding air. The wolves were shifting. Bone crunching, ligament stretching, skin peeling sounds filled the air. Her father couldn't shift, not with the silver bullet in him.

His flesh was strange to her senses. She ignored that distraction and tried to find the silver. She wasn't particularly sensitive to it as a witch, but the werewolf in her should be. The frustrated sensation inside her mind surged to the fore. Lily faltered. It was too strong, too powerful for her to rein in. If she let it go, it would take over. While her father bled and writhed under her hand, a battle went on in her skull.

Find the silver bullet! Have to find the silver bullet.

There it was, lodged deep into muscle. She could feel it there, like a throbbing beacon. Now she just needed to extract it somehow. She dug her finger in, trying not to think about the flesh, the living, breathing person she was invading. Panting, she used her magic to pull the silver to her fingers. The flesh gripped it, unwilling to let it go free. "Dad, relax. Help me by relaxing."

Her father spluttered a bunch of curses that she had never heard before. He yelled and writhed and finally Domhnall relaxed, and she used her power again and the bullet moved. Her father cried out in pain. The poison spread out quickly as she moved it. Come on, you piece of useless shit, help me! Her inner wolf surged. Her mind flashed silver, wiping out every other sensation.

When she woke up, flat on her back, a massive brawl surrounded her. "Domhnall?"

She lifted her blood-covered hands. In one was the bullet.

A familiar voice called out. "Da!"

It was Connor. He came running up, still in human form. "Da!"

He cried and wailed. A wolf leaped over their heads, its jaw connecting with a vampire. The stench of dead, stagnant blood wafted into the air as an arm tore off. Even she could smell vampire now.

"Where were you?" Lily asked as she crawled over to her father.

Connor blinked. "What are you doing here?"

"I came to help. Where were you, Connor?"

"I was at the back, behind the others."

"No, you weren't."

Connor gaped at her. He looked down at his father and then back at her. She could see the lies forming in his mind, his attempt to hide what he had done.

"I was ... I must have been taking a leak when you came."

Lily shook her head. "How did the vampires know about me, Connor? How did they know what I am?"

Connor shook his head, screwed up his mouth. "Dunno."

"I think you do. Did they beat it out of you?" she tried to sound sympathetic, giving him an out.

"No, it wasn't me!"

"Were you bugged?" she asked, more and more certain that he had betrayed Gene, had betrayed her. Maybe their father, too.

"No. I wasn't anywhere but here. You've got it wrong. Maybe you hit your head."

Domhnall groaned and then rolled to his side. He tried to get up. The moonlight brushed along his skin. He was going to transform, as the were magic would help him heal.

"They shot him, Connor, with a silver bullet. Is that what you wanted? Him out of the way?"

Connor stood and backed away from his father. A growl filled the air as her father called his wolf. So close to him, big man that he was,

Lily caught the backwash of power and recoiled. The White Wolf of Donegal was a sight to behold. She thought he looked more like a white lion. Enormous shoulders, a mane of white hair tapering down his spine. Huge paws and a big muzzle. He howled and gnashed his teeth.

Eyes wide, Connor turned and bolted, transforming on the run. It was a very neat and clever transformation. Between one stride and the next, legs and arms became forelegs and hind legs. With a shake of his shoulders, his head became a wolf, his clothes a shredded pile.

Lily's heart hurt. Would she ever see her brother again? Why had he told the enemy? One day she might find out the reason.

Once he had shifted, her father leaped into the throng of vampires and werewolves. A shaft of magic split the air, and a vampire broke into shadow pieces. She knew that magic. Witches closed in from the sides. A few more strikes and the remaining vampires fled. Like a flap of capes, they became shadows flitting into the night.

Body parts and one or two wolves lay on the grass, darker lumps in the dark.

In the confusion of her father's wound, Lily had forgotten about Gene. She turned, scanning the surroundings. What if he had been killed while she was distracted? Reeva would never forgive her. She would never forgive herself. She picked out Rolf's wolf. He was limping, head turning this way and that, searching. He had to be looking for Gene.

"Gene!" she called. How would she be able to pick out his wolf in the dark? On instinct she ran over to the dark wolf-sized lump nearest her. "Gene?"

It was an enormous wolf. Its chest rose and fell in rapid movements. She ran a hand along his head and, when she reached his shoulder, he turned and licked her hand. He had a large gash along his side and one of his legs looked broken. It was Gene. Hurt, but alive.

Silvio Bentino was a savage bastard when threatened. He must have come armed with more than just teeth. She checked Gene again and there didn't appear to be a gunshot wound. Thank the Goddess, the witches fought along with the werewolves.

"Over here," she called to Rolf. Rolf, still in wolf form, came over and started licking Gene's wounds. There was no sign of the old vampire.

She checked her surroundings, and Elvira had not come to her aid. Not a great time to confirm that she didn't have the power to mind call after all.

Lily dug out her phone and pressed the speed dial. Someone answered. "We need help with the wounded werewolves. Oh and thanks for the reinforcements."

CHAPTER 22

Lily slept in Elena's old bedroom at Elvira's house. Elena was Grace's cousin who had moved out years before and now lived with her husband, Jake, who only found out that he was a warlock after they met. They now lived with their three children on the North Shore. Their story was often told in the Sydney Coven. A bad warlock called Drew, who'd gone really dark, had cast a love spell on Jake, catching his own half-sister, Elena up in it. Although at the time, Drew didn't know he was related to Elena. Elena had tried to restrain herself from taking advantage of Jake. However, it had been resist or die of lust. In the end, though, it had come out fine.

It was close to the full moon, so Gene and the rest were not in human form and in no state to discuss anything. She lay on the bedcovers, letting the yellow-tinged moonlight play over her skin. Wind-tossed branches swayed and disturbed the flow of the moon on her legs. The moon didn't feel any different to her than previously. It came in the window bright and pure and nothing else. No tingling of power on her skin, no urge or desire to transform, no raging in her mind from her inner beast, or insane thoughts. If anything, the extra light caused insomnia.

It was a relief, actually. She didn't have to worry about randomly turning into a werewolf. That thing was stuck inside her, a disembodied entity lurking. The news from Elvira was that her father, Gene, and Rolf were healed and feeling fine. Being in wolf form now was way easier, so close to full moon. A lot of energy had been expended in the fight with the vampires. Werewolves and witches had joined forces. A first as far as Lily knew. Her brother, Connor, was still missing, presumably in wolf form as well. Thinking of her new-found brother dropped her mood. Had he really betrayed her and, if so, why? Jealousy? She was a woman and even she knew that among werewolves, women inhabited the lower ranks. Except for Abbie, she recalled. Reeva too. She couldn't categorise them as trodden down by the weight of wolfish patriarchy. But if not jealousy, then why? He had seemed so nice, so easy and eager to love.

A depressed feeling came over her. On top of Connor, she was forever separated from Gene. She couldn't join his world as a stunted half-werewolf. Reading between the lines, her job was done. Gene didn't need her anymore. He knew who the bad guys were, and he'd deal with it. Reeva didn't need her now either and, in fact, the den mother reckoned she shouldn't exist.

If only she could have said goodbye to Gene, though. It might have given her some closure. Unable to sleep, she picked up her phone to do some personal administration. Checking her banking app, she noticed a series of deposits had landed in her account. Her eyes widened when she saw the total. Both Gene and Reeva had paid her in full, with a bonus by the looks of it.

Blinking back tears, she pressed the top of the phone to her chin. It was over. After about twenty minutes of feeling sorry for herself, she sniffed and then set about paying off the debts of the moneylending victims. She was too late to save Violet Tremblay but, hopefully, not too late for the others. She had their details and also knew the number of the moneylender's account.

To help stop more people becoming victims, she sent off the dossier on the illegal moneylending to the police, including the names of their victims, their debts, the images from the files showing the threats of bodily harm. Not to her friend on the force, Michael, but to the head of the Illegal Moneylending Unit. She doubted it would end the business entirely—the underworld always found a way—but a few of the nasty people involved might get caught.

Come morning, the noise from the television leaked into the room. The morning news by the sound of it. She got up, showered and joined Elvira in the lounge room.

Elvira passed her a coffee when she entered. "The police commissioner just had a news conference. He announced that the Mayor of Sydney has revoked the keys to Sydney from Silvio Bentino because of his links with organised crime."

Her heart leaped. "That's great news. Is the police commissioner resigning as well?"

Elvira shook her head. "No. He's had a fright, though, you can tell. And he also surrendered that list when asked."

"You retrieved it? And any copies?" she asked.

Elvira frowned. "Of course I did. Gene asked and, well, he's so handsome how was I to resist?"

She returned to the kitchen and called out. "You want some breakfast?"

"No, thanks. I'm good." Lily was far from good. She needed time to recover, to adjust and also to decide what she was going to do next.

Continuing to listen to the news, her eyes widened when another tall glass of potion appeared in front of her. "You need this. You must have used your magic during that confrontation."

Lily took the glass, sipped and winced. "I don't think I did." She drank off the potion, anyway.

"Are you sure?"

Lily frowned, trying to remember the exact flow of events. At some stage, her memories were chaotic. "Come to think of it, I tried to access the wolf part of me in desperation to save my father. I would say I blacked out, but it was more whited out."

Pursing her lips, Elvira nodded. "That is strange. No urge to transform?"

"None."

"Are you sure? I hear it's hard to resist when you are surrounded by alphas as you were. Their magic combined should have pushed at you, almost coerced you."

Shaking her head, Lily considered this. "No, it appears I'm tone deaf as far as alpha magic goes. I mean, initially Reeva thought it was Gene's alpha magic that connected with me, causing erotic dreams." She shrugged. "I don't recall feeling anything out of the ordinary besides fear, and definitely no urge to transform. I had an urge to bash a few heads together, though."

"Well, dear, I suggest you rest up for a few days and take it easy. Grace is heading home this morning. Declan led our attack to support Gene and his wolves. Poor thing was missing her man, so she is returning home with him. So the grandchildren won't be here to disturb you as they are going home with their mother. I've got to pop out for some coven business. There's plenty of food in the kitchen. I'll be back before you know it. If Rory comes home, don't mind him. He's been away on coven business, and I expect him home today."

Rory was Elvira's second husband. They were childhood sweethearts kept apart by circumstances.

Once Elvira had gone, Lily ran a bath. She threw in scented bath salts, turned on some music and lit a few candles. After soaking in the bath for an hour, topping up the hot water several times, she thought about getting out. It had been relaxing, even though her mind strayed to Gene and memories of their lovemaking. "Goddess woman. It was one bloody night. Get over it!"

In all the chaos, she hadn't zapped Gene's sperm after their night together. She did that now. Some witches used their power to stop ovulation, or to stop conception. Others like Lily used a spell to kill sperm.

"Hello?" a man's voice echoed up the hall. Lily gasped and hoped he hadn't heard what she said.

"Don't come in!" Lily called, quickly grabbing a towel to cover herself. She did not want to have one of those moments with Rory.

Outside the door, footsteps halted. "Is that you, Lily?"

"Y-y-yes."

"It's me, Rory. Elvira said you'd be here. I'm just letting you know I'm home. Okay?"

"Thank you."

Lily lay back and then decided it was time to dry off and go nap.

With the wolves deep in moon-enforced wolf form, she wasn't expecting much to happen or to receive updates on Connor's whereabouts. No news was good news.

After a long nap, she was up again after waking to the sound of pots clanging in the kitchen. She was hungry, not surprisingly, as she hadn't eaten for a while. Full moon was that evening so she wasn't about to hear from Gene or any of the others. She shouldn't be expecting contact but she held out hope.

When she entered the lounge room, Rory lay stretched out on the couch. "Hello, Lily." He got up and shook her hand and smiled sweetly at her. "I swear you are even lovelier than the last time we met."

Lily sucked in a breath, momentarily uncertain. She had known Rory for a few years after his marriage to Elvira. He had never paid her a compliment about her looks before. "Thank you," she replied.

She turned to the kitchen. "I wouldn't if I were you," he said, as if reading her mind.

Turning back, she gaped. More noise from the kitchen. She jerked her thumb towards Elvira. "I thought I should offer to help."

"Believe me, she won't appreciate it. If she wants something done, she'll issue orders." He said this cheerily, which indicated that this amused him, and this amusement came from experience.

"Set the table, Rory." Elvira's voice issued from the kitchen.

"Yes, dear," Rory went over to the sideboard to fetch the dishes and cutlery.

"Are you there, Lily?"

"Yes."

"Come here and take this tray in for me, please?"

Rory looked up. "Pleases are reserved for guests."

Lily sent him a confused smile and went to help Elvira. There were three platters. One of chicken, one of potatoes and another of greens. The aroma of the chicken teased her senses and her mouth watered. Hints of smoked paprika, roasted capsicum and garlic. Elvira pointed to the larger platter of chicken and Lily took it and carried it out. She went back for the greens. The older witch followed with the platter of crispy roasted potatoes and a gravy boat full of sauce.

Soon they were seated around the table. "Have you told Lily the news, Rory?" Elvira said, adjusting her chair. "Oh, and pass the potatoes."

"No, I haven't," Rory replied, hefting the large platter and passing it to his wife. "I thought you would like the pleasure."

"What news?" Lily asked, hating the way her heart skipped a beat. Was it news about Gene? Her father? Connor?

Elvira narrowed her eyes and peered at Rory. "Do you mean you've kept the poor girl in suspense all afternoon?"

Rory shrugged and opened his arms in an 'I don't know' gesture. "I didn't mean to."

"The poor girl. Pass the sauce, luv?"

Rory passed the sauce.

"What news?" Lily glared at them both.

Elvira passed her the potatoes. "Just that there's been a mass exodus of vampires. Right after the police commissioner's announcement."

"Bentino?"

Elvira waved a hand. "Not him. He'd never leave. I hear he did something bad and can't show his face back in Southern Europe at all. His power here is curtailed, though, as he's no longer able to go where he pleases without an invitation. His progeny, Bianca-what's-her-name passed out of life, sadly. One of his other fledglings took off with the fleeing vampires. Found a new sponsor, apparently."

"What does that mean, exactly?" Lily asked, thinking hard. The influx of vampires must have been at Bentino's invitation and now he was in disgrace they were leaving. She wished she knew the truth of it, though.

"There's more!" Elvira said, gesturing with her fork. "The police have arrested Pavel Ludic and charged him with murder and racketeering, drug dealing, and I lost count of the charges. He's been denied bail along with several cronies."

Lily sat back in her chair. "That's good news. So Bentino has less influence now."

"For the moment," Elvira said before cutting up some chicken breast and layering the sauce on it. They ate in silence for a while.

"They found your brother," Rory said, breaking the silence. Elvira's head shot up in surprise.

"Really?" Elvira asked breathily. "I hadn't heard that."

Lily swallowed a mouthful of potato. "Connor?"

Rory nodded. "Yes, he's locked up with some other werewolves. The story is, he betrayed who and what you are, but not intentionally. His drink had been spiked. He was just a young man at a pub, hoping to impress. With his lovely Irish accent, he was the centre of attention. However, the crowd he was with knew who and what he was. Normal booze wouldn't affect him, but there's a plant around here that, when ground up and added to a drink, will overcome a werewolf's better judgement."

Lily let out a sigh. "Thank the Goddess. I knew he was guilty, but I'm glad it wasn't intentional. So I guess the entire coven knows what I am now, too."

Elvira sighed. "The elders do. But not everyone, unless you tell them."

Lily glanced between them. She hadn't thought about the consequences of what she was being widely known. It wasn't until Bentino wanted her for a perverted reason that she realised how rare and valuable she was to the wrong people. The potential for danger was not lost on her either. She had always wanted to fit in, particularly with the coven, but hadn't quite made it. Her true nature becoming general knowledge would not change anything for the good. She would be just as different and on the outer as she had been, probably more so.

"Do I need to tell them?" she asked.

Rory shook his head. Elvira spoke. "No. You don't have to tell anyone. You don't have to be ashamed of what you are, either. You are you. Unique. Lovely and talented. I know it's hard enough in this world to accept who you are, to understand your nature. You will need time to come to terms with yourself, just as anyone does."

Lily leaned forward. "Are you saying I'm no different from anyone else?"

"No, I'm not saying that. I'm saying we all have a similar journey. We all have our own uniqueness to deal with. Whatever you decide to do with your life, you are always welcome here in the coven and with us."

Lily couldn't stop the tears that erupted. One minute she was calm, maybe slightly riled, and the next she was crying because Elvira knew her, knew her deep down and that was disturbing and also comforting. The older witch stood up from her place and came over to envelop her in a hug. "I know," she said calmly. "It's been hard for you. Living with us, but not being truly one of us. And then finding out about your parents, about how you came to be here in Australia and how different you are and how some people see you as a threat or an opportunity to further their goals. You have such love in you, Lily. You have fight and a strong sense of what is right. This will serve you in life."

"Thank you," she replied through her tears. Elvira let her go, patted her head, and resumed her seat. Lily toyed with her food, sniffing occasionally and trying not to think about anything at all. Despite the pep talk, she felt awful. She knew the feeling would recede, and she'd pull up and get on with her life. Right now, she was wallowing in misery.

Rory looked at her and she barely acknowledged him. When he stood up from the table, she looked up, startled. He met her eye. "I think we need ice cream."

Elvira tossed her napkin on the table. "Indeed, we do. Chocolate for me. A sundae with three flavours for Lily, I think, with whipped cream, chocolate sauce and crushed nuts. The full Sydney Coven special sundae, please."

"Coming right up."

Lily met Elvira's eye. The older witch winked at her. "When I say 'please', he goes all out. Just you wait and see."

Lily giggled. It was nice to see how they got on so well. From previous experience, she knew they enjoyed their little digs at each other. The sundae Rory presented to her was amazing. A mountain of ice cream, three peaks—one each of strawberry, chocolate and vanilla—buried under a huge layer of whipped cream and salty crushed peanuts. Lily picked up her spoon, forgot all her troubles and delighted in eating the sundae to the last drop of topping and pieces of nuts. Smiling, she sat back. She didn't know if Rory had spelled the ice cream and didn't care. She felt good. Elvira ate her ice cream with relish, too, and she gave Rory the eye and a rather salacious smile.

Reading the room, Lily excused herself and left them to it. She hoped her room was far enough away from theirs. She didn't want to hear them enjoying each other. Not when she couldn't enjoy herself with Gene. *No*, she thought. *I'm not going to think about him.* Men in general weren't worth wasting sleep over, and Gene was no different. She was going to pick up one of the romance books that sat on Elena's bookshelf and read until she finished or fell asleep. Dressed in her pyjamas and wrapped in a blanket, she stretched out, ready to be drawn in to the world of Johanna Lindsay's *Warrior's Woman*.

CHAPTER 23

Around two a.m. strong moonlight shone in through the window and, awake from the heat, Lily gazed out into the yard. It seemed cooler out there and the stars in the sky and the wind shifting the leaves would soothe her, so she climbed out the window, bringing a blanket with her to stretch out on the grass. Once outside, her nose detected salt in the air, drifting in from the harbour. The strong scent of the grass and the hint of rotting leaves also made themselves known. There were other scents in the air as well.

A rubbish bin next door with the lid slightly ajar. The sulphur fumes of the exhaust of a car down the road. It was weird to have such an acute sense of smell. She put it down to the night air and lay down. There she stared into the night sky, spotting satellites, the international space station and other space junk as they sped across the firmament. Her eyes drifted closed, until a sound woke her. A dog shoved its face through the azaleas lining the yard, rustling leaves and disturbing blooms. It paused there as if sniffing the air and came forward slowly, head down, strong shoulders propelling it forward. As it broke cover, she saw it was a wolf. Her gaze narrowed. Surely this couldn't be Gene. Her gaze went heavenward and although it was past the full moon, it was still very full. She'd only seen him in his wolf form twice, but it was him, she was sure. He sniffed around her feet, then around the edges of her blanket, and then came up and put his face near hers. She reached out and patted him just below the ear. He opened his mouth and yawned widely, his breath smelling like dog and raw meat. Their eyes met and in his, she saw those flames again and her breath caught.

He lay down next to her, head resting on her chest. Lily, feeling sleepy, curled up around him, her hand on his back, his fur tufted between her fingers.

Sunlight spilling into the yard woke her in the morning. She squinted in the bright light, trying to recall why she was outside. Memories resurfaced: her climbing out, a wolf coming to visit her. But she was alone on the blanket. The powerful scents of the previous evening had waned. She inhaled and thought she caught a whiff of wolf. Had she dreamed him up? Yet, when she gathered up her blanket, she detected traces of fur on her fingers. Maybe she hadn't imagined it, after all.

Inside, the aroma of cooking bacon made her stomach growl. She raced into the shower and then, after dressing in shorts and a top, she entered the sitting room.

"It's a heatwave again," Elvira said, wearing a cotton sundress.

Rory shook out his newspaper. "I hope this weather breaks soon. The papers suggest it will be another couple of days."

"Help yourself, Lily," Elvira said, indicating the place set at the table, complete with orange juice and fresh toast. Lily sat and reached for the glass. It tasted good, like freshly squeezed. She was going to miss being spoilt when she went back to her apartment. If she went back there. She had an invitation to visit Ireland, and that was still large in her mind. Would she, wouldn't she? What was stopping her?

"Elvira, is it possible that a wolf could get into the yard through the wards?"

Elvira came out with a pot of scrambled eggs and ladled them onto plates. "Depends on the wolf. If it was one I know, then, yes. Gene and his mother can come into the yard. Not the house at night, unless invited." She put the spoon back into the empty pot and met Lily's gaze. "Did you have a visitor?"

Lily nodded. "I was hot, so I went into the garden and lay on a blanket. I think Gene came to visit me in wolf form."

"You think?" she asked as she walked back into the kitchen.

Lily angled her head to keep Elvira in sight. "Well, yes, because I could have dreamed it. He was gone when I woke up."

Elvira came in with bacon and started dishing it out. "Mmm ... hard to pin down, isn't he? Your father and brother are due after breakfast. They want to meet me, thank me and all that, and say goodbye to you."

"Then they're back to themselves already?" she asked as the older witch sat down.

"The stronger ones can revert to human quickly if they need to. From what I hear about Domhnall, he's an impressive one."

Lily recollected how he looked as a wolf and silently agreed that he was very impressive and powerful.

"Do you think it's over, Elvira?" she asked after a while.

Elvira looked up. "No, it's only beginning. But it's good to know we can work with the werewolves, guard each other's backs. I had an email from Dane Archwright. There've been more attacks in Europe, and more attacks at the Collegium."

Lily sighed. She hoped the darkness plaguing their kind would give them some respite. There were things she needed to do.

Within the hour, there was a knock at the door. Elvira went to open it. "Come in, come in."

Lily stood in the lounge room, after getting up from her chair. She was having mixed feelings. Shyness, fear, anger, and a whole raft of things. Her father drew her into a big hug and squeezed until she couldn't breathe. Behind him, her brother waited for his embrace. It was the first time she'd seen him since she found out he betrayed her, albeit accidentally.

"Please forgive me. I'm so sorry, Lily. I—"

"Just give me a hug. It could've happened to anyone."

They took their seats, Domhnall seeming too big for the chair he sat in. "If I may call you Elvira," Domhnall began.

"Of course, it's my name."

"Elvira, I wanted to pass on my sincere thanks for your help in our battle with the vampires. Thank you for healing us and guarding us in our vulnerable moments."

Elvira waved a hand. "It was valuable exercise that proved we can trust each other and work collegiately."

"Aye, indeed, that is so. Thank you for the care you have taken of Lily all these years. You and the coven. You are most welcome to visit us in Donegal and stay as long as you like. Every courtesy will be extended to you."

Elvira appeared very chuffed by this invitation, and Connor chipped in with his thanks as well. Lily volunteered to make coffee and while she was in the kitchen, Connor came in to help.

"Hey, sis," he said, not quite meeting her eye.

"Hey, you," she replied and then ground the coffee.

"I didn't mean to betray you, just saying."

Lily met his eye and smiled. "I heard. I know you didn't mean it. They drugged you."

Connor leaned against the cabinet, folded his arms across his chest, and gazed at the floor. "I didn't realise how special you were, you know? We don't know each other well, but I want you to know I'll be there for you, if you need me. I hope you can forgive me."

"Of course I forgive you, and thank you for apologising, too. It helps."

Connor dropped his arms to his sides. "Thank heavens for that. Your boyfriend nearly ripped my head off."

"My what?"

"Big Gene Cohen. Da had to get between us. He was gunning for me."

Lily creased her forehead as she considered this. "I have no idea why he's worrying about it. I've not seen him since the fight and haven't spoken to him before that since ... well since."

Connor blinked, obviously surprised. "You're kidding. He acted like he was your mate or something. Took it real personal like."

Lily switched on the coffee machine, which made conversation difficult. She hated all these unnerving feelings in her gut. Why couldn't relationships be clear-cut with everyone knowing how they stood?

After coffee was served and consumed with fresh lamingtons, Domhnall and Connor stood to leave. "I must say, I like that cake you served. I've never had it before."

"It's a local thing," Elvira said, flapping her hand to dismiss any hard work on her part. As she didn't bake them, Lily suspected she'd ducked into the bakery earlier.

"Could you walk us out, Lily?" her father asked. "There's something particular I want to say to you."

"Sure," she replied and followed them into the driveway.

Domhnall turned. "I've a few things to say now. First is, just call me Da as Dad feels weird to me. Second, I know this is your home and I'll not pressure you to come live with us in Ireland." He lifted a hand before she could respond. "I'll welcome ye if you want, and I ask that you visit. And visit us soon."

Lily smiled. "I'll visit you soon. I was thinking of coming back with you if you can share your flight details."

"Ah! I can do that." He sent his itinerary to her phone. "I won't hold you to it, but I'll be glad of your company and so will Connor and all the family back home."

She went to hug him, and he gathered her up and swung her off her feet. The sensation of being in his arms with her feet in the air was exciting and unnerving. Yet, it felt right. She felt at home with him. The scent of him and her brother embedded in her memory.

"You're such a wee thing. Just like your mother was. We'll have to call you wee Lily."

"You better not call me that. Sounds like I pee my pants or something."

Her father laughed, not able to stop until Connor whacked him on the back.

Their ride arrived and Lily wiped a tear as she waved them goodbye. She glanced at her phone. Their flights were in two days' time, so she'd have to get cracking if she was going to get on their flights. After they drove off, she sighed loudly. She'd forgotten to ask him about her enhanced sense of smell. It wasn't something to do with the night. It seemed like it was there to stay.

Back inside she logged onto the computer but hesitated before booking the flights. What if Gene called her? There had been no word from him, Reeva or any of them. She was on her own now. If her Da could find human form again so quickly, she was sure Gene could. The silence spoke volumes to her. She really had been a one-night stand. Shaking off thoughts of Gene, she booked her flights to Dublin. She'd work out how to get to Donegal when she got there. It looked like her father might drive, rather than fly, because his booking information had not included a connecting flight to his home county.

Her life was at a crossroads. She wished she could at least say goodbye to Gene. What if she liked Ireland and didn't want to come home? She'd have to get her identification and Irish passport sorted, and that would take a while.

She'd just hit pay on the flights when a text came in. She picked up her phone. It was from Abbie to tell her she and Rolf were returning to Canberra as they had urgent pack business. *Thanks for saving my favourite jacket! And Rolf sends his regards.*

Lily snickered. She didn't think Rolf approved of her and he barely spoke to her. Abbie she wasn't sure about. Not quite friends, maybe, but the potential was there. She replied with thanks and best wishes for their trip. As she didn't have her things with her, she told Elvira she was heading back to her place. "I've got some things to organise."

She decided against telling Elvira that she was going to Ireland. Not that she didn't trust her, but it felt like a betrayal. The coven and Elvira had cared for her, and it felt awkward to say she was heading to Ireland. Also, she was pretty sure she'd tell Gene if he asked. Not that he was going to ask, though she wouldn't put it past Elvira to tell him, because she was a matchmaker at heart. All the elder witches were, as they were desperate to see their young ones take partners and produce children. She laughed out loud. Children. She'd grown up expecting she would have children, even though she was different to the rest of the coven. It was so much of the zeitgeist. Children were necessary for survival and strength.

At home, she looked at her possessions, trying to work out what to pack. She didn't vary her clothes much. But she chucked in the dress she'd worn for the gala. She wasn't sure why; for the memory, perhaps. The way he'd looked at her when she'd worn it had been gratifying. She fixed up a few personal details, like paying bills in advance and writing a note to Elvira in case she didn't come back. As she gazed out her kitchen window to the street, she realised she really was at a precipice, the deep dive into changing her life. It was exhilarating and scary. It would be hard to leave Sydney behind; even harder to leave him behind.

Not that there was a him, really. It was best to get out of town and get over it and shove him into the past, in the lessons-learned section. She nodded and tipped the container of rotten milk down the drain and turned to emptying all the old food out of her fridge.

CHAPTER 24

Returning to human form after the full moon was a chore. Gene was tired. So tired because he'd had to shift to fix his injuries, issue orders and then turn back because of the moon's pull. The mind of the wolf was quiet, untaxed by all the problems and issues Gene in human form had to deal with. There was pack business, which always rose to a crescendo around the full moon and after. Feuds, fights, alleged sexual assaults to be investigated and marriages. Justice to deal out and see done. One sexual assault that was reported to him was particularly unusual.

One of the she-wolves had a thing for a human male. With her attraction and the moon's pull, her sexual desire became uncontrollable and before she had turned wolf, she had attacked the man, restrained him and fucked him, whether he wanted it or not. Not the usual rape issue, to be sure, because it was predominantly the males at fault. Within the pack, the females got to choose their partners, even though at times the male thought he was the one making the choice. As long as they were both consenting, there wasn't an issue. The she-wolf's punishment was restitution to the man, and she would be caged five days before the full moon until she learned to curb her appetites.

Luckily, the male victim was happy to take a cash settlement and forget the weirdest fuck of all time, or so he had said.

All this, and his personal business, took him away from thinking about Lily and what he was going to do about her. He sent off an email that had been waiting for a reply for three days. A commotion alerted him to his mother arriving. He put his head in his hands and groaned. Fighting with his mother now was hard when he was bone-tired.

She walked in without knocking, dressed elegantly in some designer suit and floaty, flowery scarf, hair done, make-up perfect. Perfect for waging battle. "We need to talk, Gene," she said and lowered herself gracefully to the chair in front of his desk.

"Obviously, since you are here. In my office."

"Don't get smart with me, son. You forget yourself and what you owe to me and this pack."

He let out a sigh and sat back in his chair, appearing relaxed, although he was anything but. "That's a big accusation. I don't feel that I've let the side down. Everything is running smoothly."

His mother put both feet on the ground and leaned forward. "You are letting her slip through your fingers."

"Her?"

"You know exactly who I mean."

Gene shook his head. "Forgive my confusion. Didn't you tell me she wasn't for me? And didn't you lose your shit when I ended up bedding her?"

"I said that, but it was you who lost their shit when you bedded her. Not me."

He blinked. That was true. What he'd seen in Lily's eyes had freaked him out. What he felt had scared him to his toes. It was like he had met his end and his beginning in one moment. A moment that coiled around his innards and yanked hard. Of course he had run. That didn't mean he didn't think about her, didn't picture her in his mind, that he didn't remember how it felt to move inside her. He recalled her soft fingers in his fur. Why had his wolf sought her out? Why did he sleep with her on a blanket, soaking up her warmth? When he had woken, human and naked beside her, he'd run, and he was still running.

Not running would mean he would have to face it, face the situation, and think and feel. He was not ready for that yet.

He coughed, uncomfortable at the direction of his thoughts, their conversation. "I don't have time right now to deal with this, with you or her."

Reeva scoffed. "Make time. She's leaving for Ireland, and I think if you let her go without fixing this, you will lose her forever."

"What? She's leaving? When?"

Reeva sniffed and checked her phone. "Tomorrow. Her flight departs at one-thirty p.m."

"You had this from Domhnall?"

Reeva nodded. "I upgraded his flight to first class, which means he and Connor are leaving tonight instead. She planned to travel with them, but I thought you'd have a better chance if she was on her own."

Gene wrinkled his forehead. "Better chance? At what?"

Reeva rolled her eyes. "I didn't think you were that dense. Of securing her. Making her stay or, better yet, going with her."

Gene put his hands in his lap so his mother didn't see his hands shaking. "Why, Mother?"

"Heavens! Are you really that dense? She's the one for you, Gene. That's why there was a fire in your eyes and why you saw that answering flare in hers. It's why you ran away. You've been so busy sticking your cock into any woman who'd let you, you weren't prepared when the right one came along."

"I'm not that bad."

Reeva nodded decisively. "Yes, you were that bad, until you met Lily. I knew there was something special about her. Now we know there is. She's one of a kind. In banning you from fucking, I knew you'd just want her more. Admit it. It worked."

Gene's mouth fell open. "You were manipulating me? And her? She took that to heart, you know. A punch to her feelings, of not been accepted, not being good enough."

Reeva eased her neck and crossed her legs. "That was unforeseen and I'm sorry to have hurt her feelings. You can repair any misunderstandings when you see her. With Domhnall being her father, she's like royalty. It's a fantastic alliance, and she's smart to boot."

Gene slumped forward, head in hands, elbows on the desk. Of course his mother manipulated them. Of course Reeva was thinking about the benefit to the pack, to him, to their family. He knew, too, that Reeva genuinely liked Lily. "Mother, I can't just take off. There's business to attend to."

Reeva scoffed. "Who taught you the business? I did. Who was den mother before you became alpha?" She pointed to her own chest. "I can manage things here. Take a holiday with her. Just don't let her slip through your fingers."

Gene lifted his head. "I thought you'd hate it if I told you I loved her."

Reeva sank back into her chair, her expression alight with a smile. "You are misguided. I'm so happy to hear that. I only want you to be happy, and finding love is a sure way to make us both happy. It will probably make Lily happy, too. Your behaviour devastated her."

Gene groaned inwardly. It wasn't easy facing up to the consequences of being a prick and hurting those you loved. Eating humble pie wasn't a favourite pastime, either. He knew his mother was right. Now he knew Lily was leaving, he couldn't stall any longer.

"Okay, let me tie up these things and write up a handover note for you, and I guess I'll head her off at the pass."

"Don't stuff this up, Gene. I expect grandchildren. Lots of them."

Gene shuddered. "Mother, don't push it. I'm not sure what the future will bring."

"With your libido and her Irish ancestry, there are bound to be triplets first time out of the gate."

Gene frowned. Lily couldn't be that fertile, could she? He shook his head in denial.

Reeva glided out of her seat and was out the door before Gene could open his mouth to argue.

He couldn't allow himself to think of Lily, not until he had sorted all of this business to hand over to his mother. He trusted her to handle things, but he still needed to communicate his wishes, suggestions, and ideas. It was five in the morning by the time he'd finished. Enough time to go home to his Bondi house, shower, pack, and organise himself.

LILY SAT NEAR THE AIRPORT BOARDING GATE AND PEERED AT HER phone. She couldn't believe what she was reading, so had to double-check the message. *Sorry we had to take an earlier flight. See you on the other side.*

Her Da and Connor had already left. She'd arrived early, so they could get a meal and hang out before the flight. Now she had too much time on her hands, and she hated sitting at the departure gate, as it was exposed and uncomfortable. "Dammit."

Smells lingering in the air were giving her a headache. She went to the bathroom and washed her face. When she came out, she spotted a guy. A weedy guy in jeans and a T-shirt. He loitered around the windows. She was certain he was a werewolf. Her gaze ranged out again, and she spotted someone else who she was sure gave off werewolf vibes. She didn't recognise either of them; she hadn't met them. It was something characteristic that she couldn't name. This weirded her out. She tried to ignore them, but then there was the smell. A guy eating a burger three rows behind distracted her with the aroma of charred beef. Perfumes mixed with smelly burps and farts were an olfactory soup she couldn't bear. She needed to get a grip.

She picked up her holdall and made her way to the lounge, bought herself a pass and stepped inside. There it was quiet, there was food and drink, and she could pretend she wasn't at a busy airport for a short while.

After getting a bite to eat, she relaxed back into a chair and watched planes take off and tried not to think about her problems.

GENE WAS AT THE COUNTER AT THE ENTRANCE TO THE LOUNGE. He knew Lily was inside, but the receptionist wasn't letting him in. "I'm sorry, sir. Even with a membership, you need to be flying today yourself, or be accompanying someone who is flying today, to enjoy the lounge."

"I just want to talk to her."

"I could page your friend."

"No, no." That might not work. "What about if I buy a ticket?"

"I can process a ticket for you, sir. Where are you flying to?"

Gene frowned, but made a snap decision. His plans, such as they were, were in disarray. He had to be spontaneous and think on his feet. He checked the details his mother had sent. "Can you get me a first-class seat on this flight to Dublin?"

The woman keyed up the flight information. "I'm sorry, sir. First class is fully booked."

"What about business class?"

"We have two business class seats available as there was a cancellation this morning."

"Fine, can you upgrade Ms De Vere to one of the business class seats and put me in the other one?"

"I'm sorry, sir. I cannot do that without her permission."

Gene sagged and thought of his next option. "Okay, book both those seats for me. I take it if I invite her to take the other one, that would be all right with the flight crew."

"Oh, yes, provided you're not going to harass this woman. I wouldn't want to help you stalk her."

Gene gasped. "What? Of course I'm not going to harass her. I want it to be a surprise."

The woman processed the tickets and took Gene's passport. He had packed some things, just in case, but had hoped to change Lily's mind. It looked like he was going to Dublin. It was lucky that Reeva had moved the father and the brother to an earlier flight, leaving him with a clear path. What if Lily rejected him? He remembered the way she had snuggled into him when he was in wolf form. Maybe he still had a chance with her, even though he had run off like a coward.

He checked his watch. The ticketing was taking time and soon they would be boarding. "Excuse me for taking so long. Just a bit longer. How will you pay for the flights, Mr Cohen?"

He slid his credit card along the desk and tapped his fingers. It took another twenty minutes for the ticketing to complete. "Is there anything else I can do for you, sir?"

"Can you book me a room in Dublin? Five stars. City. Two nights."

The woman typed away. "Sir, I can book you into a five star hotel for fifteen-hundred Australian dollars per night. It has excellent ratings."

She showed him the hotel page. "That will do. Thank you."

He grabbed his boarding pass and ducked out into the gents as the boarding call had started. Bumping into Lily now would be awkward. Much better to do it in flight. If she brushed him off, he'd have to abide by her choice. He'd be able to try again in Dublin, maybe.

This feeling in his gut unnerved him. Despite all his affairs with beautiful women, he had not contemplated this moment, when his future happiness depended on one person.

Lily took her seat, after queuing until the ground crew called her row. She had an aisle seat and the middle seat was free. As she was still keyed up, relaxing was hard. She was going to see her mother, and it suddenly occurred to her how momentous that might be.

Thinking of Domhnall confused her, too. Why did he leave on an earlier flight without letting her know? Surely he knew how big a deal this trip was for her. Maybe she hadn't made it clear enough that she was coming. The book she had brought to read lay on her lap. She fidgeted until the plane taxied. As they took off and veered over Sydney, she tried not to think of Gene and failed. He was down there, oblivious to her leaving. Mentally, she wished the coven goodbye, and knew she'd be back before anyone noticed her absence. Unless she stayed away, of course. Her heart gave an anxious beat at the thought.

The smells in the aircraft snagged her attention. The guy seated in the middle section, three rows forward, had passed wind. She could smell it. Ewww. The meal service was being heated, and the competing smells overwhelmed her. The woman two seats behind her had obviously eaten raw garlic, because the stench filled Lily's nostrils. It was most unpleasant having such an acute sense of smell. Where had it come from? It was some awakening of her werewolf. She couldn't decide which. A man stood up four rows ahead and she could smell the stale perspiration wafting from his armpits as he reached for the overhead locker.

"Excuse me, Miss De Vere?" A flight attendant was leaning down close to her ear.

"Yes?" The woman wore perfume. Not unpleasant and not too much, but she could smell it like her face was in a flower bouquet.

"There's a gentleman in row six who asks if you would like to sit with him for a bit."

"A what?" Lily asked, not sure with the engine noise she had heard correctly.

She repeated the message. "I have to go now, as the food service starts soon. It's up to you. If there's a problem with that gentleman bothering you, please let us know."

Utterly perplexed, she undid her seatbelt. It could be her father, but that didn't make sense. Maybe Connor was on the flight.

As she made her way up the aisle and turned into the cubicle that was row six, she saw him. It was as if she had been punched in the gut. She didn't know whether to collapse or run.

"Lily, please. I just want to talk to you." She hesitated, stomach churning, yet his cologne was so familiar and welcome. Breathing out slowly, she nodded once, and slid into the seat next to him. She had wanted to say goodbye, after all, and here was her chance. Business class was quite a set-up. It was a private cubicle, complete with a curtain for a screen.

"What are you doing here?" Lily asked.

Gene smiled tightly. "I think you know. We have business to discuss."

"Business? Am I still the hired help?"

"Of course not. I meant that in a general sense."

"That's complimentary. I'm general business now."

Gene rolled his eyes. "No. Stop. Would you like a glass of champagne?"

She caught sight of the bottle in a cooler. "Okay. I could use something."

He poured her a glass and handed it over and took one for himself. "To the future," he said and tilted his glass towards hers. She clinked hers in return. Then she looked around the cubicle again and back at him. "Are you going to Ireland?"

"Whatever it takes to be with you."

Lily downed her champagne in one long swallow. She lowered the glass and levelled a stare at him. "Let me get this straight. You're coming to Donegal to be with me?"

"Yes," he replied.

Lily met his gaze, silently measuring him. "But you ... ran off." The hurt was there, coiled and waiting, but so was hope.

"I did. Not my proudest moment. What we shared ... well ... it scared me. I didn't understand it and it frightened me."

"I scared you?" Lily asked slowly, in a tone that suggested she didn't believe him. It was hard to credit that the mighty, obnoxious, over-confident Gene Cohen had been afraid of anything, particularly her.

He studied her face, as if trying to read her thoughts. "I haven't felt that before. What I saw in your eyes, well, it touched me." He pressed his hand against his chest. "Mother said it is because we're a match. Our wolves recognise each other."

"Your mother said that? But I thought she was against me."

Gene let out a light laugh and dug out his phone. He showed her a message from Reeva. *Tell Lily welcome to the family and that she'll make a great daughter-in-law.*

Lily held the phone as if it was a bomb ready to go off. "But I don't understand. She seemed so angry after we spent the night together."

"She was—furious at my behaviour. She suspected what would happen if we got together. That you were the one for me. She wanted me to want you by banning me."

Lily grabbed the champagne and refilled her glass, drank off the foam. "This is hard to take in." She took another sip. "I don't know if I believe all that mate thing you've got going. That Reeva was manipulating both of us, I believe."

Gene reached over and took her free hand. "I love you, Lily. I want to be with you. I think I've known it since we first met, but I couldn't figure it out. Mother says banning me from touching you was a way to get me to want you. But while that might have honed my desire, I wanted you from the first." He kissed her hand.

"But ..." Lily felt tears clogging her throat. "I thought you were a dick, but there was more to you than that. I can't tell you what moment it was or how that changed how I felt. The werewolf side of things didn't matter to me. I'd care for you if you were a man or a witch or ..."

"Don't say vampire."

Lily chuckled and wiped at her tears with the backs of her hands. "What I am is scared. Knowing that some people would like to use me or end me. That takes a lot to process."

"It does. But I'll be here to support you, if you'll let me."

Lily began crying in earnest. Gene moved closer and held her tight. "It's okay now. I didn't think about the hurt I caused you running off like that. I can understand if you hate me now. If you don't want to be with me."

Lily hiccupped, stared at him wide-eyed and wiped her face. "Kiss me, please."

"I thought you'd never ask." Gene grabbed her to him, mashed his lips against hers, and she kissed him back. Food arriving drove them apart. "I suppose I need to return to my seat," Lily said.

"No. This seat is yours, if you want it. They flatten out and we can sleep later. Together."

Lily tried to eat the delicious food, but her emotions were all over the place. Gene loved her. Reeva accepted her as a daughter-in-law. How did she feel?

When Gene kissed her, all felt right with the universe. When he held her, she felt at home in his arms. She reached out and ran her forefinger along his arm. "Did you come to me in the garden?"

"Yes. I woke up naked beside you and had to get away before you woke up screaming."

"I wondered. At first, I thought it was a dream, then knew it wasn't. I didn't hear from you, so I had to make decisions about my life. About going to Donegal."

Gene nodded, and brushed his hand against her chin. "Yes, I know. Your father asked you to come to Ireland. My mother is minding the business and the pack while we're away. She reminded me she taught me the business in the first place. I remember her guiding my father, too. She's the real power."

"You aren't angry?"

"Why would I be angry? It's your life. You decide. I want to come along with you, if you'll have me. My womanising ways are over. I pledge this to you. I am yours, body and soul."

"What about children?"

"You want a baby?" His eyes were wide with alarm. She saw him swallow.

"Yes, maybe twins. I want them to know they belong. That they're wanted and loved and nurtured. I need to do that, to give that to them."

Gene rubbed her back, making sympathetic sounds. "I understand your motivation. But does it have to be twins?"

She looked up at him. "No. More than one, though. You seem a bit taken aback. In the coven, that's all they think about—having babies to grow the community."

Gene laughed, a twinkle in his eye. "Mother will be pleased."

"But won't she object to me being only half wolf?"

Gene picked up his phone again and scrolled. He showed her another message from Reeva. *Remember, I want a lot of grandchildren. Tell Lily that.*

"What about you, though?" she asked. "What do you want?"

"To be honest, I've not contemplated having children of my own. My lifestyle sort of meant that it wasn't on the cards. Mother nagged. I ignored her. Rolf told me we don't get to choose if we have children or not. I have you now and something has changed in me. I want you. I want whatever our life brings. Children, responsibility, love, and joy. With you by my side it will be amazing. I'll be the best husband, the best lover and the best father."

Lily smiled and for the first time in a few days, joy filled her up. She leaned in and kissed Gene on the lips. "I'm afraid I have to tell you something."

Gene's eyes widened. "What?"

"I love you. I had to fight it. Couldn't win against my feelings for you."

Later, they snuggled together in their fold-down beds. "Do you want to join the mile-high club?" Gene asked.

Lily gaped at him. "You can't mean that."

He slapped their beds. "They are quite sturdy and it's private in here."

She looked around. The cubicle was a screen and not sound-proof either. "No way. We wait until Dublin. Got me?"

"Absolutely, ma'am." Calm and quite chaste, they slept entwined until breakfast was served. The smell of bacon and sausages was quite strong, and Lily woke up suddenly, pulling a face. "What's wrong?" Gene asked.

"My sense of smell is crazy acute right now."

Gene narrowed his gaze and quizzed her on the details, his eyebrows rising as she finished. "Are you pregnant?"

"Pregnant? No, I can't be." She furrowed her brow as she tried to think of dates. "I took care of it, a bit late to be sure, but I zapped those sperm of yours with magic. My magic reserves were low but I'm pretty sure I got them all." She didn't feel any different, except for the sense of smell.

"So witches have a spell for contraception?"

"Yes, a few different ways. The spells cover most human diseases too."

Gene studied her silently and then proposed another explanation. "Maybe it's a wolf thing, you know. I suspect that with each full moon, your sense of smell will become acute."

"Every month?"

He nodded. "Sort of like a were PMT."

She thumped him on the arm. "You're joking."

Gene put his arm around her shoulder and squeezed. "I'm not. It's also a symptom of pregnancy."

"Damn." Evidence that she was a wolf inside, after all. If she had fallen pregnant so easily there was no interspecies issues to overcome. "I can use the abort spell just in case."

"No. Just leave it to fate." Gene's mouth closed in, and she seized it, their lips colliding, hot and moist.

"You're sure about that?"

"Absolutely." Something had happened while they slept, a calm acceptance that he wanted her as much as she wanted him. That this was the right thing for her and him.

In the transit lounge in Dubai, Gene ordered massages after their showers, and these concluded just as it was time to board the next flight.

By the time they entered their hotel room in Dublin, Lily's skin was on fire and only rubbing her naked body against Gene's equally naked body was going to soothe her. Gene had a similar thought, she guessed, because they were on each other as soon as the door to their hotel room shut behind them. Tearing at their clothes, kissing and nipping and touching, desperate for contact, desperate for relief. Their coupling was hot. It was flames. It was carpet burns, because they didn't make it to the bed.

After slaking that first drive for sex, they climbed on the bed and started again. The desire had built to a crescendo and her emotions twirled within. She loved him, and he loved her. He loved her for who she was, despite what she was. He was going to give up his womanising ways to be with her. *This was really happening*, she thought as she guided Gene inside. She moaned as he filled her; the excitement rising from her core to her chest and then out of her mouth as she cried out in ecstasy. Mad desire, longing and fulfilment. Riding Gene until he cried out her name. Once again, seeing the essence of him in his eyes. This time, he didn't run. He stayed.

EPILOGUE

Meeting her mother was a moving moment for Lily. Gene hung back to give her space. Her mother was interesting. She had been imprisoned for being a dark witch. Apparently, she had done some bad things. Whether she repented of them, Lily didn't know. She wasn't there to judge.

"Shauna! You are so beautiful and so like your Da." They embraced and her mother drew her fingers through Lily's hair. "I'm sorry they took you. I couldn't find you. I had no idea where you were, or even if you were alive. Not until Donny told me a month ago now. I've done a lot of crying and a lot of soul-searching since then."

Lily wiped her eyes. Meeting her mother brought home how much she had missed after she was abducted. Thoughts of how she might have turned out if she had stayed came to mind. It was weird how she felt about meeting her mother. She felt pity, sadness, and fondness. There was no strong recognition or feelings of love that she had expected.

In Donegal, there was a huge welcome. "I'll be giving you a wedding, too," her father said a few days after they arrived. "Must tie up that canny son of a bitch before he slips through your fingers."

"Da!" she exclaimed. "Don't talk like that about Gene. It's not polite. Besides Reeva will have your guts for garters if she heard you."

"Ah, polite is it? And what do you call it when you two are at it all the time that the bairns in the pack can't catch a wink of sleep? You encourage my wife to be a very demanding woman. I'm exhausted."

Lily laughed and blushed at her father's teasing, and then her gaze locked with Gene's. She saw the fire in his eyes and let her own flames leap up to meet his.

"By the way, Lil. Did you know you're pregnant? Can smell it on you more than I can smell him."

Lily's faced paled. She turned to Gene, but he stood there and shrugged. "Why did you have to tell her that? Now the cat's out of the bag."

Domhnall laughed and whacked Gene on the back. "I hope you've got more of that very fertile sperm, laddie. I'd like a big brood of grandchildren to carry on me name. By her scent, she be carrying triplets."

Lily's legs buckled, and Gene grabbed her so that she draped along his side. "Triplets?" Gene said in a trembling voice. "That can't be right."

Lily spared him a look and winced. Now, Gene looked ready to faint, his normally tanned complexion pale. Then he met her gaze and winked. His complexion back to normal and a smile in place. She wasn't so ready to be told she might be having triplets. Pregnant with one child perhaps, maybe twins but a multiple birth? They'd find out when they had a scan.

Gene drew himself up. "What do you mean carry on your name?" he queried, turning to Domhnall. He tapped his chest. "You mean my name."

"No ... mine," Domhnall repeated.

"Guys," Lily said and rested her head on Gene's chest and cuddled him. "Our name."

ACKNOWLEDGMENTS

This book was a long time coming and if you have been waiting for it, I apologise. I really liked Lily De Vere as a character and I felt that possibly I could have done a whole series with just Lily and Gene. However, it wasn't meant to be, but, perhaps, they will turn up in other stories. I hope you like the joining up of the Spellbound in Sydney with the Cursed One Series. I think it works.

Many thanks to my excellent beta reader Nicole Murphy. You are awesome and so quick. A bit thank you to Keri Arthur for her advice and mentorship and to my editor Debbie.

Special thanks to my partner Matthew Farrer for being an inspiration and entirely understanding.

Dani Kristoff
November 2024

ABOUT THE AUTHOR

Dani Kristoff is a Canberra-based author, who delights in reading and writing paranormal romance. She's been writing since late 2000, which means some 24 years, although she's been concentrating her efforts on science fiction, fantasy and horror. Published both traditionally and independently, she's has a PhD in creative writing from the University of Canberra. Her research area was feminism and romance. Her partner is also a writer and they get up to geekery whenever possible.

Dani has six books in her paranormal series, Spellbound in Sydney and Cursed Ones. Destiny's Blood, Cursed Ones Book Three, unites the two series.

ALSO BY DANI KRISTOFF

Cursed Ones Series

The Sorcerer's Spell

The Changeling Curse

Destiny's Blood

Spellbound Series

Spirtbound

Bespelled

Invoked